I0663633

Prophecy

Soul of the Witch Saga - Book 4
C. Marie Bowen

Pixler Publications

Prophecy

Soul of the Witch Saga – Book 4

by C. Marie Bowen

This book was previously published as *Soul of the Witch, Book 2.*

ISBN-13: 978-1-945215-094 – Paperback

ISBN-13: 978-1-945215-087 – EPUB

Edited by Liette Bougie

Cover Design by C. Marie Bowen

Published by Pixler Publications

Discover other titles by C. Marie Bowen at www.cmariebowen.com

Contents

Chapter 1

Dr. Frank Phelps

—

Present day – Fort Worth, Texas

Dr. Frank Phelps rushed down the hall and squeezed between the elevator doors just before they closed. He took a quick breath, reset the computer bag on his shoulder, and then pressed the button for the third floor.

The medical conference in Geneva had been a treasure trove of both practical psychiatry and theoretical psychology. He'd been able to obtain a series of audio lectures on cutting-edge psych research. A now familiar Swiss accented voice spoke through his earbuds and explained the latest hypothesis on counter-intuitive diagnoses.

He caught sight of his disheveled image in the reflective elevator door.

I should have stopped by the house.

He ran a hand through his thinning brown hair and straightened his jacket and glasses. Thankfully, he had no appointments—just a quick check-in with Marcia, and he would have the rest of the day and weekend to himself. *Ding.* He adjusted his collar as the elevator doors slid open.

When he entered his office, his receptionist, Marcia Brice, rose to her feet and hurried around her desk. Her wide, blue-eyed gaze and pale face stopped his progress through the reception area.

He pulled out the earbuds and his pulse quickened. "What's wrong?"

"You've not seen the news?" Her eyebrows rose toward her hairline.

He shook his head and flinched when the phone rang.

Marcia ignored it and after two rings the tone discontinued. "The service has picked up our calls for the last five days, on advice from the attorney."

"Whose attorney? What's happened?" Dr. Phelps set his shoulder bag on a chair, never taking his gaze from Marcia.

"One of our patients, Courtney Veau, was found inside an abandoned property in Denver. She's dead, Frank."

"What?"

This doesn't make sense.

"I saw her but two weeks ago." His mouth went dry and his pulse quickened when he recalled the photo of a house and the map of Denver she had placed on his desk.

"I tried to reach you."

"I was at a conference. I switched off my cell."

"I left messages at your hotel." Her voice rose as the phone rang again. They both ignored it.

"I never checked—" Dr. Phelps ran his hand over his face. "When? When did this happen?"

Marcia picked up the remote and turned on the DVD player. "Courtney's... body was found on the twenty-third. Her funeral took place yesterday, here, in Fort Worth."

Dr. Phelps directed his attention to the television. The flat-screen showed a distance shot of the residence, the house cordoned off by police tape. A small crowd gathered to watch the officer's work. The house appeared a perfect match to the photo Courtney had slapped on his desk.

Marcia handed him the remote. "Greta said I should record this news report, and have you watch it when you returned to the office. She wants to speak with you before you take calls from reporters or the Denver detective."

"Greta?" He echoed—heart still racing. "Detectives?"

"Greta James, Courtney's attorney. Well, *former* attorney. Just watch." Marcia pointed toward the flat-screen.

"This was the scene last week when the body of Russell Veau's daughter, Courtney, was found in an abandoned house near downtown Denver. Our viewers may remember Russell Veau from his 90s hit TV show, The Psychic Connection.

"Following an anonymous tip, police were sent to this address on Pence Street in Denver, where the young heiress was found and pronounced dead at the scene."

The screen changed to a familiar blonde-haired woman in the newsroom. *"That was Kent Davis, our reporter on the scene last week at the house where the body of Courtney Veau was discovered. The Denver police have ruled out homicide and are waiting for toxicology results to confirm if this was a possible suicide or overdose.*

"As our viewers will remember, Courtney Veau, a Fort Worth resident, sustained serious injuries earlier this month in an automobile accident. She was admitted to the hospital for observation, then released three days later."

Dr. Phelps sank into one of the waiting room chairs and increased the volume. "Her injuries weren't serious," he muttered at the television.

"The staff physician at JPS, Dr. Milton Chambers, released Courtney for follow-up care to a Dr. Frank Phelps. Dr. Phelps, a psychiatrist and psychologist, has been unavailable for comment. Police have confirmed that prescription medications were found on the scene, but they will not confirm if a suicide note has been discovered."

"Who's on Courtney's HIPAA form?" Frank whispered as Marcia slid into the seat beside him.

"Greta James. Her attorney."

"Did she ask for my notes on Courtney's visit?" He turned to Marcia and decreased the volume on the set.

"You know she did. It's the first thing she wanted." Marcia's cell phone rang, and she pulled it from her pocket. She held up a finger to Dr. Phelps. "Hello? Yes. Yes, he is." She looked at her boss and handed him her cell. "Greta James, for you."

"I think I should speak to our own attorney first." Dr. Phelps stared at Marcia's cell.

"Then just listen to her," Marcia suggested. "You've done nothing wrong, and she gave me advice when I couldn't reach you."

With reluctance, Dr. Phelps took the phone and held it for a moment to his ear before he spoke. "Hello?"

"Dr. Phelps?" a soft professional voice responded.

"Yes. Ms. James, is it? How may I help you?"

"I hoped we might meet. I have information—not released to the public—which may interest you regarding Courtney Veau's death. You have two voicemails from her I would like to hear."

He heard the familiar elevator chime in the hallway and through the phone. His eyes turned to the office door. "I'm unaware of any messages, Ms. James. If you'd like to make an appointment to meet, I'll hand you back to Marcia. She maintains my schedule." He rose from the chair just as the office door opened.

Greta James smiled at Dr. Phelps, closed her phone and dropped it into her briefcase. "No need to bother Marcia, unless she would be willing to make a pot of coffee."

Greta stepped across the waiting room and held out her hand to Dr. Phelps.

He returned the phone to Marcia and shook the attorney's hand. "Ms. James."

"Please, call me Greta." Her smile was filled with concern, and a touch of grief.

She was tall. Almost as tall as his own six-foot height. He glanced at her shoes and confirmed she wore a high stylish heel. Her calves were toned. Her modest length skirt flared around her knees but tightened along her slim hips. By the time his gaze made it past the curve of her silk blouse and crescent moon necklace, to her amused hazel eyes and full-lipped smile, he was convinced there was some sort of mistake. Women like this didn't walk through his door and ask to be called by their first name.

Greta tipped her head toward his private office. "Shall we?" She released his hand, smiled at Marcia, and strode into the next room. Her shoulder strap slid down her arm as her leather case landed in the guest chair. "Oh, and Marcia? Please lock the front door." Her gaze switched to Dr. Phelps. "I apologize for giving orders in your office, but Detective Hernandez is in town to speak with you. You should expect a visit from him today." She took a seat in the other guest chair, crossed her legs, and then turned her head to meet Frank's eyes. "This shouldn't take too long, but I don't want to be interrupted."

Frank tore his gaze away from Greta and looked toward Marcia. "Courtney's file?"

"On your desk." Marcia changed the time on the 'We'll be back at' sign on the door to noon, then locked the door and stepped to the coffee maker.

Frank took a moment to gather his senses.

What the hell have I come home to?

The unexpected and upsetting events left a hollow feeling in the pit of his stomach. His young patient was dead—one who had been vibrant and full of life.

Is her death my fault?

He lifted his black framed glasses with the back of his hand and rubbed his tired eyes, then gripped his case and walked into his office.

Courtney Veau's file sat in the middle of his desk. He took his seat and flipped open the file. He didn't need to read his notes; he could remember his conversation with Courtney word for word.

"Let's start with the messages she left you," Greta suggested, her voice soft.

Dr. Phelps nodded but didn't reach for his cell phone. Instead, he focused on the woman across the desk. She was dressed to distract him, and her smooth cultured voice had an almost hypnotic quality to it. Soothing. Manipulative. He used hypnosis and distraction enough to know when he was being coerced. Ms. Greta James certainly had game, but she appeared far too young to be Courtney Veau's trust attorney. Despite how lovely she looked, she didn't add up.

"I think not, Ms. James." He raised his hand to forestall her protest. "I'm sorry—Greta. I've not heard those messages myself. I'm sure you understand my need to be cautious. Malpractice lawsuits are rampant, and I must vet everything I hand over to my client's—*former* client's attorney. Please understand, I've only just learned of Courtney's death."

Greta nodded and ran the heel of her hand across her cheek and her nails along her temple, dislodging a few auburn strands of hair. As though a mask fell away, her fatigue became apparent. "I understand, and I do apologize. I've simply been on my feet since Detective Hernandez contacted me a week ago. Why don't I go first, then?

"My family has worked closely with the Veau family for years. I became Russell Veau's attorney when my father took on other clients. Even before any direct contact with the Veaus, I grew up with their—peculiarities—through my father's practice."

She paused as though considering her words. "When Courtney's parents were killed in the plane crash, I became the estate and trust manager. Courtney has always been more to me than a mere client." She reached over, pulled a tissue from her bag, and then dabbed her eyes and nose.

"I'm sure this is difficult for you—"

"As I said, I'm just tired." The tissue disappeared into her fist, and liquid gray eyes assessed him. "Dr. Phelps—"

"Call me Frank."

"Thank you, Frank. Let me assure you; Courtney's death is not your fault. There's nothing you could have done to prevent her from making this decision."

Frank's breath caught for a moment. "You believe it may have been suicide."

Greta shook her head. "No, not precisely." Her voice remained slow, considerate. "Courtney comes from a long line of powerful mediums—spiritualists, if you will. Their power is inherent. In the normal course of events, she would have learned these skills from her father, but she never had that chance."

They paused while Marcia brought them coffee. When she left the office, she closed the door behind her.

Greta set her Styrofoam cup on Frank's desk and cleared her throat. "Let me tell you what I know, and what I gleaned from several sources. Correct me if I am mistaken."

Elbows on his desk, Frank laced his fingers and rested his chin on his thumbs. "Go ahead."

Greta sat forward. "Courtney Veau barely survived a serious car accident. Her heart stopped twice. Both the EMTs and the ER staff feared she had sustained a traumatic brain injury, but the MRI scans came back clean. She spent the next three days in the hospital under observation, but was released with only a deeply bruised leg, facial abrasions, and a black eye."

Frank nodded and shifted in his chair. "The rounding doctor was Dr. Chambers."

"Yes, I've spoken with him." Greta smiled and nodded at Frank's interruption.

"Dr. Chambers referred Courtney to me due to emotional instability. He felt the imbalance could have been caused by her near-death experience. I've done several research papers on the subject. He thought I might be able to help her."

Greta shook her head and raised her eyebrows. "But it wasn't a typical near-death experience, was it? Courtney claimed to have returned to a past life. She even brought you proof in the form of a photograph and map to a house in Denver."

"Yes." Frank pressed his lips and looked away. "She didn't reveal her plan to travel there."

They were both silent for a moment, and then Greta spoke. "The detective told me they've preliminarily dismissed drug overdose as the cause of death—pending the toxicology report. There were no marks on the body and the prescriptions in her possession were practically untouched. I know they've had the MRIs reviewed by their own experts. Nothing was missed. COD is likely to remain a mystery."

"Unless there is something on my phone that could tell us what happened."

Their gazes locked. The fatigue and grief he recognized in her eyes made him reach for his phone. "All right. This goes against my better judgment, but I'm curious as well." He turned the device on. As soon as the screen lit up, he touched the voicemail icon, turned the speaker on, and hit play. There were ten messages. The first two were from men. He paused then skipped them. On the third recording, they heard Courtney's voice.

"Uh—hi Dr. Phelps? This is Courtney Veau. Don't be upset, but I wanted to let you know I'm in Denver." Her voice went up a pitch and her words tumbled out with excitement. "I found the house—the one in the picture I showed to you—and they had a room for rent—so I took it. I can't believe I'm really here. The landlady said the rent was month-to-month when she gave me the key. I'll call you when I get back to town. Buh-bye."

Frank's gaze lifted from the phone to Greta. "They said on the news the house was abandoned."

"It is. I've read the police reports. They don't know how she got in and out. The doors were locked and so corroded they had to bust them down to gain entrance. They did find a single silver key in her purse, but it didn't fit any of the locks. A landlady, she says. That's interesting."

Frank skipped three more calls, and then heard Courtney's voice again.

"Hi, Dr. Phelps. It's me again." Her voice was slow and strained this time—nasally, as though she had been weeping. "I'm hearing voices, well... one voice. He whispers to me—I mean to Nichole. I have my father's journal, and I've tried to make Merril hear me, but it hasn't worked. I know he loved me in my other life. I know the time I spent there was real. But I don't know what to do now. I think I might come home. Call me when you get this."

Frank covered his mouth with his hand and shook his head. Courtney's words pierced him.

Could I have stopped her death with a phone call?

His chest ached, and his eyes burned. "She doesn't sound good."

Greta didn't appear to notice his distress. She tipped her head to try to read his phone. "No, she doesn't. What is the date on the message?"

He looked at the screen. "April twenty-first." The glass on the phone went dark and he slid it into his bag. "So, what happened between the twenty-first and the twenty-third?"

Greta ran her fingers across her brow and sat back in the chair. "She found the photo."

Frank's head came up. "What photo?"

"The official police report states they found Courtney in the attic, an old photo clutched to her chest. The report goes on to describe the photo, but here—" She reached into her bag and withdrew an antique framed oval photograph. She laid it on the desk in front of him and pointed to a woman, seated between two standing men. "This is Nichole Harris. The photo appears to have been taken in the early 1870s." She tapped the raised glass above the tall gentleman on Nichole's left. "I suspect this handsome young man is Merril."

"How did you obtain this?" He glanced from the photo to Greta.

A shadow of a smile moved across Greta's face. "There's no official crime scene. Nothing held as evidence. The building, and all the items in the attic, including this photo, belong to The Hawthorn Group—an investment company. I reached out to THG and offered to repair the doors that were damaged when the officers entered the house in search of my client. In return, I asked to purchase this photograph—an out-of-court settlement. They agreed."

"Why would you want it?" His gaze returned to the photo. The blonde woman's eyes seemed to draw him in. He took in every inch of the photograph.

"I don't. It's not for me."

The tone of her voice drew his attention back to her face. Her eyes smiled first, and then her lips. "I read another report, filed by an officer who never entered the house. This officer maintained crowd control and checked ID badges of those who required access to the house during the site investigation. According to his report, an elderly woman approached him. She informed him, in no uncertain terms, that the photograph 'in the poor girlie's hands', should be given to her doctor for the long table under his clock."

Frank's gaze shot to his credenza beneath his office clock and then back to Greta. "How is this possible?"

Greta shrugged. "By the time Detective Hernandez read the report, the elderly woman had vanished. I'm surprised the officer even mentioned her comment. The old woman must have made quite an impression on the young man."

Greta closed her bag and stood. "Thank you for your time, Frank, and for sharing Courtney's phone calls with me."

"You're welcome." Frank came to his feet. "You seem relieved. Do you have a better understanding of what happened to Courtney?"

"Actually, I do." She gave him a genuine smile. "You remember, I told you her spiritual powers were inherent. Although she never trained with her power, she really only needed two things—desire and belief. We know she had the desire." Greta tapped the oval glass above the photo. "When she found the photo, it suspended her disbelief and she knew she could find her way back to him."

"Then, you're saying that—" Frank blinked and shook his head. "You believe Courtney returned to her previous life?"

Greta shrugged, picked up the long strap of her bag and hung it on her shoulder. "I have no reason to believe otherwise."

"But, that's not possible." He rounded his desk and stared into Greta's gray eyes.

She smiled. "Suspend your disbelief, Frank. You didn't cause this, and you couldn't have averted the outcome." Greta picked up the photograph and placed it in Frank's hands. "Courtney's gone back to her life as Nichole. She returned to Merril, and she wanted you to have this."

Chapter 2

Amy Harris

—

June 12, 1875 – Denver, Colorado

Amy Harris stood in the hallway outside the bedroom door, an empty ceramic water pitcher clutched to her chest. When her knees threatened to buckle, she locked them tight and leaned her back against the wall.

Calm yourself.

Her eyes fluttered closed, and she urged her heart to regain a slow even pace. She pushed a ragged breath through clenched teeth and pressed lips. Her inhale hitched as she struggled to fill her lungs.

You will not cry. The worst is over.

Her body trembled, and her heart rate accelerated, despite her attempt to quiet her mind. The terror that had overwhelmed her in the dark confines of the locked wardrobe clawed at her throat.

With a gasp, she opened her eyes and searched the empty hallway. Daylight shone through the broken bedroom wall and illuminated the corridor with an unfamiliar glow.

Everything has changed.

From the bedroom behind her, Nichole coughed the last blood from her lungs, while Merril repeatedly assured Nichole, and himself, she would be all right. The opening in the exterior wall channeled the worried shouts of neighbors, who had been drawn to the sound of a single gunshot, followed by the crash of the porch collapse.

Jim must be hurt. I need to move.

The tall Highlands foreman, Jimmy Leigh, had gone through the window, taking the madman Blackwood Jones with him. But Jim's heroic attempt to save Nichole had come too late. The thought of Nichole's battered, and bloody body filled Amy's mind along with memory of Merril's anguished cry. Amy would have fallen to her knees in defeat as Jason pulled her from the wardrobe, were it not for the Entity.

The Entity's composed presence had calmed her mind and given Amy the strength to push her husband away. She'd directed Jason to go outside and aid Jim as she turned to Nichole's broken body. The moment she had placed her hands on Nichole's lifeless chest and pushed her *earth-vision* into Nichole, Amy felt the Entity move across her consciousness and interlace with her own limited magic. No longer a simple spectator, the Entity not only saw through Amy's eyes, but it also healed through her hands.

Amy relaxed her grip on the urn enough to brush the auburn hair from her face. She paused and held the trembling hand before her eyes. With a thought, she pushed her vision past her skin to see bone and tendons—the absolute extent of her ability. She had neither the *fire-skill* to knit bone, nor the *air-skill* to fill Nichole's collapsed lung. She had only *Earth* and *Water*.

The Entity had observed the damage inside Nichole through Amy's vision, then extended its reach and used the delicate touch of fire to knit her splintered rib and mend her lung. In the end, it had been the Entity who pushed air into Nichole's chest and sparked the beat of her heart.

Whoever... or whatever had invaded Amy's mind, had healed Nichole and then departed with a whispered promise. *"I will find you."*

Another tremor moved down her spine, and she gripped the empty urn with both hands.

Find your center—calm yourself. Jim needs you. Nichole needs you. Your husband—

Amy's thoughts ground to a halt. This entire unspeakable episode could be laid at his feet. Her anger at Jason steadied her.

Two more quick breaths, a prayer to the Goddess for strength, and she pushed herself away from the wall. Her composure returned as she navigated the steep staircase with the urn cradled in her arm. At the base of the kitchen stairs, she paused when Jason helped Jim through the broken back door.

"Is Nichole all right?" Jim grimaced as he limped forward, his bloody side toward Amy, with his opposite arm thrown across Jason's shoulders for support. He faltered and took another quick step into the kitchen.

"She'll recover—with rest." Amy's gaze cataloged the big man's injuries with growing concern. A scraped chin and bloody elbow were minor. And although he favored his right leg, it was the blood on his left side and down his leg that concerned her the most. "She's in better shape than you. Jason, sit him at the table. Jim, you'll need to remove your shirt."

Albert Fielding, their closest neighbor, stood in the broken doorway. His clothes were covered with blood from assisting Jim into the house.

"Hello, Mr. Fielding. Thank you for your help." Her calm voice held no trace of her pent-up fury. She handed him the ceramic urn, retrieved the bucket from under the kitchen counter, and held it up for him to take. "Would you be so kind as to bring me water from the pump at the well? It flows much faster than the pump in the kitchen."

Mr. Fielding took the bucket in his other hand and disappeared out the back door with a nod.

She turned her gaze from the retreating neighbor, flicked a brief glance at her husband, and focused on Jim's muscular frame. "What happened to Jones?"

Jim held his bloody shirt above his head as he twisted to view the gunshot wound along his side. Although the flow of blood had slowed, his denim trousers were soaked red from his belt to his boot. "He's dead. The fall broke his neck."

"I can't say I'm sorry about that." Amy's hand touched the skin above the wound as her *earth-sight* penetrated. The injury had already begun to mend. "This will require stitches." A quick appraisal of his other injuries told her his knee had been wrenched but would also heal at a remarkable pace. She raised her gaze from the wound to Jim's eyes.

His dark stare held hers for a moment before he turned his head and nodded. "Do what you have to."

Jason's blue eyes, so similar to Nichole's, turned from the deep slice along Jim's ribs to Amy. "Shouldn't we take him to the hospital?" Blond curls clung to the perspiration on his forehead, his face still red from the race to the house.

Anger hardened Amy's heart. "No. That won't be necessary." She stood and stepped to a tall linen closet tucked beneath the stairs. "I can manage a few stitches." She brought Jim a folded linen cloth. "Hold this to the wound until I return." The back door squeaked on its broken hinge. "Thank you, Mr. Fielding." She took the urn from the neighbor's hand and pointed toward the floor. "Please, set the bucket next to Jim's chair." She held the urn to her chest, withdrew additional linen towels from the closet, and then turned to mount the stairs. "I'll be right back."

"Here, let me help," Jason offered, a footstep behind her

Amy stopped and faced her husband. "No. Thank you. I can manage." She tipped her head toward the back door. "You should wait out front for the coroner and police chief. I imagine they'll be along shortly."

"But Nichole—"

"Is in good hands." Amy turned from Jason's injured gaze and looked up the steps. "Besides, I doubt Nichole would care to see you just now." Her clipped tone brooked no argument. Thankful the urn was only half-full, she pressed the linens under her arm, grasped her skirt with her hand, and ascended the steps.

Merril and Nichole's soft voices caught her ear as she passed the first room. She paused and looked in on the couple.

Merril sat at the head of the bed, his back rested against the headboard. He held Nichole in his lap, the bedcover wrapped around her to keep her warm. His long dark hair, loose and dusty from the race to her side, curtained both their heads as he whispered to her.

They both looked up as she entered the room.

"I have water and towels for you. I'll put these in the room down the hall. This room needs to be—repaired." Her gaze flicked toward the hole in the wall, then settled on Nichole.

Nichole's mouth moved without sound, and her crystal blue eyes filled with tears. She reached out her hand and whispered, "Amy."

Amy set the urn and towels on the dresser and took Nichole's hand. "My dear, what's the matter?" Amy sank to her knees beside Nichole and wrapped her arms around her. "Shh, now. You're safe."

Nichole's blonde curls nodded against Amy's shoulder. "I know," she rasped, her voice thick with emotion. "I just missed you so much."

"You missed me?" Amy exchanged a confused glance with Merril.

Nichole pulled back and wiped a tear from her cheek. "I have to explain so many things."

Amy smiled and placed a hand on each side of Nichole's face. "We'll have time to talk soon, my dear. For now, you need to move to a different room and clean up." Amy stood and stepped back. "Blackwood Jones is dead." She waved her hand toward the missing wall. "Jones and Jim went out the window and took the wall out as well. The porch broke their fall."

"What?" Nichole cleared her throat and looked from the hole in the wall back to Amy. "Is Jim all right?"

"He took a jolt from the fall. He's injured, but nothing is broken," Amy assured Nichole. "The worst harm was from the bullet wound."

"Jim's been shot?" Merril asked, shock and concern evident in his tone.

"Yes. Luckily, the wound is only a deep graze, no penetration. It could have been much worse." Amy retrieved the water and towels. "I'm going to put this down the hall. Merril, if you could help Nichole change rooms, and then fetch her travel case, I would be most appreciative."

Chapter 3

Alyse James

—

Earlier that day - South of Toronto, Canada

Alyse James snuggled deeper into her grandmother's settee and took a sip of hot mint tea. Dark clouds hung heavy in the sky and a slow rain had fallen all day. Cuddled beside her were her two cats, Sabine and Anaïs, both black and completely content to lounge beside their mistress on this rainy afternoon. Her grandmother's *grimoire* lay across her lap. A forbidden treasure she paged through each time *Mémé* and her two uncles left the house. Today, they had taken the wagon to Toronto for a delivery and told her not to expect them back until after dark.

Uncle Bernard had tasked her to cut the fabric for the chair cushions to be delivered with the dining room set next month. Her uncles made fine furniture. She and *Mémé* produced the delicate petit point cushions. The fabric cuttings for the chairs were stacked by the canvas frame near the fireplace. Furniture craft earned their living, but it was not who they were... or not *all* they were.

Alyse had grown up with their family secret. Raised by her grandmother, Chantal James, and twin uncles, Bayard and Bernard, Alyse learned basic spellcraft before she could walk.

She had a strong affinity for both *Fire* and *Air* elements but lacked even the most rudimentary skill when working with *Water* or *Earth*. Uncle Bay teased her lack of *water-skills* unmercifully, but she knew what she lacked in *Water* or *Earth*, she more than made up for with *Fire*. For five years now, since her twentieth birthday, she had practiced her *fine fire-control* becoming more than adept at its manipulation.

She finished reading one of the fine control spells in the grimoire and consigned it to memory. She repeated the spell several times before she opened her dark eyes and focused on the lamp's flame across the room.

"*Viens à moi, feu!*" she whispered, and held out her hand.

Anaïs raised her head and watched as a portion of the flame jumped from the lamp to Alyse and danced in the palm of her hand.

Words weren't required to enact the spell, French or otherwise. She just liked the way French rolled at the back of her mouth. "You see, Anaïs? I can gather one flame from another and make it grow." With a wave of her finger, the small flame in her hand stretched taller.

Unimpressed, Anaïs rested her head on her paws and shut her eyes.

Alyse closed her fist and snuffed the flame. She browsed through several more incantations and diary entries, when the spell to heal caught her eye. She'd read this entry before, even tried it several times on the injured animals her beloved pets gifted her. They always died. Sometimes quite horribly. "*Don de guérison,*" she said softly, which meant 'Gift of healing'. She turned the page and moved on to find an interesting *air* spell. She could work *air magic* as well as she could *fire*.

She gasped as her heart rate accelerated. Both cats hissed and jumped from the couch. Her vision tunneled as cold perspiration broke across her brow. A soft whimper escaped the back of her throat and she panted in terror.

Is this me? No. *Who then?*

She rode with someone in a dark space.

Amy... Amy... The name whispered through her mind.

Enough light entered to see the woman's hands test the dimensions of the tight space. They were locked inside a wooden box.

Beyond the dark prison, the sounds of a fight—no, a beating. Fist connected to flesh and a cry of pain. Again, and again. Helplessness consumed her, and she sobbed in sympathy and terror.

A crash shook the floor beneath her. Pounding footsteps and a primal scream shocked her into silence. The shattering of glass outside her prison, and a single gunshot, galvanized her into motion. She screamed and pounded on the walls. "Let me out!"

The door opened, and she blinked, blinded by the sudden brightness. A breath of freedom filled her lungs as strong arms pulled her from the box and embraced her.

A man's breathless voice asked her—*asked Amy*—if she'd been injured.

Emotion erupted in her chest, and she clung to the man's dusty jacket as her knees buckled.

Alyse pulled back, separating herself from the terrified woman's emotions. She'd heard her uncles talk about casting spells while *twyned*—how they could see through each other's eyes. They hadn't warned her about the emotional entanglement of a shared perspective.

As best she could, Alyse lent the woman a calm strength.

You are safe. Be calm.

The woman turned to a blonde-haired girl who lay across the bed. One eye swollen shut, the other half-opened. The girl's dress was torn from the throat to the waist, her breasts covered with blood.

A tall dark-haired man wrapped the dead young woman in a blanket and lifted her to his chest. Tears left tracks on his dusty face and a low moan escaped his lips.

Her *twyned* partner—*Amy*—refused to give up. She directed the man to put the body down on the bed, to empty her mouth of blood. Straddled above the body, she placed her hands on the girl's chest and stomach.

In that moment, Alyse's world changed. Through this woman's *earth-magic*, she could see the damage inside the girl's body. Without thought, she pushed her *fire-skill* through her partner's hands and their magic twisted together. They were *twyned* and they were twins. Her twin's *earth-vision* allowed her to observe the damage inside. Healing the woman became child's play. Together, they worked through her wounds and repaired the internal injuries. In the end, Alyse sparked the woman's heart and filled her lungs with air.

When the girl on the bed took a breath and began to cough, Alyse pulled back. She gazed at the frayed auburn braid and dark-eyed mirror image of herself.

"I will find you," Alyse whispered, then pulled away and broke the *twyne*.

***

Alyse sat at the petit point frame and pulled bright colored thread through the cloth with a long needle. The mudroom door at the back of the house opened and familiar voices raised in a loud discussion echoed down the hall.

"Of course, I told him no. We've the Chesham contract to complete next month. There's also the summer solstice right around the corner. We'll not have the time," Bernard argued.

"But you didn't ask me, that's all I'm saying." Bayard's voice grew louder. "You don't get to make all the decisions yourself."

Alyse's grandmother sailed into the living area, already divested of her coat, boots and hat. Chantal James stopped beside Alyse and brushed the hair from her forehead and kissed her brow.

"You work late, my dear. I'm sorry we were delayed. Your uncles stayed to discuss additional orders with a former client we happened to meet at dinner. Did you have a nice day?"

Alyse looked up at her beautiful *mémé*. At eighty-one, she looked no older than sixty. With an elegant posture, she stood straight and slender; her snow-white hair swept up into a loose bun atop her head. Witches age slower than unskilled humans, if they chose.

"I wanted to wait up for you, *Mémé*. I've had an interesting day, and I have a question I need to ask." Alyse wove her needle into the material and paused as her uncles came into the room.

Bay and Bern still argued about the furniture contract. Without breaking eye contact with Alyse, Chantal held her hand toward her sons. Their discussion came to a halt, and they looked from their mother to their niece.

"Is something amiss, darling? Did something happen?" Chantal tipped her head slightly as she observed Alyse.

Alyse moved Sabine and Anaïs from her lap and stood to face her family. She loved them dearly. It hurt to know they had lied to her. All of them. Her entire life.

"Who is Amy?" she asked, her voice tight with controlled anger. Her grandmother and her uncles exchanged uneasy glances, but Alyse kept her gaze locked with Chantal's.

Mémé has the answers.

"Where did you hear that name, dear heart?" Chantal asked with a cautious smile.

All the lamps and fireplace flared for several seconds and then returned to their former state.

"I have a twin. Never mind where I heard her name. I should have heard it from you." Alyse's words were darts, aimed at her grandmother. "I should have known her *all my life.*"

Sabine and Anaïs yowled and ran from the room.

Once again, flames flared, far too high for safety, and fire flickered between the fingers of Alyse's clenched fists.

"Calm yourself, young lady!" Her grandmother gestured with her arm and doused every flame in the room with a thought.

The room went dark, except for the fire Alyse held in her fist. Even her powerful grandmother could not extinguish Alyse's flame. She raised her fist, opened her fingers, and bid the tiny flame on her palm to grow. It illuminated her face and reflected in her eyes.

"I didn't know you were lying because I never looked for lies from you—from any of you." Her gaze passed over her uncles, then returned to Chantal and her voice lowered. "I trusted you. But make no mistake, I will *truth-read* everything *any* of you tell me from now on. You know I can." Alyse tossed her flame at the fireplace and it flared back to life, along with all the lamps in the room.

Chantal turned away from Alyse and walked into the dining room. "Bernard, make us some tea. This is going to be a long night." With unruffled elegance, she took a seat at the head of the table.

Chapter 4

Minister Tremble

—

Near New Orleans, Louisiana

The old man, asleep on a cot, blinked his eyes open as the prisoner gagged and convulsed on the dirt floor across the room. Late afternoon light slanted through the filthy window and left the room in dim shadow. He turned his head toward the corner where he kept the girl, her ankle chain staked to the floor to prevent escape.

His Lord's good work required a prophet. When he purchased the girl, he'd been assured she possessed a seer's ability. So far, she remained a disappointment. The girl had been Minister Tremble's guest for eight long months and not a single vision had she shared.

"What's wrong with you, girl?" The minister listened to her moan for several moments before he sat up and brushed at his dirty robe. "I already fed you, didn't I? I watered you too."

The prisoner's back arched and she inhaled sharply. "Um—uh, uh—"

With a spryness that belied his skeletal frame, the old man sprang from his bed to the cabinet along the wall and struck a match to the lantern. He held the lamp high to illuminate the small cabin, as he squinted at the girl.

Her dress, the same she'd worn when he bought her, lay in shreds across her back, from hip to shoulder. The cutting edge of his belt had bitten deep to rip material and flesh and left bloody welts on her skin. With skin dry and peeling, and her tightly curled black hair falling out in patches, she looked closer to fifty than fifteen.

"Speak up, you witch—you succubus." He dared approach no closer. Several times the demon within her had tempted him to couple with her. She aroused in him the desire to forget his self-imposed abstinence with visions of her naked flesh. He had beaten her, and himself, until temptation passed.

He squawked in surprise when she flipped onto her back. His mouth dropped open as her eyes rolled back in her head and tremors wracked her body.

A bloody froth ran from her mouth, across her hollowed cheeks and onto the dirt floor. Her cracked lips moved, and he edged closer, anxious to hear her words.

"Uh—mm—uh, ba... ba..." She gasped, then began again. "Be—behold the power of the—of the *Twyned*. Their time has come." She choked, and a spray of blood spattered her face. After several choked breaths, she continued, "Know them by their b—birth—crowned beneath the full moon, on the witches' High Sabbat."

Another seizure shook the emaciated girl and the old man scampered back against the wall. This was more like what he had expected months ago. He must prepare for the coming of his Lord. He needed prophetic counsel to show him what he must do to assure a place for himself at his Lord's Table for their triumphant feast.

Her convulsion slowed. Her mouth moved several times before she spoke. "The Demon has awakened. By Fire and Earth, he shall be defeated—lest the *Twyne* fail—then death shall reign." Blood filled her mouth. She became still, and her eyes dimmed.

The old man fell to his knees and gave thanks, unconcerned his seer lay dead. He had been blessed with a prophecy and the coming was nigh.

I must not hesitate to act.

He struggled to his feet and stumbled to the corner of the room, where he pulled a locked metal box from above the cupboard. The key hung on a leather string around his neck, tucked safely beneath his robes. He withdrew the key and opened the box.

With few earthly needs, his savings had grown to a respectable sum. He hoarded the donations collected each Sunday beneath his revival tent near the edge of the swamp. The old minister counted out fifty dollars then added twenty-five more. He would pay half when he commissioned the Lord's work, with the remainder paid upon completion.

He put the box away, and without a glance at the body in the corner, he stepped from the cabin into the swampland, and headed south toward town.

It was a short walk to his *pirogue*, a flat-bottomed canoe he kept hidden beside the bayou. Once on the water, he paddled swiftly down the channel to the canal. Another thirty minutes saw him secure his craft at the canal public dock, and shuffle down the cobbled street toward the riverfront. He had a particular riverboat in mind.

A parishioner had spoken to him last Sunday about a bounty hunter who lived in New Orleans. The church member begged prayers for the man, who played the devil's games aboard riverboats and carried the mark of Lucifer on his face. They'd even gone so far as to warn him they'd seen this gambler on Allen Tremble's boat, the minister's own cousin. Minister Tremble promised to pray for the Godless sinner, and now he intended to hire him. It would suit his purpose just fine if the spawn of Lucifer became the instrument through which he fulfilled his Lord's commands. God's way was surely mysterious.

The sun had begun to set as he hurried along the dock to the boat he believed belonged to his cousin. At the gangway to the craft, a large muscular watchman greeted patrons as they boarded the riverboat.

The minister bowed his head when he made eye contact with the man, and then approached with his eyes downcast. "Excuse me, young man, could you tell me if this is Allen Tremble's boat?"

The big man, dressed in a crewman's gray uniform, regarded the ragged minister with visible disdain. "Captain Tremble is the owner of this vessel. What business do you have with him?"

"I was—that is—I heard there might be a man on board who seeks employment. I am Captain Tremble's cousin, and if the Lord wills it, I may be able to supply work for this man."

The watchman nodded as a few passengers departed, and then returned his attention to the minister. "Do you have the name of this man, or do you want to speak with your cousin?"

"Oh, no, don't bother the captain. I would, however, like to speak with a man they call Hunter, if he's on board. He has a notable scar on his face."

For the next few minutes, the man ignored the minister and welcomed several people on board by name. Finally, he turned to the persistent old man, glared at him for a moment, and then waved to a crew member who stood across the gangway. The young man stepped over to the watchman who bent down to whisper in his ear.

"No," the crewman replied. "The game hasn't started. They're waiting for the last player to arrive."

"Fine, then. Would you tell Mr. Hunter there's an individual, dockside, who wishes to speak with him?" The watchman raised an eyebrow and cast an annoyed glance at the minister. "He says he wants to offer Mr. Hunter a job."

The crewman nodded and disappeared inside the boat.

The watchman and the minister waited in silence and watched foot and carriage traffic along the waterfront. A rented carriage came to a stop several feet from the gangway, and a handsomely dressed gentleman stepped from the coach. He held out his hand to assist a woman from the vehicle, and then proceeded to the gangway with the young woman on his arm.

The gentleman smiled, tipped his top hat to the watchman, and presented him with a card from his vest pocket. "Samuel Kline," the man said with a smile. "And guest." He then proceeded up the gangway into the riverboat.

The watchman slipped the card into his pocket and looked down at the minister. "That's the last passenger." He turned away from the old man and crossed the gangway.

"But—but—" Minister Tremble stammered as the watchman ignored him and disappeared into the dark interior of the boat. He rolled his hands and looked around for assistance or inspiration. This opportunity had been set before him, he couldn't let it pass. With a quick inhale, he tucked his chin and set foot on the gangway to follow the watchman inside. He stopped when a man appeared out of the darkened doorway.

The man stood as tall as the watchman, but wore formal evening attire. His straight black hair had been combed back and tied in a queue at the collar of his jacket. An old scar ran from the outside of his left eye to his chin, and showed pale beside his tanned skin. His dark gaze locked with the minister's as he stepped across the footbridge. "Are you the man who asked to speak with me? I don't believe we've met," the gambler said, without hesitation.

"My name's Minister Tremble. I've been assigned a glorious task by our Lord. He has put you in my path to assist me. That is, if you are Mr. Hunter."

The dark-haired man's eyebrow rose, and he nodded. "I am. Unfortunately, we are about to shove off. Can this glorious task wait a few more hours?"

The old man licked his lips and hesitated a moment before he nodded. "Where should I wait?" He looked around to hide his displeasure.

I must pray for patience.

"This would be up to you, *monsieur.*" Hunter shrugged wide shoulders and pointed up the wharf as he turned toward the boat. "You could wait at the Riverside Boarding House, two blocks east, or you could wait on the dock." The gambler crossed the gangway, then glanced back at the minister. "We'll be back in about four hours. If you're here when I return, I'll listen to what you have to say. *Au revoir.*"

Minister Tremble watched him disappear into the dark interior of the vessel. The crew pulled the gangway in and secured the entryway. The paddleboat inched away from the dock and began its slow turn into the Mississippi.

The minister watched the boat, while he recited Bible passages to himself, and repeated a portion of the seer's prophecy. "By Fire and Earth, he shall be defeated."

Chapter 5

Morago

—

The Snake Pit

The demon opened reptilian eyes. Its rest had lasted seven hundred years.
What has awakened me?
Balled together with other slumbering demons—snakes coiled at the mouth of hell—Morago eased away from the others.

He slithered from the knotted coil and raised his head to contemplate the gate. Bound in hell, it stood as a barrier between his kind and the world of men. Each of his demon brethren would confront a gate different from his, as individual as the demons themselves.

No stranger to the world of men, Morago had entered on numerous occasions. A hunter by nature, he coveted power. Any power he acquired remained his by right, by the law of the predator, the conqueror. His prey always had the ability to defeat him, and they always knew he approached.

His release from hell would have been preceded by prophecy. A foretelling for those who knew where to look and how to listen. This type of contest had played out many times over the centuries. Each triumph added a new skill to his arsenal. Each defeat returned him to hell.

He considered himself the most magnificent demon in his coil. His abilities provoked much envy among his lesser brethren.
They would take my power if they could.
Yet, he remained undefeated.

Anticipation shivered down his serpentine body. Desire for a new talent, one which existed solely in the world of men, filled him. The opportunity to obtain new ones struck but once a millennium. Only by defeating his opponent and consuming their soul could he take their magic as his own. For that was where true power resided—in the soul.

Possession had been his first skill acquisition for use in the world of men. He earned the ability to possess another over a thousand years ago in this very hall. The demon he defeated served him as a slave now, along with two dozen other demonic souls, who had been felled by his prowess. Under his command, he could unleash them with a thought to do his bidding. His demonic horde amplified his authority and served at his will.

More—I need more magic, more skills.

Powerful in hell, the capabilities he used against his brethren demons were forbidden to him on Earth. Once he entered the realm of men, he became vulnerable because of his limited power.

But the potential reward!

With deliberate thought, he reviewed his earthly skills. *Limited mind-reading*—he could skim the minds of unwarded humans—know their thoughts. *Seduction*—when in possession of a human body, none could withstand his charm. He had only one skill which remained potent in both worlds—*absorption*. The moment of his opponent's defeat, he would absorb their power, along with their soul.

The abilities he coveted were many: prescience, invulnerability, teleportation, and shape-shifting, to name a few.

I want them all.

Each new skill built on others. As his power increased, new abilities became easier to acquire.

A sensation crawled along his skin and flared his scales with desire. It spoke to him of elemental manipulation. The power of the witch. He coveted those skills more than any other, even though it meant a dangerous adversary awaited him. His eyes dilated in anticipation, and his forked tongue tasted the air.

As the Prophecy of the Twins came into fulfillment, a painful shock shot through his scales. Elemental power *twyned*, and the gates of his personal hell swung open. Morago slithered into the world of man, prepared for the hunt.

This was not the first time prophecy had released him from hell. Each time before, he could pinpoint the location where the prophecy manifested, but not this time. Two distinct positions—miles apart—burned into his mind as he slid along the bottom of the ocean, away from his prison. He swam north along the coast, toward the nearest point of revelation.

Morago left the water of the North Atlantic and coiled in the mud beneath a pier. Sailors and merchants passed along the boards above his head. Their thoughts slipped through his mind, dreams of sweethearts, business deals, travelers. A busy port, chosen well for his purposes.

A merchant nearby directed the loading of his wagon and reviewed the route for his deliveries. A route which would take him inland, in the direction Morago desired to go.

Serpent skin split and fell empty as Morago's evil essence turned to vapor. The initial possession of a living being could not take place while in his primordial form. His pure essence had to be inhaled to gain control of a living creature. Once inside a warm-blooded host, he could jump from mind to mind with only a thought. He could not maintain a vapor form for long, and there lay his greatest danger. To release the primordial form too soon, and not take command of a suitable host, would return his soul to hell.

The low floating vapor meandered along the waterfront and spread unnoticed toward the road. His target, the unsuspecting merchant.

The man stepped off the pier and into the dusty street as he followed the dockworker, along with his merchandise, to his wagon. Both the worker and the merchant passed through a dense patch of fog. The merchant became choked and began to sneeze. He pulled his handkerchief from his pocket and held the material balled in his fist to his nose.

"Dieu vous bénisse!" the workman called over his shoulder as he loaded crates onto the wagon.

God bless you, the workman called.

The merchant chuckled and returned the handkerchief to his pocket. *"Merci."*

Undetected, Morago rode beside the merchant's consciousness and peered out through the man's eyes, filled with malevolent anticipation.

Chapter 6

Alyse James

—

Bayard served everyone tea, and then seated himself beside his brother. Alyse sat across from Bernard, at Chantal's right hand. Alyse sipped her tea and waited with hard-won patience for her grandmother to begin her tale.

Chantal tasted her tea then set the white porcelain cup on the saucer before she raised her eyes and looked at Alyse. "This tale begins before your birth, so I shall start there. When your grandfather and I were first married, we lived in Boston. We owned a small print shop and provided patriotic pamphlets and what news we could gather during the second war with Great Britain."

Alyse shifted with impatience, and then stilled as Chantal narrowed her eyes with displeasure.

"Eager to assist with the war effort, we pledged ourselves to a local coven and directed our energies to aid our troops. At this time, a young woman who was part of the coven became quite ill. Her family brought a physician to her bedside, but he gave them no hope. Healing spells did not restore her health. No matter what we tried, the girl continued to weaken.

"Toward the end, she suffered dreadful trembling fits. The coven gathered to ease her passing as best we could. There were six members present when she spoke her last words—*The Prophecy*—and then perished."

"What prophecy?" Alyse urged when her grandmother paused.

Chantal shook her head. "I'm not sure I can recite her exact words." Chantal's gaze met and held Alyse's. "At the time, I thought I'd never forget. She foretold the birth of powerful twins." Chantal closed her eyes and took a deep breath. "Let me see, how did it go?

"You will know them by their birth—crowned beneath a full moon on the witches' High Sabbat. Their *twyne* shall wake the Demon. By Fire and Earth, he shall be felled—lest the *twyne* fail—then death shall reign." Chantal's cup rattled against its saucer as she lifted it. "Or something very similar."

No one spoke for several moments.

Alyse took another sip but found it hard to swallow; her throat had grown so tight. She glanced from her teacup to her uncles.

Bayard stared at the table, while Bernard met her gaze with a serious expression in his dark eyes. Their balding scalps fringed with brown-gray trimmed hair—identical.

Chantal cleared her throat. "Twelve years later, I became pregnant with twins—your uncles. As you can imagine, your grandfather and I were terrified. Thank the Goddess, I gave birth to my boys just past midsummer, beneath a crescent moon. Six years later, I gave birth to your mother, and we set thoughts of the terrifying prophecy aside.

"Your grandfather passed in '41. Margaret married her merchant in '45, didn't she?" Chantal looked to Bay and Bern who shook their heads and shrugged.

Chantal turned back to Alyse. "When your mother became pregnant, we were overjoyed. But as the pregnancy progressed, it became clear she carried twins, and would give birth near Samhain."

"I was born on Samhain," Alyse stated.

"Yes, you were." Chantal's hazel eyes held old sorrow and memories. "Beneath the light of a full moon."

"And you separated us because—"

"—because if were you to *twyne* as children, you would have called the Demon. Even with four adult witches to protect you, it would not have been enough. Our spells at that time were limited in power—gentle spells to encourage health and healing, abundant crops, and potions of affection. We rarely dabbled with our deep elemental power and took great care to hide our true nature from the eyes of men.

"After your birth, our path changed. Your uncles and I turned our minds to offensive and defensive spellcraft—deadly spells which others of our kind would find abhorrent. Still, the power you share with your sister—*when you twyne*—is what will be needed to defeat the Demon."

"You've been training me," Alyse whispered. Her gaze passed around the table.

"As best we can." Uncle Bay raised his gaze to hers. "We don't have your disability, of course."

Bernard elbowed his brother. "Ah, hush, Bay. We don't have her power, either."

"Without *Air* and *Earth*, the girl has serious limitations," Bayard argued.

"I need my sister," Alyse acknowledged, and the room grew quiet once again.

"You need your sister," Chantal repeated. "Did you *twyne* with her today?"

Alyse nodded. "She didn't understand what was happening. I knew because you had taught me about it." She looked at Bay and Bern. "I frightened her. She didn't know me."

"The only one to teach Amylia would have been your mother, Margaret, and she keeps her talents hidden from her husband. Whatever Amylia knows, she learned in secret and practiced alone." Chantal laid her hand on Alyse's arm.

"I have to go to her." Alyse turned to her grandmother. "I promised to find her. Is she in Boston with my—with my mother?" Unexpected tears welled in Alyse's eyes. She blinked rapidly and turned her face away from Chantal.

"As far as I know, she's still there. I've not seen your mother since the night we left with you."

"The night of my birth?" Alyse swallowed and blinked at the tears, pushing them from her eyes.

"The moment of your birth," Chantal corrected, and patted her arm. "We had a wet nurse and carriage hidden down the street. You see, Bay and Bern *twyned* at 18 months, maybe earlier. We couldn't risk that possibility."

"And my parents—they agreed to this?" Alyse turned and searched her grandmother's eyes. Their explanations were sound, but her heart ached for a mother she'd never known.

"When it became apparent her children would be born on Samhain, during the full moon, and drastic measures would need to be taken to keep you both safe, Margaret's heart broke." Chantal picked up her napkin and held it to her nose. She cleared her throat and opened calm eyes.

"The closer she came to your birth, the more Margaret cried. Your father had no idea how devastated we all were. He believed Margaret's tears were a result of her pregnancy, and nothing more.

"The night of your birth, I delivered you, and your mother held you for only a few minutes—until her labor began again. Then, you were bundled up and given to the wet nurse. You, Bayard and the wet nurse set out for this farm immediately." Chantal paused and then added, "Your mother named you Alyse. She thought it the most beautiful name she'd ever heard."

Alyse's throat closed and she shook her head, fighting back the tears.

A mother and sister I've never known.

In the end, she gave up and put her head down on the table and sobbed.

Her grandmother's hand smoothed her hair. "It had to be done, dear one. It broke everyone's heart. And now, you need to be strong and find your sister. You're being hunted."

Alyse's head came up, her eyes red from weeping, and stared at her grandmother. "Hunted?"

"Yes child. The Prophecy. The reason you were separated. The moment you *twyned* with your sister, it set off a chain of events. I have no doubt the Demon is coming, just as I have no doubt you and your sister will face him and defeat him."

"By Fire and Earth." Alyse wiped her face and sat up.

Chantal nodded. "Just so. Now, it's late and I think we should all get some rest. Tomorrow, Bay will need to advise the Chesham's their order will be delayed—indefinitely. Allow them to cancel and go elsewhere if they can't wait until you return."

Bay's brow furrowed as his gaze turned to his mother. "What do you mean?"

"From where?" Bern added.

"When you return from teaching your nieces how to cast as a working pair. Some *twyning* exercises will be in order as well, I presume. Who better to teach them how to fight together? Besides, we can't send Alyse off to find Amylia by herself."

"She thinks of herself as Amy," Alyse whispered and turned tear-filled eyes to her grandmother. "Won't you come with us, *Mémé?*"

"Ah, now dear one, I shall not. I will only slow you down. I'll stay here and wait for your return. I do look forward to meeting your sister."

Chapter 7

Nichole Harris

—

Nichole held the damp washcloth to her face and groaned. The time overlap threatened to wreck her mind. The pace and emotion of everyone around her were distant and out of step with her memory. In her mind, she had experienced today's events with Amy and Jim weeks ago. The Highlands barbecue, the dawn escape from the ranch, and even Jones's brutal ambush were less immediate to her than the flight from Dallas and finding the photo of Merril. Her recollections needed to be reordered, and she had more than one set of memories to prioritize.

Nichole's experience advised, *"You'll just have to make do. Collect yourself and keep going."*

While Courtney's muttered, *"Holy-shit! Did this just happen?"*

She required time to put herself back together in perspective with—this life. Courtney and Nichole weren't separate.

They're both me.

Past and present. A few days should settle her senses, align her with this time, this body, and distance herself from her past.

My future?

She fought the impulse to confide her newfound realizations with Merril and Amy—to continue the conversations started with half-understood truths.

I have those answers now. At least, some of them.

She wouldn't be at peace until those conversations were finished, but she also knew those would have to wait. The emotional momentum of here and now had to take precedence.

When Merril had brought her trunk, he hesitated to leave her alone, but she encouraged him to help Jason. She assured him she wanted privacy to wash and change, when in truth, she needed this time and solitude to acclimate her time-lanced senses.

The water in the basin turned pink when she wrung the washcloth. She removed the torn, blood-soaked blouse, along with the shredded camisole, and tossed them aside. Her breasts and shoulders were speckled and smeared with blood.

Movement in the small dresser mirror caught her attention, and she stepped closer to peer at her reflection. The blood in her hair hadn't had time to harden and dry. She rolled her fingers over the hair beside her temple, and then she looked at her red-stained fingertips.

Is all this blood mine?

She searched her face in the mirror, checked her nose and teeth. If she lost this much blood, shouldn't there be some evidence? Some injury?

She wiped her body clean and rinsed what blood she could from her hair, and then dried herself with the last towel. There were no injuries on her body that would account for this amount of blood.

Speculation is useless.

Merril and Amy would know. They were both with her when she awoke.

She turned to the trunk and paused. Her thumb slid over the initials engraved above the latch.

N.H.

Her thumb came away clean, but she rubbed it against her finger anyway. *So weird.*

As Courtney, she had pried the rusted latch open this morning—over a hundred years from now.

This time, the clasp opened easily. Still, Nichole hesitated to lift the lid.

Don't be silly.

She closed her eyes and opened the trunk. Breath held, she looked down. In the center of her lavender skirt laid the photograph of Kevin, Merril, and herself. When she lifted the photo, her hand trembled, and she gripped the frame with both hands.

This is the photo she'd found in the attic—this item led her back to Merril. If she unpacked it, would that change what Courtney found when she came looking? If she didn't discover the photo in the attic, would she not have opened her eyes in Merril's arms today?

Before she changed her mind and had the trunk along with all its contents hauled to the attic, she placed the photo on the mantelpiece. Her gaze shifted from the photo to the closed bedroom door.

I'm still here.

She stood still for a few minutes, but nothing changed.

Would I know if it did?

With a shrug, she returned to the case for clean clothes. She bypassed the lavender outfit, and instead, chose the dark blue skirt with a white camisole and blouse.

While she dressed, her mind traced loops of time and possible alterations she'd made to the timeline from her visit before. There was no way to know, and no value in obsessing over it. She ran the brush through her damp hair and looked at her reflection in the mirror.

Suck it up, Veau, and get on with the life you died for.

Despite her intention to slip back into Nichole's life—*her life*—unresolved questions haunted her.

As afternoon slipped to evening, she convalesced beside Jimmy Leigh at the kitchen table, trapped in a haze of emotional anxiety. An internal dialogue played in her head as she watched the day wind down from the sidelines.

The police chief knocked at the recently repaired back door and stepped into the kitchen. He spotted Amy coming down the stairs and removed his hat. "After speaking with your husband, I've determined the break-in and death of the intruder to be a consequence of a robbery gone awry." He glanced at Nichole and Jim. "Your unexpected return home resulted in a most unfortunate confrontation."

Nichole raised an eyebrow at his choice of words.

Unfortunate? Yeah.

"I find no need for further investigation." The officer tipped his hat and left the kitchen.

She exchanged glances with Jim and Amy, but nobody spoke.

An unidentified intruder. Tidy. Less paperwork.

Jason and Albert Fielding came in and went upstairs to look at the damaged wall.

Merril stayed downstairs and accepted a cup of water from Amy while he waited for Jason and Albert. "The undertaker just left." Merril informed them. His gaze turned to Nichole. "He and his helper tossed Jones in the back of their wagon." He set the empty cup on the counter. "Jones will have an unmarked grave at the edge of the city cemetery."

Nichole clenched her teeth and looked at the table.

Better than the prick deserved. Whatever.

She looked up as the sound of boots echoed down the stairs.

"We're off to the lumberyard." Jason planted a quick kiss on Amy's cheek as Merril and Albert left the kitchen. "Albert knows several contractors. He said he would contact a mason and a glazier to schedule repairs, if I approved."

If Jason approved?

Nichole ground her teeth but held her silence.

Albert Fielding's plump wife, Wilma, dropped off a casserole and a bag of warm biscuits for their supper. She apologized for not coming inside, but Albert would still want dinner at home tonight. The beef and vegetable casserole filled the room with a mouth-watering scent. Nichole's stomach growled.

Albert hurried home to his dinner after the men boarded up the front bedroom.

Merril and Jason took seats at the table while Amy unwrapped Wilma's casserole.

Tom Baker arrived at the town house just as Amy set plates and utensils on the table. Tom filled his plate, took a biscuit, and wedged himself into the corner.

Nichole watched Amy scoop a serving onto her plate, then pull a chair from the corner to sit at the counter. Perhaps Amy preferred to eat by herself rather than sit close to Jason.

Can't say I blame her.

Jim, Jason, and Merril sat at the table with Nichole. She watched Jason eat as her annoyance built and her appetite fled. Jason could have prevented everything. Although he took no active role in the threat—that either Nichole marry Kevin, Merril's brother, or be committed to an asylum—his apathy had allowed it to happen. Anger ignited in the pit of her stomach, and she thought she might be sick. No one noticed her hard stare at her cousin, and the conversation went on around her.

"Midnight and Sadie." Merril looked up at Tom with hesitation and regret in his green eyes. "Are they... all right?"

Tom swallowed and split his gaze between Merril and Jason. "You're damned lucky you were near someone who had enough sense to take care of your animals."

"Tom," Jim's low voice held a reprimand.

Tom looked to Jim, then down at his plate. "Yup. They're dehydrated and exhausted, probably wind-broken, but they'll live."

Merril dropped his fork and rubbed his face with both hands. "Thank the Lord. I'll go by the livery in the morning and check on him—on them both."

Nichole glanced around the table, when Amy caught her attention. Amy tipped her head toward Jason, then nodded at Nichole. Her meaning clear—ask him now.

"So—Jason," Nichole's soft voice began conversationally, and then rose with resentment. "Explain to me just what the *hell* you were thinking."

Jason's head shot up, and their ice-blue gazes locked. "Mind your language, please."

Indignation brought Nichole to her feet. "You *will not* tell me what to do." She clenched her teeth. "Not *ever* again." She pointed her fork at Jason. "You were going to let them put me in an asylum."

Jason indicated her abandoned chair. "Calm down. I would never have allowed that to happen."

"Really? You turned your back while Clemens and Renata drugged me." Nichole fought back angry tears.

I will not cry.

"I had no idea what they intended. They acted before I could stop them."

"So, you weren't going to let them send me away? You only used that threat as leverage to force me to marry Kevin."

Jason nodded, his face scarlet beneath his fair hair. "Renata and Kevin wanted the marriage." He glanced up at Nichole then back to the table. "I never agreed to participate. I warned Renata if you refused to marry Kevin, I wouldn't force you."

"How noble of you." Anger throbbed in her head. She tossed her fork onto her plate, placed her hands on the table and leaned toward her cousin as her voice rose. "And how unfortunate you failed to mention that small detail to me."

Jason's jaw clenched. "You're mistaken. I never intended—"

She pounded her fist on the table. "Then why didn't you stop them?" Tears filled her eyes.

"Renata blackmailed me," Jason whispered.

"What could Renata possibly know that's worth all of this?" Nichole looked at Jim and Amy, then back to Jason.

Jason sighed and shook his head. "All right. I'll tell you everything. If you want a full confession, and a list of all my sins, then you'll get it." He looked around the table. "You're all aware of the bank failures?"

"Weren't they caused by the fire?" Amy's voice softened as she stared at her husband.

"Not entirely, but both the Boston and Chicago fires played a role in the downward economy. The Boston fire is where everything began for me." Jason and Amy exchanged glances, then Jason turned back to the group at the table. "There were many factors—Grant's Coinage Act, the railroad failures, reconstruction, and inflation, among others. They all contributed to my personal economic collapse."

"Now you've lost me." Nichole lowered herself to her chair and pushed her half-eaten dinner to the center of the table.

"A brief explanation then." Jason sat back and looked around the table. "President Grant moved the States from a silver and gold standard for valuing our currency, to a pure gold standard in '73. My investments in three silver mines proved a substantial loss.

"Until two years ago, railroad bonds seemed a sure investment, but their value had been over-inflated. Railway expansion appeared a foregone conclusion, until Grant raised interest rates to slow inflation." Jason shook his head. "Banks with large debt, especially those with investments in railroads, went bust. Over fifty railroads failed. They're just gone. Sixty more have filed bankruptcy since the stock market's ten-day close, two years ago.

"Unemployment is above eight percent. New construction is down, except for this area of the country. Real estate values have plummeted, to say nothing of corporate profits. The country—" Jason spread his arms wide, "—the world is in a great depression, and all my personal investments have failed."

No one spoke as everyone in the room considered Jason's words.

Nichole shifted in her seat and folded her hands on the table. "You lost a lot of money."

"All of it, and more." Jason shot a quick look at Amy. "I borrowed capital from an investment firm, Pierce and Peabody, to reinvest—in an attempt to mitigate so many losses."

"Let me guess." Nichole rolled her eyes. "They had a few 'just can't lose' opportunities for you."

"Yes." Jason nodded. "But those failed as well."

"How much do you owe them?" Nichole asked.

"Twenty thousand dollars, before interest," Jason admitted. He cast another brief glance at Amy.

Jim let out a low whistle.

Merril shook his head and muttered, "Twenty *thousand* dollars?"

Amy gasped. "Jason, how could you?"

"It gets worse," Jason said when the exclamations quieted. "P&P put pressure on me to do unethical things for them in Boston. If I worked for them, they would pay down a portion of the interest I owed.

"I didn't know what to do, and then I received an invitation from Uncle Quincy to come West and help with The Highlands' bookkeeping. I jumped at the opportunity." Jason's voice trailed off, and the room fell silent. After a moment, he shook his head and continued.

"P&P followed me here, or their letters and threats did. They demanded payment but implied they would reduce the interest rate if I provided them with certain... information on potential investments out west." He shrugged and looked around. "All I knew about running a ranch I learned from Uncle Quincy. I'm ashamed to say, I sent P&P information on both the Shilo and Highlands' ranches."

"What kind of information?" Merril asked and sat forward.

"The number of head, wages, expenses and income on The Highlands. Rough estimates of the same for The Shilo. I've no idea why they valued this information. It isn't as though your ranches had stock options with curbstone brokers or the Boston Stock Exchange." He shook his head. "Their interest is unimportant now. What *does* matter is Renata learned of my correspondence with P&P. She threatened to expose me as a spy. That alone wouldn't have been enough, but she knew more."

He didn't look up when he paused, and the room remained silent. With a quick inhale, he raised an apologetic gaze to Nichole. "After Uncle Quincy died, I reinvested a large portion of The Highlands' assets, to diversify our portfolio."

"You'll explain how *my* ranch is now *our* portfolio," Nichole replied sarcastically.

"All right then, *your* portfolio. After what happened in '73, I knew it to be the height of foolishness to have all of your money tied up in one asset. I even spoke to you about it, but I doubt you remember."

"Oh, I remember," Nichole replied. "But I didn't understand what it meant, and you *knew* I didn't."

"You're right." Jason hesitated. "I—didn't put the new investments in The Highlands' name. I hold those in my name alone."

"You what?" Anger brought Nichole to her feet. "My father trusted you. I trusted you. You're a liar and a thief."

"Embezzler is the actual term, and in my defense, I did speak to you about my objectives. Uncle Quincy and I discussed which investments he favored before his accident." Jason rose and faced Nichole across the table. "Both of you were aware of my goal, and I have every intention of paying The Highlands back, plus interest."

"Your good intentions turn to shit, Jason, in case you haven't noticed."

Jason's jaw flexed, and he balled his fist. "Mind your language."

Nichole's lip curled. "Kiss my ass."

Merril's chair scraped back as he came to his feet. "Jason, sit down before you do something you'll regret." Merril turned to Nichole. "This isn't the best time to have this conversation. It's been a rough day for everyone."

Jason resumed his seat, but Nichole remained standing. If she sat, she might not get back up. Fatigue heightened her emotions, and she only wanted to curl up beside Merril and fall asleep.

She heaved a sigh and spoke down at Jason. "You'll transfer everything back to The Highlands' name." Nichole paused until he nodded, then continued. "You'll no longer have unrestricted access to The Highlands' accounts. Every transaction will require my signature."

"You're not putting me out?"

"I should, but I won't." A yawn caught her by surprise and she covered her mouth. "Oh, excuse me. If you have more confessions, they'll have to wait until tomorrow. I can't stay awake any longer." Nichole circled the table toward the stairs and held out her hand to Merril.

"What rooms will you be in?" Amy asked. "We've more people than beds."

"We'll be in the far back bedroom. The one I changed in." Nichole grasped Merril's hand and followed him up the stairs.

"Nichole, you can't share a room with Merril. You're unwed." Jason came to his feet and tossed his napkin on the table.

Nichole turned and looked at Jason from the bottom step. "Are you serious?" She released Merril's hand and stepped down onto the floor.

"Let it go, Nic. I can sleep down here." Merril offered.

"No," she said softly to Merril, then turned to Jason. "You have no authority over me. I can, and I will, do as I please."

"He's concerned for your reputation." Amy stood and looked from her husband to Nichole.

"My reputation?" Nichole matched Jason glare for glare. "He should have had more care for his own." She turned to Amy and her face softened. "For you, I'll offer him this."

Nichole reached back and took Merril's hand, then cast her gaze around the room. "Merril and I were married the night we spent with the Cheyenne. Gifts were exchanged, and I was given my Indian name by their shaman, White Eagle. You may address me as Lost Wind, wife of Dark Moon." She narrowed her eyes at Jason as she performed a slight curtsy, and then turned her back and mounted the stairs.

"Legally, I don't believe that counts," Jason called.

Nichole would have turned back, but Merril didn't release her hand. "Let it go, sweetheart. You can fight with your cousin tomorrow. I have other things in mind for tonight."

Chapter 8

Hunter

—

Hunter left the River Queen soon after the riverboat docked. Instead of his usual quick stroll up the street to the boarding house, he crossed the gangway and leaned against the rail. He lit a cheroot and nodded farewell to acquaintances while he waited for Sam Kline to exit the boat. Hunter had spotted the tall blond man when he boarded, but Sam had managed to avoid Hunter all night.

Hunter had met U.S. Marshal Samuel Kline nigh on ten years ago. They had a working relationship that bordered on friendship, until three years ago. Sam remained pleasant when they encountered each other at the boarding house or livery stable, but their friendship appeared to have ended.

He's been like this since that Christmas in Beaumont.

The last time Sam had acted like himself, Hunter thought they would ride back from Texas with that little spitfire redhead Sam had been so taken with.

I wonder what happened to Nell?

Sam never spoke of her, and Hunter knew better than to ask.

Because of Sam's behavior since Beaumont, it surprised Hunter to see him with a female companion this evening. A beautiful young woman with auburn hair and dark blue eyes. Although she seemed familiar, Hunter felt positive he would remember such a beautiful woman. Curious, and happy for Sam, Hunter hoped they could resume their relationship. He hadn't realized how much Sam's friendship had meant to him, until it was gone.

Hunter stood away from the rail and crushed out his cheroot as Sam stepped from the riverboat exit to the gangway. The mystery woman held his arm, and Sam laughed as she whispered in his ear. They followed a large group past Hunter, and he stepped up beside Sam as the couple walked by.

"*Bonsoir, mon ami.* I hope you had a pleasant evening." At six-foot-one, Hunter stood only an inch taller than Sam. When their gaze met, he could tell Sam's smile did not extend to his eyes.

"Good evening, Hunter. Another profitable night for you, I imagine?"

Hunter shrugged. "I consider it a good night when I break even. And you?"

"Down a bit, but overall, an enjoyable time." Sam continued up the street, past the line of carriages, toward the boarding house. He shrugged out of his jacket and placed it around his companion's shoulders.

Hunter matched their slower pace and walked beside Sam.

We're all going the same way, after all.

He glanced at the woman on Sam's arm and found her studying him with curiosity. Unaccountably pleased the scar along his cheek faced away from the young woman, Hunter tipped his head and smiled.

She returned the nod then turned her attention to the street ahead.

Hunter had forgotten about the minister, and his job offer, until the man stepped out of the shadows near the porch beside the boarding house.

"The Lord has blessed me with patience, Mr. Hunter. I have waited here this long night. I've a bounty for you, if you would accept it. Evil has shown its face to the world, and the Lord hath shared with me a glorious purpose."

Hunter and the couple beside him stopped and regarded the emaciated man.

His torn and filthy robe smelled of the swamp and unwashed flesh. He rolled his hands together, as though unable to hold them still. His hair, thin and oily, hung to his shoulders and exposed his dirty scalp.

Hunter exchanged a quick glance with Sam, then gave Tremble a nod. "Yes, of course, and we shall speak of your purpose, as soon as you permit my friends to pass."

The man stepped to the side and allowed the couple to reach the boarding house entrance.

Hunter touched his hat to Sam and the woman on his arm. "Good night."

"Good night." The woman looked back and smiled as Sam held the door.

Sam narrowed his eyes at Hunter, tipped his head, and walked through the door. His failure to introduce the young woman appeared a deliberate omission on Sam's part.

C'est la vie!

Hunter stepped onto the porch and perched on the rail, one foot to the ground. He pulled a cheroot from his jacket and struck a match.

The minister watched Hunter light the small cigar and shook his head. "You're a Godless man, Mr. Hunter. God's will is cloaked in mystery, and not for one such as I to understand."

"Nor I." Hunter blew out smoke and watched it float beyond the porch. "So, Minister Tremble, wasn't it? Tell me more about your intentions, and please be brief. As you say, it has been a long night."

The man nodded. "She spoke a prophecy, about the ones born on the Witch's Sabbath, under a full moon." He stepped closer to Hunter. "I want you to hunt and kill them. They plan to call a demon to fight against my Lord."

"Uh-huh." Hunter eyed Tremble and blew another puff of smoke into the night. "Who is she?"

"She is a witch, gifted with sight and prophecy. A succubus of temptation, she is made for sin, and simmers with evil." Passion raised his voice and moved the minister forward. He shifted from one foot to the other, and rubbed his hands together.

"*Mon ami*, you've been in the swamp far too long." Hunter tapped the ash over the rail.

"I can pay half now, and half when the deed is done." Minister Tremble reached into his robe and pulled out a roll of bills.

Hunter chuckled in disbelief and ran a hand over his face. "Minister Tremble, if I take your contract and kill for you, it would be murder. Do you understand?"

The minister nodded. "A most splendid sacrifice, in our Lord's name."

"*Mon Dieu!*" Hunter muttered. "If I *don't* take this contract, you will find someone else who will?" He clarified and crushed the tip of his cigar against the rail.

Minister Tremble nodded, bright eyed, and rubbing his hands. "The Lord's work must be done. He put you in my path when I needed a hunter; however, if you decline to fulfill his holy task, I shall be forced to recruit another such as yourself."

"I see." Hunter considered the man for a moment. "How much will you pay?"

"I have seventy-five-dollar notes here. There will be another seventy-five for you when the evil ones have been slain."

"I'll need two hundred fifty up front and the same when I'm done."

"This is outrageous." The minister exclaimed and stepped back, eyes bulging.

"You have asked me to murder someone for you. More than one, in fact. I don't negotiate. Take it or leave it." Hunter stood from his half-seated stance by the rail and stepped around the man.

"I'll pay your price. May the good Lord forgive your thievery." Tremble hesitated and gnawed his lip. "I don't have all you require with me. I shall have to return to my home."

Hunter crossed the porch. "Bring the money, the names of your witches, and their last known location. I can start in the morning."

"I do not know their names, Mr. Hunter. Nor their location." The minister shoved the notes back into his pocket.

Hunter turned and considered the small man again and scratched the back of his head. "You don't know who or where they are?"

"The prophecy did not provide those details."

"What about your succubus of temptation? Does she have this information?"

"Surely not. She has perished by the will of our Lord and passed from this earth."

Hunter stared at the minister, eyebrows raised. "You killed her?" He ran his hand through his hair and broke the tie that held it back.

"I did no such thing. She spoke the prophecy and expired. It's how I know she spoke a true foretelling." The minister nodded with self-righteous knowledge, his eyes gleaming with excitement.

"Uh-huh." Hunter remained silent for several minutes while he considered the minister.

Swamp worms have eaten his brain. The man is insane.

Hunter would have walked away from the lunatic and his bounty except for two things. Lives were at stake—if they even existed—and this maniac would pay two hundred fifty dollars up front.

"Do you know where the body of your succubus is now?"

The man smiled and nodded. "She is at my home."

"You have a dead body in your home?"

The lunatic nodded and grinned.

"*Sacrebleu!*" Hunter whispered and ran a hand over his face. "Perhaps you could take me to your house in the morning and pay the first fee. Oh, and one more thing; I will need to see the body of the woman."

"Why would you need to see a corpse?" the minister snapped.

"If I must explain myself to you, *mon ami,* the fee will double."

"I see, yes, I see." Minister Tremble nodded and rolled his hands. "I will be here in the morning. I have a canoe we will use to reach my house. Once you have seen the woman and taken your money, I'll return you here." He paused, fidgeting with his hands, and considered the scar on Hunter's face. "Is that satisfactory?"

"*Tout à fait.* I'll see you in the morning." Hunter entered the boarding house and left the minister on the porch.

Whoever this madman wants dead must be warned.

***

Sam Kline

—

Sam escorted the woman across the boarding house common room toward the stairs. He had secured a room for her not far from his, on the second floor.

The night clerk at the front desk called to him as they passed, "Marshal Kline? You received a telegram earlier. A runner for Western Union brought it by." The clerk held out a brown envelope.

Sam detoured to the desk to pick it up. "Thank you." He returned to the woman who waited by the foot of the stairs and gestured toward their rooms, envelope in hand. "Shall we go up?"

"Sam, I don't know why you asked me to come with you tonight." She turned and mounted the stairs. "Watching you gamble is the most tedious thing I can imagine."

"I couldn't leave you locked in your room, now, could I? I thought you'd enjoy the riverboat. There is more to do than just gamble." He opened the door to her room and then shrugged. "Although, I didn't expect to run into Hunter tonight."

"Is he the friend from the boat?" She tossed down her small handbag and rounded on Sam. "You didn't introduce me."

"Cat, you're my sister. I am not going to introduce you to a man like Hunter."

"That's ridiculous. You're a man like Hunter." Cat stomped her foot. "You keep me cloistered like a nun."

"I am not like Hunter." Sam tapped the unopened envelope against his hand as he watched her cross the room to the pitcher and glasses. "Hunter claims bounties. The Marshal's office has hired him, on occasion, because of his impressive tracking skills. That's how I met him."

Cat poured a glass of water. "How is hunting men different from what you do?"

Sam chuckled. "I'm a U.S. Marshal. I perform investigations for the government."

She handed Sam the water glass. "Which sometimes includes bringing in fugitives."

"True." He slipped the envelope into his inside pocket and took the glass from his younger sister. He took a sip and decided to change the subject. "A finishing school would be perfect for you." He unbuttoned his jacket and sat at the small table.

Cat sank into the other chair and regarded him over the rim of her glass. "Boarding school was bad enough." She took a sip and set the glass on the table. "I'm not a child anymore, Sam, and I have no interest in finishing school."

"But you've missed so much, Cat. Without a debut, you never had the chance to meet any nice young men your age—from good families." Guilt weighed heavy on Sam's conscience. After the yellow fever outbreak took their parents in '67, he had been little more than an occasional visitor in his sister's life.

She waved it off. "I never wanted a debut and a nice young man my age. I want to be with you, to get to know you again."

Sam searched her beautiful blue eyes and saw his mother's eyes. He shook his head, "I'm sorry Cat. I can't take you everywhere I need to go."

"Maybe not all the time, but sometimes you can. I won't stay in a finishing school. Besides, I have skills you could put to good use." Her mouth twisted in a suppressed smile.

"Skills?" He looked at her in confusion.

From beneath the fold of her skirt, she withdrew the brown envelope Sam had just put in his coat pocket.

His hand flew to his vest, then his gaze shot to hers in annoyance. "You learned this in boarding school?" He put his hand out for the envelope.

She lowered it into his palm. "Is this an assignment?"

Sam took the envelope and held it in his hand as he considered his sister. A lovely young woman of twenty, almost too old for a coming-out. She also held peculiar notions about what she wanted to do with her life. Perhaps it would be best to keep her under his watchful eye for a time.

Sam tapped the envelope against his palm and tore off the end. A puff of breath opened the pocket, and the telegram slid into his hand. He unfolded it and scanned the type. "This doesn't seem too bad. I think you'll be able to come with me—this time."

"What does it say?" Cat bounced forward trying to see the letter.

Sam folded the missive and put it back in the envelope. He began to return it to his pocket, but eyed his sister and changed his mind. Instead, he kept the envelope in his hand. "I have been asked to speak to a gentleman near Denver about some investments he made through a particular brokerage firm the Marshal's office intends to investigate."

"Denver?" Cat breathed. "I've never been out of New Orleans."

"I know." Sam stood to take his leave. "You'll get to see quite a bit of the country. I'll make our travel arrangements in the morning. Get some rest." He backed out of the room, envelope still in his hand, and closed the door.

"Lock the door, Cat." Sam called from the hallway. He waited until he heard the bolt slide home before he turned toward his room.

Cat's laughing voice sounded through the door. "I'm going to Denver."

Chapter 9

Nichole Harris

—

Nichole awoke before she opened her eyes. The scent of his warm skin beneath her cheek, and the steady beat of his heart, sent flutters from her stomach to her chest. Her eyes eased open, and her hand came into focus. Head on his shoulder, her relaxed fingers curled slightly on his chest as her palm rose and fell with each breath.

Merril.

She flattened her fingers and felt him tighten his arm around her shoulder in a gentle hug.

"Are you awake?" He kissed the top of her head.

"Hmm." Nichole smiled. His morning voice was low and soft. She shivered as the flutters moved lower. "What time is it?"

"Early. No one's up."

Nichole tilted her head to look into sleepy eyes. "I can't believe I'm here."

"So you've said." He trailed kisses along her brow and down the side of her face to her neck. "Where else would you be?"

"Mm—" Nichole murmured as he shifted her head to the pillow.

He rose above her, his weight supported by his forearms, and lowered his head to place a kiss on the center of her throat.

She pushed the hair back from his face and guided his mouth to her own.

His lips caressed her mouth and their tongues touched in a soft dance. Nichole moaned and arched against him. After a long, caressing kiss, he moved from her lips and trailed small, warm kisses from the corner of her mouth to her ear.

"I love you." He tugged at her earlobe with his teeth then kissed the side of her ear.

"And I love you." Why had she left her camisole and drawers on last night? Exhaustion seemed a feeble excuse now that her undergarments were between her and his naked chest. She scratched her nails gently across his back and chuckled as gooseflesh rose along his shoulders.

He tasted her neck once more then lifted his weight to his elbows. His eyes, shadowed in the morning light, stared down into her own.

"What?" She pushed his hair behind his ears and tried to pull him back to her, but he resisted.

"I made a mistake a few years ago, after our first time together at the cabin." He caught her hand and kissed her palm. "I thought you knew, or understood, I wanted us—wanted *this*—to be forever."

Her hand lingered along his jaw. "It will be, Merril. It wasn't a mistake."

"But I didn't tell you. I didn't ask." He whispered into her palm and kissed it again before he raised his gaze to hers. "Nichole Harris," his voice steadied and filled with emotion, "would you do me the honor of becoming my wife?" He waited, braced above her, his gaze moved from one eye to the other.

Her throat constricted even as she grinned up at him. She managed a hoarse whisper, "Of course, I will." Happiness trickled from the corner of her eyes through her hair to the pillow.

Merril lowered his head and his mouth touched her lips, sharing her breath. "I love you," he whispered so soft only her lips felt it, then he covered her mouth with his own and tightened his arms around her.

Pounding on the back door startled them both.

Through their open window above the kitchen door, the sound of a single pair of boots scuffed against stone. "Get a move on, dang it all."

In the room beneath them, a chair slid across the kitchen floor, and then they heard the door open.

"Kelly? What're you doin' here?" Tom's voice, hoarse with sleep.

"I came to get Merril. Is he here?" Kelly asked.

"Yeah, he's here. No one's up yet. Come on in, have a seat—" Tom's voice faded to muffled sounds through the floor as the back door shut.

"I need to get up, sweetheart." Merril placed a quick kiss on Nichole's nose.

"And things were just getting good." She smiled at the wide-eyed look he gave her as he sat up on the edge of the bed.

"Your cousin is across the hall." He half-whispered and pointed at the wall, but his grin ticked up.

Nichole chuckled. "Rain-check, baby."

"Rain-check?" He raised an eyebrow at her and reached for their clothes. Merril moved her skirt from the bedroom chair and set it at the foot of the bed, then shook out his denim trousers.

Nichole watched him dress with a possessive smile. His bandaged shoulder caught her attention. "How's your shoulder?"

Merril rotated the joint and slipped on his shirt. "Stiff, but the bullet wound has healed. The bandage could come off."

"Have Amy look at it." Nichole sat up and pulled her skirt into her lap.

Jim's door opened, and his halting step disappeared down the stairs. The distinct sound of his low voice added to the muffled discourse in the kitchen.

The latch rattled on the door across the hall, and Amy's light tread hurried toward the stairs. Jason's heavier footsteps came to a slow stop outside Nichole and Merril's door.

Merril paused buttoning his shirt and turned to Nichole. His half-grin grew wide, and he raised his eyebrow and tipped his head toward their door.

She pulled the blanket to her mouth and stifled a giggle. Instead of the knock she expected, Jason's pace resumed and followed Amy's down the stairs.

As soon as Jason's footsteps faded, Merril resumed dressing. He buckled on his gun belt and tied the holster tight to his leg. "We should tell him we're getting married. He feels responsible for your reputation." He paused and looked up. "Whatever is left of it after this last week."

Nichole shrugged. "Part of me understands his concerns, and the other half doesn't care." Nichole slipped from beneath the covers and pulled on her blouse and skirt. She ran the brush through her tangled curls to establish some order.

"Have you forgiven him for what he's done?" Merril rested his hand on the doorknob and met her gaze.

"No. I'm angry he didn't stop Renata and Kevin." She braided her hair, but several strands escaped her fingers. "I'm more forgiving of his investment venture." The braid disappeared, and she tied the whole wavy mess out of her face with a ribbon. "He knows what he did is wrong. He must have been desperate, and he did talk to us—my father and I—about his diversity scheme last year. I don't think he intended to steal the money."

Merril nodded. "He's put himself over the barrel with the bank, no doubt about it." Merril opened the door. "It's damned hard to forgive him for hurting you, even though I know Renata had him hog-tied like she did us." He motioned with his hand. "After you, sweetheart."

Nichole tipped her head back and smiled at Merril as she passed under his arm.

He grinned back, patted her bottom, and followed her out of the room and down the stairs.

A fire burned in the stove and water steamed from a pot on the flat-top. Both went ignored. Jim and Jason sat at the table while Tom and Kelly stood nearby, eyes downcast and silent. Amy faced the window, her back to the room.

As Nichole stepped into the kitchen, the heavy atmosphere brought her to a halt, and her stomach dropped.

This is bad.

Merril stepped down beside her. "What happened? What's wrong?"

The men had looked up when Merril spoke, but Jason and Tom looked away again.

Kelly tried to speak, but no sound escaped his throat. He shook his head and stared at his boots.

"Merril, have a seat." Jim used his foot to push a chair out from the table for Merril.

Merril stepped to the table and sat across from Jason, never taking his eyes from Jim.

"We've had some hard news from your ranch." Jim began, then paused and shook his head. "I'm just gonna say it. Sometime yesterday morning, Kevin shot and killed Renata, then turned the gun on himself. I'm sorry."

"Wh... What?" Merril's brows drew together, and he leaned back, shaking his head. "Kevin's—dead?" His gaze turned from Jim to Kelly. "Was anyone there? Do you know why, or what happened?"

Nichole placed her hand on Merril's shoulder, and he covered her hand with his own. She glanced back at Amy and their gazes met.

Did you know?

Amy shook her head, as though she could read Nichole's thoughts.

Jason cleared his throat. "I stopped at The Shilo yesterday morning and spoke with Kevin." Jason rubbed his unshaven face with his hand. "I wanted him to know Nicki had left The Highlands with Amy—and was beyond his reach."

Nichole caught her breath.

Did Kevin kill himself because of me? Because I left?

Years ago, Kevin had seemed like an older brother, but since the accident—and his father's death—he had changed.

This can't be about me. Why kill Renata?

Merril looked to Jason. "How did he seem? What did he say?"

"He was drunk, and still drinking." Jason shook his head and glanced at Nichole. "He hadn't been to bed or changed his clothes from the barbecue, as far as I could tell. I noticed his gun belt on your father's desk." He looked down at the table. "Renata came to the library before I left, furious Nichole had ruined her plans. I didn't talk with her. I said my piece to Kevin and left. I could hear them argue as I rode away." Jason raised his sorrow-filled gaze to Merril. "Kevin hadn't been himself since your father died."

"Well, damn." Merril leaned forward and placed his elbows on the table. He covered his face with his hands. "That stupid son-of-a-bitch."

Kelly shifted from one foot to the other. His voice was soft when he spoke. "Bill rode over from The Shilo with the news yesterday afternoon. He said Henny's daughter heard your brother and Phil's woman argue. Just before the gunshots, Kevin yelled that Renata had killed your pa." Kelly paused and looked around the room. "Lloyd sent Bill to Kiowa Crossing to fetch Doc Johnson and told me to come here and find you."

"This doesn't make sense to me." Merril scrubbed his face and sat back in the chair. "I need to get back to the ranch." He stared at the coffee cup Amy set at his elbow.

"I'll go with you." Nichole ran a gentle hand across his shoulders.

Kevin and Renata both dead?

She cared for neither of them, but couldn't imagine The Shilo without them.

Jason shook his head, his face pale but determined. He looked from Nichole to Merril. "Nicki stays here."

"We're going to be married." Merril raised his head and looked at Jason.

Jason continued to shake his head. "Not today. Not before you need to leave."

"There's a Justice of the Peace on Park Avenue, just past the livery. I saw the sign as we rode in yesterday." Amy set Jason's tea on the table and smiled when he looked up at her.

"We can stop there on our way out of town," Nichole suggested.

I can only pack a few things.

She would need to leave her trunk here.

"None of the horses we rode yesterday have had enough rest," Tom chimed in.

"Not *all* of us can leave today, anyway." Amy looked from Tom to Jim. "Jim needs to heal a few more days before he gets back in the saddle."

Jim nodded. "Tom should go with Merril and Nichole. Lloyd will need him. The rest of us can follow in a couple of days."

"This marriage is a reckless decision," Jason cut in, color returning to his face. "You shouldn't marry on the heels of such devastating news. What's the rush?"

"There's no rush to marry, but I won't be separated from Merril." Nichole shrugged at Jason. "Besides, as far as we're concerned, we're already married. I told you last night."

"You were outrageous last night." Jason sputtered. Red crawled up his neck from his collar. "I excused your behavior for being distraught by my confessions. However, your compulsion to be disagreeable at each opportunity must cease."

"You what? You excused *my* behavior?" Nichole blinked, then narrowed her eyes as she advanced on Jason. "I go where Merril goes, Jason. Period. I'm not *asking* for your permission." She put her fists on her hips and glared at her cousin. Her voice dropped low. "My disagreeable behavior is no longer your concern.

Jason's face flushed dark. He looked from Nichole to Merril, then shook his head and looked down at the table, fists clenched beside his teacup.

Nichole's voice softened. "I love you, Jason, but I'll make my own decisions—outrageous or not." Her arms fell to her side. "Accept this, please, and let's not fight about it anymore."

Jim caught Nichole's desperate glance and turned to The Highlands' messenger. "Kelly, head over to the Justice and ask what time he could come by the house today." When Kelly tipped his head, Jim looked across the room. "Tom, see if the livery can loan us three horses. I think most of the animals there are ours, but they stable some of their own."

Jason looked up from the table and nodded at Jim. "In that case, Merril and I should take down what's left of the front porch and talk to Albert about a mason."

Amy nodded to her husband, then gave a soft smile to Nichole. "You and I need to find something for you to wear."

Nichole tried to find a smile for Amy but turned instead to Merril, who sat silent, staring at his fists. She crouched by his chair and took his hands. They were cold. She remained quiet, and warmed his fingers with hers until he raised his gaze. "If this is too soon, I understand. We don't need to marry today. I will go with you to The Shilo, either way. We can marry later."

Merril gripped her hand and offered her a half-grin. "No, I want this. I've wanted this for what seems like forever. I'll be damned if I'll let Kevin and Renata come between us again. Kevin made his choice. Nothing I do will change that." His voice lowered, and he spoke only to her. "My love for you and our life together is the only good thing I can see right now."

Tom and Kelly slipped out the back door as Merril and Nichole spoke.

Jason and Merril exchanged a long look, and Jason gave a slow nod of his head. "Let's look at the porch, Jim." Jason stood, and Jim followed him outside.

"I'll be upstairs if you need me," Amy stated. She dried her hands then disappeared up the stairs.

Nichole sat back on her heels and waited. Sympathy, tinged with guilt, wracked her heart.

How much worse for Merril?

Both sorrow and anger shadowed his eyes. When his gaze rose to meet hers, he swallowed twice and cleared his throat. "Kevin and I were never close. Most of the time, we weren't even civil to one another." He released her hands and rubbed his forehead. "Christ, the last time I saw him, I tried to beat him to death." Merril's stare was sightless as he lowered his hands to his knees. "Until then, I had hoped he and I would someday come to understand one another."

Nichole rose to her knees and wrapped her arms around him. "You can hate someone and love them at the same time."

He pulled her close and rested his cheek against her hair. "I know." His whispered voice was a low rumble in his chest.

"You had a difficult relationship with Kevin, but there were good times, too. I even remember a few of them." She spoke into his shirt. "Your father's death changed him."

"It was more than Pa's death. Kevin's world collapsed, and he couldn't find a way back."

"Have you even had time to mourn your father?" Nichole slid into the chair beside him. "You suffered his loss as well and now Kevin—"

He shook his head. "No." He stopped her before she could continue. "I know I need to grieve, and I will. But not today. Not tonight."

Nichole leaned across the table and touched her lips to his. "I'll be with you."

"Nichole, can you come look at these dresses?" Amy called from upstairs.

"Go find a dress, sweetheart. I'll head outside and help Jason. Jim needs to take it easy."

They both rose, and Nichole wrapped her arms around Merril's waist and hugged him close. "Don't leave without telling me," she instructed, then released her hold and ran up the stairs.

***

The front porch had been cleared, the broken lumber stacked beside the steps, and the house straightened to Amy's satisfaction by the time the Justice of the Peace arrived.

Jason's dour mood was no match for Nichole's excitement, and once Kelly started decorating, even Jason began to smile.

Amy and Kelly had pushed the kitchen table out of the way and tied late blooming lilacs and snowball hydrangeas, cut from the backyard bushes, down the staircase railing.

The Justice stood at the far side of the kitchen, across from the stairs, with Merril, Jim and Tom to one side, Amy and Kelly on the other.

At the top of the stairs, Nichole clutched Jason's arm and looked down the steep incline. From where they stood, no one below was visible, only the empty space where she and Merril would stand. She turned to Jason and studied his profile, so like her own. "Are you still mad at me?"

He turned his head to look at her, and smiled. "No. Are you?"

Nichole shook her head and whispered, "I love you, Jason."

"I know," he said, and kissed her forehead. "I love you too."

"We're ready down here," Jim called up the stairs.

"Don't let me trip." Nichole tightened her hold on Jason's arm.

"I'll go first." Jason started down the narrow stairs with Nichole's hand on his shoulder.

Since none of the men wore formal attire, Nichole refused Amy's offer to borrow a fancy dress. Instead, Nichole chose the lavender skirt and jacket with a white frilled blouse, and carried a bouquet of purple lilacs and white snowball flowers.

At the bottom of the steps, Jason waited for her to take his arm. When they reached the Justice, Jason placed her hand in Merril's. Jason kissed her forehead again then moved back to stand beside Amy.

Nichole smiled at Jason and Amy, but her gaze was drawn up to Merril's. No grief or guilt marred the joy in his eyes. His grin sent her pulse racing.

The Justice performed the short version by request.

Nichole had asked the Justice to omit the word obey, and instead say cherish, before she had gone upstairs.

Both Jason and Jim chuckled when the Justice reached that part.

Merril surprised her with a ring. As he slipped it on her finger, she ground her teeth and tried to stop her tears.

When the Justice declared, "You may now kiss the bride," Jim and Tom gave a loud hoot, while Amy clapped her hands.

Jason had to give Kelly his handkerchief to dab his tears.

Merril intended a brief kiss, but Nichole wrapped her arms around his neck and kissed him thoroughly.

Jason cleared his throat, and Nichole pulled away with a laugh.

Merril drew her back into his arms. "I have another surprise for you."

"You do?" Nichole grinned at her husband through tears of joy.

"Tom and Kelly reserved us a room for tonight at an inn on Park Avenue. We'll have a wedding dinner there, just the two of us. We'll leave in the morning with Tom."

"How wonderful! Are you sure we have the time?" Nichole's face flushed with thoughts of their wedding night. She had dreaded spending tonight in the saddle or camped beside the road with Tom. Now, she would have time with Merril. *Her husband.*

"Lloyd can handle the ranches for one night. We need this. We deserve this." He lowered his head and kissed her again.

Kelly laughed. "You two lovebirds need to keep your clothes on until you get to the inn."

Nichole hesitated. "Let me change first. I don't want to wear this on the ride tomorrow." She left her bouquet on the table and hurried up to their room.

She removed the lavender skirt and jacket, folded them into her empty trunk, and dressed in a dark brown skirt with a matching jacket and tall boots. She paused, then took the photograph of herself, Merril, and Kevin from the mantel and placed it on the lilac-colored skirt in the trunk.

Just as I found it.

She closed the lid and hurried down the stairs.

Their saddlebags were packed and on the borrowed horses, ready for the ride to The Shilo in the morning.

At the front door, Nichole turned and gave Jason a swift hug, then embraced Amy and whispered into her hair. "I left my traveling case in my bedroom. Please store it in the attic, just as it is." Nichole stepped back, Amy's hands clasped in her own. "The rest of my clothes are folded on the bed. Would you bring those with you, when you come home?"

Amy stared into Nichole's eyes for several moments, then nodded. No questions asked.

Nichole squeezed Amy's hands and let go. "Thank you."

"Be safe on the road." Amy stepped beside Jason. "We should see you in about five days."

Nichole nodded and walked to where Jim, Tom and Kelly stood talking with Merril.

"Are you ready?" Merril asked as she approached.

"One last thing." Nichole paced away, turning her back to the men. Without warning, she tossed her bouquet of flowers over her head at the group. All three men reached for the flowers, but Jim, with his long reach, gave a grunt of pain as he plucked the bouquet from the air.

Nichole's laugh faded when she spun around and saw the grimace on Jim's face.

"What the heck was that about?" Jim returned the flowers to Nichole.

"A foolish thing that brides do. I'm sorry, Jim." She hugged him. "Take care of yourself and hurry home. I need you."

"I know ya do, gal. Go on, now. Have a good evening with your husband." Jim winked at her as Merril helped her mount. She waved at Amy, then smiled at Merril as they rode toward Park Avenue.

Chapter 10

Alyse James

—

Alyse woke the next morning with a mixture of excitement and dread in her heart. She hated to leave her grandmother, but the urgent need to find her sister compelled her. In the storage closet, she found her old trunk and pulled it back to her room. All the clothes she owned fit easily into the old traveling case. Alyse added an extra pair of shoes, two sets of gloves and hats, plus two nice shawls *Mémé* had made for her last spring. Her travel attire was a simple dark blue dress with stout shoes and dark stockings. She laid her greatcoat across the bed. It continued to rain, and the ride to the train station in Toronto would be a wet one.

When she finished packing, she walked down the hall to the main room. She could hear her grandmother's chant in the kitchen. Through the front windows, she saw Uncle Bern harness the horses to the wagon. She stopped before she entered the kitchen to watch her grandmother complete her spell.

Chantal's *grimoire* lay open in the center of the workspace. All around the book were cloth circles cut from satin, three of blue and a dozen or so of white. Alyse could tell her grandmother cast protection spells by the ingredients she placed in the center of each circle. Chantal normally kept her spellcraft ingredients on the family altar to infuse them with power.

The blue satchels were for protection while traveling. She knew those would be for her and her uncles. The white ones were for pure protection and warding. A warm golden glow infused the work surface as Chantal added cloves and pine to each pouch. Tiny scrolls marked with protective runes came next, with an additional scroll for each of the blue satchels, then she placed several crystals in the center of each circle, chanting soft words the entire time.

As she finished, she held her hands over the satchels and asked for the Goddess's Blessing. The golden glow intensified for a few moments then faded away. Chantal dropped her hands to the counter and leaned wearily over her work.

"You think it's coming here? The demon?" Alyse asked.

Chantal pushed an errant strand of white hair out of her face with the back of her wrist and looked at Alyse. "I think it's a possibility," she said in her low husky voice. "There's an equal chance it will go after your sister first. I hope he comes here. At least I am prepared. Amylia—Amy knows nothing."

"You must come with us," Alyse insisted. She halted at the line of salt on the floor.

Chantal shook her head and began tying up the small bags. "I cannot travel as quickly as you and your uncles can." Each circle of cloth had a braid of yarn woven through openings along the edge. Chantal pulled the yarn tight, tied a knot and set the satchel aside to move on to the next. "Should the demon come here first, I plan to delay him, even if it is just for a few days. I can give you time."

She stopped tying the pouches and looked at her granddaughter. "You need time to reach your sister, to teach her what you already know. Time to train with her." Chantal stepped toward Alyse and gripped her shoulders. "This demon will find you, my dear. Never doubt it. It's coming for you and your sister. It has but one purpose, to find and destroy you. You need to be strong." Chantal released Alyse and lifted one of the blue satchels and pulled the closure tight. "This one is for you."

The scent of clove and pine and the forest after rain reached Alyse. The items inside pulled the satin bag lengthwise, making it about the size and shape of her thumb.

Chantal chose a silver chain from a bowl on the counter and drew it through the braided ties, then clasped the chain closed. She held out her hand to Alyse.

Alyse crossed the line of salt that encircled the workbench and stood beside her grandmother.

Chantal placed the satchel in Alyse's open palm and held her granddaughter's hand between her own.

Familiar with the ritual, Alyse covered her grandmother's hands with her other hand. She closed her eyes and inhaled a deep cleansing breath, as she waited for Chantal to begin.

"Lord and Lady, I call to thee,
and to the four elemental spirits of this world –
Air, Fire, Water, and Earth.
Attend me now Spirits.
I summon thee, and invoke your protection,
for this one so dear to my heart.
Banish all evil and protect her from harm.
Let my will be done."

"Let it be done," Alyse repeated. She could feel the heat in her hands, and knew if she were to open her eyes, a golden glow would surround their clasped hands. She waited until the warmth faded, then gazed into her grand-mother's eyes, so much like her own.

"I love you, dear heart." Chantal lifted the chain, placed it around Alyse's neck, and tucked the satchel out of sight beneath Alyse's blouse. She kissed her granddaughter's cheeks.

Chantal turned back to the workbench and closed her *grimoire*. She lifted the large book, slid it neatly into a plain white cloth bag, and cinched it shut. "You'll take this with you. I know you are familiar with it." She winked at Alyse. "Also, I have a package for your sister, and one for your mother. They're in the main room on the settee."

"It feels wrong to leave you here, *Mémé*," Alyse complained as she took the *grimoire* from Chantal.

"You're not leaving me yet. I'll come with you to the train station. Now, mind the circle, pack the book and those packages in your trunk before your uncle carries it outside. Bay, come here, please."

Bayard sat his niece's luggage down and turned to his mother. He noted the satchels, bowed his head, and stepped into the protective ring to receive his blessing.

Alyse found the packages addressed to her mother and sister wrapped in plain brown paper and tied with twine. As she picked them up, she realized she would meet her mother and sister very soon. Nervous excitement bubbled in her chest, despite the doom of the prophecy. She put the packages and the *grimoire* in her trunk. After she closed the lid and fastened the leather buckles, she laid her hands on it and fashioned a quick deterrent spell. It would make opening her trunk undesirable to anyone but herself.

Bayard walked up to her as he slid his satchel into his coat pocket. "Are you ready for this, niece?" He picked up her trunk by the leather handles on either end.

"Are you, Uncle Bay?" Alyse asked.

Her uncle winked at her and smiled. "Sometimes, it seems like I've prepared for this my entire life."

"At least you knew about it," Alyse muttered.

Bay shook his head. "Do you think that makes it better, or worse?"

"I don't know." Alyse shrugged. "I think it would have been better to know."

"And I think it would have been better *not* to know," Bay responded with a smile.

Alyse held the door open for her uncle

Bay shouted to his brother as he stepped down from the landing into the yard, "Ho Bern! Mum wants you."

Uncle Bayard stepped out into the misty rain and across the muddy yard to the wagon. He passed Bernard without glancing up. The brothers always dressed similarly, both preferring dark trousers and vests. They wore bowler style hats over their thinning brown and gray hair.

Although they looked identical to most people, Alyse could tell them apart. She felt familiar head bumps on her calf and shin as Anaïs and Sabine made themselves known to her, winding in and out between her legs. She bent her knees to stroke them, and they continued to move around her, butting their heads and letting her know they required her attention.

Chantal watched from the kitchen, with a bittersweet smile on her face. "What are you going to do with them?"

The black cats found a way to knock Alyse onto her rump and jump into her lap. Alyse laughed at their antics. "I should leave them here with you, *Mémé*. I don't think they would appreciate being locked up on a train."

"They don't need to travel by train, dear heart. They're fairies beneath their fur."

The animals stopped their antics and turned to regard Chantal.

Alyse's hand hovered over her pets' fur, and her gaze rose to her grandmother's. "*Mémé,* they are cats. Are you teasing me?" Alyse grinned.

"Not at all, dear. It is they who tease you. You love them as cats, so they remain cats. Now, however, I would send them straight away to your sister. It would be best for them, I think."

Alyse looked down at two sets of yellow eyes. They blinked solemnly back at her.

"Do they know where she is?" Alyse wondered aloud.

"I imagine they have always known, if not always, then at least since you *twyned*. They should be able to find her." Chantal nodded at the felines and cinched another satchel.

The door opened, and Bernard came inside dripping moisture from his greatcoat.

"Bay said you wanted me, Mum?" He noticed Alyse on the floor with her cats. "I thought they'd be gone by now." He passed Alyse and the cats and stepped carefully over Chantal's circle.

"How will they go? How do I send them?" Alyse wondered to her grandmother and uncle.

"They were barn owls when you were a baby," Bernard commented as Chantal prepared his satchel.

"I've seen them as rats, raccoons and starlings, dear. They will know the best way to travel." Chantal took Bernard's hand and closed her eyes.

"And you never told me." Alyse scolded her pets.

You've never been mine at all.

Anaïs licked her paw and began to groom her head, while Sabine kept her full attention on Alyse.

"Will you go to Amy and stay with her until I get there?" she asked them, not sure what to expect.

Sabine lifted her paw and batted Anaïs on the head.

Anaïs paused her grooming and looked at Alyse.

With two sets of yellow eyes trained on her, she ran her hand down each beloved animal's fur. "You should go now. We're all leaving. I don't want you here alone," Alyse explained.

In a blink, both cats disappeared. Alyse watched in wonder as two tiny lights, brighter and steadier than fireflies, floated toward the ceiling. They paused, bobbed several times, and then streaked down and out underneath the front door.

Alyse jumped to her feet and ran to the window, just in time to see two red-tailed hawks disappear into the rainy mist. They were headed south.

"Owls?" Bern asked her as he came up beside her and looked out the window.

"No. Hawks," she said, her heart full of wonder.

Bern nodded. "Good choice." He turned to Chantal.

"We're loaded and ready to go, Mum, whenever you are."

Chantal finished knotting the protection satchels and released her wards. She swept the salt on the floor into a pile, scooped it up with a stiff piece of paper, and poured it back into a jar.

She nodded at her son. "Let me get my coat and I'll be ready." She placed her craftwork on a tray and carried it across the room to the family altar. She placed the white satchels around the altar, now decorated for summer solstice with roses, wild thyme and ferns, and then slid the empty tray beneath the settee.

Alyse slipped her arms into her coat as her grandmother came back down the hall with her large black cape and hood. She handed Alyse a hat like her uncles wore and opened the door. Together, they headed out into the rain.

Alyse and her grandmother sat in the wagon with the trunks while her uncles sat on the seat above. The rain had made the road bumpy. They had to go slow to avoid puddles for fear that hidden potholes would damage the wheels. What would, on a clear day and a well-tended road, be a two-hour ride to town, became a four-hour muddy and miserable trip.

They paused briefly at the Chesham home where Bay went in and spoke with them about their furniture order. Bay said they understood about the family emergency and would be willing to wait for their dining room table and chairs.

When they finally reached the station, Bay climbed into the back of the buckboard to help Chantal to her feet. Then, the men unloaded the wagon and carried their trunks to the raised wooden platform around the train station. A wooden awning built around the station kept the platform dry for passengers and baggage.

As they gathered together beneath the awning, Chantal gave Bayard the money in her reticule. "Ask for the train departing to Boston, Bay. Find out the departure time and remember to only purchase three tickets." As Bayard moved to stand in the line for the ticket window, Chantal turned to Bernard. "I won't be able to get the wagon back home in this rain."

He nodded his understanding. "Do you want to take a room at an inn? I could stable the rig and horses until the weather clears."

Chantal shook her head, as she massaged her hands. They always became stiff and sore in the rain. "No. There isn't time to wait for good weather. Take them to the stable and see how much you can get for Pippin and the wagon. Ask if they have an inexpensive saddle for Acorn they will sell you. I'll ride Acorn back to the farm today."

Bern gave his mother a single nod and stepped back into the rain. He took the horses by the lead to walk them and the wagon across the muddy street to the livery stable.

"Are you sure about this?" Alyse questioned, as Bay returned with their tickets.

"Of course, I'm sure, dear heart. That old wagon has seen better days. Acorn will get me home without losing a wheel or breaking an axle and do it in half the time."

Bayard looked to his mother. "What are you doing?"

"Riding Acorn back home, dear. Bern is going to sell Pippin and the wagon for me. Did you get the tickets?"

Bay held up three tickets and offered Chantal back the extra money.

She refused it. "Divide it between the three of you. You will need it for meals and incidentals."

"Mum, this is quite a bit of money," Bay argued.

Chantal smiled. "I know, dear, but I won't need it, and you three will."

Alyse watched her uncle Bayard's face fall.

He just realized this is goodbye.

"Ah, Bay, dear heart, don't start." Chantal scolded and wrapped her son in her arms. "We've been together a good long time. Longer than many get to be near the ones they love. This is the best thing I can do for you and the girls."

Bay nodded his head against his mother's silver white hair and managed to say, "I love you, Mum." Then, he released her, and walked into the station.

Tears streamed down Alyse's face as Chantal reached out a hand to her.

She took her grandmother's thin, strong hand and held it tight in her own. They waited together in silence for Bernard to return.

Bernard emerged from the stable yard leading Acorn. They watched him walk across the muddy street in the rain. He wrapped the reins around the hitching post near Alyse and stepped up on the platform out of the rain.

"Did he get the tickets?" Bern asked as he shook the water off his hat, then returned it to his head.

"Yes. Bay went inside." Chantal's gaze never left her son's face.

"I hope this is the right saddle."

"It's fine, dear. I'll need you to help me mount," she said to Bernard.

Chantal turned to Alyse. "My dear beloved girl, never forget how strong you are. Have faith in yourself. Remember, Amylia is just as strong with her elements, but she is untrained. Your uncles can teach you to *twyne* and pair, but it will be different for you and Amy, because the two of you can only work as a pair when you're *twyned*." Chantal ran her gloved hands up and down Alyse's arms.

Alyse could only nod as emotion tightened her throat.

Chantal wrapped Alyse in her arms and whispered into her hair, "Remind your mother I love her. I've thought of Margaret every day we've been apart. Tell your sister about everything you and I have shared. When you share it with her, I will be with you both."

Alyse nodded and whispered, "I love you, *Mémé*," before her throat closed.

"I love you too, dear heart—so very much. Go on inside, now, and get warm."

Alyse hugged her grandmother one last time, then turned away and entered the station.

Through tears, she saw Bay at the end of a bench against the wall, his face turned away. She spun around and leaned against the window to watch her grandmother and uncle.

Uncle Bern lifted *Mémé* to the saddle and gave her the reins. He made sure her leg was secure, and her cloak covered her dress and boots.

Chantal bent to speak with Bern, and he nodded his head several times.

Bern kissed his mother's gloved hand and stepped back.

Chantal tightened the reins, turned Acorn away from the station, and rode down the street toward home.

Chapter 11

Hunter

—

Hunter dressed in an old pair of denim trousers and frayed shirt for the excursion into the swamp with Minister Tremble. He pulled on tall brown-stained boots, pushed his old felt hat onto his head, and chose three glass vials with cork stoppers from his leather satchel.

Once downstairs, he paused long enough for a quick breakfast in the common room. While he sipped his coffee, an unexpected surge of compassion filled Hunter's chest, and he shook his head. If it hadn't been for his *grand-mère,* he might have been put out on the street, or forced to live hand-to-mouth along the bayou, much like the old man.

When he finished his meal, he selected a large biscuit from the tray and wrapped it in a cloth napkin. He nodded to the desk clerk as he left the dining area and stepped outside. The sun had just risen and already the cloudless hazy white sky pressed its heat upon the city.

On the far side of the porch, Minister Tremble perched on the edge of a bench. When the door clapped shut behind Hunter, Tremble lifted his head and stood. His bony hands fluttered beside his dark, discolored robes.

Hunter crossed to Tremble and offered him the linen-wrapped biscuit.

The old man narrowed his eyes. "What's this?" He glared at the white cloth in Hunter's hand and raised his reluctant gaze to Hunter's.

"It's a biscuit." Hunter opened the cloth to display the flaky golden crust. "I thought you might like to eat before we head out."

Minister Tremble licked his lips. "I don't take charity."

Hunter tipped his head to one side and studied the elderly man. "But you do take donations, do you not?" Hunter lifted the biscuit again. "Consider this a donation, *mon ami*. Go on. Take it."

The madman snatched the offering from Hunter's hand and took two quick bites before both the biscuit and the napkin disappeared inside his dirty robes.

"It's this way." Tremble turned, hopped off the porch, and scurried down the street.

Hunter watched the old man for a moment and shook his head.

Mon Dieu! What a strange person.

He confirmed his knives were secure before he followed the lunatic away from the river.

After several long blocks, Tremble stopped at a small public dock beside a canal. He glanced back at Hunter then descended into one of the shallow flat-bottomed boats tied to a low rail. He knelt in the bow of the small vessel, knees wide, and sat back on his heels. He looked over his shoulder at Hunter. "Get in and untie us." He jutted his narrow chin toward the rail and picked up one of the paddles.

Hunter raised an eyebrow. He checked the vials in his coat pocket to make sure they would remain secure should the vessel capsize. No stranger to this type of boat, he stepped down, slipped the rope from the rail, and lowered himself to his knees. He sat on his boot heels and picked up the other wooden paddle.

"We will follow the current to my home." The old man spoke over his shoulder. "It will be harder work when we return."

Hunter put his paddle in the water opposite the minister, and they pulled away from the dock. The canal ran straight through the city, then turned sharply into the bayou and headed northeast toward Lake Pontchartrain. They were almost an hour on the water when Tremble pointed toward the shoreline, thick with moss-covered trees. They turned the canoe onto land.

The spry old man jumped from the boat and held the craft stable as Hunter walked forward and stepped from the canoe onto the soft soil. Tremble pulled the light boat ashore and covered it with netting concealed with moss. Satisfied with his work, Tremble moved onto a narrow path through the trees. "This way, it ain't too far."

Not ten feet past the first bend in the path, Hunter spotted the shack. Set off the trail, it looked to have grown from the hanging moss and foliage. The front door stood open, the interior dark.

As they approached, Tremble grabbed his stringy hair. "Oh no! Oh no!" He broke into a run toward the cabin.

Unsure of what had upset the man, Hunter slowed his pace and kept a sharp eye on the foliage and brush along the trail. He touched the knife beneath his jacket and moved between the trees toward the shelter.

The minister stopped in the doorway, his hands covered his mouth, as he turned his head from side to side. "She's gone." He glanced back at Hunter. "They took her—one of those... those... abominations took her."

Hunter stood behind the distraught old man and studied the shack's interior. Dim light from a dirty window left the room in shadow. The smell of rotting flesh permeated the air. "Whew! The smell alone will bring predators." He moved from the door and surveyed the ground beside the hovel. "It looks as though an alligator or three have been here."

Tremble disappeared inside, and a flicker of light illuminated the shack.

Hunter edged to the doorway and peered inside. A hard-packed dirt floor supported a tall cabinet beside the entrance. Along the left wall, an old cot tilted on two legs beneath a small, mud-streaked window. Across from the cot lay the remnants of a foot and leg, torn from the body below the knee, and chained by the ankle to a stake. The rotting appendage lay in a muddy pool of blood.

Hunter drew back in revulsion. "*Mon Dieu!* What have you done?" The stench of rotting meat was overwhelming. He turned to the madman and swallowed the bile in his throat. "You kept a woman chained in here?"

"The succubus had to remain until the prophecy was spoken." Tremble continued to pull at his stringy hair. "She's been taken. The body has been defiled."

Hunter turned away in disgust. "We must be quick. Grab what you wish to take and let's go." He withdrew one of the vials from his inside pocket and stepped to the remains of the woman's leg. The blood pooled beneath the foot was fouled and sticky. He had never used blood from spoiled flesh, and the thought sickened him. Teeth clenched, he held the container steady and milked a tiny amount of blood from the woman's severed leg.

The results may be uncertain, or perhaps, not work at all.

Cabinet doors opened and slammed behind him, and Hunter glanced back at Tremble, unwilling to trust his back to the man.

Whoever this madman searches for needs to be warned.

Hunter placed a stopper in the vial of dark fluid, wrapped the glass in a soft cloth, and returned it to his jacket. He stood and watched as the minister counted his money.

"Here." Tremble offered a jumble of paper bills to Hunter and stuffed the rest back in the metal box. "I'll pay the rest once you show proof the witches are dead."

Hunter took the bills, folded the wad and shoved them deep into his trouser pocket. "You should not return to this place. You'll never be free of your—abominations. Your seer will forever dwell in this place and call to the scavengers for your blood."

Hunter turned from the wide-eyed lunatic, walked outside and studied the area around the shack. Long strands of moss hung from trees and obscured his view. He edged away from the cabin just as movement to his right captured his attention. A quick scan to the left showed a clear path back to the boat.

Clear for now.

He took a step down the boat trail and pulled the long knife from its sheath beneath his coat. "Time to go. We're about to have company."

The minister hurried from his shack with a burlap bag of items and the tin box clutched in his arms. He paused at the sight of the large alligator, quickened his step past Hunter, and scurried along the path toward the canoe.

Hunter followed more slowly to be sure they had not caught the 'gator's eye, but the big fellow entered the cabin to retrieve a final meal.

At the boat, Tremble stood waiting. His arms clasped around his belongings. He tipped his head toward the netting. "Set the boat in the water. Hold it still for me."

Hunter stared at him for a moment, then slid his knife into its sheath. He uncovered the light canoe and set the bow on the water.

Minister Tremble placed his items in the center of the craft, then took his place at the front of the vessel.

Hunter stepped into the craft, picked up the wooden pole in the bottom of the boat, and with feet braced apart, pushed them away from the shore and into the bayou.

They fought the current on their return, but Hunter's strength pushed them steadily forward. He could not shake the memory of the delicate ankle chained and rotting on the shack's dirt floor. He kept his thoughts to himself and used his anger and disgust against the water as he rowed. When they reached the public dock, Hunter climbed from the boat and turned his angry regard to the crazy man. "You're not getting out?"

Tremble shook his head. "When should I expect you to return?"

Hunter clenched his jaw and lifted one shoulder. "I don't know who I'm looking for or where to find them. I wouldn't get too anxious if I were you. This could take some time."

"I must remind you the matter is urgent. The Lord's work is laid before you. The demon has been called forth."

"Evil disguises itself in many ways, Minister Tremble." Hunter stared down at the scrawny man in the canoe. "Ask at the boarding house in a few weeks. If I learn anything, I will send a wire, and have it delivered there."

The madman nodded and pushed his canoe away from the dock with the paddle.

Hunter watched him glide away along the canal for a moment then turned and made his way back to the boarding house.

The clerk at the front desk looked up as he entered. "Welcome back, sir."

Hunter moved to the desk. "I'll need laundry service, today if possible, and I'll need my boots cleaned."

The clerk leaned away from Hunter. "At once, sir. If you would place your soiled laundry in the hemp bag and the boots in the hallway beside your door, I'll send Wanda up to fetch them. They will be returned by morning, at the latest."

Hunter shook his head. "I'll need them tonight."

"It will cost extra."

Hunter grinned at the clerk. "Might you have a train schedule available?"

"Of course, sir." The clerk handed Hunter a leaflet with departure times, destinations, connections, and pricing.

"Thank you." Hunter took the schedule and made his way to the stairs. He noticed Sam Kline and his woman having lunch in the dining area, but Hunter continued up the stairs to his room. The shack's rank odor lingered on his clothing and he didn't want to spoil her meal.

Once in his room, he removed the vial of dark fluid from his jacket and laid it on the bedside table. He placed the money in his long wallet, stripped himself of his clothing, and followed the clerk's instructions for laundry service. Then he closed and secured the door.

He stood naked as he made quick use of the room's water and clean smelling soap, even washing the rancid smell from his hair. He draped a towel around his neck to catch the chilled droplets from his wet hair as he turned his attention to his work.

Hunter pulled his travel bag from under the bed and opened it. He withdrew his leather folder, tossed it on the bed, and set the bag aside. He untied the folder, retrieved a white satin pouch, and dumped the rest of the contents onto the bed. Five sackcloth sandbags along with a dozen maps slid from the folder. Most of those were small area maps of different locations which he had drawn himself. He pulled the largest from the stack and unfolded the heavy paper. Not knowing where to begin his search, he would have to cast a wide net.

He spread the map across his bed and placed bags of sand on each corner to hold it flat. The chart had been painstakingly drawn over the last ten years, as he traveled the country and northern territories, collecting bounties. Many sections showed only rivers or boundaries and were marked with a number that corresponded with one of the smaller maps.

Hunter opened the small window and hoped the light breeze would disperse the noxious odor from the vial once he uncorked it. He picked up the white satin sack and measured its weight in his hand. With a short prayer, he withdrew his pendulum from the bag.

He had crafted the instrument at age sixteen. An arrowhead that once belonged to his great-grandfather. A pink rose quartz from his beloved *grand-mère*. Both items attached with wire to a watch chain that had belonged to his father. No one touched the pendulum except Hunter, and it never failed him.

He uncorked the vial and tipped it to allow only one drop of blood to touch the arrowhead. The thick bead of rancid blood set for a moment on the stone, then hissed as it dissolved into the arrowhead. He recapped the glass flask and set it aside.

Hunter took a deep breath to calm his mind. Then another. He positioned himself before the map and held the quartz portion of the pendulum. The arrowhead swung free at the end of the chain. He held the apparatus as still as possible over the center of the map and closed his eyes.

Seeress, I seek the ones you spoke of in the prophecy.

He allowed his urgency to build in his mind. Spirit voices whispered to him—warning him of danger—but he already knew. He'd always known the risk inherent in this magic. His *grand-mère* had taught him of the dangers long ago. It didn't matter. The innocent had to be warned of the minister's deadly intent.

Help me, Seeress. By your own blood, I beseech you.

Anxiety grew in his chest, and he imagined it flowed into the pendulum. "Where are they?" He spoke aloud to both the instrument and the blood of the woman who had died, chained to a dirt floor shack.

The pendulum began to circle the map and Hunter opened his eyes. He held a steady hand as the arrowhead's swing became oblong, then a line, from the northeast to the center of the country. Those he searched for were in more than one location. This would make warning them much harder.

He reached down and folded the map in half, adjusting the sandbags to hold it flat. Only the Western half of the country lay revealed, from the furthest tip of Texas to the Canadian border. Again, he let the pendulum swing and watched its movements. At first, the arrowhead circled in a counterclockwise direction. Soon, its wide circumference decreased, and the spiral swung slower and tighter. Hunter moved the pendulum in one direction, then the other until the spiral motion stopped. He dropped the tip to the map.

Denver.

He flipped the map over and repeated the divination for the east coast. This time the pendulum did not stop, but moved in a line between the southern end of Lake Ontario to the Boston area.

Hunter cleaned the arrowhead meticulously and slid his pendulum into the satin bag. He folded his map and returned all the items he used for divination to the leather folder, then placed it in his travel bag.

He sat on the bed, still naked, and picked up the train schedule. A train leaving for Dallas would depart late this evening. From Dallas, he could take another train on the same line to Kansas City. Once there, he would have to change lines and board the Union Pacific straight into Denver. He considered Boston and Toronto but felt Denver to be the wiser choice. There could be two individuals on the east coast, or one person who traveled between two points. No, the best and closest target appeared to be in Denver.

His head came up at a knock on his door. He wrapped the towel around his waist and unbolted the door.

The laundress held his bag in one hand and his boots in the other. Her eyes traveled up from his bare feet to the towel, then to his broad, muscular chest, with an appreciative smile. The smile faded, however, when she saw the scar on his face.

"You need these back tonight, sir?" Her eyes never strayed from the scar that ran from his left eye to his chin.

"Yes, thank you. I will need them no later than seven this evening."

"There will be an extra fee for the rush order."

"There always is."

She bobbed her head. "By seven."

"Thank you," Hunter replied and closed the door.

He dressed and reviewed all that needed to be accomplished this evening. His first stop would be the train station to buy his ticket. He checked his wallet and slipped it into his vest. On the way back, he would stop at the livery. The owner needed to understand Hunter's expectations—feed, exercise, and care for Roulette as though she were his own. He already regretted leaving *la belle Roulette* behind. This time, however, it would be best to travel by boat or rail. Time was of the essence.

After visiting the stable, he would return to the boarding house and pick up his cleaned clothing. The room was his for a monthly fee. He need only tell the clerk he intended to travel on business. Then he would return to the station for the 8:15 train. His final destination—Denver.

Chapter 12

Morago

—

The merchant and his wagon traveled far too slowly for Morago. He urged the man to whip the team to greater speed. However, their pace remained unsatisfactory.

The chatter of demons inside Morago's mind suggested he punish the merchant for his pace.

The lips on the possessed merchant formed a smile as Morago's demons crackled with glee. But Morago did not wish to waste time torturing this human. Instead, he remained focused on his destination and the prize that awaited him there.

In the end, he left the merchant to vomit at the side of the road, and took possession of a small fox, asleep in a den nearby. The fox proved much faster, and raced directly toward Morago's beacon, unhampered by human roadways.

However, when a deer bounded past the exhausted fox, the demon jumped again. Morago possessed the doe and left the fox to die in the bushes. When the deer's heart threatened to burst, he shifted to another animal, an elk this time, and allowed his demonic host to take part in the race. Two dozen elk ran headlong for Toronto, until one by one they failed and fell to their death. As the last elk fell, Morago and his host leapt to a crow, which wheeled in midair and turned west.

Chapter 13

Nichole Harris-Shilo

—

Nichole took Merril's hand as she stepped off the boardwalk along Park Avenue and crossed the dusty street. The sweet music of a fiddle and harmonica from down the block drew them from the dining room at their hotel into the cool Denver evening. As they strolled past the celebration, a bride and groom raised their glasses in a toast surrounded by their wedding guests. Laughter blended with the music, and the couple kissed on a side yard platform.

"Are you sorry we didn't have a church wedding?" Merril ran his warm hands up her arms.

She leaned back against his chest and shook her head. "No. Not at all. Everyone I care about was there."

"Our marriage will cause a scandal among the Cattlemen's Association." Merril's voice was low in her ear.

"I know. I thought about that, too." She shivered as the memory of Kevin's announcement at The Highlands' barbecue flashed through her mind. "I don't care what anyone thinks, honestly. I only care about you." She tipped her head back and smiled at the concern on his face. "Really, it's okay."

"You're chilled. Let's go back." He ran his hands down her sleeves one last time, then offered her his arm.

She slipped her hand into the crook of his arm and they retraced their steps to their small hotel.

Inside their room, a banked fire in the wood-burning stove removed the chill and warmed the room.

Nichole unbuttoned her jacket and glanced at her saddlebag stacked on top of Merril's in the corner.

Should I find my nightgown?

She shrugged the light coat from her shoulders and turned to Merril. His emerald eyes locked onto hers as she tossed the jacket onto the chair.

Probably not.

"Have a seat. I'll pull your boots off." His grin ticked up on one side, and he hung his hat on a hook beside the door.

Nichole's face warmed, and butterflies fluttered low in her chest as she sat on the chair and lifted her foot to her husband.

Merril grabbed the heel of her boot and slid the leather free from her foot with a quick movement. Her heel dropped into the palm of his hand. He lowered her foot as she raised her other boot. Her second boot dropped beside the first, and he bent to kiss the top of her stocking-covered foot.

"Now yours?" she asked.

Merril shook his head, pushed his boots off, one at a time, toe to heel, and kicked them aside. "Mine are old. They come off easy."

Nichole lifted her skirt and untied the garter just below her knee. She rolled the stocking down and slipped it from her foot, then glanced at Merril.

His interest shifted from her foot to her face and back to her foot.

She wiggled her toes at him, stuffed the garter into the stocking, then lifted her skirt above the other knee.

Merril groaned.

"Torturing you is kind of fun." Nichole grinned as she rolled the other stocking leisurely down her leg and set it aside. She looked up as he shrugged out of his shirt.

He unbuckled his belt and undid the top button, loosening his trousers.

Her gaze scorched a path from his tightened trousers, across his tanned chest to his laughing green eyes.

"You're right. This is fun." His grin widened as he crossed his arms and leaned his back against the wall. "Your turn, darlin'."

Nichole stood, reached back and unhooked the buttons on her skirt. She stepped out of the material and folded it on the chair with her jacket. The blouse followed. She smiled over her shoulder at Merril. "Would you unlace me?"

He stepped close and loosened the ties on her corset as she unpinned her hair and let it fall across her back. Merril swept the curls to one side and nibbled along her neck to her shoulder.

Gooseflesh ran down her arms, and her breath hitched as his tongue swirled across her skin. The corset slid over her hips to the floor, and Merril's warm hands slipped beneath her camisole and cupped her breasts. She turned her head and lifted her face to his. His soft lips found hers as his thumbs stroked her nipples.

When she turned in his arms, he lifted the camisole over her head, and pulled her tight against him. His mouth slanted across hers with desire.

Nichole wrapped her arms around Merril's neck and pulled his hair free from a black ribbon. She ran her fingers through his long hair and pressed herself closer.

He unfastened the button on her drawers and guided them down her hips.

She trailed one hand down his chest to his trousers and caressed the tight denim. The answering rumble deep in his chest made her legs weaken.

His hands disappeared from her hips, and then the entire burning length of his body pressed against hers. He lifted her leg and ran his hand down her back and between her legs, inflaming her passion.

"Such nice long arms," she whispered, as her other leg gave way. "I'm going to fall."

"No, you're not. I have you." Merril picked her up and set her on the bed.

Squeeeeak.

"You've got to be kidding me." Nichole laughed.

The bed squealed again as it took Merril's weight. "Do you want me to stop?" He rose to his elbows and grinned at her as he pressed himself part way into the center of her desire, then withdrew.

"Don't tease me, Merril." She tried to wiggle onto him, but he pulled back.

"I don't want you to be embarrassed in the morning."

Her eyes opened and stared hard into his.

Green eyes glittered with gold as he almost entered her, and then withdrew again. "You need to tell me what you want me to do."

"I need you to break this damn bed, Merril."

He laughed as he filled her, and then groaned as he wrapped his arms around her and tucked his head into her neck.

She didn't hear the bed squawk in time with their lovemaking and didn't care if it did.

After their passion cooled, he drew the cover over them and pulled her close.

Nichole curled into his side, her leg over his, her head on his shoulder. "I love you, Merril."

"And I love you, Mrs. Shilo."

She looked up at him and smiled as he dropped a quick kiss on her nose.

"What?" he asked. "I see you've got something on your mind."

"I do." She cuddled closer. "Remember what I told you at the barbecue, before I went in the house?"

"Mmm." His head fell back on the pillow as his hand ran up and down her arm. "You told me you remembered things that never happened. You were worried about what White Eagle had said about you."

"That's right." She paused and chewed her nail for a moment, then looked up at him. "Let me ask something else. Have you ever heard of reincarnation—of being born again into another life?"

"Actually, I have." He looked at the ceiling, his arm around her shoulder. "I worked for almost a year laying a spur of the Central Pacific line. My partner was a Chinese man named Chen. He spoke in broken English, but we understood each other well enough. He told me he hoped for great things in his next life."

"Good—then this might not be an impossible explanation." She pushed up onto her elbow and stared into his sleepy eyes. "When Jones hit you and you lost consciousness—imagine that when you woke up you were in ancient Rome."

He raised his head slightly and looked at her. "Instead of The Highlands?"

"Yeah. Say you opened your eyes, and you were someone else, thrust back into a life and body of the person you used to be—in a previous life."

Merril's brow furrowed as he stared at Nichole. "Is that what happened to you? You woke up in a previous life?"

Nichole nodded. "I did."

Merril folded his arm behind his head and studied her eyes. "What was it like? Do you know who you were?"

Nichole nodded. "I know." She looked down at her hand on his chest. "I woke up on a cattle ranch and met a man I couldn't live without." She lifted her eyes to his. "I married him today."

"What?" Merril blinked and shook his head. "But that's—now."

"It's who I am now. In this life, I'm Nichole Harris. But I have memories from another life."

"A previous life?"

"*This* is my previous life, Merril. I had to make a choice—stay where I was or come back to you. White Eagle was right, the choice was mine. I chose to be with you."

Merril's head fell back, and he regarded the ceiling.

Nichole watched his eyes as he considered what she had told him.

When his gaze returned to her, he remained silent.

"Did I blow your mind?" She ran her hand along his stubbled jaw.

"Blow my mind?" His brow creased.

"Yeah... ka-boom." She held her fist to her head and pulled it away as she opened her fingers. "I don't mean to upset you, but I need you to know."

"I'm not upset, I'm—I don't know—in a state of wonder, I suppose. Do you remember your name, your life?"

Nichole nodded. "My name was Courtney Veau. I had parents, grew up, went to school." She tore her gaze from his and looked down at her hand. "I never gave any thought to things like past lives, until I woke up in the hospital and remembered the time I spent as Nichole. When I realized you were lost to me—forever—it was the worst thing that ever happened to me, in either life." She studied his face. "I love you, Merril and I didn't want to live a life without you in it. I found a way back."

He tightened her in his arms and closed his eyes. "I'll thank God every day of my life that you did."

Chapter 14

Chantal James

—

Chantal turned Acorn into the corral and unwound her legs from the sidesaddle.

When did I become so old?

She slid to the ground and held the saddle to steady herself.

No time to rest. Too much to do.

She saw to Acorn's comfort and turned him loose in the small enclosure. Thankfully, he had plenty of food and water.

The trip to the station had been long, but the ride back felt longer. Every bone in her 81-year-old body ached as she hurried toward the house. She had made this farm a home for her boys and her granddaughter for twenty-five years. She took pride in what she had accomplished, and how much she'd been able to teach Alyse and her own twin sons. Chantal had one last gift for her children, and she intended to give it now.

She raced to the well pump, filled a bucket of water and carried the heavy, sloshing pail into the house. Once she sealed her home, she would not be able to leave it. She made a final trip to the garden to collect a few vegetables which could serve as a quick meal. She closed her eyes and cast her senses into the breeze that blew from the east. He drew near, and his evil stench already tainted the wind.

Hurry!

She slammed and bolted the door. With her back against the entrance, she let her lungs calm while she surveyed the room.

So much to do before I face the monster who would harm my family.

Her mouth lifted in a snarl.

I will crush this devil.

She checked the kerosene in the lanterns to make sure they were full, then placed what remained in open containers and located them with care throughout the house.

Next, she took a bag of salt from the pantry and cut a tiny hole in one corner. She drew a line of salt across the front and back door thresholds, and along every windowsill in between. She set the bag in a large bowl on the counter beside the vegetables.

She rummaged through Bernard's room to find the hammer. With small nails, she attached each of her protection satchels to the lintels above the doors and windows. The hammer slipped from her damp hands and crushed her finger. Pain exploded in her hand and she gasped in shock.

No time.

She grasped a new nail with her third finger. As blood ran down her arm, she pounded in the last nail.

She lit a fire in the fireplace, and tossed clove and pine into the fire, saying a prayer to the Goddess for protection against the coming evil. She knelt on the floor before the hearth and repeated the prayer. The magic glow began in the fire. "Good," she whispered, and grinned.

She pulled one of the smoldering sticks free and made sure no burning ember clung to the smoking wood. Only charred wood would accomplish her purpose. Carefully, as she continued to chant her prayer, Chantal drew a rune of protection on each pane of glass and door in the house. She smudged each satchel as well, tying all the protection back to herself by smudging the same rune on the back of her left hand. That task completed, she returned the blackened brand to the fireplace and offered her thanks. Next, she turned to the furniture.

She leaned her weight against the sofa and pushed with all her strength. "Move for me, you heavy..." She grunted. It slid beneath the window. The rest of the furnishings moved easily, and she cleared the center of the floor. She tossed cushions and pillows into the empty space and arranged them in a circle. The two largest cushions faced the door. She placed the bowl with the bag of salt inside the circle of cushions.

PROPHECY   83

She turned to her altar, one that Bayard had built for her several years ago. It had been constructed in two pieces and allowed her to remove the top from the base. She cleared the decorated altar, carried the upper part into the center of the room, and leveled the four corners on two large cushions. When the altar felt secure, she covered the table and cushions with an altar cloth she had made. The satin cloth displayed a pentacle stitched into the middle.

Chantal walked through the house and gathered everything she would require in a small woven basket, and then stepped into the circle of pillows and knelt before her altar.

It took several moments to calm her spirit. Her shattered nail pulsed in time with her rapid heartbeat. From the basket, she withdrew one of five colored candles. She held each, in turn, in the air. "Red for fire." The flames in the fireplace flared as she placed the enchanted wax in the pentacle's lower right corner. "Blue for water." With the candle held high, water drops ran down her arms as she lowered it to the pentacle's upper right tip. She placed the green candle for earth and a yellow candle for air. Wind circled the scent of pine from inside the closed off room. Her hair blew as she lifted the final candle. "White for the Goddess, the spirit within us all." As she placed the final candle, a tingle ran across her scalp.

Next, she retrieved the small cauldron to hold her spent matches and an athame, her ceremonial knife. Finally, she took out three photographs, one of Alyse, one of her boys, and one they had taken as a family in Toronto two years ago. She sat those in the center of the pentacle where she would have normally placed her *grimoire*.

As she worked, darkness had stolen the light from beyond the windows.

Time, I need more time.

Chantal closed her eyes and took a calming breath. As she released air, she concentrated on her internal balance, the center of herself. The next spell required full focus, and her nerves played havoc with her senses.

He's coming and soon.

Chantal couldn't cast a ward and lay the protective circle until the fight was about to begin. Once she was bound to the ring, food and water would be out of her reach. Chantal ground her teeth. I'll need every drop of strength to fight this devil.

Instead, she invoked the quarters and cast her personal protection spell. The circle would come last, if she had time.

Chantal struck a match and whispered to the flame.

"Spirits of the East, I call you.

Attend me, Elements of Air.

Hold me in your protection and offer me

The breath of life and transformation.

Guard this body and let it not be defiled

By the evil that shall soon stand at my door."

She lit the yellow candle and dropped the match into the cauldron, and then she struck another match.

"Spirits of the South, I call you.

Attend me, Elements of Fire.

Hold me in your protection and offer me

The light that banishes darkness

Guard this body and let it not be defiled

By the evil that shall soon stand at my door."

Chantal lit the red candle and dropped the match into the cauldron.

The wind picked up outside, and an unspeakable urgency assailed Chantal. She struck another match and spoke quickly.

"Spirits of the West, I call you.

Attend me, Elements of Water.

Hold me in your protection and offer me

The cleansing rain that replenishes the earth.

Guard this body and let it not be defiled

By the evil that shall soon stand at my door."

Chantal lit the blue candle, dropped the match, and struck another.

"Spirits of the North, I call you.

Attend me, Elements of Earth.

Hold me in your protection and offer me

The strength of stone to compel my purpose

Guard this body and let it not be defiled

By the evil that shall soon stand at my door."

She lit the green candle, dropped the match, and struck another.

"God and Goddess, be welcome in my home,

Lord and Lady, in all aspects of your creation

Hold me in your protection and offer me

The reborn spirit of my father,

And the loving embrace of my mother,

Guard this body and let it not be defiled

By the evil that shall soon stand at my door."

Chantal lit the white candle and dropped the match.

The glow from the candles did not extend to the dark corners of the room, but she feared nothing there. She took up the knife, just as what sounded like hail began to beat against the front windows. From the light of her candles, she could see grasshoppers, rather than hail, threw themselves at the glass.

The demon had arrived.

Without hesitation, she ran the edge of the sharpened blade through the fire of the white candle, and then held the tip to her forearm and carved the runic symbol against evil and possession into her skin.

"Protect me, threefold Goddess

From the evil of possession.

Do not allow this body

To be used against those I love."

Taking the blade in her left hand, she carved the same symbol again into her right forearm.

"Protect me, Father of life and rebirth,

From the evil of possession.

Do not allow this body

To be used against those I love."

Chantal sat the blade down and listened to the wind and rain outside. She closed her eyes and visualized the protective weave of power that ran from each rune and satchel throughout her house, held tethered to her left hand.

The fire still burned in the fireplace, and she called on the element of fire with her right hand to light all the lamps in the house.

Outside, a chorus of howls changed to wild yipping.

Coyotes.

Chantal came to her feet and picked up the salt bag from the bowl. She walked clockwise and chanted the protection spell for her circle as she drew a line of salt on the outside of the circle of pillows, which included her altar and candles. She set the empty salt bag in its bowl and turned to face the door.

The yipping howls grew closer.

A flutter of wings in the chimney, then a half-dozen bats flew into the fire, knocking cinders onto the floor. Two bats made it through and flew at her head. Chantal cast out her right hand, and their wings burst into flames. They fell and flopped along the floor for a moment, then, they were still.

The sound of breaking glass in Alyse's bedroom startled her, and she tugged the protective lines of power in her hand—tested them. The glass had broken, but the ward still held.

The front door began to vibrate in its frame, so hard and fast, the edges hummed. Then the bolt gave way and the door splintered and blew open. Wind and rain rushed into the house. Several lamps fell over and went out. The altar candles burned steady, as though the wind could not penetrate Chantal's protective circle.

Through the open door, she could see the coyotes circle the yard in the rain. One of them jumped at the front door, but was stopped by the weave of the protection spell. The coyote dropped dead just outside the door, its fur singed and its eyes white. A chorus of howls went up.

How many are out there?

She had thought to face a single demon, not a host.

She stood and squared her shoulders toward the door, legs braced as if for a blow. Her left hand held the protective weave, her right hand ready to cast in battle.

She heard Acorn scream once, then a yip of pain. A moment later, Acorn walked past the front door as the rain soaked his coat. The horse turned its head and looked at Chantal, and a gleam of fire reflected in her eyes.

"Oh, no," Chantal muttered.

I'm sorry, Acorn.

The horse ambled out of sight. Moments later, a pounding began against the wall of Bayard's room. The demon inside Acorn would try to kick down the wall.

Another coyote rushed the front door and flopped dead next to the first one. Again, the baying went up in the yard, but to Chantal, it sounded like laughter.

The pounding of hooves against the wall stopped, and for a few seconds all she could hear outside was the rain. She gasped as a shadow passed before the window. The low sound of boots on the wooden step, toe to heel, echoed through the open door.

A man stood in the doorway. He wore a long raincoat with a shoulder cape and a drooping felt hat. He looked familiar, but in the darkness of the stoop, she couldn't tell who he was. When he raised his head to look at her, she recognized the miller's son, but he was the miller's son no longer.

"Hello, Chantal. I see you've been expecting us." It grinned and reached out a hand against the protective magic at the door and nodded. "Very nice. We're all impressed with your skill. But you aren't the one we were promised, are you?" He tilted his head and searched her eyes. "No, you're not. But you're close—family, then?" An evil grin split his face. "Your daughter? Or your son, perhaps?" He stepped back from the door. His gaze locked with hers. The flicker of her candles reflected in its dark eyes.

"It's only a matter of time, Chantal. You know that. I'll have you and your power, and I'll know who you're protecting." He chuckled. "It's just a matter of time."

His laughter sent a shiver down Chantal's back, as the yipping howls took up their chorus again, and Acorn began kicking the wall.

Her fortress had become a trap, but she knew it would. She needed to hold him here as long as she could, to give her children time to escape.

The repetitive sound of Acorn's hammering hooves became soporific—almost hypnotic. As soon as the thought occurred to her, she lifted her head.

The demon stood at the door and grinned at her, and the yipping resumed in the yard. "Well, it was worth a try, don't you think?" he said conversationally and stepped down into the yard. He spun around and looked at Chantal through the doorway and the pouring rain. Then he threw up his hands.

All the glass in the house shattered. Chantal cried out as glass from the front windows littered the floor outside of her pillows. The head of a dead elk rested across the window's broken sill. Above the animal, the white satchel swung precariously, and then fell.

Over the body of the elk came a coyote. It hurled itself directly at her face, and she threw fire from her hand at its head. It fell writhing to the floor. Two more leapt through but vanished into the darkness. A third came over the elk and jumped at her. It died in fire beside the first.

A scratching sound on the floor drew Chantal's attention away from the window, and she saw one of the coyotes pawing at the salt circle, trying to break it. She threw an arc of fire at the animal, but it disappeared down the hallway with a yip.

The sound of Acorn's kicking stopped. Into the room, from Bayard's bedroom, came a rhumba of rattlers. They slithered along the salt circle, dispersing it as they wove back and forth around her.

She felt the weave of protection break as a coyote ran past with a white satchel in its mouth. Then came the sharp piercing pain of a bite on her ankle, followed by one on her calf. All the snakes were inside the circle of cushions. Another rattler sank its fangs into her thigh.

As she turned to her altar, the demon grabbed her by the throat and held her still.

"You see, Chantal. That didn't take very long at all."

With a thought, Chantal ignited the kerosene.

The open containers set strategically around the house were placed under beds, near curtains or surrounded by oily rags. In moments, flames licked up the side of the walls and crawled along the spilled oil from the overturned lamps. A whoosh of air drawn into the house by Chantal detonated the blaze.

***

Morago

—

Unable to possess Chantal's body due to the runes carved on her arms, Morago snapped her neck, then put his mouth over hers and inhaled sharply, sucking her soul, abilities, and mind into his arsenal.

He let her broken body fall across her altar.

The flames fully engulfed the house as Morago strolled out the front door, but he controlled the fire now, and it didn't harm him.

As he stepped into the yard, he twisted to look at the farmhouse. Laughing, he raised his hands, drawing the flames higher in jubilation.

I search for twin girls. I'll find them in the town of Boston.

Chapter 15

Nichole Harris-Shilo

—

The next morning, Merril helped Nichole dress in the brown skirt and jacket she'd worn the day before. She pulled on her riding boots while Merril stepped outside to speak with Tom.

The sun broke over the horizon as Nichole closed the hotel door behind her and greeted Tom.

While Merril listened to Tom plan the ride, he secured their saddlebags.

"We can make it to The Shilo by tonight." Tom tightened the cinch, dropped the stirrup, and mounted. "We'll stop halfway, and again at your branding site. Unless you want to go by way of Kiowa Crossing."

Merril helped Nichole climb onto her sidesaddle. He straightened her skirt over her boots and gave her leg a pat. "No. I would rather head toward The Shilo. I know you and I can make the ride, Tom, but Nicki's not used to being in the saddle. We'll need to rest more, maybe stop for the night."

"Let's try to get as far as we can." Nichole understood the urgency Merril felt to return home and take care of his brother and The Shilo.

"You'll let me know if we need to stop?" Merril confirmed, looking up at Nichole.

She opened her parasol and set it on her shoulder. "Of course."

They stopped the first time at the campsite Amy had pointed out as the halfway point. Tom had packed a lunch for them and took care of the horses as Nichole finished off a second piece of fried chicken.

Merril tossed a cleaned chicken bone into the weeds. "How are you doing?"

"My back aches and my rear end feels flat, but I'm doing better than I thought."

"Good." He gave her a sympathetic nod. "You'll tell me if you need another break."

"I will." Nichole cast a bone into the tall grass behind her and stood. "I'm going to stretch a bit more before we head out."

They stopped again at The Shilo branding site. Quite a few head of cattle ranged nearby, but there wasn't a wrangler within shouting distance.

Tom pulled his mount beside Merril. "Do you find this odd?"

"More than odd." Merril nodded toward the branding fire. "Those irons should be back at the ranch. It's as though the wranglers mounted up and lit out at a moment's notice." Merril's gaze found Nichole. "How are you doing?"

Nichole forced a smile and nodded. "I'm all right. Ready to be done with the ride, but I'll make it. Are we stopping here?"

"I'd like to keep going, if you think you can. The Shilo is less than an hour from here."

"I can. Let's go." When Merril turned away, Nichole cringed. Her back ached from her hips to her neck, and her legs and rump had gone numb.

They arrived at the Shilo late in the day. The empty bunkhouse cast a long shadow across the yard. They pulled rein near the corral and sat in the empty silence.

"Where is everyone?" Nichole pondered as she watched Merril dismount. The bunkhouse door caught her attention as it swung back and forth, abandoned in the summer breeze.

Tom dismounted while Merril moved to help Nichole from her mount. He held her weight as she got her legs under her and moaned when cramped muscles stretched.

Tom gathered the reins to the three horses, saw to their immediate need, and then turned them loose in the corral.

Nichole followed Merril onto the porch.

He paused at the doorway. "You should wait out here." Merril loosened the silk scarf around his neck.

"Why? What do you think you'll find?"

"I'm not sure. Doc wouldn't have buried Kevin without me here. I think Kevin's body will be inside. Maybe Renata's as well."

Nichole stepped to the library window, put her hand to the glass and peered inside.

The window looked as though it had been blackened on the inside with paint, and then she realized the blackness moved. She jerked her head back and let out a sound of disgust.

"What?" Both Merril and Tom voiced, as Tom followed them up onto the porch.

"Flies." Nichole shivered and moved back. "Thousands and thousands of flies."

Both men peered through the flies on the library window.

"The door is closed." Tom looked to Merril.

Merril nodded and stepped back. "They removed the bodies from the library, but the room hasn't been cleaned." He pointed across the yard. "Why don't you both wait by the corral? I need to go in and see about... the remains, but you should stay out here."

"Yeah, I'll be over there." Nichole made a face at the flies and moved carefully off the porch. Every bone in her body ached, and the skin on her ass and legs felt raw. The material of her drawers stung her skin as she moved across the yard. She stopped near the trough and turned to watch the men.

Ignoring Merril's instruction to wait outside, Tom pulled his bandana over his nose and nodded for Merril to lead.

When they disappeared inside the house, Nichole rubbed her rump and groaned. She cast a glare at the torture device called a sidesaddle and swore she would begin to wear denim slacks and ride astride. She turned back to the house just as Tom stepped out the door.

He walked to the railing, pulled the neckerchief from his face and hung his head, taking in large gulps of air.

She looked back at the door.

Where's Merril?

She straightened her back as Merril walked out the door.

He had a burlap bag over his shoulder. His long strides took him across the yard, past her, and into the corral. He tied the bag behind his saddle, then pulled the scarf down and rubbed his face against his shoulder. When he turned to find her gaze, his eyes were dark. He shook his head, then captured the reins of her horse, and walked out of the corral to where she waited.

"What did you find?" she asked when he stood beside her.

"Kevin's and Renata's coffins. Doc must have brought coffins with him from The Crossing. He tacked their names to the top, so I wouldn't have to open them to find my brother." He swallowed, then looked back toward the open door. "I'd like to bury them, if not tomorrow, then the day after."

"What's in the bag?" Nichole gestured toward his saddle.

"Clothes, mostly. There's not much here I need."

They watched Tom shake his head and start for the corral.

"Where's everyone else? Henny and Katy?" Nichole asked.

Merril shrugged. "Don't know. No one's in there. We can't stay here, either. It's going to be dark by the time we get to The Highlands."

Nichole stared at the horns of the sidesaddle. "How far is it to home?"

Merril's eyes filled with concern. "You're hurt, aren't you?"

"I'm fine." She couldn't cry in front of Merril. "How long until we're home?" *We can't camp here. That would be horrible.*

"A couple hours at the most." Merril searched her eyes. "Can you make it?"

Nichole nodded and gripped the saddle horn of her rent-a-horse. "Help me up." She cringed as she took her seat and hooked her legs in the horns.

I can ride for two more hours.

After the first hour, Nichole could glimpse the lights from The Highlands at the top of each small rise. They shone like a beacon in a sea of blackness and brought home to her just how isolated they were on the flat empty prairie.

When they finally reached the yard, both Merril and Tom dismounted, but Nichole didn't move.

Merril took hold of her horse's bridle and looked up at her in sympathy. "Are you stuck?"

"Actually, I am. My butt is asleep, and the insides of my legs are on fire. I'm afraid to move." She joked, but when she looked down at Merril, his image swam in unshed tears.

"I knew it would be too much. We should have stopped." He raised his arms to her. "Lean on me, I won't let you fall."

Nichole dropped the reins and reached down for Merril's shoulders. He gripped her waist and lifted her from the saddle. He lowered her to her feet, but kept his arms around her, and she leaned into his chest.

"I never want to do that again," she whispered. "The buckboard hurt less than that saddle."

"Can you walk, or do you want me to carry you?"

Tom collected the reins and drew all three horses toward the barn.

"Give me a minute." She stomped her feet and grimaced. "Let the tingling stop first."

They stood in the darkened yard for several minutes, then Nichole took a few halting steps.

Merril scooped her up in his arms. "Here, let me help." He crossed the yard and porch and set her on her feet at the door.

Instead of opening the door, she turned in his arms and laid her arms around his neck, then drew his head down for a slow lingering kiss.

The long kiss ended with several smaller kisses, and then Merril drew his head back and gazed into her eyes.

"Today totally sucked, my love." Nichole smiled and pushed a strand of hair behind his ear.

"I would have to agree." His grin ticked up. "But things seem to be getting better." Merril bent to kiss her one more time. "We have an audience," he murmured into her hair.

Nichole glanced toward the window, but only saw the curtains fall back into place. "Well, then, let's go inside." Nichole turned around and opened the front door.

June, Jeanne, and Cookie all stood near the dining room table as Nichole limped through the door. June's face was flushed and disagreeable, but both Jeanne and Cookie appeared overjoyed Nichole had returned home.

"You made it in time!" Cookie took both sides of Merril's head with her palms. She pulled his head down and planted a big kiss on his forehead, knocking his hat to the floor.

Nichole hugged Jeanne and nodded hello to June. "Just barely."

"Where's Amy?" June asked.

Merril retrieved his hat from the floor and chuckled at Cookie. "Amy and Jason stayed in town to allow Jimmy Leigh to heal. Jones shot him just before Jim took him down."

The women exclaimed in unison, and Merril gave them a brief explanation, leaving out most of what Nichole had endured.

When he finished, Cookie touched his arm. "Did Kelly find you?" The smile left her face.

"He did." Merril nodded. "He stayed in town to help Jason and Amy. Tom came back with us." No one spoke, and after a few moments, Merril continued. "We stopped by The Shilo on the way here. No one's there. Do you know where Henny and her family are? Where Bill is?"

Cookie shook her head and looked at Merril with sorrowful eyes. "Henny and her family came here after they left The Shilo. Henny said they couldn't stay there, what with your brother and you being gone. She didn't know you'd gone to Denver to save Miss Nichole. Renata told everyone you'd run off for good."

"Are they still here?" Nichole asked.

All three women answered, "Yes." But Cookie continued to explain. "Lloyd told them to move into the family bunk, now that most of the wranglers have taken off for a short break."

"That's fine." Nichole stepped forward and grimaced.

"What about Bill?" Merril put his arm around Nichole and stopped her from attempting to walk.

"Lloyd sent Bill to Kiowa Crossing to get Doc. When Bill came back, Lloyd told him to bunk down here until you got back and sorted things out."

"That's good." Merril nodded, and then a smile lit his face.

"We do have some good news to share." He hugged Nichole a bit closer. "Nichole and I were married yesterday in Denver."

Jeanne's eyes welled with tears as she hugged Nichole and whispered, "It's about time."

Nichole laughed and choked up. "Thank you, Jeanne," she said as the women released each other from their hug.

Jeanne furrowed her brow at Nichole. "For what?"

"For everything you've done for me since we left Boston. You were a rock when my mother became ill. I don't know if I ever told you how much your help and friendship has meant to me."

The women hugged again, and Jeanne whispered, "You have your memory back."

Nichole nodded, unable to speak.

"Hello, there. I don't think we've been introduced," Merril said.

Nichole looked up and saw Lawna's anxious face peeking down the stairs. "Merril, this is Lawna Caine, both she and her husband work here. Lawna, this is my husband, Merril Shilo."

Lawna bobbed her head, and her smile relaxed, although she cast an anxious glance toward June and Cookie.

Nichole tried to take another step forward, but it became more of a hop. The skin down the inside of her thighs felt burned and stiff.

"Allow me, Mrs. Shilo." Merril swept her up in his arms. "I believe I shall carry you up the stairs once again."

"What's wrong with her?" Cookie asked.

"Saddle sore, Cookie. A full day in the saddle has rubbed her legs and rump raw. Do you have ointment for burns?"

"We have Amy's salve. Let me fetch it." Cookie and June both disappeared through the doorway to the kitchen.

Nichole tucked her head to Merril's shoulder as he mounted the stairs. She pulled her feet in as tight as possible, but he didn't bump her head as he made the narrow climb.

Lawna pointed to Nichole's room when Merril reached the second floor. He rounded the handrail and set her down on her bed. "I am going to leave you to the care of Jeanne and Lawna, my love. I need to speak with Lloyd and Bill."

Nichole held his neck and kissed him. "Thank you."

Both Lawna and Jeanne giggled at her show of affection for Merril.

When she released him, she said, "Don't leave the ranch without me, and come back here when you are done with Lloyd, okay?"

"Yes, ma'am," Merril's sideways smile lifted, and he tipped his hat to Nichole lying on the bed.

"Ladies," he said to Lawna and Jeanne as he left the room.

"I am so happy for you," Jeanne said again, unable to keep the smile from her face.

"Thanks." Nichole moved, and hissed through her teeth as her drawers pulled at her chapped legs.

"Let's get your clothes off." Jeanne shoved the door closed and helped Nichole stand. She unfastened the skirt as Nichole unbuttoned the jacket.

Nichole tried to step out of the skirt, but shook her head and lowered her leg. "I can't."

"There's blood dried to your drawers on the inside of your legs." Jeanne looked up at Nichole. "This will need to be soaked off and bandaged."

"It's really sore," Nichole gritted through her teeth, and closed her eyes.

"Lawna, go tell Cookie we'll need some warm water and bandages, as well as Amy's ointment," Jeanne instructed.

The door opened and closed as Lawna left the room.

"Where's Hope-Anne?" Nichole asked as Jeanne pulled an old comforter from beneath the bed and spread it over the fine cover on Nichole's bed.

"Sleeping, I hope. The babe has been colicky. There's some tension between June and Lawna. I think nerves may be drying Lawna's milk. Now, lie back on the bed and let me try to loosen the drawers."

"Dang, this hurts." Nichole scooted onto the comforter and tried not to pull at the dark stains on her drawers. Both legs burned and stung along the inside from just above her knees to mid-thigh.

"Oh, Nicki, this is going to hurt," Jeanne whispered. "Let me cut them off, then soak the dried cloth away from your skin."

Nichole nodded, and Jeanne disappeared from the room. Nichole listened to her run up the stairs at the end of the hallway, and moments later, she returned with a large pair of sewing shears.

"Down the sides first?" Jeanne wondered aloud.

"I think so. Help me back up, that will make it easier."

Jeanne helped Nichole to her feet, then cut away the drawers, avoiding the four inches or so on either side of her legs. Next, Jeanne took a clean pair of drawers and cut the legs off well above the knee and helped Nichole step into them and pull them up and over the bloody parts of her leg.

Nichole had just laid back down when footsteps sounded on the stairs, and then Lawna and Cookie came into the room.

Lawna had several linens draped over her arm and carried a pitcher with warmed water.

Cookie looked at the bloody patches of cloth stuck to Nichole's legs and exclaimed in dismay, "My lands, child, I know you didn't tell Mr. Merril you needed to stop."

"No, I didn't. My legs were so numb I didn't realize they were this bad."

Cookie and Jeanne each took a leg and soaked the crusted material from Nichole's skin. Once they washed the area clean, Cookie covered the burns with Amy's salve and bandaged the sores with soft linen. She wrapped strips of cloth around her legs to hold the bandages secure.

Nichole stood as Jeanne removed and folded the old blanket, and then unlaced and removed Nichole's corset.

Nichole slid between the cool, clean sheets. Her legs felt better already, but her head swam with exhaustion.

"I'll bring up a dinner tray," Jeanne said at the door.

Nichole nodded and closed her eyes.

Chapter 16

Alyse James

—

The novelty of traveling by train proved a poor diversion for Alyse. Anxiety at leaving her grandmother behind kept her chest tight as the miles rolled past. Perhaps her uncles were wrong, and the demon wouldn't go to the farm. She glared out the window.

Maybe there's no demon at all.

She would meet her parents and sister in Boston, and then return home to the farm and her grandmother.

Bayard wiped his eyes. "We shouldn't have left her." He ran a hand over his balding scalp and hung his head. "We should have made her come with us."

Bernard gave a pat to Bay's knee. "It's what she wanted, Bay. She's planned for this day since the girls were born."

"I know," Bayard muttered. "We all have. I just can't believe we'll never see her—"

"Baked goods. Anything you'd like, dearies?" A woman with a straw basket stopped beside their seats. The basket held small loaves of bread and muffins, and what appeared to be berry tarts.

Bernard purchased two loaves of nut bread and set them beside Bay.

Alyse turned back to the window. The daylight outside the glass faded to twilight. They would sleep on the hard bench for two nights and arrive in Boston the day after tomorrow. Then they would return to the farm. Deep inside, she knew the truth her grandmother and uncles had lived with for twenty-five years.

It's all true.

"How much do you think Maggie's changed?" Bernard wondered aloud.

Alyse watched her uncles from their reflection in the window.

Bayard shook his head. "I don't know. Her husband's name—isn't it—Prescott?"

"I think so." Bern nodded. "Let's hope they still live where the twins were born. We'll start the search there."

Alyse had never heard her father's name.

Her name.

She'd grown up a James. Alyse Prescott sounded foreign to her ears. She leaned her head against the window and closed her eyes. Despite the hard bench, the slow motion of the railcar and the monotonous clickety-clack of the train lulled her to sleep.

They arrived at the Boston station early the second day and collected their luggage from the porter.

Alyse rolled her eyes as her uncles debated the best way to travel to their sister's home.

A hansom cabbie referred them to a nearby livery to rent a wagon. He explained to Bernard that their luggage would make it impossible for them to hire a cab or ride the omnibus.

They located the livery, rented a single-horse buckboard wagon and stacked their trunks in back. The late morning traffic proved light and easy to negotiate. They traveled north from the train station toward the Charles River and turned onto Beacon Street.

Alyse gazed at the city with wonder.

This is where Amy grew up.

How different would her life have been if she'd grown up here instead of the farm?

Bernard slowed the wagon to a walk. "We're here. Up ahead on the left." He halted the wagon several doors down from their sister's home.

"No. This doesn't look right." Bay glanced around at the other houses and down the street.

"I'm positive. That's Mag's house," Bern replied.

"What are we waiting for?" Alyse urged, trapped between her uncles on the seat.

Bernard set the wheel brake, wrapped the reins around the upright post next to the seat, and stepped down. He offered his hand to his niece.

Bay dropped from the wagon on the other side and attached a feedbag to the horse's head.

"You should stay behind us," Bern warned Alyse as they crossed the street. "We don't know if your father's home."

"Why would it matter?" Alyse quickened her step to pass her uncles.

Bernard grabbed her arm. "We don't know what Mags told Prescott about you." He directed Alyse behind the tall brothers. "For example, where you've been for the last twenty-five years."

Bayard nodded. "Even if your mother's the only one home, you're going to be a shock to her."

The brothers stepped up to the front door, shoulder to shoulder, and knocked.

Alyse put her back to her uncles and crossed her arms, but she couldn't stand still. She spun around and tried to spy around Bernard, but he put his hand on her bowler hat and pushed her back.

Bay knocked again.

From inside the house, they heard a woman call, "Coming... coming." Then the door opened.

"Hello, Maggie." Bay pulled the bowler from his head.

"Don't faint, Mags." Bernard reached out to steady his sister. "Are you alone?"

"Is Mum all right? Is she with you? Is Alyse..." Margaret's voice trailed off as Alyse peered around Bayard's side.

Margaret gasped and covered her mouth. Tears filled her eyes.

"Can we come in, Mags?" Bern asked. "Let's not do this out here. We're looking for Amylia."

Margaret backed into the house, her gaze on Alyse's face. When the door closed behind Bern, Margaret opened her arms and embraced Alyse. "Oh, my beautiful daughter." Margaret wept as she hugged Alyse.

Alyse's throat closed, and she simply held on to her mother while she cried.

"Is your husband home, sissy? Are you alone?" Bernard circled his sister and niece as Margaret gained control of her emotions. "There are matters most urgent. We need to speak with you and Amylia."

Margaret pushed Alyse to arms' length and ran her gaze over her daughter. "You're so like your sister." She brushed strands of hair from Alyse's damp face.

"Mags..." Bern cautioned again.

Margaret turned to Bayard and embraced him, ignoring Bernard. "Bay, you haven't aged a bit. How I've missed you." Then she turned to Bernard and smiled. "You old stick in the mud. Always business with you. Give your sissy a hug." They embraced, and Margaret kissed the side of his face.

"Come into the parlor, where we can sit." Margaret led them through an arched opening into a seating area. Long windows faced the street and filled the room with light. Even as she sat, Margaret never took her gaze from her daughter's face.

Alyse smiled through her tears and consigned everything about her mother to memory. An inch shorter than Alyse, Margaret carried more weight in her hips than either Alyse or Chantal. Her mother had dark eyes, like the rest of the family and wore her brown-gray hair up, just like *Mémé*, in a loose bun.

Why does my mother look older than my uncles?

Alyse cast a quick glance at her uncles as she took a seat beside her mother.

I'll have to ask.

Margaret took Alyse's hand. "Robert's not here. He's at the warehouse. I don't expect him back until late this evening, so we have time to talk." Margaret tore her gaze from Alyse and looked from Bayard to Bernard. "Tell me, why are you here? Where's Mum?"

"Mum stayed at the farm." Bernard's tone was low and cautious. "She said she couldn't travel so far or as fast as our need. It's urgent. We believe she's buying us time. We must speak with Amylia."

"Amy?" Margaret's voice rose as she spoke. "I thought the whole reason for separating my girls was to keep them safe from Mum's prophecy."

"She tried to stop them from *twyning*—like Bay and I do—but it didn't work." Bernard shook his head in frustration. "They *twyned* anyway, despite the distance."

Bayard reached out and touched his sister's arm. "Maggie, the Prophecy is happening. *Now*. It's too late to keep your girls apart. They need to learn to work together."

Bernard rose after his brother spoke and paced around the couch.

"How can this be?" Margaret turned to her daughter, her voice soft. "You *twyned* with Amy?"

Alyse felt her face heat as she nodded. "I didn't mean to, but she needed me. I didn't know I had a sister until I was with her and *twyned*. Can I see her?"

Margaret's eyes filled with sadness, and she shook her head. "Amy isn't here, darling. She married a banker's son two years ago, a young man named Jason Harris. They moved to Denver last year to help Jason's uncle with his cattle ranch." Margaret dropped her gaze to their clasped hands. "She writes, but I still miss her so."

"What?" Alyse questioned. "Amy's not here?"

Margaret's head came up. "No, she's not." She looked at her brothers, then back to Alyse.

"Amy lives in Denver?" Bern asked as he paced behind the settee.

"Yes. I have her address." Margaret turned from Bernard and looked again at Alyse.

"If you could give that to us, we'll need to be on our way," Bernard said.

"That's what I thought." Margaret pressed her lips and wiped at her face with one hand. She kept a firm hold on Alyse with the other.

"We can stay for a bit." Alyse corrected her uncle.

Bernard stopped pacing and looked crossly at his niece but held his tongue.

"*Mémé* sent you a present... Mother. It's in my trunk. Uncle Bern, could you get the package, please? It's addressed to Margaret." Alyse cast a trembling smile of thanks at her uncle, then turned back to her mother.

Bayard sat forward and reached for Margaret's other hand. "It's wonderful to see you Maggie. Are you doing well? Are you happy?" Bayard grinned and winked at Alyse. "Does your husband treat you as he should? We can take care of him if he doesn't. You know we can."

Margaret laughed through her tears. "Of course, I'm happy. Robert is a good man and a good father." She looked back to Alyse as more tears welled in her eyes. "I'm so sorry you never got to know him. Oh! I have a photograph." She stood and crossed to the mantel. When she returned, she brought a photograph of herself, her husband, and a young Amy. She handed the frame to Alyse.

Alyse looked at the photo of the family she should have been a part of. It was several years old. Amy wore calf-length skirts and braided hair—but the face? She saw it every morning when she glanced in her mirror.

"Does he... does my father know about me?" Alyse looked from the picture to her mother.

Margaret shook her head. "No. Robert doesn't know both our daughters survived their birth. He knows nothing of The Prophecy, or of our family's—peculiar skills."

Bern came in the front door with the brown paper package in time to hear Margaret's last comment.

"You never trained Amy in her skills?" Bern handed his mother's package to Margaret.

"I taught her to scry with water. She has only two elements, *Water* and *Earth*," Margaret explained.

"I have *Fire* and *Air*." Alyse looked at all the faces around her.

Margaret raised an eyebrow at her daughter. "How curious. Do you have precognition as well?"

Alyse shook her head. "No, but I can *truth-read* people—when I try."

"Amy has precognition? That's unexpected." Bayard looked from his sister to his brother.

Margaret nodded as she took her seat and began to untie the knotted string around the package. "As is the ability to *truth-read*. I have very talented children, it seems." She smiled at Alyse as a knot came free. "Amy's visions began at a young age. The poor girl didn't understand at first, and they frightened her." She glanced at her brothers. "What was I to do? I worked with her to glean the important things from ordinary. Aside from scrying, I also taught her herb lore. She always had the *earth-sight*, but could never heal, though Lord knows she never stopped trying."

Margaret released the string from the package and pulled back the paper. "I taught her what was safe for her to know." Folded inside the paper package lay a finely knitted shawl, white across the top, the shawl grew progressively darker until at the very bottom of the 'V' the yarn was black.

Margaret gasped in delight as she picked it up. From inside the wrap fell another package and a letter. She retrieved them from the floor and unfolded the letter. She scanned it, then read it aloud.

Margaret, my beloved daughter,

How I wish I could see you again. Please know I have loved you and thought of you each and every day we have been apart. You are always in my heart.

The thing we tried to prevent has come to pass. Your girls have twyned. The Prophecy is set in motion and will end only with the defeat of the demon.

Inside this package is my gift to you. The wrap has been crocheted with an element of protection. Please wear it whenever you feel uneasy, it will help calm and protect you.

I have also enclosed a protection satchel. Keep this close to your heart. And lastly, I have included a satchel for Robert. Tell him it is a scent you love and put it in his coat pocket.

This is all I can do to keep you both safe.

All my love, Mum

Margaret swallowed and held the shawl under her nose for a moment and inhaled, then opened the smaller package. She withdrew a satchel on a long chain. The protection amulet looked similar to the one Chantal had given Alyse. Margaret hung the talisman around her neck and tucked the satchel inside her blouse. She looked at her brothers and her daughter.

"And so it begins." Margaret's voice shook with emotion.

"It began when your girls were born," Bayard said.

"It began with The Prophecy," Alyse corrected. "But now we have the chance to end it. And when it's over, I want to come back and visit with you and my father. Would that be possible?"

Margaret took Alyse's hand and smiled. "Of course, my dear. We will find a way to explain this to Robert when you come back."

Margaret hugged Alyse one more time then stood and walked to a writing desk. She handed Bernard several of Amy's letters.

Bernard wrote down the address on a slip of paper and placed the note in his vest pocket. He returned the letters to his sister. "Thank you, Mags."

Alyse and Bayard rose and followed Bern and Margaret to the door.

Margaret reached for her daughter and hugged her tight.

Bayard wrapped an arm around Alyse. "We must go, niece."

She nodded but couldn't stop her tears. She paused inside the door and looked back.

Bernard spoke quietly with his sister. "Mum thinks the demon will go to the farm first. We all believed Amy still lived in Boston. Mags. The demon will know we came here. It will follow us."

Margaret's face paled. She looked from Bernard to her daughter and Bay, who stood inside the door. She closed her eyes and nodded. "Mum knew too, hence the gifts."

Bernard wrapped his arms around his sister. "I know you don't practice the craft like we did growing up but take what precautions you can. I don't want to see you hurt." He kissed her head and followed Bay and Alyse out the door and down the street to the wagon.

At the train station, they reviewed the departure schedule, stops and lines they would need to use to get to Denver. The Central Pacific would take them all the way to Cheyenne, then they would change lines and head south to Denver on the Colorado Central Railroad.

Bernard purchased the tickets for the train and the transfers at the counter, and they turned their luggage over to the porter to be loaded into the baggage car. The train would depart at 6:45 that evening.

Alyse watched Bernard purchase hot pies from a vendor in the station and carry them back to their seats.

"Four days to Denver. I didn't get a Pullman car, just the standard seats." He handed each a hot pie. "I want to save Mum's cash if we can. We may need it."

Chapter 17

Catherine Kline

—

Catherine Kline left her brother reading yesterday's Daily Picayune in their open compartment. She couldn't bear to watch him read another minute.

Going somewhere besides New Orleans, and the novelty of traveling by train, filled her with a constant hum of excitement. She could not sit quietly as the world passed by her window.

Cat made her way to the front of the car, and tipped her head to the elderly couple seated near the forward door. She threw a quick glance over her shoulder at her brother and slipped onto the small observation platform between cars.

Her breath caught as an exhilarating rush of air swirled by her. The trees the train passed were no longer draped with moss. They had made the line transfer in Jackson and were now headed west toward Shreveport. A new scent, as unfamiliar as the trees, swirled around her and she inhaled the crisp fragrance.

The small landing boasted a safety rail on each side, but was open to the platform on the next car. She stepped across the opening above the linkage and entered the adjoining car.

Catherine passed forward through three cars before she encountered a locked door with a sign that stated, "NO ADMITTANCE." Unwilling to return to her seat, she stood on the platform in the fresh air and felt the rumble of the wheels beneath her feet.

It wasn't long until her stomach rumbled as well, a reminder breakfast waited with Sam.

I should go back. Sam will wonder where I've gone.

She retraced her steps through the cars and caught sight of a familiar face.

His back would have been to her when she passed through on her way forward. Now, he stared out the window, as though deep in thought. His reflection in the glass showed the long scar from his eye to his chin. The side of his face turned toward her—tanned and unblemished—was beautiful. An unfamiliar tingle assailed her stomach and her heart fluttered.

Curious.

His chin wore a day's worth of stubble. His thick, black hair had been brushed back and secured with a leather tie at his nape. Shorter hairs escaped the binding and feathered along his face, softening the sharp angle of his jaw. He had a perilous and mysterious air about him that drew her. Sam had a dangerous feel about him as well, so that proved no impediment. However, the mystery seated before her filled her stomach with nervous flutters.

Cat smoothed her windblown hair and gripped her skirt. With an easy smile, she stepped to the empty bench across from her brother's friend and seated herself.

Inquiring blue eyes, deep set and lined by thick, dark lashes, turned from the window to her.

Cat felt her smile falter, but only for a moment; then, she held out her gloved hand. "I'm afraid my brother failed to introduce us the other night. My name is Catherine Kline, but my friends call me Cat."

His smile crinkled the corners of his eyes. He sat forward and took her hand in his. "Well, you are quite a surprise this morning, Miss, or is it Mrs Kline? Are we friends then? Should I call you Cat?"

"It's Miss Kline." Cat's grin grew wide as the warmth of his large hand penetrated her glove. "We might be friends, if I knew your name. Are you and Sam friends?"

He tipped his head, as if to consider the question. "No. Not really. We've worked together—twice, I believe." He shrugged and placed his other hand on top of Cat's. "No one calls me by my given name, *ma chère*. Both friends and acquaintances call me Hunter."

Cat glanced at her trapped hand, then back to Hunter's amused eyes and dimpled her cheek with a half-smile. "My brother is a hunter of sorts, as well, sir. Since Hunter is not your given name, I shall venture to guess it is something of a title, not unlike doctor, or conductor." She shook her head and leaned closer, resting her other hand upon his. "If we are to be friends, sir, and I were to allow you to address me as Cat, I would need more from you than your title." Cat lifted her chin and smiled a challenge.

Hunter gave her hands a gentle squeeze, released them, and leaned back in his seat. "Is your brother on board, Miss Kline?" His eyes sparkled, and the smile on his face met her challenge.

"He is. Our compartment is three cars back. We travel to Denver. And you?"

"Denver, *ma chère?* I travel there as well." His eyes narrowed, and his white teeth flashed a grin. "Perhaps it is more than coincidence I ran into you and your brother on the riverboat."

Cat waved her hand in annoyance. "Sam likes to gamble, Mr. Hunter. He visits the riverboat whenever he's in town." The way he watched her made her neck and stomach tingle. "I must say I found watching the card games disappointing. Perhaps, if I had played a hand and placed a wager, it would have kept me better entertained."

Hunter rubbed his hand across his mouth and cleared his throat. "You are an adventurous woman, Miss Kline. Are you from N'Orleans?"

"I am, sir. And you?"

"*Oui.* I grew up in the city." He sat forward and studied her face. "May I ask what takes you and your brother to Denver?"

Cat looked around the railcar. No one sat nearby. She leaned toward Hunter, her voice low. "You know of my brother's work, Mr. Hunter?" She waited for him to nod. "He's going to Denver regarding an investment firm. He's always rather vague about his work." Cat sat back and arranged her skirt. "For my part, I refused his offer to attend a finishing school. I have set my mind toward discovering the world." She gestured at the countryside passing beyond the window. "Isn't this exciting?"

***

Hunter

—

Hunter glanced out the window, then back to the young woman seated across from him. *Mademoiselle* Kline's beautiful face radiated excitement and held his interest far more than the view outside his window—much more than her brother would find acceptable. "Is this your first trip away from home?"

Two gentlemen came to a stop beside Hunter's compartment. "Excuse me, miss, but these are our seats."

Without hesitation, Cat moved from the bench across from Hunter to the seat beside him.

Hunter could no longer hide his smile. He found Catherine Kline delightfully forward, yet completely unaware of it.

Natural innocence.

When her brother came to find her—and he would—Sam would be irate to discover his younger sister practically seated in Hunter's lap. Hunter laid his arm along the back of the seat behind Cat and turned toward her.

With two strangers seated across from them, Cat lowered her voice and leaned closer, her shoulder brushing against his chest. "Why, yes, it is my first trip outside of New Orleans, although I always imagined I would travel to New York. However, I'm not disappointed with Denver as my first destination." Her gaze rose from her gloved hands to his face, and she smiled.

He waited for the flinch at the sight of his scar, but it never came.

Remarkable.

"Nor am I, Miss Kline." He caught curious glances from the men across from them and drew his head back—away from her inviting smile. "I'm concerned, however, that your brother will become anxious as to your whereabouts." Hunter found Cat a dangerous combination of innocence and aggressive curiosity. A mix he would like to explore more thoroughly. Sam, however, would undoubtedly put an end to their blossoming acquaintance.

Cat came gracefully to her feet and tipped her head. "You are correct, Mr. Hunter. I don't want to worry Sam. It has been my pleasure to see you again, sir."

Hunter rose when she stood, as did the men sitting across from them. Cat smiled, nodded to them all, and turned to continue through the passenger car.

***

Catherine Kline

—

Cat closed the door at the front of her passenger car just as Sam threw down his newspaper and stood. She nodded to the elderly couple again, and advanced to her seat.

"Where have you been?" Sam straightened his jacket and lowered himself back to his seat.

"I took a walk through the train cars." She sat on the bench and picked up the bag of cold sausages and biscuits. "Did you know you can pass between cars? There are four in front of us. I've not yet explored the cars behind us."

"It's not safe to walk between cars on a moving train." Sam accepted the napkin with a biscuit and sausage from his sister.

Cat shrugged. "Perhaps, but it's not overly dangerous either." She bit into her biscuit. "Rest assured, I am quite cautious." As she swallowed the dry bread, she considered how she might escape her brother's watchful eye and visit Hunter again.

Near midmorning, the conductor stepped into their car and cleared his throat. "Attention, please. We will pull into the Shreveport Station shortly. The train will remain at this station for thirty minutes. I encourage passengers to exit the train and to purchase food, drink, and handcrafted items from vendors in the station. This will be your last chance to get anything you might need before we reach the Fort Worth terminal." The conductor walked at a leisurely pace through the passenger car as he spoke. "Since we are scheduled to pull into Fort Worth at 2:05 tomorrow morning, I would highly recommend making any necessary purchases at this stop." When he reached the door at the end of the car, he turned back. "The engineer will sound the whistle once to signal those who remain in the station they should return to their seats for immediate departure."

Cat searched through her carpetbag and found her small reticule and counted her coins. She looked at her brother and dimpled her cheek.

Sam rolled his eyes and withdrew his wallet from his vest pocket.

***

Sam Kline

—

Sam had just grasped Cat's hand as she stepped from the train to the platform, when he caught sight of Hunter exiting from the train several cars from their own. "Did you see Hunter on the train?"

Cat released his hand. "See who?" She walked to the short line around a woman who sold fried chicken in small baskets.

Sam followed. "Hunter. The man we met on the riverboat." His height gave him an advantage, but he lost sight of the dark-haired man.

Why would Hunter be on this train?

Cat purchased a small basket of fried chicken. She moved to a farmer's stand and selected several vegetables and a basket of wild berries. The farmer also sold cloth bags, so she bought one and placed all her food items inside. At the next vendor, she got three glass bottles of spring water, two flavored sodas, and two bottles of beer. She arranged all the items in her bag and handed it to Sam. "Would you carry this, please? It's too heavy."

"Why did you buy so much?" He took the bag from his sister.

"You will ask why I didn't buy more before we reach Fort Worth," Cat admonished him. "Can you take those to our berth? I want to look at those blankets."

"I'm not comfortable leaving you alone." Sam's brow creased as he stared at his sister.

Cat shook her head. "Don't be silly. I'll be right here. Oh, look, jewelry!"

Sam heaved a defeated sigh as he turned and made his way back to their car. He checked with the conductor, who had his watch in hand. They had fifteen minutes before they needed to reboard. Plenty of time for Cat to finish shopping.

Sam hurried to their berth, stowed the food bag under their seat, then went back to the station to find his sister.

***

Hunter

—

Hunter spotted Cat as she haggled for two quilted blankets. He followed her as she crossed to a display of earrings and stopped beside her.

Cat paused to look over her left shoulder, then turned to her right and smiled at Hunter. "I thought I felt someone watching me."

"You were correct, *ma chère*." He gestured to the jewelry display. "Do you see anything you like?"

"Hmm. Perhaps." Cat looked up at him through the corner of her eye and grinned.

Caught off guard, a burst of laughter escaped Hunter. "You continue to surprise me, *ma belle Cat*." Hunter chuckled and shook his head. "What am I to do with you?"

"As to that, I'm sure I couldn't say, Mr. Hunter. I don't have a great deal of experience with men, if the truth be told. However, I do have an insatiable curiosity," Cat responded in her straightforward fashion and an inviting smile.

Before he could say anything, she handed him the two colorful quilts she held in her arms. "Would you hold these, please, Mr. Hunter? I believe I shall purchase a pillow as well."

While Cat bargained with the vendor over two pillows, Sam walked up and looked Hunter over with his steely blue eyes. "You didn't mention you'd be traveling to Fort Worth the other night." Sam hooked his thumbs in his belt.

Hunter regarded Sam warily. "Nor did you mention your travel plans when we last spoke, *mon ami*."

Cat completed her transaction with the pillow vendor. "Ah, Sam. Just in time." She shoved the pillows in Sam's midsection. "Here, take these. I found your friend from the riverboat."

Both men spoke at the same time.

"He's just an acquaintance, Cat."

"We're only acquainted, *Mademoiselle* Kline."

"Hmm. Yes, well, I do appreciate your help, Mr. Hunter. I look forward to seeing you on board." Cat took back the blankets from Hunter and turned to her brother.

"I'm done shopping, Sam. I'm going to take these back to our seats." Cat smiled at both men, her eyes lingering on Hunter, then she turned away and strolled toward the train.

Hunter watched her skirt sway from her narrow waist as she walked away.

"How does she know your name?" Sam asked.

"She introduced herself earlier. I must say, your sister is a woman beyond my experience." Hunter met Sam's gaze.

"Let's keep it that way, shall we? I don't want to have to shoot you." Sam grinned.

Hunter tipped his head toward Cat. "Shooting me won't solve your problem, *mon ami*. Your sister has a definite mind of her own. A beautiful, educated woman with an insatiable curiosity."

Sam turned and lifted an eyebrow at Hunter.

Hunter chuckled. "Her words, not mine. You have your work cut out for you, Sam."

The men watched Cat climb the steps with the quilts in her arms and disappear into the railcar.

"As I am finding out," Sam sighed in resignation.

The station had emptied as passengers returned to the train with their purchases. Sam waited while Hunter made several food purchases, then they walked together toward the train as the engineer sounded the whistle.

"Do you remember the old man we encountered at the boarding house?" Hunter glanced at Sam as they paused to allow others to board the train.

"I do," Sam replied.

"I met with him yesterday."

"Are you working for him, then?" Sam asked.

"Yes, and no. I would speak with you about it, if you would be so obliged. I believe the man to be insane."

"Sounds interesting. If you come by later this evening, Cat should be asleep. We can discuss it then."

"Until then," Hunter replied.

"All aboard!" The conductor shouted.

Hunter held his purchases and took an easy jaunt down the platform to his railcar. He glanced back to see Sam lean out from the train.

He watches me.

Hunter nodded to Sam and climbed into the second car.

***

Catherine Kline

—

Catherine asked Sam to lower the overhead sleeping berth, so she could nap before they changed trains in Fort Worth. It had been a boring afternoon under Sam's watchful eye, and the continuous rocking motion of the train made her weary. She took off her shoes, closed the curtain, and curled around her new pillow and quilt. She fell asleep just before the sun went down.

Hushed voices woke her. She opened her eyes in the darkness and listened to the men who sat below her. Their voices were clear. She lay still so she could eavesdrop.

"You went with the old man into the bayou?" Sam's voice was low.

"I did. He needed more money for my fee, and I wanted to see the body."

Hunter's voice set tingles spiraling from her stomach. She stuffed the edge of the quilt in her mouth to quiet a giggle.

"Body?" Sam questioned.

"The old man believes there are witches who will call a demon. His information source was the woman he held chained in that tiny bayou cabin. According to Minister Tremble, she died after telling him this nonsense." Tainted with disgust, Hunter's voice sounded angry.

"Then why take the bounty?" Sam asked.

"He said if I didn't find the witches, he would hire someone else. He doesn't want these people brought in, *mon ami*. He wants me to kill them."

"Huh," Sam grunted.

Cat heard glass clink.

Sam spoke again. "Do you want a beer? Cat bought two, and she doesn't drink it."

Cat bit down hard on the quilt.

"Thank you." Hunter replied.

"So, he met your increased fee." Amusement tinged Sam's voice.

"Well, there is that." Hunter laughed.

"Do you know who they are?" Sam questioned.

"No, I don't have names or descriptions, other than evil demon summoning witches," Hunter replied. "There is more than one individual, though. I believe there may be two or three. One of them is in the Denver area. The others are somewhere on the East Coast."

"He told you that?" Sam asked.

Hunter was slow to respond. "No. Tremble could offer no information on the witches."

Another long pause in the conversation. Cat turned her head to better hear their voices.

Sam cleared his throat. "You went to the cabin to get blood."

Blood? She must have misunderstood.

"Yes, but the body was gone, well—most of it."

"You tell the most unbelievable stories, Hunt."

"I swear to you, *mon ami*, he had a foot chained to the floor in that cabin. The rest of the body had been gnawed off and dragged away by alligators," Hunter hissed.

"Shh, you'll wake Cat," Sam admonished.

Cat cringed and buried her face in the pillow.

"Sorry."

Both men were quiet for a few moments. She imagined they listened for her to call out as they sipped the beer she had purchased for them.

"I'm telling the truth," Hunter insisted. "I've never seen anything like it, and that's saying quite a bit."

"But you did obtain the blood?" Sam asked again.

"Some. Enough to know there is more than one individual involved. I'll try again once I reach Denver. Perhaps then I can narrow it down."

More silence.

They must be drinking their beer.

"Cat mentioned you are going to Denver also," Hunter said softly.

"We are. Investigative assignment. Nothing intriguing or dangerous. It seemed a perfect opportunity to spend some time with Cat."

"You never even told me you had a sister," Hunter replied.

"Twenty minutes to the Fort Worth station," the conductor called loudly from the front of the car. "This train continues on to points west through to El Paso, Texas. Those of you who are making connections, please be sure to check your area and take all your belongings with you. We will be enjoying a brief stop in Fort Worth."

Cat felt Sam knock on the bottom of her fold-down bed, and she opened the curtains to peek out. Hunter had disappeared.

"Wake up Cat, time to pack up and change trains."

Chapter 18

Amy Harris

—

Amy opened her eyes. Jason lay beside her in the dark. His light, even snore was not enough to disturb her.

What awakened her?

Did Jim or Kelly have need of her? She listened to the silence, but she was the only wakeful being in the house. With a soft sigh, she closed her eyes and reached out with her mind.

Who stalks my dreams?

Sorrow tore at her awareness. Her heart grew heavy, suffused with anguished regret—silent tears spent for the lost years and the unfairness of never knowing her mother or father.

Moved by sympathy, Amy reached out. The moment she touched the grief-stricken soul, she recognized the Entity.

Made aware of her presence, the Entity firmed their connection.

In Amy's mind, the Entity appeared as a mirror image of herself. "Who are you?" Amy whispered. Her heart pounded hard in her chest.

The Entity mocked her movements. It raised its hand and touched the surface of the mirror as Amy did.

"I am Alyse," her likeness responded.

Amy lowered her hand and so did the image in the mirror. "Are you... me?" She had never encountered anything like this before. Had her mind splintered when Jones locked her in the wardrobe?

The mirror smiled like her, and at her, and shook its head. "I am not you, and you are not me. We are separate."

"I heard you weeping," Amy persisted. "Why are you so sad?"

"Is that what drew you? My tears?"

A surge of sorrow filled Amy's chest. "Alyse?" Amy questioned.

"Yes?"

"Are you—are you in my head?"

The question appeared to catch Alyse by surprise. The tears stopped, and she smiled at Amy. "Actually, I think you are in mine, dear sister."

"Sister?" Amy questioned. "I have no sisters."

"I understand." Loss bound them together as the image nodded. "Nor did I, until you called to me. I felt your fear. You feel my sorrow. We've lived a lie, Amy. They lied to protect us."

Amy studied Alyse. "They?"

"Our mother. Our grandmother." Alyse replied.

"Grandmother Prescott?" Amy questioned.

"No. Grandmother James—*Mémé*." Alyse gestured, and the image of a slender, elderly woman coalesced beside her in the mirror.

"My mother's mother?" Amy searched her memory. "Is that her?"

"Yes. She raised me." The mirror rippled with pain and loss.

"Are you saying—you're real?" Stunned, Amy shook her head. "Where are you, if not in my head?"

The figure in the glass looked around, and then turned back at Amy. "I'm on a train. The sun has just risen, and my uncles are asleep. I believe we're still in New York, but I'm not certain."

"You're coming here?"

Am I dreaming?

"You're not dreaming." Alyse touched the mirror again. "And yes, we're coming to find you, Amy. I promised I would, remember? We'll arrive in Denver on Sunday."

"I won't be in Denver on Sunday. We'll be at the ranch by then."

The mirror rippled again, and panic blurred the image. "Why?" Alyse pressed both hands against the polished surface. "I must find you!"

"You'll find me." Amy projected comfort. "Let me show you where I'll be." She passed all she knew about the route from Denver to The Highlands to Alyse with a thought.

"I see." Alyse nodded. "Wait for me there, please."

Jason murmured in Amy's ear and snuggled closer. He ran his hand beneath Amy's nightgown, over her hip and along her waist to her breast. He cupped the soft globe in his hand as his lips caressed the back of her neck.

Amy caught her breath and the reflection shimmered with arousal.

"What is that?" Alyse's eyelids fluttered closed, and she inhaled sharply.

"My husband is awake. I must go." Amy explained.

Jason rolled her toward him and ran his hand down her stomach, coming to rest between her legs.

"No, wait!" Alyse urged.

The connection with Alyse broke as Amy's attention focused on her husband's touch.

He kissed her neck and ran his fingertips from one eager nipple to the other, then slowly back down her stomach to the dark hair between her legs. He slipped his fingers inside her and stroked her sensitive silkiness. "I love you, Amy." He kissed down her jaw until he found her lips.

Amy moaned with pleasure and turned toward him, tangling her nightdress. Impatient, she rose to her knees, pulled the disruptive garment over her head and tossed it to the floor. She looked down at Jason. The soft morning light reflected against the blond stubble along his jaw and wild, curly hair.

He smiled and ran his hands up her stomach to lift her breasts. "You were talking in your sleep."

Amy bent to place her mouth on his chest. She licked and kissed her way to his neck. "I don't talk in my sleep." Her hand moved down his body and gripped the evidence of his desire as her lips moved up to find his.

Their kiss deepened, and Jason groaned at Amy's firm touch. Her mouth led his on a chase for several moments, then she lifted her head and studied his eyes. "What did I say?"

Jason chuckled. "You want to talk now?"

"Well, no—"

He rolled her to her back and centered himself above her. "That's good."

Amy forgot what she had asked—forgot everything, except Jason.

***

Jason read the Rocky Mountain News at the kitchen table while he sipped his tea.

Jimmy Leigh ambled down the stairs and glanced around the kitchen. "It smells good in here."

Amy smiled over her shoulder and picked up an oven-cloth. "It's just biscuits and jam." She opened the oven, pulled out a tray of biscuits and placed it on the counter to cool.

"We ought to head back to the ranch today." Jim took a seat at the table across from Jason.

Jason lowered the paper and raised an eyebrow as his gaze traveled over the tall foreman. "You feel up to it?"

"I've been four days without fever. My leg's about as good as it's going to get. It's time to head home." He looked up at Amy as she set a cup of coffee at his elbow. "Thank you."

All the repairs, except for the porch, had been completed. Albert Fielding had agreed to supervise the porch construction, scheduled to proceed in several days. Nothing, except Jim's recovery, kept them in Denver.

Amy put a basket of biscuits in front of the men and added a jar of honey and a jar of grape jam.

"There are ten Shilo-Highlands horses stabled at the livery." Jim picked up a biscuit. "We only need four to get back, two for the buckboard, and one each, for Kelly and me. Do you want to take the other six with us, or leave them here?"

"Leave them, I suppose," Jason replied. "Merril borrowed three of theirs. Tom or Kelly can return those next week and bring home the rest of our stock."

Kelly came downstairs, his hair a wild mess. He ran his hands through a few strands, but it refused to stay down. He sat at the table and Amy set a coffee in front of him. He nodded his thanks and reached for a biscuit.

As the men discussed their return trip, Amy's thoughts turned to Alyse and their strange communication. Amy had tried to reach out to her again, several times in fact, but never found Alyse.

I know it wasn't a dream.

She finished her biscuit and brushed her hands on her apron. Unable to sit still, she picked up her gardening gloves and hat and stepped out the back door.

In her garden, she pulled a few weeds, collected dill and mint leaves, and pinched a few marigold heads. Just as she dropped the herbs and flowers into her apron pocket, she noticed two black cats. They sat motionless at the back of the yard and watched her with intense interest.

Curious.

Amy pinched a few more flower heads and looked over the rest of the garden. Things were either past their prime or yet to ripen. She rose and turned toward the house, and then paused to look back at the cats.

They still watched her with wide, yellow eyes. One of the cats stepped forward and minced its way through the garden to wind itself around Amy's ankles. After a couple of turns, it stepped back, sat and curled its tail around its paws, and looked up at her.

"You're a most peculiar pair." She removed a glove and stroked the animal's head. The cat arched itself against her hand, and Amy smoothed the soft fur along its back. As she touched the cat, she received a strong visual impression. She saw herself with these cats, curled in front of a fireplace, reading an old book.

They were with Alyse.

She blinked away the vision and looked down at the cat. "Do you belong to Alyse?"

The first cat meowed, and the other cat ran forward to join its twin. They both looked at her.

She knelt beside the cats and ran her hands down each feline. "We are leaving today to return to the ranch." Amy glanced around.

Goddess, let no one see me speak to these animals.

Both cats purred as she scratched their ears.

"Alyse said she would be here on Sunday. I can't take you with me. Jason wouldn't know what to think about cats in the wagon." She laughed as both cats flopped over for belly scratches and batted at each other's heads.

"You are silly things." She rubbed their silky bellies one last time, then returned to the house.

Jason looked up as she shut the door. "Can you be ready to leave in two hours?"

"Yes, I can." She took the marigold heads from her apron and set them on the counter. When she looked out the window, the cats were gone.

Chapter 19

Nichole Harris-Shilo

—

Nichole woke late the next morning. The pain in her back and legs had lessened, but ached enough to remind her of yesterday's long ride. The indent in the pillow next to hers and the rumpled blankets told her Merril had slept beside her.

How odd.

Her sleep had been so deep she hadn't noticed he shared her bed. She pushed herself erect and pressed her hands into her sore back. A peek beneath the bandages on her legs showed healthy scabbed skin. Last night, the wounds had been bloody and inflamed.

Amy's ointment. Merril is right, she's a healer.

The door hinge creaked, and Jeanne peeked inside. "You're up?"

"Just now."

Jeanne stepped into the room and closed the door. "Can I help you dress?"

"I don't know what I'll wear. I left most of my clothes in Denver."

"You've a wardrobe full of beautiful dresses." Jeanne held out her hand to the cabinet.

Nichole raised an eyebrow. "Mm. No. There should be a black skirt and blouse in that saddlebag."

Jeanne pulled the wrinkled garments from the leather satchel Merril had laid across the vanity. "This mess?"

Nichole rubbed a hand across her face. "Well, sh—oot."

"I'll lend you one of mine until this can be ironed." Jeanne disappeared out the door. "But I don't know why you won't wear your pretty dresses."

Nichole used the bedpan while Jeanne fetched new clothes and made use of the water in the bowl to wash away yesterday's dust.

I need a shower or a long soak in a hot tub.

By the time Jeanne returned, Nichole had changed into clean undergarments. Together, they dressed Nichole in Jeanne's gray skirt and white blouse.

"Have a seat. I'll brush your hair." Jeanne pulled out the vanity chair and picked up the hairbrush.

"Thanks." Nichole didn't hesitate to accept Jeanne's help. Although she could brush her own hair, it felt right to let her friend help her. "Is Merril outside?"

Jeanne scooped up the curls and began to brush from the ends. "No. He left this morning with Tom and Bill. He took the wagon and... his Indian friend to The Shilo."

Nichole watched Jeanne work in the mirror. "Do you know why?"

Jeanne nodded. "Merril told Tom they were going to bury the bodies—his brother, that woman, and the Indian."

The brush snagged Nichole's hair, and she winced.

"Sorry."

"It's okay."

"Merril told Bill to saddle up and head to The Crossing. He's to talk with Reverend Michael about a funeral service. Bill's to meet them at The Shilo on his way back from town."

"The Shilo is deserted."

"That's what we heard." Jeanne glanced at Nichole. "Bill is the only Shilo wrangler who didn't leave after..." Jeanne hesitated then opened the vanity drawer and drew out a few hairpins. With a twist of her wrist, Nichole's wayward curls were corralled into a loose bun. Jeanne set the last pin and met Nichole's gaze in the mirror. "Is that secure?"

Nichole nodded. "It's good."

Down the hall, the sound of Hope-Anne's plaintive cry was followed by June McKay's harsh shout. "For land's sake, doesn't that baby ever be quiet? What kind of mother are you?"

Jeanne rushed out the door and into the hall before Nichole could stand.

Nichole paused just inside her door.

In the hallway, Jeanne took Hope-Anne from Lawna's arms, and turned back toward the stairs. A storm brewed in Jeanne's eyes. She cast a brief angry glance at Nichole, and then hurried down the stairs.

Lawna followed with an armful of laundry, her eyes downcast.

June raised her voice. "You shouldn't help her, Jeanne." June stood on the narrow stairs at the end of the hall that led to her attic room. "You know she shouldn't be here."

Nichole stepped from her room.

June's eyebrows rose, and she sniffed. "I didn't see you there, Miss Harris."

"I could—sense that, June. Please remember to address me as Mrs. Shilo from now on."

Lips pressed into a bitter line, June bobbed her head then mounted the attic steps.

Nichole spent the day outside with Hope-Anne on her lap while Katy and Lawna helped Henny turn new soil to expand the garden behind the family bunk.

***

Late in the afternoon, the men returned from The Shilo. Tom slowed the wagon enough to allow Merril to step off the buckboard, and then shook the reins to continue to the barn.

The kitchen door closed behind Nichole. "I'll take the babe," Jeanne offered.

Hope-Anne reached for Jeanne as soon as she approached.

"You're her favorite, I think." Nichole released the babe, picked up one of the clean linen towels from table, and walked toward Merril.

He set his hat on the well and used the hand pump to splash water on his face. Droplets ran beneath his open shirt and down his broad chest. He pushed wet fingers through his thick hair, and grinned at Nichole.

Nichole tossed him the towel. "You didn't tell me you were leaving this morning."

Green eyes looked at her over the towel. "I tried. I couldn't wake you."

"Jeanne told me you went to dig the graves."

Merril flipped the towel over his shoulder. "We buried the bodies as well. Reverend Michael will meet us at noon tomorrow to say a few words."

"I'm surprised you buried Toma. I thought Indians only used burial platforms."

"Where did you hear that?" Merril snagged his hat and walked toward the kitchen.

"I don't know. Movies I guess, or old T.V. shows."

Merril cocked his eyebrow at her. "What are those?"

"Unreliable, apparently."

Merril stopped before they reached Jeanne and Hope-Anne. "You need to tell me about your other—memories—if you're going to talk about them. I don't understand what you're saying to me. It's unsettling."

"You're right. I'm sorry."

"And yes, Toma's spirit had enough time to depart before he returned to the earth. He should have been honored by his family, but I don't know if he had any, or where to find them."

"I understand."

He opened the back door for Nichole. "I opened the house up—all the windows and doors." He followed Nichole through the kitchen into the dining room. "Tom helped me clear out the library. We stacked the furniture behind the bunkhouse. It needs to be burned." He stopped and raised his hand to his forehead. "I left the log book and ledgers in the wagon." He spun on his heel.

Nichole grasped his arm. "Wait. Does Tom know they're there?"

"He does."

"Then sit. Let me get you something cool to drink. Tom will bring them to the house."

Merril nodded and shoved his hat to the back of his head as he fell into the chair. "I couldn't read them."

Nichole turned back. "Read what?"

"The ledgers. Pa and Kevin used some sort of shorthand. The numbers I can tally, but the notations don't mean anything to me."

Nichole left him at the table and asked Cookie to bring refreshments. When she returned to her husband, she sat beside him and took his hand. "Don't worry about the notations. We can go over them with Jason when he comes home."

Cookie brought in a pitcher of cool water and a small basket of bread and honey. She nodded to Nichole, then returned to the kitchen.

"I do need a favor from you, though." Nichole spread honey on a piece of bread and handed it to Merril.

"What's that?"

"I need a wall built to divide the family bunkhouse. We need to move the Caine family into their own place. Henny and Katy are on one side, and the Caines will move to the other."

Merril nodded and sipped his water. "I'll ask Tom and Timothy to do it. I want to take another look at those ledgers before your cousin gets back."

***

The next day, Reverend Michael performed the burial service at The Shilo Cemetery. The service was short and centered around asking the Lord's forgiveness for the sinful and welcoming the lost into the shelter of His arms.

There were only a few in attendance besides the Reverend and Merril. Nichole represented the Harris family. Henny, Katy, and Bill from The Shilo, paid their respects.

Nichole kept her head down during the short service. The only one who deserved Heaven was Toma, in her opinion. She didn't know what the Cheyenne believed, but she was pretty sure Renata and Kevin would burn in hell, regardless of Reverend Michael's entreaties to the Lord.

After the ceremony, the mourners walked back to The Shilo yard, and Reverend Michael took his leave to return to Kiowa Crossing.

Henny and Katy climbed in the back of the buckboard and whispered prayers while they waited to return to The Highlands.

Nichole tucked herself beneath Merril's arm as he gazed at the ranch house. "Are you going to leave it open?"

Merril kissed the curls on her head. "No. Bill and I will close it up."

Nichole took her seat on the wagon and watched as Merril and Bill entered the house. She had no desire to go inside. With everything at The Highlands Ranch—the horses, chickens, both pigs, even Henny's tomato plants now grew in a new spot—the ranch felt abandoned. The only things that remained were the ghosts of people she wanted to forget.

Bill walked out the front door first and crossed to the corral. He checked the cinch strap on his mount, rose into the saddle and shook the reins. "See you at home." He touched his hat to Nichole and rode out of the yard.

Merril came out just as Bill rode past. He waved to the wrangler, then crossed to the buckboard. He climbed onto the seat, took the reins, and followed Bill onto the road home. "No one wants to come back here." His voice was low so only Nichole could hear.

"I can't blame them. The place gives me chills."

"Luckily, we have some time before the drive. The Shilo herd is scattered, but close. I bet Jim and Lloyd have The Highlands herd buttoned up and ready to move."

"We don't have enough bunks at The Highlands for all the wranglers, do we?" Nichole tipped her head to look up at Merril.

"Bunks won't be a problem. We'll be driving to one of the railheads."

"When will you leave?"

Merril's long silence caught Nichole's attention. "What's wrong?"

"I'm not sure when we should leave. I've never made that decision." He was silent as he reined the team around a long rut in the road. "I know there are three stockyards within driving distance, but I was never asked or included in those decisions. I'm a wrangler, Nic—not a rancher."

Nichole watched the tick along his jaw and recognized the worry in his eyes.

He never wanted this, and now he was responsible for two ranches and a dozen lives.

She curled her arm around his and leaned her head on his shoulder. "We'll be fine. Jimmy Leigh will know what's best to do, or have suggestions. We'll make it work."

She looked up at his face when he chuckled.

"I'm supposed to be the one who comforts you, Mrs. Shilo."

"You *do* comfort me, Mr. Shilo."

Chapter 20

Morago

—

Morago plundered Chantal's thoughts and memories despite her feeble attempt to shield her mind. Her sons and granddaughter had taken a railed conveyance to the human settlement of Boston to find the other grandchild. The grandchildren were the prize then—the witches that held such raw, elemental power.

And they are afraid of me.

Glee changed to disappointment, and he clenched the miller boy's teeth. Such a shame the old woman had defaced her arms with protective runes. Runes that prevented him from possessing her body. The anguish of her children, as they watched their mother—their grandmother—perform abominations upon them, and upon herself, would have been exquisite. Still, he wasn't quite done with the old woman yet.

The demon's chuckle scored across Chantal's soul, and she writhed in pain.

Mounted on the old woman's horse, still possessed by his servant, Morago followed the path outlined in her memory to the place she had last seen the child.

They stopped on the road before entering the small settlement. Eyes closed, Morago projected his awareness through the train station, appalled at the number of humans and the cacophony of unfamiliar thoughts. The demon horde chattered inside Morago's head in frustration.

Things have changed much since I last walked the earth.

As he skimmed the minds of the humans inside the crowded station, he faced a choice. He could either possess an individual as they boarded the train, or he could ride silently inside one of them, as he had the merchant.

Morago's lips drew back with a hiss of distaste, and he clenched a fist. He would not hide inside another mewling mortal again. However, to mimic a human to hide among them disgusted him even more. These domesticated primates were beneath contempt. To ape them would demean Morago's own extraordinary existence.

He turned once more to Chantal. Amid her screams of resistance and failure, Morago discovered another path to follow her children. Lips twisted with indecision. Should he follow this child to the destination in Chantal's memory, or turn inland and move toward the other beacon that burned within his mind?

Chantal's thoughts held no clue as to the second beacon's significance, and these witches were running. The compulsion to chase prey proved insurmountable. With a thought, both Morago and the horse turned as one and raced back toward the farm.

The demon rode the horse southeast around the lake until the animal failed, then he discarded both the horse and the miller boy's body and jumped to a doe—and then a hawk.

Morago continued toward the destination for two days, abandoning animal bodies when they faltered. The preferred animals—a hawk, deer or wolf—were not always nearby when the spent beast fell. At those times, he settled for a slower beast until a swifter creature could be taken.

On the outskirts of Boston, the demon possessed an animal that traveled within the city without reprisal. Inhabiting a large domesticated canine, Morago raced toward the residential area along the Charles River.

Although darkness had settled on the city, there were a number of people who strolled in the warm night air.

Morago grew cautious as he approached the house. Nose to the ground, the dog crossed the narrow lawn and crawled on his belly beneath the decorative bushes around the foundation of the home.

His wet nose touched the brick, and it jerked back with a yelp. A warding spell, like the charm at Chantal's farm, protected the residence. Head lowered to its paws, Morago extended his senses into the dwelling.

Two humans took nourishment and drank a dark, fermented liquid.

Delighted to discover he could skim their minds beyond the feeble ward, he found nothing of interest in the male. The female, however, had power—limited and rarely used. Her thoughts wandered far from the discussion with the male. Sadness and longing beat against her mind, as she replayed the recent visit with her daughter.

The demon growled and gnashed its teeth. The child had been here but was now gone. The chattered frenzy of underlings inside his head distracted and enraged Morago even more. With a thought, the horde within were rendered mute and paralyzed in agony.

He yearned to shred this house, and those within it—to destroy this city and all the insipid beings who strolled the night. But he did not possess enough power, and that realization infuriated the demon.

I loathe.

I hate.

I hunger.

Pain seized his chest, and when it ceased, Morago no longer inhabited a living host. His rage had burst the dog's heart. He had been less than judicious with the new power and allowed fury to take hold.

A lesson learned, and now, an inconvenience.

Bereft of a host, Morago writhed in primordial serpent form inside the dead dog. He crawled through the animal and departed from the mouth onto the dirt under the bush. What had been a warm evening felt chilled against his scales. Morago coiled beside the dead beast, vulnerable and filled with rancor. Left with no choice, he slithered down the lawn to the street and curled beneath a flowering shrub near the sidewalk to wait.

Several people strolled this summer evening, but Morago needed a specific type of individual. A solitary human, healthy enough to walk some distance without attracting unwanted attention. Impatience became unbearable. Only couples meandered close enough, and none to his liking. He writhed with frustration.

At last, a single gentleman approached, and Morago shed his skin and rose as an oily vapor to blend with the evening mist from the river.

The man inhaled the rancid vapor as he strolled past the Prescott home. Four hours later, the man regained his senses near the edge of town, dehydrated and vomiting. A large crow cawed from a split rail fence then jumped into the air.

Morago headed west.

Chapter 21

Catherine Kline

—

The train blew a long whistle as the black engine led the cars into Dallas. Sam and Cat readied their belongings as the wheels came to a stop. The Texas and Pacific Railway station stood a quarter-mile from the Missouri, Kansas, and Texas station. An omnibus awaited the passengers for the predawn transfer.

Cat followed several travelers from the station to the bus. Her bag in one hand, her pillow and blanket over her other arm.

Why build train stations so far apart?

Irritated and sleepy, it seemed the height of poor planning to her. She enjoyed traveling by train, but line transfers were inconvenient.

Especially in the middle of the night and across town.

Sam followed with his own bag and bedding. Inside the coach, Sam found Cat a seat beside an elderly woman.

Cat smiled hello to the gray-haired traveler while she kept a sharp eye on the station door.

Where is Hunter?

She watched through the long bus windows as two porters pushed a luggage cart from the T&P station to the omnibus.

The thump and scrape of trunks loaded on the upper deck echoed through the carriage. Eight travelers, besides her and Sam, waited on the bus.

Sam checked the time on his pocket watch then returned it to his vest. Still standing, he turned to face the bus door.

Cat followed Sam's gaze toward the T&P station.

He wonders about Hunter as well.

The coachman began to close the door just as Hunter rushed from the station with his travel bag and a vendor sack.

Sam gripped the door. "One more." He nodded toward Hunter.

"My apologies, *monsieur.*" Hunter removed his flat-top, wide-brimmed hat and climbed inside.

The woman beside Cat sniffed with distaste and turned away from the new arrival.

Cat raised an eyebrow at the woman's behavior. When she glanced at Hunter, his gaze met hers. She grinned, despite herself, and looked down at her hands.

"I thought you might have taken another line," Sam said to Hunter.

"No, *mon ami*, the MKT to Junction City is the fastest route north."

His low voice, flavored by his peculiar mix of Cajun and French accents, sent chills across Cat's neck. Her gaze returned to her brother and Hunter as the bus began to move. The men stood in the aisle, braced for the short ride to the MKT station.

"What car are you on?" Sam inquired. He pulled their tickets from his vest.

Hunter glanced at Cat, then his eyes cut back to Sam and he smiled. "The third car."

Sam read the tickets. "Cat and I are in the second." He returned the tickets to his pocket.

As the bus slowed to a stop, Cat glanced up and caught Hunter watching her.

He grinned and settled his hat back on his head. When the door opened, he winked one dark blue eye at her, stepped from the bus, and disappeared.

She rose and hurried past Sam to the exit, but Hunter had vanished down the platform into the night.

Cat followed Sam as he escorted the elderly woman to the porter at the first passenger car.

"Thank you, young man."

"My pleasure, ma'am." Sam tipped his hat and they continued toward their car.

"The air feels different." Cat observed when they reached their car.

"It's drier than at home. Wait until you feel the arid Denver air; then, you will know the meaning of dry." Sam chuckled. "Are you tired?"

"Exhausted. I could sleep for a week."

A porter helped Cat up the steps to the car.

"The second area, there—on the left," Sam directed as he followed her inside.

Cat slid her bag beneath the seat and tossed the pillow against the window.

Sam folded down the overhead sleeping berth and attached the ladder. "Do you want to lie down?"

"I do." She removed her boots and climbed into the sleeper.

"I'll wake you for breakfast." Sam handed her a blanket and pillow, and drew the curtain.

Cat fell asleep before the train pulled from the station. She dreamed of Hunter's unusual blue eyes, laughing at something she said. She leaned forward and ran her finger along his scar, tracing the imperfection down his skin to his jaw. Her gaze followed her finger to his lips—full, and well defined. They parted as she leaned closer.

Three sharp taps on the underside of her bed evaporated her dream. She gave an exasperated grunt and slid the privacy curtain aside to glare at her brother.

"Time to get up. Hunter stopped by. I told him to come back in twenty minutes. He has blueberry muffins for breakfast. I thought you might want to..." Sam waved his fingers at his head, "...freshen up before we eat."

Cat rubbed her eyes and felt her hair. Her fine, straight, auburn locks defied curling irons and pins, yet tangled each night even when braided. Without comment, she crawled from the compartment and found her shoes and bag under the seat. She pulled the hairbrush, several hairpins and a washcloth from her bag.

"Where's the privy?" Cat's sleepy gaze rose to her brother.

"The conductor said there's a ladies' room in the car behind us."

"I must see this." Cat came to her feet. "I'll be right back." She flashed a rushed smile and hurried down the aisle toward the next car.

She found the ladies' room at the end of the next car, past the men's room and a small passenger section. Once inside, she stepped to the vanity and stared with discouragement into the mirror.

What a bedraggled mess.

The single braid she had twisted into a bun yesterday had frayed and slipped overnight.

Well, what did you expect?

Worse, she discovered a red mark on her cheek where she had slept against her hand. Pulling the few pins that remained from her hair, she ran her fingers through the tangled braid.

Two women entered the room, nodded to her in the mirror, then seated themselves at the vanity behind Cat.

Cat brushed the tangles, twisted wavy strands into a chignon at the base of her head, and secured it with several hairpins.

Better.

A ceramic bowl with a pump lever provided water for her washcloth. She held the damp cloth to her face, as the conversation behind her caught her attention.

"He smiled at me, I'm sure of it."

"Which one, the tall blond or the devil with the scar?"

"Heavens, no! Not the marked one. I would have died of fright."

Cat lowered the cloth and studied the women's reflection in the mirror.

The dark-haired woman nodded. "His face is terrifying. I swear, I shall have nightmares."

Cat shook her head and wrung her cloth. She forced a smile when she nodded to the women and left the room. No stranger to female gossip, she'd heard enough whispers about her handsome brother while at school.

Do some women ever grow up?

The scornful remarks about Hunter brought her blood to a boil. Those women were blind—and stupid.

She entered her car and saw the objects of the ladies' room conversation sitting across from each other, heads close in conversation.

"Good morning," Cat greeted Hunter as she slid her brush and damp cloth inside her bag.

The men sat back, and Sam moved closer to the window, affording Cat a place to sit.

"*Bonjour*, Miss Kline. Would you care for a muffin?" Hunter held open the vendor bag from last night.

"Thank you." Cat took a pastry, pinched a portion from the top and popped it into her mouth.

"Do you know where you're going to stay in Denver?" Sam asked.

Hunter shook his head and set the bag aside. "No, not yet. I've never been there, and I'm not sure where I'll find—" his eyes shifted to Cat, then back to Sam "—my associates."

Sam nodded. "We'll take rooms at an inn I know, spend the night, and wash the travel dust from our hides. I have an address to check in town, but I suspect we'll need to travel to the informant's cattle ranch, east of town."

The men were so cautious with what they said in front of her. Cat nibbled on the muffin and nodded as though she hadn't overheard their conversation the other night. It occurred to her to ask Sam if he would allow her to remain at the inn, instead of traveling with him to the cattle ranch.

A suggestion best made to Sam in private.

"If it is agreeable with you, *mon ami*, I shall take a room at the same place. Where I begin my search will not matter."

Cat faced the back of the railcar and saw the two women enter. She smiled and nodded as they approached. Her grin widened as the dark-haired woman raised her head and passed by, stone-faced. Cat's chuckle caught both of her companions' attention.

"Do you know them?" Hunter asked.

Cat turned her head and saw they had moved on to the first car. "I know their type." She turned back to Hunter and her brother. "They were in the ladies' room. They think you're handsome, Sam." She popped another bite of muffin into her mouth and grinned at her brother.

Hunter's laughter warmed her. "All the ladies find your brother *très beau.*"

Sam's face went cold as he stared at Hunter. "Enough."

Surprised at her brother's tone, Cat stared at Sam.

What's wrong with him?

Since when did Sam care what women thought of his looks? She and Sam had joked about her foolish friends at school before. When had he become so testy?

Hunter ignored her brother's anger and pulled a newspaper from the vendor bag. "For you, Sam. I read it last night." He rose and nodded to Cat. "Perhaps I will see you both later."

Cat watched Hunter move through the car and exit, without turning to look back at her. She switched to the seat across from Sam. "What's wrong with you?"

"What do you mean?" He asked as he opened the Dallas Daily Herald. He flipped through the pages, then returned to the front page and began to read.

"You snapped at him. We were only teasing you." Cat propped her elbow on the windowsill and gazed out, her chin in her hand.

"And I'd had enough. Now, let me read."

There was more here Cat didn't understand, but questioning Sam would get her nowhere. They were all tired of traveling—maybe that was Sam's problem.

Outside, the landscape had changed again. Shorter trees with dark twisted branches covered the low hillsides. "What kind of trees are those?"

Sam looked up from his paper. "Mesquite."

The train picked up speed as they moved north. Their last train had slowed to pick up mail and parcels every few miles. This train appeared determined to reach its destination as quickly as possible.

"Why is the train moving so fast?" Cat asked.

"We're crossing Indian Territory." Sam cast a quick glance at Cat and returned to the newspaper. "Less chance of an incident if we stay at full speed."

Cat looked out the window again with renewed curiosity.

I've never seen an Indian.

But as the morning passed, she grew restless and bored. "I need to visit the ladies' room, Sam."

He nodded and turned to the last page, then set the newspaper aside and pulled his hat over his eyes. "That's fine. I'm going to take a nap. Don't get lost."

Cat chuckled. "Don't worry." When she stepped outside, the rush of wind caught her breath and tugged at her skirt. The air tasted different. She inhaled a deep breath, then crossed to the next platform and went inside.

She pulled the door closed and stepped past the men's room. The few seats between the salons were almost empty of passengers. To her left, a man slept across the seat, and in the second berth to her right, she spotted Hunter.

Hunter appeared to sleep as well. He reclined, his back to the window, and his hat pulled down to shadow his face. His long legs, stretched to the aisle, were crossed at the ankles.

Cat stopped beside Hunter's bench. She let her gaze travel up from his black boots and muscular legs to his dark vest and jacket. His white shirt stood in stark contrast to his tanned skin and suit. Both of her men needed a shave, she noted, then blinked in surprise to find his alert eyes gazed at her from beneath the brim of his hat.

"*Bonjour, Mademoiselle* Kline." He smiled and pushed his hat from his face as he pulled in his legs.

"Oh, Mr. Hunter. I thought you were asleep." Cat felt her face heat.

"So I gathered." Hunter chuckled and gestured to the seat across from him. "Would you care to join me?"

"Thank you." She indicated the ladies' room as she arranged her skirts. "I came through earlier but didn't see you."

"I may have been in the men's room." Hunter shrugged and smiled, his attention focused on her face.

Heat flared on her cheeks and Cat cleared her throat. "Are there more passenger cars besides ours?"

"Yes, there are," Hunter confirmed. "There are five altogether, one in front of yours and two more behind this one."

"Have you been the other way?" Cat pointed past the ladies' room.

"No, I haven't. Would you like to explore?" Hunter looked past her shoulder, then returned his attention to her.

"Yes, I would." Cat stood and proceeded past the room to the exit. She glanced back and found Hunter right behind her. She turned the latch and Hunter's arm pushed the door open above her head.

When the door closed after them, Cat paused as the air swirled around them. The low hills and misshapen trees expanded to the horizon on both sides. She didn't continue to the next car. Instead she stared into the distance, summoning her courage.

"Did you wish to cross to the next car?" Hunter asked and stepped toward the gangway.

Cat turned to face him. "I have a confession and a request." She ran her hand down her skirt and looked away. "I've considered how best to proceed with both."

"You intrigue me, *mademoiselle*. What would *you* confess to *me*?" Hunter's eyes crinkled at the corners as he smiled and leaned against the door.

Cat took a deep breath and watched her knuckles turn white from her grip on the railing.

Just say it.

"As to the confession, I admit I've never kissed a boy before—or a man, for that matter." The wind felt cool on her face.

I must be as red as a beet.

"I'm not altogether sure how to go about it." She chanced a quick glance at his face and looked away. "I imagine it to be quite different than kissing the girls at school."

"You've kissed girls?" Hunter stood away from the door.

Cat nodded. "Most of the girls tried it. Some enjoyed it more than others, of course. The idea began as a way to practice for when we would someday kiss a boy." Cat ran a hand across her forehead. "This has gotten off topic, I'm afraid."

"Did you—like to kiss girls?" Hunter stepped closer, clearly intrigued by her confession.

"No! I mean, not really." Cat glanced up at him. "That is, however, where my request comes in." She blew out her breath and gripped her skirt. "Mr. Hunter, would you kiss me?" Cat raised her gaze and looked into his eyes. "I am afraid kissing—well, anyone—would not be to my liking." She took a quick breath, unable to stop talking. "The girls at school seemed to enjoy it very much, but I never did. So you see, my curiosity has blossomed to such an extent—" She licked her bottom lip. "—I thought kissing you might be much more enjoyable." Her chatter ran to an end as he stepped so close she felt the heat of his body.

"You've thought about kissing me?" Hunter asked. He slipped an arm behind her back and drew Cat tight to his side.

"In all honesty, I dream about it," she whispered, unable to look away from his eyes.

"And... do you think you might like it?" The breath from his whisper was warm against her skin as he lowered his face.

"I already do," she breathed as his lips touched hers.

Hunter's mouth brushed hers, the barest touch of skin against skin. His tenderness encouraged her to relax. When she did, he tugged her lower lip with his teeth, then brushed the sensitive skin with his tongue. Slowly, he deepened the kiss.

Cat leaned into him with enthusiasm and wound her arms around his neck to pull him even closer.

When her tongue touched his, he moaned and released her lips to trail warm, moist kisses across her earlobe and down her neck.

She leaned her head back to allow him better access. The wind caught her chignon and pulled the pins from the bun to whip the ends of her long hair around them.

Hunter held her along her back to her neck with one arm. His other hand slid up her side and cupped her breast gently. *"Mon beau chaton."* He exhaled and drew her close. He wrapped his arms around her shoulders and tucked her head beneath his chin. They stood silent for several moments as he smoothed her hair.

Into the silence, Hunter muttered, "Your brother is going to kill me."

Cat pulled her head back and considered the black center of his dark blue eyes. "Then don't tell him. It's my life, Mr. Hunter, not my brother's."

He chuckled and tightened his hold on her once more. "It's not that simple, *jolie demoiselle*. I wish it were." He took a deep breath. "You should call me Alexander. I think we're more than just friends now."

Beneath his chin, Cat smiled.

Chapter 22

Amy Harris

—

Amy floated in the soft space between dreams and reality. She knew she rested in the back of the buckboard beside Jason, snuggled underneath blankets in the predawn chill.

She opened her eyes, but instead of seeing stars, her view looked down upon the campsite where she slept. Kelly and Jim were awake. Kelly stirred the small fire and set the tin to boil water for coffee and tea.

A vision of some sort?

Her view widened, and she saw herself and Jason tucked together in the wagon. Then her line of sight lifted toward the rising sun and shot east.

The grassy plains blurred as it passed beneath her. The sun rose swiftly to its zenith then lowered.

Nighttime. She continued east as the moon rose and flashed across the sky.

Sunrise. The terrain below changed. She flew above a city, and then trees and a wide slow-moving river. Another day ended, and the ground below grew dark. She looked up and watched the stars and the moon race west.

Morning again, and train smoke captured her attention. It moved toward her, heading west. Her movement slowed, and she descended from the sky to pass beside the train. Boxcars flashed by, then coach cars. She slowed and reversed direction to move beside the train. Through glass windows, she saw the uniformed porter walk along the aisle. She went through metal and into the car.

Few travelers were awake at dawn, most slept curled in their seats. Through the cars she floated, an invisible spectator. Her vision turned and focused on a sleeping girl—her head rested near the window against her travel bag. Amy looked down on herself—no, on Alyse. Her twin slept in the seat alongside their uncles.

Alyse opened her eyes and her sleepy gaze lifted to Amy's vantage point. Amy watched Alyse mouth her name—*Amy.*

Then the vision moved out of the window. She sped east once more. The sun passed overhead and into night, then rose and traced its path across the sky.

Toward evening, she slowed, and her sight lowered from the horizon to the ground. Beneath her, a large gray wolf ran west, pushed beyond its limits. The exhausted animal blew a bloody froth from its nose with each labored breath. It chased no game, and no danger pursued it. The beast acted out of character, as though possessed by an irresistible force. The wolf stumbled and fell. A gush of blood spewed from its mouth, and it gasped its last few breaths.

From a nearby grove, a doe leapt away, wild eyed, racing west. The bray of her young fawn fell on deaf ears. As with the wolf, the animal appeared driven by a force Amy could neither see nor understand.

From high above, she followed the string of animal possessions, one after another, as they ran west. A deep dread took shape in Amy's mind as she felt a keen and eternal darkness move toward her.

Her chest tightened, and she struggled for breath. A frenzied panic took hold of her.

It comes for me.

"Amy, what's wrong?" Jason's voice reached her.

The vision shredded, and she tried to blink gummy eyes. She gasped for breath and growled as if she had been one of the animals possessed.

"Sweetheart, are you ill? Wake up." Jason held her in his arms.

Her eyes opened, and she pushed Jason away. In desperation, she pulled herself up and leaned over the side of the buckboard to vomit. She felt Jason gather her hair and hold her head steady as she emptied her stomach again.

When the cramp inside eased, she lowered herself to the bed and allowed Jason to wrap his arms around her. Her hand shook as she took the cup of water from Jimmy Leigh.

"Thank you, Jim." Tears threatened, and she closed her eyes.

Jason steadied her hand and helped her sip the cool water.

"I'm not sure what to do," Jason's whisper held an edge of panic. "Tell me what you need. Will you be all right?"

"I will be. Just give me a moment. It will pass. I had—a bad dream."

"I hope to hell I never have a dream like that." Jason held her close and rubbed her arms.

The tremors eased, and she took another sip from the cup. "I'm better now." She smiled her thanks to Jason.

Jason hugged her a last time and slid to the end of the wagon. He pulled on his boots, found his hat, and walked to the fire.

Amy didn't attempt to move yet. She couldn't. Her heart fluttered each time she thought of her vision.

I wish Nichole and Merril were here.

Guilt from withholding the truth about herself from her husband assailed her, but there had never been a reason to tell him about her abilities. Her secret couldn't remain hidden much longer. She finished the water from the tin.

Jim tightened the cinch on his saddle then approached the wagon. "There's no rush, gal. We can head out once you feel better."

"I'm better now." She shrugged the blanket aside. "It was only a bad dream."

Jim's gaze captured hers "Take your time. We won't leave until you're ready." He pushed back his hat with his gloved thumb and looked at the angle of the sun. "We should get home just past noon."

Amy moved down to the end of the wagon, slipped on her shoes and laced them. She lowered her feet to the ground, and then gripped the side of the wagon and waited for her head to stop spinning. Whatever physical manifestation bound her to the vision persisted. Uneasiness settled in her belly. To cover her discomfort, she pulled the blankets to her and folded them.

Kelly tossed his bunk roll into the wagon and handed her the coffee tins to stow.

"Look at that." Jim's voice held a hushed urgency. He stepped beside Amy and pointed back the way they had come.

Amy followed the line of his arm and saw them. In the center of the dirt road, two black wolves sat still as statues, watching the group break camp. "Oh my!"

"What is it?" Kelly asked.

Jim held up his hand to Kelly to be silent then pointed at the wolves. In moments, all four travelers stared at the two large animals seated in the road.

"That's just plumb unnatural." Kelly hunched his shoulders turned toward his mount.

"Do you think they'll follow us?" Jason wondered aloud.

"I think they will. Yes." Amy responded, her thoughts on Alyse as she stared into the wolves' yellow eyes.

Both Jim and Jason turned and stared at her.

Amy heaved a sigh. "There were two black cats at the house in Denver." She looked from Jason to Jim and pointed toward the wolves. "The cats acted strange, like these animals. I think they're the same, somehow."

"The cats and the wolves are the same." Jason raised his eyebrow. "Are you sure you feel all right?"

Amy narrowed her eyes and clenched her teeth into a smile. "Why, yes, Jason, I'm fine."

Jason ran his hand through his hair and reset his hat. "Good. Then let's go home." He shot Jim a hard glance and walked to the front of the wagon to help Kelly harness the team.

"You know more than you're saying, don't you?" Jim queried, his gaze still on the pair of wolves.

"Almost always," Amy replied with resignation.

One wolf stood and nudged the other, and then they moved off the road into the summer grass.

"They act like those two cats, Jim. I swear. I know it doesn't make a bit of sense." She shook her head and turned back to organizing the wagon. She heard Jim move away as she finished stowing the bedding and gear. When she looked back, Jim and Kelly were mounted and talking beside the doused fire.

"Ready?" Jason took her arm and helped her climb into the seat. He shook the reins after the horsemen passed by and followed them onto the road.

Amy kept a look out for the wolves, but if they trailed behind, they remained well hidden. Jason's silence gave her time to review her vision and the warm sunlight on her face felt like courage. Whenever she thought of the possessed animals racing west, her stomach twisted. She had to warn Jason that an unspeakable evil was heading toward them, not far behind a twin sister and uncles he didn't know existed.

How do I explain?

"If you sigh one more time, I'm going to stop the wagon." Jason looked at her with concern. "What's wrong?"

Tell him now.

Her mouth opened, but the words caved in on themselves. She shook her head and blinked at tears. "Just the dream," she whispered and looked across the yellow grass. When she glanced back, Jason still watched her.

"Your parasol is beneath the seat in case you need it."

"Thank you." She retrieved the umbrella and slid it open.

"If you want to tell me about your dream, I'll listen."

Amy nodded and brushed a tear from her cheek. "When I can."

Ahead of them, Jim pulled rein and dropped back to Amy's side of the wagon.

"Do you see 'em?" he asked.

Amy shook her head.

Jim pointed up.

Both Amy and Jason looked up to see two dark hawks circle high above them.

"So... now you think the wolves turned into hawks and are following us?" Jason scoffed at Jim.

Jim looked hard at Jason. Without another word, Jim urged his mount forward to ride again with Kelly.

Amy ignored the men and watched the hawks. They could just be hawks, riding high on the air currents, but they stayed above the small group of travelers.

"I've had just about enough of Jimmy Leigh," Jason grumbled.

Amy turned to her husband and leaned close to his arm. "Try to be more open-minded, Jason. There are many things in this world we don't understand."

Jason glanced at Amy. "It's not just the hawks and the wolves." Jason stared ahead at the horsemen. "He encourages that nonsense with you, and I know why."

"My practical love. So logical. So rational." Amy tangled her fingers into curls that trailed over his collar. "What would you say if I told you something completely outlandish and asked you to believe me?"

Jason turned to her and searched her face. "Are you serious?"

Amy pressed her lips and inclined her head. "I am, and I would like to tell you a thing about me you don't know." She held his gaze until he looked back at the road.

"Go on, then. Tell me." His voice was soft.

"When I was a young girl in Boston, I began to have dreams while awake. Visions of people and things would rush into my head. I didn't understand it, and they frightened me terribly. I told my mother."

Jason glanced at her, then back to the road. "What did your mother say?"

"She told me the visions couldn't hurt me, and I should never tell anyone about them. She asked me to come to her each time I had one, and tell her what I saw, and she would write it down."

"And you did this?" Jason asked.

"I did. I told her everything. It became apparent I saw things before they happened."

"Why do you say, 'apparent'? What did you see?"

"Oh, Jason, many things. Unimportant ones, mostly. Things my mother would explain later, but as a child, I didn't know or care. It comforted me to know she believed me and took great care to write down whatever I said. It helped me to not be alarmed by them."

Jason's voice rose. "Margaret encouraged you?"

"She taught me how to live with my visions," Amy explained patiently. "They're part of who I am, not something she could change. When I grew older, she taught me how to interpret them. How to know when I saw something important, and when they held only trivial information."

Ahead, Kelly pointed to a washed-out portion of road.

"Give me an example of trivial information." Jason guided the buckboard around the missing portion of road.

"Let me think." Amy tapped a finger on her lips, then nodded. "I must have been about ten years old when I saw who left their dog's droppings on the commons walking path."

"You saw them at the park?"

"Yes, but I sat in the parlor with my mother. I didn't know the man, but I described him and the dog to my mother. She wrote it down. A few days later, an article appeared in the paper. The man had been fined for leaving his dog's droppings on the walking path. The article provided a description of him and his dog, just as I had."

Jason chuckled. "Visions of dog crap. All right, then give me an example of an important one." After a few moments of silence, Jason nudged her with his shoulder. "Go on."

Amy nodded, but didn't look up as she spoke. "Before I returned to the ranch for the barbecue, I had a vision in Denver. A strong one. An important one." She looked up at Jason and saw she had his full attention. "I saw Merril and Kevin, both distraught over the death of their father. I saw the fringed carriage of Nichole's flip over. I saw Merril tell you he couldn't find her pulse." Her gaze locked with his.

Jason shook his head. "I'm speechless. Are you telling me you can see the future, and no one knows about this except me and your mother?"

"Nichole and Merril know," Amy admitted.

"You told them and not me?" he questioned sharply.

"I had to warn Nichole about Jones. She wanted to know how I knew he'd come after her. I told her about the visions to convince her the threat was real. Then Nichole told me what an old Indian said to Merril about her." Disappointment filled her, and she shook her head and looked down at her hands. "Oh, Jason. Sometimes it's just easier to talk about this with people who don't scoff at me and think I've lost my mind. Both Nichole and Merril are open-minded. I never thought you would be."

They rode in silence. Amy cast a glance at Jason every so often.

He must understand.

The muscle in his jaw worked rhythmically. After several miles, he spoke without turning his head. "What do the wolves have to do with this?" He shot her a scathing glance. "And how much have you confided in Jimmy Leigh?"

"Jim knows nothing of this from me." Amy glared at her husband, then turned and looked up at the hawks still circling above them. "As for the wolves—" Amy hesitated until she felt Jason's eyes on her. She turned to face him. "I think my sister sent them." She lifted her chin and met his stare.

He raised his eyebrows and laughed. "Your sister? You don't *have* a sister." He chuckled and looked back at the road.

"I wasn't raised with a sister. But I've come to believe I have one, nonetheless."

"Your visions again?"

Amy looked across the prairie. In the distance, storm clouds rose in the afternoon heat. She could sense the moisture. The flow of power moved eastward, away from their path. "No. It's different with her, but I think it's all connected somehow."

Their conversation lapsed into silence. Amy looked at Jason occasionally, but he kept his eyes on the road before them. Soon, the outbuildings of the Highlands came into sight, and then the house.

As they pulled onto the long drive up to the yard, Jason slowed the wagon to a stop, then looked at Amy. "Did you have a vision this morning? Is that what made you sick?"

A flurry of nerves fell through her chest to her stomach.

Tell him.

She turned toward Jason and nodded.

"And you decided to tell me all this—now—because of something in your vision?" Jason's voice was low and serious.

"Yes," she whispered.

"How bad is it?" Jason laid his arm along the back of the seat behind Amy. "What's going to happen?"

Amy shook her head. Relief flooded her, and she held her hand to her mouth. "I don't know, exactly." Tears threatened her eyes, but she refused to turn away from Jason's blue gaze. "There's something coming, but I have no name for it. It's like nothing I've ever seen. I think it's why Alyse is trying to find me." Amy shook her head and the tears slid down her cheeks. She looked down at her hands, fingers twisted in her lap. "I only know it frightens me, and not many things do."

Jason wrapped his arm around her shoulders. "Her name is Alyse?"

Amy looked up from her hands and nodded. "Yes. She's on a train now, and will arrive in Denver in a few days."

Jason relaxed back against the buckboard seat and glanced up at the clear blue sky.

Amy followed his gaze. The hawks were gone.

Merril and Nichole crossed from the back of the house to greet Jim. Nichole glanced at them and waved, but continued with her husband and Jim past the corral and into the barn.

"Do I still have a place here, Amy?" Jason watched the group disappear into the shadowed interior of the barn.

Amy could see both fear and regret etched on Jason's face. He had aged visibly in just a few weeks. "I think we do." She took his hand. "It will be different than before, of course. But the wounds will mend. Nichole loves you. She wants you here with her."

Jason searched Amy's eyes. "You said *we*."

"Yes. We will stay, or we will go—either way, *we* will be together."

Jason smiled as he lifted the reins to put the team in motion, but Amy laid a hand on his arm.

"I'm sorry, but I still don't feel well. I should lie down for a bit. Would you make my excuses to the family?" The effects of the vision clung to her, each time she thought of the animals, nausea churned in her belly. She wrapped one arm across her stomach and pressed her right hand to the pounding ache in her temple.

"Certainly, my dear. Here, let me help you down." Jason set the brake, stepped down and around the wagon, and extended his hand to her. "Have a good rest." He kissed her forehead and released her hand as she stepped onto the porch. "I'll see you at dinner."

Amy climbed the stairs to their room. Her head throbbed. Did her vision cause these physical symptoms, or was this nervous exhaustion from all that had taken place in the last week? She closed the door to her room and lay fully clothed on the bed.

When Amy woke, the slant of the sun through the window told her it was late afternoon. She regretted the delay in speaking with Nichole, but she felt better for having rested. She repaired her hair, washed her face and hands, and went downstairs to find Nichole.

In the kitchen yard, someone had raised a tarp on wooden posts to provide afternoon shade. Hope-Anne balanced on her hands and knees in the center of a colorful quilt. Katy sat across from her and encouraged the babe to move toward several shiny objects.

Nichole sat beneath the tarp at the table and watched the children play. Beyond Nichole, past the well, Lawna and Jeanne chatted and laughed together as they pinned wet sheets on the clothesline.

Amy hugged Nichole's shoulders, then took a seat on the bench beside her. "Is Katy staying at The Highlands?"

Nichole nodded. "She and her mother. I'm glad Henny and Cookie get along or we'd have kitchen wars. Henny gave Cookie several new recipes Merril especially likes." Nichole turned to Amy. "Are you feeling better?"

"Yes, I am. Thank you." Amy nodded toward Katy. "Who remains at The Shilo?"

"No one." Nichole glanced at Amy, then looked back toward the baby. "Everyone who stayed after..." Nichole sent Amy a knowing look and a small shrug. "They came here. Lloyd put Henny and Katy in the family bunkhouse, but it's a large building. Tom and Timothy put up a wall to make two areas. The Caines have already moved into their new room."

"I didn't see Henny when we came in."

Nichole pointed across the yard, past the family bunkhouse and chicken coop, toward the large vegetable garden where a wide-brimmed straw hat moved between rows. "She's taken over the garden."

"Good. I'll speak with her about the herbs I want to plant." Amy leaned closer to Nichole. "Walk with me for a moment." Amy rose and strolled to the corner of the house, then waited.

"Katy, would you keep an eye on Hope-Anne?" Nichole asked as she rose. "Don't let her get in the dirt."

"Yes, ma'am," Katy replied. Her bright smile and attention remained on the baby.

Nichole followed Amy around the side of the house. They stopped in the shade provided by the big cottonwood.

"What's wrong?" Nichole asked.

"Something's coming. Something—evil. I should have warned you the moment we arrived. I told Jason, but I don't know what else to do, or how to prepare for it." Amy pressed her finger and thumb against her forehead. "I'm not sure Jason believed me."

"What is it?" Nichole whispered. Alarm filled her eyes. "Is this something you saw?"

Amy shook her head in frustration. "That's the problem. I'm not entirely sure what I saw."

"Tell me." Nichole took Amy's hands.

Amy nodded and gripped Nichole's fingers. "Honesty, then. First, you need to know I have a twin sister."

Nichole's eyes widened, but she remained silent.

"Her name is Alyse. She has abilities, like mine, only she's much stronger. Alyse is the one who healed you in Denver."

"Alyse... wasn't in Denver." Nichole replied hesitantly.

"I know," Amy spoke faster, her words tumbled out. Her heart raced with the need to confess what she knew to Nichole. "Alyse felt me panic and reached out to me. Our magic twisted together somehow—I had no idea who or what healed through me. When she said she would find me, I was terrified. Then later, I felt her sorrow and reached out to her. We spoke." Amy stared at Nichole.

What if she doesn't believe me?

Slowly, Nichole began to nod. "You have a telepathic connection with your twin. A sister you didn't know of until now."

"Telepathic?"

"You communicate with your mind."

"You understand what this is?" Amy leaned forward, eyes wide. "How do you know of such things?"

"I know about this from—" Nichole shook her head. "That can wait. What about your vision? Is your sister the evil you saw?"

"No, it's not Alyse. The evil follows her. It's using animals as transport—possessing their bodies and driving them west. I become ill when I think of it."

"Holy shit, Amy. I'm not sure what to say."

"You believe me, don't you?" Amy tightened her hold on Nichole's hands. "You must."

"Of course, I do. I *absolutely* believe you."

The tension in Amy's neck eased and she exhaled. "Thank you."

"Does your sister know what follows her?"

"I don't know." Amy admitted. "If she knows, she didn't speak of it."

"Can you ask her?"

"No. I've tried to speak with her again, but I can't. Our communication only seems to work when the other is upset or in need."

"Wow." Nichole released Amy's hands and rested her fingers across her mouth, her eyes unfocused and distant. After a moment, her gaze met Amy's. "Did you tell Jim?"

"No. Only Jason."

"Jason wouldn't have been my first choice to discuss something like this." Nichole chuckled. "How did he take it?"

"Better than I thought he might," Amy said with a smile. "But then, he saw how the vision affected me. Also, the wolves were so very odd. Watching them may have made him open to other strange possibilities."

"What wolves?" Nichole questioned.

Amy explained about the cats at the house in Denver, and how when she touched them she could see her sister with them. Then she told Nichole about the black wolves, and how the hawks appeared to follow them.

"We should watch for this pair of animals as well." Nichole suggested as they walked back to the kitchen yard.

Lawna sat on the bench with a sleepy Hope-Anne at her breast.

Jeanne and Katy were walking the garden with Henny.

As though Nichole shared Amy's thought, they continued through the kitchen yard and across the main yard to the barn.

It was time to talk with Merril and Jimmy Leigh.

Chapter 23

Catherine Kline

—

The change from the MKT line to the Central Pacific Railroad in Junction City went smoothly. Even though the transfer again took place at night, they were able to purchase food and water from the depot vendors and board the westbound train in record time.

The excitement of traveling by rail had worn thin. Cat wanted a bed and a bath more than anything else she could think of. Worse yet, Hunter sat in the same car as her under the watchful eye of her brother.

As the sun rose behind them, the low East Kansas hills flattened, and the plains unfolded into a vast sea of grass. At first, the endless vista of blue sky and golden prairie thrilled Cat with its stark beauty. Then it became boring. She curled up on her seat and fell asleep.

The sudden jar and squeal of the brakes woke her. "What's happening?" She sat up and brushed a strand of hair from her eyes. She looked from the window to her brother.

Sam set his paper aside and stood. Hunter passed their seat and disappeared through the forward exit. "Stay here, Cat. I'll find out why we're stopping." Sam followed Hunter out the door.

Passengers called questions to each other, creating a cacophony of voices inside the car.

"No need to worry, folks." The conductor's call boomed from the rear door and quieted the worried voices. He spoke at a normal volume as he strolled up the aisle. "The engineer sighted a herd of buffalo on the south side of the train. Since we're ahead of schedule, we'll make a short stop to allow you to observe these animals. For those who wish to fire upon the herd, you will be required to exit the train."

The car jerked again as its forward momentum ceased.

Cat rose from her seat, along with several people seated on the north side of the train, to look out the south-facing windows. The herd grazed far enough from the train she could not distinguish separate animals. The sea of golden grass vanished in the distance into a dark blemish across the prairie. As she turned away to retake her seat, the crack of a rifle resonated through the passenger car. The sound startled Cat and she spun back toward the windows. The observers pressed closer to the window to see the shooters beside the train.

"The animals are too far for the hunters to injure, *ma chère*."

Cat looked up at Hunter and smiled. "I thought so. They're not even close enough to see properly."

Hunter chuckled. "Their odor will not be missed, I assure you."

Cat grinned and took her seat, away from the exclamations of the onlookers. "Where's Sam?"

Hunter sat across from Cat. "He made it known to the conductor that he is a U.S. Marshal. The conductor asked him to monitor the activities outside."

Gunfire continued outside the train. The watchers shouted advice from the open windows.

Hunter turned sideways in his seat, one leg angled on the bench, to look out over the observers' heads.

Cat's gaze etched Hunter's profile, committing it to memory. He had brushed his black hair back and tied the long strands with a leather strip at his collar. Her contemplation followed his smooth brow and straight nose down to his full, well-defined lips. The only mar to his perfect profile—the scar running down his cheek.

I wonder what happened?

"If Sam sees you look at me like that, *ma très chère*, he may well shoot me." Hunter grinned and turned toward Cat.

Her face warmed, but she raised her chin and refused to drop her gaze. "Why?" she asked. "You've done nothing to warrant such a reprisal from Sam."

"Not yet, but should you continue to regard me with such—affection—I might." His grin grew into a broad smile.

"Really?" She leaned forward, her smile matching his. "Like what?"

"*Mademoiselle* Kline." Hunter sat forward and took her hand. "You appear to be under the impression I am a nice, honorable man. I must warn you, I am neither of those things."

Cat squeezed his hand, leaned closer and whispered, "By making such an admission, sir, it means you *are* a nice, honorable man." She leaned back and looked down at their hands, his fingers large and tanned compared to hers. "A villainous lout would not warn a lady of his ill intent." Her gaze darted to his and she smiled.

Hunter raised an eyebrow, but his expression grew serious. He spoke softly, his attention on their hands. "Is that so?" He caressed her palms, and stroked between her delicate fingers. "Perhaps your logic is flawed, *ma chère*. An unscrupulous man may hope to gain a young woman's sympathy by admitting to an imperfect character." He raised his somber expression to Cat.

Cat shook her head. "I don't believe that." Her smile faded.

He makes excuses.

"If you want me to leave you alone, I will." She tipped her head and looked away, north across the prairie. "I know I've acted immodestly, just as the girls at school behaved brazenly toward Sam. He found them annoying." She looked back at Hunter and captured his gaze. "Mr. Hunter—Alexander—I don't want you to think of me as Sam's annoying little sister." She pressed her lips and took a quick breath. "I'll leave you alone and cease looking at you with such... devotion, if that is what you wish."

"Ah, *ma bien-aimée*, and there lies the problem." He shook his head and turned her hand palm up. His finger traced a line around the pad of her thumb. "I don't want you to take your affection from me, and I don't think of you as Sam's younger sister." His stern glance lifted to her face. "Although I should."

Cat's heart swelled at his words. She gripped his hand and met his grim expression with a joyous smile.

He shook his head, released her fingers and ran his hand across his jaw. His head turned toward the passengers who continued to shout encouragement at the shooters. When he spoke, his words were low. "Cat, I have nothing to offer a well-bred young woman like yourself."

The song in her heart dimmed, along with her smile, as he pinned her with apologetic eyes.

"I live from one job to the next. There is no single place I call home. *Mon beau chaton*, you deserve a better life than the one I could give you."

Cat's joy evaporated. She took a breath to speak, and it caught in her throat. Unable to look a moment longer into his well-meaning eyes, she dropped her gaze to her lap and cleared her throat. "So you do want me to leave you alone, if only for my own sake."

"No, *ma chère*."

Her head came up, and she searched his face.

Hunter leaned close and whispered, "What I want is to tear the clothes from your body and make sweet, passionate love to you." He leaned back and took a deep breath. "There. Now do you see what kind of villainous lout I have become?" Hunter glanced briefly back at Cat, then leaned forward and covered his face. "*Mon Dieu!*"

Cat's eyes had gone wide with possibilities. "*All* of my clothes—and yours too? Both of us?" She leaned forward and whispered, "Naked *and* kissing?" She wasn't sure he heard her speak until he groaned. There didn't seem to be enough air in the railcar. She placed a hand over her open mouth as her imagination took flight, and then she nodded. "Yes. I believe I should like to try that." Her sight returned from the delightful imagery his suggestion conjured and settled on the man across from her.

He shook his head. "Dissuading you only gives you more ideas." Hunter rubbed his face with his hand then met her gaze. "What am I to do with you?"

Cat grinned in an effort not to laugh in jubilation. "I believe your last suggestion would work quite well, for a start."

Hunter shrugged and held out his hand. "We can't do that, *petit chat*. As I've already explained, I've nothing to offer you in return."

Cat shook her head. "Mr. Hunter, I've never asked anything of you in return for my affection. However, if there's a problem on your side of this... relationship, and you feel you need to offer me more than you currently have, then obtain it. I can do nothing about your perception of what I deserve. All I can do is tell you what I'm willing to do."

"You seem willing to do most anything, *très chère*." He retorted and threw a look of frustration at her.

"You have no idea what I would be willing to try." Her grin grew until she bit her finger and looked out the window with a chuckle.

Naked and kissing. Who would have thought?

"*Merde*," Hunter muttered. "And it's not Mr. Hunter, Cat. It's... Veau. Alexander Veau. Hunter, as you pointed out, is my title. But please, *petit chat*, be discreet. No one knows that name."

Through the open window, Cat heard the conductor encourage the people outside to finish their target practice and reboard the train. The aisle filled with men stowing their weapons and returning to their seats.

Hunter rose and stepped into the crowded aisle. Moments later, Sam slid onto the bench across from Cat.

"Did you watch any of that nonsense?" Sam fanned his face with his hat. Perspiration beaded his face.

"Some of it."

The whistle blew twice, and the car jerked several times as the wheels were set in motion.

Sam dropped his hat beside him on the bench, ran his hand through his hair and smiled at Cat. "I'm ready to eat. How about you?"

Cat shrugged. "I suppose. It must be close to dinner time." She searched beneath the seat and pulled out a basket of baked chicken.

After they ate, Sam returned to reading the paper, while Cat took up a sampler she'd started a month ago. She tried to keep her thoughts away from Hunter removing her clothes while they kissed, but her imagination wouldn't leave the image alone. She shifted in her seat and took another stitch in her sampler.

Soon, the clouds turned orange, and then pink, while the sky grew dark behind them. When the conductor walked through the car and dimmed the lights, Cat put away her sewing and pulled her blanket and pillow from under Sam's seat. She curled on the bench, her head pillowed beneath the window. Denver remained several hours away. They were scheduled to arrive before dawn.

Cat woke in the middle of the night. Sam snored softly, scrunched into the seat across from her. She untangled herself from her blanket, slipped on her shoes, and made her way to the lavatory. As she passed Hunter's seat, she saw only his hat and his blanket on the bench. When she left the lavatory, she stepped to the end of the car and opened the door.

Hunter stood at the rail, looking up at the night sky, a thin cigar between his fingers.

Cat closed the door behind her and moved to stand beside him. The horizon was visible only as a line of blackness where the stars ended. She turned and looked across the multitude of tiny lights in the sky. "Why do I see more stars here than at home?"

"The air is dry and clear. There is no haze to block your view." Hunter crushed out his cheroot and continued to look upward. "Also, there are no streetlights to compete with the stars."

Cat shivered. "It's colder too. I didn't realize the night air would be chilled in the summer."

Hunter wrapped his arms around her and pulled her close to his chest. He rested his chin on the top of her head and leaned his back against the railcar.

"We will be in Denver in a few hours," Cat murmured into his chest.

"*Oui*," Hunter whispered.

Cat pulled back and looked up into the shadow that covered his face.

He lowered his mouth to hers.

She tasted sweet smoke as his lips brushed hers.

Why did he have to be so stubborn?

Cat pressed her breast against his chest and wrapped her arms around his neck.

He took her upper lip in his mouth, then released it to capture her lower lip. His hand cupped the nape of her neck, and he tipped his head to match his mouth to hers. His soft inhale sealed their lips momentarily. He groaned, as though in pain, and pulled her tight against him.

An unfamiliar sensation clutched deep inside Cat. She moaned as his mouth savored hers and pressed her hips against him seeking something she couldn't name.

Hunter groaned once more, then broke the kiss. He pressed her head against his chest and inhaled deeply.

Cat listened to his heart race. She squeezed her eyes tight and swallowed a hard bit of emotion that clamored for release.

Neither spoke. All that needed to be said had already been laid before them.

When Cat gained control of her emotions, she stepped from Hunter's arms. She raised her hand and caressed the side of his face, down the scar, through the bristle of his unshaven face to his mouth.

He grasped her hand, turned it, and touched his lips to the tender center of her palm. "Good night, *Mademoiselle* Kline." He released her hand, tipped his head in a salute, and opened the door.

"Good night, Mr. Veau," Cat whispered, and returned to her seat.

***

Just before sunrise, the train pulled into the Denver station. Cat gathered her things and followed Sam from the train.

On the platform, beside the depot wall, Sam set his bag and blanket down. He pulled a stamped metal luggage claim from his vest.

Hunter joined them and set his carpetbag beside Sam's. "I'll get the trunks if you procure the wagon, *mon ami.*"

Sam nodded and handed Hunter their metal tab. "Cat, stay with our belongings."

Cat dipped her head and placed her blanket and bag alongside Hunter's.

The men disappeared in different directions—Hunter, down the platform toward the luggage car, and Sam through the depot toward the street.

Cat organized their luggage into a neat pile and watched the people depart the train. Before long, she spotted Hunter as he walked alongside a uniformed porter. The porter pushed a wheeled cart piled high with their trunks.

When they reached Cat, Hunter loaded their carpetbag to the cart and took Cat's arm. "This way, *petit chat.*" He escorted her around the side of the depot and down a ramp to the street.

Travelers with their luggage, and a line of wagons and hansom cabs filled the curb in front of the train depot.

Sam spoke to the driver of a two-seat wagon.

As she and Hunter approached, Sam waved at the porter to bring the luggage to the back of the wagon.

Hunter assisted Cat onto the rear bench as Sam helped the porter load the trunks. Hunter spoke briefly to Sam, then pulled himself onto the bench beside Cat.

Sam tipped the porter and climbed beside the driver. "The Wagon Wheel Hotel, near Colfax and Park."

The driver nodded. "I know the place." He shook the reins and they pulled into traffic.

At the hotel, a sleepy night clerk assigned each of the travelers a room and handed them keys. He rang a bell on the desk, and a man appeared from the next room and took charge of unloading their luggage from the wagon.

"You're in room eight, Cat." Sam handed her a key. "I'll pay the driver and have the bellhop deliver your luggage."

"What room do you have?" Cat glanced at Hunter as her brother checked his key fob, but Hunter had his back to her as he spoke with the driver.

"I'm in room 12 upstairs." Sam replied.

"All right, then. Good night."

Cat found her room and waited for the bellhop. As soon as he departed, she closed and locked the door. The small room had everything she needed—a washbasin and a bed.

She shed her travel-worn garments and made quick use of the water and soap on the dresser. She pulled on a nightgown and plucked the pins from her hair, scratching her fingers deep against the scalp. With a promise she would seek out the bathing facility when she woke, she pulled back the heavy down coverlet and crawled into the soft bed.

Hunger woke her. She clambered from the bed and reluctantly dressed in clean clothes from her trunk.

Sometime today, I shall find a bathtub.

A knock at her door interrupted her toilette as she brushed the tangles from her hair. She opened the door and smiled at her brother. "Good morning."

Sam waited in the hallway dressed in tan trousers and jacket with a dark vest and white shirt. "You should have asked who knocked," Sam scolded, mock anger in his blue-gray eyes.

Cat returned to her hair. "I knew it was you." She twisted it onto her head and secured the bun with hairpins.

"Because you can see through doors?" Sam rubbed at the four-day old bristle on his chin and raised an eyebrow.

"Because I'm hungry, which means you must be starved. I expected you."

"There's a restaurant down the street that serves breakfast and lunch. The time is right for either." He hesitated in the doorway. "Are you about ready?"

"I am." Cat picked up her reticule.

"After breakfast, we'll go to the address I have for Jason Harris. The Marshal's office indicated he may be at his ranch, but I should check the town address first." He followed her down the hallway and out the door to the street.

"You can check the address without me. I heard the night clerk mention a bathing room attached to the hotel. I fully intend make use of a tub after we eat."

"Hunter's going to the house with me."

Cat stopped and turned to her brother. "Why do you say that?" She felt the heat in her cheeks.

Dash it! How does he know?

Sam stopped and looked back at his sister with a wide grin. "I'm trained to observe. Did you think I wouldn't notice after four days confined with you two on a train?"

"Why didn't you say something?" Cat advanced on her brother.

Sam shrugged as they resumed walking. "I'm not your father—and I trust Hunter."

"You trust him and not me?" Cat threw a snide glance at Sam. "I thought you were only acquainted with him. How well do you know Hunter?"

"Well enough, Cat. He's a good man." Sam opened the door to the small restaurant. Arriving between breakfast and lunch, they had their choice of seats. Sam hung his hat on a peg by the door and escorted Cat to the back of the establishment. He pulled out her chair, and then sat with his back to the wall.

Both Cat and Sam ordered the breakfast omelet.

After the waitress left their table, Cat grinned and whispered to Sam. "I've grown quite fond of Hunter." Relieved she could speak of her affection lifted her heart and made every possibility more real.

"I like him, too." Sam smiled at his sister's enthusiasm. After a moment, his smile dimmed, and his eyes became solemn. "I would hate to see him get hurt."

"Don't say that." Cat sat back and shook her head. "I would never do anything to hurt Hunter."

"You may not intend him harm." Sam thanked the waitress who set water on their table. "A young woman might not realize how much a man cares for her, or how her actions could—make him suffer."

Cat's brow furrowed as she stared at her brother.

This isn't about me at all.

He took a sip of water and looked away.

"Who was she?" Cat asked, her voice heavy with sympathy.

His gaze returned to his sister. "I'm not talking about me."

Cat narrowed her eyes. "I think, perhaps, you are."

"It doesn't matter. My point is Hunter doesn't receive a great deal of attention from women. Especially not from beautiful young girls like yourself." Sam straightened as the waitress approached with their plates. "Just be sure how you feel about him."

The waitress slid their plates onto the table in front of them. "Anything else?" She glanced from Cat to Sam.

"No, thank you," Sam replied, and picked up his napkin.

Cat watched the waitress return to the front of the restaurant to seat new guests. "This is not an infatuation, if that's what you're implying."

Sam swallowed his first bite of omelet and leaned forward, knife and fork in hand. "I think you may be too young to judge. You're just out of school."

"Now you do sound like a father." Cat cut her omelet and glared at Sam. "Can I at least remain at the hotel while you chase after that Harris man?"

Sam swallowed and shook his head. "No. You'll come with me."

"Fine." Cat popped a piece of egg in her mouth.

"We won't be gone more than a few days. I only need to speak with Mr. Harris about his involvement in what appears to be a financial swindle run by an investment firm out of Boston." Sam cut another piece from his omelet. "Hunter will be busy with his own affairs while we're gone."

After they finished eating, Sam paid for their meal, and they walked back to the hotel in silence.

***

Hunter

—

Hunter folded the newspaper and set it on the table when he saw Sam and Cat enter the hotel lobby.

Cat pushed open the door herself, without waiting for Sam. Her lips were pinched and her eyes blazed.

Sam shook his head and followed Cat across the lobby.

The siblings had been fighting. Probably about me.

Hunter stood as they approached. "Are we ready to go?"

Sam nodded. "It's just us. Cat wants to take a bath."

"Which I would highly recommend for both of you." Cat smiled at Hunter, then walked to the desk clerk.

"We might as well get this over with." Sam turned and headed back out the door.

Hunter glanced at Cat's back as he slid his hat on his head, then he followed Sam out the door.

Sam waited on the walkway and pointed up the street when Hunter stepped outside. "There's a stable a block down."

When they reached the livery, they made arrangements with the stable master to have two horses tacked up for in town use for a few hours. In no time, they were in the saddle and heading toward Park Avenue.

"Did you do your map divining?" Sam asked.

Hunter grinned at his friend's description of his odd power and use of the pendulum. "I did. Both last night and this morning. I think there are three individuals, all east of Denver. Two are moving quickly in this direction."

From Park Avenue they turned right on Pence Street.

"It's possible they will all return to Denver. If there's a town hall here, they may have a current map of town. If they don't, I'll need to sketch one."

"And if your bounties stay east?" Sam asked.

"Once they stop moving, I'll track their location." Hunter glanced at Sam.

Sam nodded. "If Harris isn't at this house, Cat and I will head for his ranch this afternoon. We'll have to camp out overnight. Sam laughed. "I'll enjoy watching Cat sleep rough. I don't think she's ever sat around a campfire."

"Your sister is something else." Hunter smiled at the thought of Cat sitting in the warm glow of the fire.

"As you've said, more than once." Sam looked over at Hunter. "I've been meaning to ask you what your intentions are."

Hunter pressed his lips and shook his head. "I told her she could do better than me. I had nothing to offer a woman like her."

"And what did she say?"

"She told me to fix it," Hunter replied, and grinned when Sam laughed.

"Then I'm back to my original question... what are your intentions?"

Hunter reset his hat on his head and chuckled. "I guess I better do as she says and fix my problem. Is there still an opening at the Marshal's office for a field agent?"

"There may be. I know they've asked about you before. They know you and consider you a good candidate for a position like this." Sam winked at Hunter. "You come with a fairly high recommendation."

"Fairly high, *mon ami*?" Hunter chuckled. "I'll send them a telegram this afternoon and see what they say. I want to have a permanent job before I ask to court your sister."

Sam cocked an eyebrow at Hunter. "I thought you were already courting."

"She doesn't take no for an answer."

"Don't I know it?" Sam pulled an envelope from his pocket and checked the address. "It's just ahead. The house being repaired."

As Sam dismounted, a thin, balding man turned away from the construction work and greeted them. "Hello, gentlemen. How can I help you?"

"Are you Jason Harris?" Sam asked as they shook hands.

"No, sir. My name is Albert Fielding. I'm supervising Mr. Harris's porch rebuild."

"I see." Sam returned the envelope to his pocket. "Is Mr. Harris available?"

"And you are?"

Sam pulled a leather wallet from his coat and showed Albert Fielding his badge. "Samuel Kline, U.S. Marshal. Mr. Harris may have some information on a case I'm investigating. Do you know where I can find him?"

Albert Fielding bobbed his head. "He and his wife left a couple of days ago for his cousin's ranch, east of here. The Harris-Highlands Ranch. You know of it?"

"I do. Thank you, Mr. Fielding."

Hunter turned his mount as Sam stepped into his saddle.

They returned the horses to the stable, and Sam rented a buckboard wagon and team for several days. At the hotel, Sam advised the desk clerk he and his sister would be checking out. However, he expected to return in less than a week's time. Then, Sam went to tell Cat they would leave for the ranch today.

After Sam left, Hunter turned to the small lobby to wait. He looked up from his paper when he heard Cat's voice. She gave the desk clerk her room key, and requested a bellhop fetch her trunk to the lobby.

When she turned, her gaze found Hunter's and she walked toward him with a smile on her beautiful face.

What does a woman like her see in me?

Even dressed in her travel-weary outfit from the train, she moved with regal bearing.

He rose to his feet as she approached.

"We'll be leaving soon." She took the seat across from him.

"Sam said you could be back in five days."

Cat nodded. "Will you be here when we return?"

"I'm not sure." He wanted to say yes, but the lives of those he hunted were at risk. "If I depart to follow a lead, I will leave a message for you at the desk."

"A message for me... or for Sam?" Cat's eyes asked questions he couldn't answer yet.

"*Mon beau petit chaton,* any message I leave at the desk will be for you." Perhaps he would hear back from the Marshal's office before she returned. Until he had more to offer her, he didn't want to give her false hope.

Sam entered the lobby from the hotel hallway, spotted Hunter and stopped behind Cat. "I'm going to walk up to the stable and get the wagon." He glanced down at Cat. "The bellhop will take our luggage outside. The wagon should be ready." He raised his regard to Hunter. "Would you keep an eye out for me?"

"I will see you when you pull up, *mon ami.*" Hunter indicated his line of sight through the front window.

Sam nodded and crossed the lobby to the exit.

Hunter looked from Sam's back to Cat. "He knows about us."

"Us." Cat smiled. "Yes, he does. He's known all along, or so he would have me believe."

Hunter's gaze broke from Cat's blue eyes and focused out the window. He stood, held out his hand, and then drew Cat to her feet.

"I am going to miss you, Alexander Veau," Cat whispered.

Hunter brought her hand to his lips. He kissed her palm, never looking away from her eyes, then folded her fingers over the kiss and touched his lips to her knuckles. "And I shall miss you, Catherine Kline. I look forward to your return."

Cat inclined her head and smiled at Hunter.

Hunter glanced out the window and muttered an oath. "Your brother is here already."

She nodded, looking down. "I will see you soon. Take care of yourself."

"I will," he murmured. "And you—"

Cat clasped his hand quickly, then turned and made her way across the lobby and out of the hotel doors.

Hunter followed to watch through the glass.

Sam stood beside the wagon as the bellhop secured their trunks for the journey. When Cat approached him, he helped her to her seat, then rounded the wagon and climbed up beside her.

Hunter stepped out the door and onto the wooden walkway as they pulled away. As he knew she would, Cat looked back and waved. Hunter lifted his hand and held it high until she turned away.

Hunter returned to his room and pulled his maps from his leather binder and his pendulum from its silk pouch. He opened his big map of America and laid it across the bed. The vial of blood had dried to a congealed sludge. He twisted the stopper into the glass and put it away. He had used the pendulum before without blood, and this vial had been contaminated from the start. The whispers in his head urged caution, but they had urged that from the moment he set eyes on Minister Tremble.

He held the pendulum in his hand and closed his eyes. His mind became calm, and his heart rate slowed. He let the arrowhead slide from his hand as he held tight to the rose quartz above the map. The instrument began to circle.

Seeress, show me again the location of those you spoke of in the prophecy.

The urgency of his quest built in his mind. He felt the pendulum change direction and opened his eyes. The pendulum swung in an oblong circle, wider on one side, as though forming a triangle. There were clearly three points, all east of Denver. The furthest point was this side of the Mississippi River.

Two are still moving this way.

Their positions were closer than they had been this morning.

He put away his maps and pendulum. He had already begun to sketch a street map of Denver to add to his portfolio. The sooner he found these individuals and warned them about the minister and his prophecy of a demon, the quicker he could turn his full attention to *Mademoiselle* Kline.

Chapter 24

Alyse James

—

Alyse and her uncles stepped from the train onto the wooden railway platform outside the Denver station. Underneath her sturdy boots, the rigid boards felt as though they moved with the familiar motion of the train.

A sensory illusion.

Alyse grinned and looked up at her uncles from beneath her bowler hat.

Bernard pointed toward the station. "Bay, wait beside the door with Alyse. I'll find our trunks." Bernard handed his brother his small bag and disappeared into the crowd along the platform.

Bayard took Alyse's arm and steered her to an empty place on the side of the building. "Did Amylia tell how we are to find her?"

Alyse nodded then became distracted by the crowd. A woman rushed away from the train, three children in tow, like a string of ducklings. A porter, pulling a low-wheeled cart, followed a lanky gentleman wearing a tall hat. Loud laughter behind her caused her to turn. At the corner of the station, several men with gun belts strapped to their hips and curved brim hats discussed last night's entertainment.

She pulled her attention from the loud men and concentrated on her uncle. "She showed me the house where she lived. There's a livery near her home where several of her horses are boarded."

Behind her uncle, a round man in a vest held the door for an elderly woman, whose overskirt and collar were trimmed with bright red pleated ruffles.

Too many people and distractions.

The clamor along the platform and the throng of anxious people assailed her senses. She closed her eyes for a moment to shut out the cacophony, then opened them and kept her gaze on Bayard's calm, familiar face. "Amy suggests we rent a wagon from the stable and use two of her horses for the trip to her ranch."

Bayard nodded, as he stood on his toes and looked down the platform. "Bern's coming."

A tall, young porter in a Union Pacific uniform pushed their luggage cart and followed Bernard.

Bernard looked from Bay to Alyse. "Where to?"

"Amy suggests we find transportation to the livery near her house on Pence Street." Alyse looked over her shoulder at the line of horse-drawn vehicles waiting for fares along the street.

"We'll need a wagon for the trunks," Bay commented.

"I see one." Bernard slipped around the gregarious men on the corner and hurried down the ramp toward the street.

"This way, then." Bayard nodded to the porter and took Alyse's elbow.

"I want to see the house," Alyse commented as Bayard helped her to the high buckboard seat.

After Bernard tipped the porter, he and Bayard climbed in the back and sat on their trunks.

The driver looked over his shoulder. "Where to, gentlemen?"

"The livery stable on Pence Street and Park Avenue," Alyse directed the driver. "Do you know it?"

The driver nodded, made a clicking sound with his tongue and directed the team away from the line of vehicles.

They encountered a considerable amount of construction and traffic along the main thoroughfare. Wagons with lumber, and groups of horsemen, slowed their progress.

Alyse found her attention returning time and again to the mountains. They had passed through mountains during their train ride west, but nothing compared to these.

Before long, the driver turned onto a diagonal street, and pulled to a stop beside the livery a few blocks down.

Bernard leaned forward from the back and paid the fare while Bayard jumped down to help Alyse descend from the seat.

Her uncles stacked their trunks next to the building, and Alyse stepped inside to speak with the stable master.

The stableman greeted her as an old friend. "This is a surprise, Mrs. Harris. I thought you'd left town with your husband." He paused and stared as Bay and Bern walked into the stable yard and stopped behind Alyse.

"I—um. Yes," Alyse improvised. "My husband traveled to the ranch, but I stayed to meet my uncles at the train." She paused, unsure how to proceed with introductions. Amy would have known the man's name.

The man put out his hand to Bayard. "Nice to meet you. I'm Clay Matthews."

"Bayard James, Mr. Matthews, and this is my brother Bernard."

"Call me Clay." He shook Bernard's hand then stepped back and turned his attention to Alyse.

"What can I do for you, Mrs. Harris? Are you ready to take your horses back to the ranch?"

"Only two." Alyse smiled and fidgeted with her skirt. Pretending to be Amy caused her stomach to knot. "And a buckboard for the luggage."

"That won't be a problem. You'll want your usual provisions for a two-day trip?"

"Yes, please." She pointed up the street. "We're going to check on something at the house. We shouldn't be long."

"I'll have the wagon tacked up by the time you get back." The stableman turned and pointed toward two boys who watched across the yard. "Hitch the Harris's brown and the dappled to the small wagon."

Alyse turned and paced out of the yard and onto the street. "We'll need to stop at the general store on the way out of town for items the livery may not provide," she reminded her uncles.

At the end of the first block, Alyse stopped. "Wait a moment. I need to catch my breath."

Bayard put his hands on his knees and nodded.

Bernard lifted his bowler and ran his sleeve over his bald head. "It's like there's no air."

Alyse nodded "It's very thin." A brief rest restored her, but they walked slower along the second block. She hadn't noticed while sitting on the train, but even a short walk proved the difference in the air.

By the time they stood in front of the red brick house with the 'H' on the door, Alyse's breath was labored and her heart beat fast.

Broken lumber and debris leaned against the side of the house. The recently rebuilt porch cover had yet to be painted.

Alyse pointed to the second-floor window. "Amy stood in the room upstairs when we *twyned*."

I saw the damage from inside, through Amy's eyes.

"Hello," a voice called from behind them.

Alyse turned and watched a man cross the street.

He must be a neighbor. Oh Goddess, he'll know I'm not Amy.

Alyse gripped her skirt with both hands and smiled a welcome.

The thin, balding man appeared surprised, but smiled and continued into the yard. "Miss Amy, I thought you left with Jason." The man looked from Alyse to the twins beside her and raised his eyebrow.

Make it a nosy neighbor.

She cleared her throat. "I did, but Jason dropped me off at a friend's house near the station. My uncles from Boston were due in today. I wanted to show them the new porch before we left for the ranch." Alyse smiled what she hoped was a confident expression. After days on a train, she knew she looked as bedraggled as she felt.

The neighbor turned to Bayard and put out an open hand. "Albert Fielding."

"Hello, Mr. Fielding. I'm Bayard James. This is my brother, Bernard."

"Mr. Fielding." Bernard and the neighbor shook hands.

"I had cousins that were twins. Never could tell them apart." Mr. Fielding chuckled. "Oh say, there was a federal marshal here just yesterday looking for your husband."

"Really?" Alyse raised her eyebrow. "Did he say what for?"

"No, not really." Mr. Fielding rubbed his chin. "Just wanted to ask Jason a few questions. I told him you were at the ranch."

Alyse nodded. "Perhaps I will see him tomorrow, then."

"I expect you will, if he headed that way." The neighbor took a step back. "Well, I've got to get back to my own projects now. Nice meeting you, gentlemen."

In the middle of the street, the neighbor turned back. "Oh, before I forget, tell Jason I have the painters coming tomorrow to paint the porch." He waved and continued toward his house.

Alyse raised her hand. "All right, Mr. Fielding. I'll let him know."

Bayard waved as well. "These westerners are kindly folk."

"Only because they think she's Amylia." Bernard countered.

"I'm not used to pretending to be someone else," Alyse confessed as they started back to the stable.

"There's nothing to it, really. People believe their eyes before anything else," Bay told Alyse as they walked. "These people don't even know your sister has a twin. It's much harder to convince people who suspect duplicity."

Alyse laughed. "You sound like you have plenty of experience tricking people."

The wagon was ready when they arrived. Alyse thanked Clay for loading their trunks onto the wagon.

"Have a safe trip, Mrs. Harris," Clay called as Bernard guided the team away from the livery.

Bayard stayed with the wagon while Alyse and Bernard hurried into the mercantile for supplies. They purchased a pot for heating water, a basket of fried chicken, several strips of salted beef and a bundle of firewood at the recommendation of the clerk. Firewood, the clerk explained, was difficult to come by heading east.

They decided to get as far as they could while the sun lasted. At sunset, they would camp and get an early start in the morning. With the directions embedded firmly in Alyse's mind, they headed east out of town toward the ranch and her sister.

Chapter 25

Sam Kline

—

Sam poured the remainder of the hot water on the coals and stepped back as steam and smoke rose into the morning sky. He cast a cautious glance at Cat.

She sat at the end of the wagon, legs tucked beneath her skirt, a blanket wrapped around her and a tin cup of hot water between her hands.

Her silence said more to him than her complaints would have. "Cat, I'm sorry I forgot you don't like coffee."

Cat's eyes flashed at him, then back to her cup. "It's not just about the coffee," she muttered into the cup, "How would you know what I like, anyway?"

Sam rested his hands on his hips and stared at his sister. "You could have slept by the fire if you were cold."

"On the dirt?" Her outraged glare scoured him with disbelief. "Have you lost your mind?"

Sam shrugged and turned to the horses to hide his smile. "You would have been warm, at least." He removed the horses' hobbles and led them to the front of the wagon. "We should get to the Harris Ranch by noon," he said as he passed the end of the wagon.

"Marvelous."

Sam's grin widened at his sister's tone. He turned his attention to harnessing the team and hitching them to the wagon. When he finished, he wiped his hands against his denim trousers and looked up.

Cat had taken her place on the seat. The blanket still wrapped around her back. Her hair brushed and plaited into a thick braid, which hung over one shoulder. She narrowed her eyes when their gazes met. "I would have liked more hot water."

Sam pulled on his gloves and climbed onto the seat beside her. "I should have asked before I poured it out. I'm sorry."

Cat lifted one shoulder. "Let's just go. The sooner we get there, the sooner we can get back to civilization."

***

Just before noon, they passed a recently abandoned ranch. Tumbleweeds blew across the yard and stacked against the bunkhouse. Sam's directions from Judge Anders mentioned The Shilo Ranch, but Sam understood The Shilo to be a working ranch. "A couple more hours and we'll be there."

"Will there be people?" Cat had shed her blanket hours ago, and now hid her fair skin beneath a parasol. She turned her gaze from the empty ranch and raised an eyebrow at her brother. "I hope they have beds."

Sam glanced at his sister. "Depending on what this Harris fellow has to say, we may not be asked to spend the night."

"You should have let me stay in Denver."

"I should have left you in N'Orleans."

He caught his sister's glare and gave one back.

Cat turned away, and they rode in silence.

After a while, Sam spotted a thin trail of smoke ahead. Soon, the house and outbuildings came into view. He turned the team off the main road and onto a drive that wound up a shallow rise to the yard. Several horses circled inside a large corral, and men worked in front of the big barn in the distance. "See Cat, there are people here."

She rolled her eyes. "Please, be nice, Sam. I'd like to sleep in a bed tonight."

Sam pulled the team to a stop in front of the house just as the front door opened.

A tall, dark-haired cowboy stepped onto the porch, a rifle held in the crook of his arm. He nodded to Sam and walked to the end of the porch near the wagon. "Hello, folks. Can I help you?"

Sam stared at the man. A vague sense of recognition assailed him, but he couldn't put a name to the face. There was something about the way he walked, and the way he wore his gun belt.

Maybe not just a cowboy then, but so damned familiar.

"Good afternoon." He set the wheel brake and tied the reins to the post beside the seat. "We're looking for the Harris Ranch. Specifically, for a Mr. Jason Harris. Might that be you, sir?"

When Sam spoke, the man on the porch stepped back and shook his head. "Well, I'll be damned." A smile transformed his face. "Sam Kline. I haven't seen you since Albuquerque. That had to be, what—eight years ago?" He leaned the rifle against the house and stepped down beside the wagon. "How the hell have you been?"

Sam froze when the cowboy said his name then recognition sparked, and a name fell into place. "Merril?" Sam dropped from the buckboard.

The men embraced and pounded each other on the back.

"What are you doing here?"

"Why do you want to see Jason?"

They spoke at the same time and laughed.

Sam stepped back and measured Merril with his gaze. "You've gained some height, kid. What are you doing at the Harris Ranch? Do you work here?"

"It's my wife's ranch." Merril chuckled and shook his head. "I can't believe it. I thought I'd seen the last of you when you rode out of Albuquerque." He gestured to the woman who watched from the doorway, and then waved for her to come outside.

The lovely blonde-haired woman crossed the porch with a cautious smile and nodded to Sam and Cat. She stepped from the porch and took Merril's hand.

"Sam, this is my wife, Nichole Shilo—formerly, Harris. The man you are asking for is her cousin. Nicki, this is Sam Kline, an old friend of mine from Albuquerque."

***

Nichole Harris-Shilo

—

Nichole smiled hello to the man beside her husband. He stood almost as tall as Merril, with light-colored hair and expressive blue-gray eyes.

He tipped his hat to her. "Pleased to meet you, Mrs. Shilo." His attention returned to Merril. "You're married? I remember you as a hotheaded kid who had just learned to shoot straight." Sam laughed again, then held out his arm toward the woman seated on the wagon. "This very patient young woman is my sister, Catherine. Cat, this is Merril Shilo, and his wife, Nichole."

The woman beneath the parasol smiled at her brother then nodded to Merril and Nichole. "I'm pleased to meet you both."

"Come inside." Nichole released Merril's hand and stepped onto the porch. "We're about to have lunch. It would be great if you would join us."

Sam stepped around the wagon and helped his sister down. "Thank you. Cat can join you while I see to the team."

"Nonsense." Merril picked up the rifle. "Our stablemen will see to your rig and horses." Merril raised his arm and waved toward the barn.

Tom and Lloyd waved back and headed their way.

Nichole stopped beside the doorway and waited for the young woman. "After you."

"Thank you." Cat gave Nichole a shy smile and stepped inside.

Once inside, Nichole spotted Lawna setting the table. "Lawna, would you set two more places, please? We have guests for lunch." Nichole smiled her thanks at Lawna, then looked with affection to Merril's animated face as he and his friend entered the house. She turned back to Catherine and tipped her head toward the stairs. "Come upstairs and you can wash off the dust before we eat. I'm familiar with the long ride from Denver."

"Yes, thank you." Cat rested her closed parasol on the entry table and followed Nichole up the stairs.

In her room, Nichole poured water into the bowl and pulled a clean wash-cloth from the drawer, then stepped aside.

"Thank you." Cat wet the cloth and applied it to her face with a sigh. "I was not prepared for how dry and dusty it is." She rinsed off her neck and then her face again.

"I know just what you mean." Nichole sat on the end of the bed while Cat washed. "So, I take it you're not from Colorado."

"No. We came up from N'Orleans by train." Cat picked up Nichole's hairbrush and gave her a questioning look. "May I? Mine's in the wagon."

"I don't mind," Nichole said with a smile. "How does your brother know Merril?" Nichole stared at Catherine's reflection in the mirror as she unbraided her long brown hair.

Cat's brown mane swung around her face and she tugged the brush through her tangled strands.

Nichole felt dizzy with *déjà vu*. Cat's rounded chin and almond-shaped eyes—Nichole had seen those reflected in a mirror before. The familiar stroke of a brush down fine, brown hair that snarled at the ends conjured a memory of the woman Nichole used to be. Nichole's posture stiffened as she put a hand over her heart. *Amazing.* She knew Cat's hair would glint like fire in the sunlight, just like Courtney's, only Cat's nose and the color of her eyes were different.

Who is Catherine Kline to me?

"I'm not sure how Sam knows your husband." Cat tugged at a tangle then set the brush on the vanity. "Sam certainly didn't expect to find him here." She lifted her hair and twisted it at the nape of her neck. She paused when her gaze caught Nichole's face in the mirror. "Is something amiss?"

Nichole shook her head. "No. Not at all. You just—seem very familiar to me."

Cat stopped twisting her hair and considered Nichole. "Have you ever been to N'Orleans?"

Nichole shook her head. "No, I haven't." She leaned forward, opened the drawer, and set several hairpins on the vanity for Cat to use.

"Thank you." Cat finished the twist and inserted a few hairpins. "Then I doubt we're acquainted. I've never been this far from home." Cat turned and smiled at Nichole. "I'm ready. Thank you for letting me freshen up."

"You are certainly welcome, Miss Kline."

"Please, call me Cat."

"Only if you call me Nichole. Mrs. Shilo is too new, and I won't know you are talking to me." Nichole instructed with a laugh over her shoulder as she left the room and started down the stairs.

"You're newly-wed?" Cat asked.

"Very new. We've been married less than a week."

"Oh my! Congratulations and best wishes. Your husband is certainly a handsome man."

"Thanks." Nichole smiled back at Cat. "I think so too."

As they descended the stairs, Nichole noticed Lawna had added the two place settings for lunch. Usually, five ate at the main house since Nichole had convinced Jim take his meals with the family. She had also insisted that Merril sit at the head of the table. As far as Nichole was concerned, the place belonged to either herself or Merril.

Jason and Amy had yet to return from their morning ride. Jim, Sam, and Merril stood at the far side of the table. Their lively conversation appeared to be about something Merril had done in Albuquerque while learning to shoot.

Cat and Nichole stopped at the base of the stairs and watched their men laugh together.

"It is good to see Merril enjoying himself," Nichole confided to Cat.

"Likewise, for my brother. He's been so reserved these last few years." Cat smiled at Nichole and tipped her head toward the men. "Sam opened up a bit with Hunter on the train, but nothing like this."

"Someone travels with you and your brother?" Nichole asked as Cookie entered the room with a tray of sliced ham, followed by young Katy carrying a bowl of mashed yams.

"Not really with us," Cat explained as they moved to the table. "Hunter and Sam are acquainted through Sam's work. Hunter's in Denver on his own business." Cat's eyes sparkled, and a blush rose on her cheeks. "I hope to see him again when we return to town."

"I see." Nichole smiled at the young woman's excitement.

She likes this Hunter.

Merril held his arm toward the women. "Miss Kline, I'd like to introduce you to our foreman, Jimmy Leigh. Jim, this is Sam's sister, Catherine Kline."

Cat stepped forward and took Jim's hand. "How do you do, Mr. Leigh?"

"Jim, please. Nice to meet you, Miss Kline."

"Please, call me Cat."

A burst of laughter preceded Jason and Amy through the kitchen doorway. They paused as they came into the dining room, and Amy pressed at the dampness on her skirt. "We have guests, Jason." She smiled and nodded to Sam and Cat.

Jason stepped around Amy and held out his hand to Sam. "This is a surprise. We rarely have guests. Jason Harris. It's nice to meet you."

Merril made the introductions as everyone took their seats. Jason laid the napkin across his lap and smiled across at Sam. "What brings you to The Highlands, Mr. Kline?"

"Thank you." Sam took a basket of rolls from Amy, set one on his plate and passed it to Cat. "Well, to be honest, you do."

"I do?" Jason chuckled and glanced toward Merril. "I don't understand."

"It's true." Sam looked around the table with an easy smile. "I admit my surprise when I found Merril at the front door. I didn't recognize him at first, and thought he might be you," Sam joked. "He's grown a foot in eight years."

"You're acquainted with Merril," Jason passed the bowl of yams to Amy, "but you're here to speak with me?" His face paled as he stared at Sam, and his voice lowered. "What is it you want?"

Sam rested both forearms on the table, his hands empty and open. "There's no need to discuss business during lunch, Mr. Harris." His voice was soft and calm. "A private word after we eat would be fine." Sam's gaze never left Jason's face.

"I've no secrets from my family, Mr. Kline." Jason took a sip of water, perspiration beaded his brow. "You can tell Otis I don't have his money." The glass trembled as he set it back on the table.

Nichole glanced between Jason and Sam Kline.

What the hell?

She turned to Jim and Merril, relieved they were aware of the tension down the table.

"I'm not here for money, Mr. Harris." The big blond man slid his chair back.

Jason rose and stepped back, knocking his chair to the floor.

As the crash of wood on wood reverberated through the dining room, all the men came to their feet.

"Please keep your hands where I can see them, Mr. Harris." Sam held one hand toward Jason, the other edged toward his holster.

Amy spun in her chair and looked up at her husband. "Jason, what's going on?"

Across the table, Cat gasped. "Oh my." Her attention not on the men but focused instead on the table.

Nichole followed Cat's gaze.

Oh my, indeed.

The water in Cat's glass spun, fast enough to create a vortex to the bottom of the glass. Nichole looked down the table. A tiny funnel descended in each water glass. She turned to Amy.

Is she doing this?

Amy looked only at Jason. She appeared unaware of the water's peculiar behavior.

"No, Jim," Merril stated.

Nichole turned to her right and looked up at her husband.

Merril had his hand on Jim's shoulder, and he gave Jim a small shake of his head. His green eyes flashed between Jason and Sam. "Is there a problem, gentlemen?"

"No. Not at all." Sam raised empty hands to Jason. "Mr. Harris has mistaken me for someone else." Sam opened his jacket and withdrew his wallet. "I'm a U.S. Marshal." He displayed his badge to Jason, then to Merril and Jim. "I'm not here on behalf of Otis Pierce or P&P, and I am not going to harm you or your family." He closed the wallet and replaced it in his jacket.

Jason picked up his chair, sat down, and rubbed his face with both hands. "I thought the worst."

The vortexes slowed until the water became still in each glass.

Cat's gaze rose from her glass to Nichole and her eyebrow arched. "Tell me you saw that," she whispered.

Nichole nodded and touched a finger to her lips.

"Mr. Harris, I'm here to investigate accusations of mismanagement, investment fraud, and other alleged crimes committed by P&P over the last few years." Sam turned from Jason to Merril. "And yes, before you ask, I was a marshal eight years ago."

"You didn't act like one." Merril's words were clipped and hard as he resumed his seat.

"I know." Sam nodded. "I couldn't tell anyone I was with the Marshal's office. I'd been assigned to keep watch on a group of men, local ranchers, southeast of Albuquerque around Lincoln County."

"You never said a word when you left. You just disappeared."

"I'm sorry for that." Sam sat and lowered his head. "I received word our parents had contracted yellow fever. I had to return to New Orleans to take care of my sister. Cat had just turned twelve." Sam glanced at Cat and then back to Merril. "After our parents passed, and Cat was placed in a boarding school, I went back to Albuquerque to find you, but you had already gone."

Merril pressed his lips and nodded. "After you left I wasn't sure what to do. I traveled northwest, into California, and helped with a gold mining operation for a couple of years. I even laid track for the Union Pacific for a time. Eventually, I headed back to Texas to find my family had moved to Colorado."

Nichole took Merril's hand and squeezed it.

Jason set his elbows on either side of his plate and leaned toward Sam. "You're investigating P&P and you believe I might have information about them and how they operate?"

Sam looked from Merril to Jason. "Yes, I do. I hoped to interview you and get specifics—dates, names, investments you were offered—and any overt pressure they applied to involve you in their activities." Sam picked up his fork and smiled at Jason. "But as I said, we can discuss all this after we eat."

Jason turned to Nichole and smiled. "In that case, could you pass the rolls, Nicki?"

***

After lunch, Jason and Sam disappeared into the office and closed the door.

Nichole and Amy took Cat on a tour of the house and garden. They walked partway down the rows of knee-high tomato plants.

Amy pointed around the garden. "The carrots are in, and the scallions. The green beans are just about ready."

Cat touched Amy's shoulder. "It's peaceful here, and your home is beautiful."

"Thank you." Amy smiled at Cat. "But the house and ranch belong to Nichole—or her new husband, I suppose." Amy's smile widened to a grin.

"I'm not sure Merril wants anything to do with the ranches right now. He keeps telling me 'I'm only a wrangler'." Nichole laughed, and her gaze settled on Cat.

She's so familiar.

"You should suggest to your brother to stay a few days. I know Merril would be pleased to spend time with Sam."

"I'll ask him." Cat nodded. "Even though I'd like to get back to Denver—" Color blossomed on the young woman's face. "A few nights in a bed would not go unappreciated."

"Good." Nichole grinned at Cat's blush. "I hope Sam agrees."

"One thing though—" Cat lowered her voice. "Do either of you know what made the water spin in the glasses?"

"What do you mean?" Amy looked from Cat to Nichole.

"I didn't think you noticed," Nichole said to Amy. "You had your attention on Jason."

"But you saw it." Cat turned to Nichole. "Have you ever seen anything like that?"

Nichole caught Amy's gaze. "When the men stood up and you reached out to Jason, the water in the glasses spun like a flushed toilet."

Amy's eyebrows rose to her hairline.

"Like a what?" Cat stepped closer to the women.

Nichole shook her head. "I meant, like a drain in the tub."

"Ah," Cat nodded. "Yes, it was like that, only you could see it through the glass."

Amy shook her head at Nichole, and cut her eyes toward Cat.

Nichole arched a brow at Amy, and smiled at Cat. "I heard tremors could cause water to spiral. Perhaps Jason's chair—"

"Hey!" At the back of the house, June McKay stood on the stoop at the back door. She waved a dishtowel above her head, and then balled the towel into her fist on her hip. She tapped her foot and glared across the yard.

Amy waved at June. "We'd best head back and see what she needs."

Near the house, Lawna played with Hope-Anne on a blanket beneath the raised tarp.

"Such a beautiful baby," Cat said to Lawna as they passed into the shade.

June glowered at Lawna then cut her gaze to Amy. "I need a moment to speak with you." Bitterness twisted her lips.

Nichole reached down and touched Lawna on the shoulder. "Would you mind escorting Miss Kline to the barn? She might enjoy seeing the puppies."

Lawna stood and lifted her daughter to her hip. "We would love to. Wouldn't we, baby girl?" She kissed Hope-Anne's neck and the baby giggled.

"Can I hold her?" Cat asked as the women walked away from the house.

Nichole turned to June, and her smile faded as she followed Amy to the house. How Amy lived with the bitter and resentful woman for a year in Denver boggled Nichole's mind.

Amy paused near the stoop smiled up at June. "What's the difficulty, June?"

"I would prefer our conversation be private." June sniffed and stared at Nichole.

"Certainly, June. Let's go to the music room." Amy included Nichole with a glance. "We won't be interrupted there."

June released a grunt with her sigh and disappeared through the kitchen.

Amy and Nichole followed her to the music room.

June waited beside the door for Amy and Nichole to enter, and then she closed the door and faced the two women. "As you know, I've been displeased with the situation at the Highlands since our return from Denver." June turned her shoulder to Nichole and addressed Amy.

Amy nodded. "Go on."

Nichole leaned her hip against the piano and rolled her eyes behind June's back.

"I made my feelings known to you when that loathsome family was allowed to live in the same house as decent folk. We both know the reason those—people—moved into this home." June paused in her tirade to glare at Nichole.

Nichole smiled at June and kept silent.

"The next thing I know, we take in those colored maids from the Shilo Ranch. I swear, she has elevated those people to the same place as white folk." June pointed a finger at Nichole.

"Anything else?" Nichole murmured.

"Just yesterday," June stabbed her finger into the palm of her hand, "Jeanne asked if I would bring down the sheets from the guest rooms so Lawna could wash them. She believed I would actually touch those filthy sheets. This type of expectation is beyond the pale." June threw her arms in the air.

"You're so full of crap." Nichole pushed away from the piano and faced June.

"I made my complaint to Amy." June pointed at Nichole. "I don't believe you've attained your rightful mind. You sleep with that Shilo boy and allowed him to take Mr. Jason's place in this household."

Nichole stepped forward. "No one cares what you believe, June. You've crossed one too many lines as far as I'm concerned. You no longer have a place in my household. Pack your things and move them to the bunkhouse. Arrangements will be made to take you to Kiowa Crossing or Denver at our earliest convenience."

"Your father hired me when he built this house." June's lips pulled back from her teeth. "You don't honestly intend to turn me out?"

"It is time you moved on, and yes, I do intend to turn you out." Nichole took another step forward and stood in front of the taller, older woman.

"I was Amy's companion for a year." June insisted.

"Add that to your *résumé*. You'll need it. In fact, you should ask Mrs. Harris to provide your reference. I would only be able to describe you as a bigoted old bitch who only wants her own way." Nichole shook her head as she watched June's face.

What an old hag!

"Well, I never!" June gasped.

"And now you have. We're done here. You have twenty minutes to pack your things and get them out of my house. Oh, and June, one last thing. If you bother anyone else with your nonsense, they'll send you back to me." Nichole indicated the closed door behind June. "Get moving."

June spun on her heel and yanked open the door. She stomped through the parlor and up the stairs.

Nichole and Amy listened to June march across the hallway upstairs, then the sound disappeared.

At least she didn't break anything. Yet.

"Do you think you may have been too harsh with June?" Amy asked.

"No." Nichole shook her head. "I don't have to put up with her hateful attitude. I don't trust her, and I won't have her around *decent* folk."

"It's your decision, of course." Amy leaned against the windowsill. "You no longer seem confused by conflicting memories."

"Oh, I still am." Nichole pointed to the photographs on the mantelpiece. "Although, I do know who they are now."

Amy looked at the photographs and smiled. "So, your memory has returned."

"Yes." Nichole crossed to the baby grand and touched the red oil lamp. "Both memories." She looked over her shoulder at Amy. "I still have two sets. Nichole's—" she turned and leaned against the piano "—and all the recollections from my other life. Courtney Veau's life."

Wide-eyed, Amy took a step forward. "A life before this one?"

"After." Nichole shrugged one shoulder. "Perspective is everything and explanations are hard." She crossed the room and took Amy's hand. "Let's just say I chose to return to this life. Courtney's life was in a future time."

Amy gripped Nichole's hand. "Why that... that's a miracle."

"It is." Nichole nodded. "But I won't lie. There are challenges. Merril says half the time he doesn't know what I'm talking about." She grinned at Amy. "Speaking of miracles, you did spin the water at lunch, right?"

Amy blushed. "I assume so. I knew Jason feared for our safety, and I—"

Nichole shook her head. "No explanations or excuses are necessary, dear friend. You have an amazing gift." She paused and grinned into Amy's frightened eyes. "Your sister will be here soon. There will be two beautiful and gifted women on my ranch. You have nothing to fear from anyone here."

"Yes. Of course, you're right." Amy blinked rapidly and nodded.

"You also told me you saw something else. Something evil."

Amy took a deep breath, closed her eyes. "Yes. It follows Alyse, or appeared to."

Nichole's voice softened. "You've no time left to deny who you are."

Chapter 26

Catherine Kline

—

Catherine carried Hope-Anne on her hip as she and Lawna crossed the yard to the corral. "She's beautiful." Cat passed the child back to her mother when they reached Merril and Jim beside the split rail.

Lawna smiled as the babe wrapped her chubby arms around her mother's neck. "Thank you. She can be a handful. Wave bye-bye, sweetheart, bye-bye."

Hope-Anne smiled at Cat, hid her face in her mother's shoulder, and stuck a thumb in her tiny mouth.

"She's still working at that." Lawna laughed. "And she's shy." Lawna pulled the thumb from her daughter's mouth and waved Hope-Anne's hand. "Say bye, Miss Cat. Bye, Mr. Merril. Bye, Mr. Jim."

Merril and Jim had turned from the corral to greet Cat. They waved at Lawna and the baby.

"What are they doing?" Cat leaned against the fence beside Merril and tipped her head toward the men in the enclosure.

"That's Tom and his father, Lloyd. They take care of our livestock. Jim ran across that wild filly this spring during roundup. She'd been separated from her herd, and Jim brought her home. Tom's been working to get her used to a halter and lead."

"She's a striking animal. Her mane is whiter than a wedding gown." Cat smiled as the horse shook its brown head. "She doesn't seem wild to me."

In the pen, the men saddled the mustang and tightened the girth. Tom led her around while Lloyd closed the gate and walked toward the onlookers.

"Tom has saddled her several times over the last week but hasn't mounted," Merril told Cat. He nodded hello to Lloyd.

"Tom thinks it's time to climb into the saddle." Jim chuckled. "We thought we'd watch the show."

"She's never been ridden?" Cat straightened her posture and held on to the fence. She'd never seen an untrained horse. In fact, she'd never considered the need to train one.

"Training takes time and small steps." Lloyd smiled and tipped his hat to Cat, then looked back at his son. "This is one of the last things they learn, to allow the weight of a rider."

In the corral, Tom put his foot in the stirrup and grasped the horn. He whispered to the horse, then swung his leg over the leather and settled into the saddle.

The mare gave several small bucks and twisted her neck. Her eyes bulged as she tried to see behind her.

"She might not be ready," Lloyd commented as she bucked again and twisted the other way.

"She's ready," Jim proclaimed.

Tom stayed in the saddle and talked to the horse with a soft, calm tone.

"What's he saying?" Cat glanced at Merril.

Merril chuckled. "Probably things a young lady shouldn't hear."

The horse settled down and took several easy steps. Tom continued to whisper and pat her neck.

Suddenly, Tom swore and slapped his neck. "Damn." He looked toward his father and yelled, "Wasp!"

"Get down!" Lloyd grabbed a blanket from the rail and ran toward the rider.

The mustang screamed and bucked hard, then jumped straight into the air and twisted.

"She's been stung," Merril muttered and slid between the rails into the corral.

"Get off her, son." Lloyd moved forward, then backed away from the frightened horse.

"I'm caught." Tom kicked at the stirrup then disappeared beneath the horse as she rolled. The mare came up and bounded away, without the rider.

Tom lay still on the ground.

Merril raced to Tom as Jim ran to help Lloyd catch the panicked animal.

Lloyd stood between his son and the horse's flailing hooves. He waved the blanket and yelled each time the frantic filly approached the man on the ground.

Jim grabbed the trailing reins and pulled the horse's head down to his chest. He held the halter tight and murmured softly. When the mare settled, Jim led the horse toward the corral gate.

Cat anticipated his need. She ran ahead, opened and held the gate as Jim led the horse out of the corral and into the barn. After Jim passed, she hurried to the men in the middle of the corral.

Tom lay on his back, his face ashen. His gaze remained fixed on his father's face.

Lloyd folded the blanket and placed it under Tom's head.

Merril ran his hand down Tom's arms and pressed his chest and stomach.

"It's my leg," Tom said through gritted teeth.

Cat's gaze involuntarily sprang to the young man's leg. A shudder crawled down her spine to her tailbone. Below his knee, his left leg turned at an unnatural and grotesque angle.

"I know about the leg." Merril and Lloyd shared a brief glance. "I'm looking for anything else you don't feel yet. Let me know if I touch something tender." He looked over his shoulder at Cat. "Miss Kline, would you find my wife and Amy? Tell them what's happened. We'll need their help."

With a quick nod, Cat rushed from the corral. She ran across the yard, up the step and in through the back door. She paused in the kitchen and stared at the cook.

"What's wrong, child?" The big woman wiped her hands on her apron.

"Where can I find Miss Nichole and Miss Amy? Mr. Shilo needs them outside."

The cook tipped her head toward the dining room. "They went through there just a bit ago. What's happened?"

"Thank you." Cat didn't pause to explain, but hurried down the short hall and into the dining room.

Amy and Nichole rounded the stairs and stopped when they saw Cat.

Cat took two quick breaths and pressed her hand to her chest. She could feel her heart race beneath her palm. "One of the men has been injured at the corral." She nodded at Nichole. "Your husband asked me to find you both. He said they need your help."

The two women exchanged glances, then rushed past Cat.

"Thank you," Nichole called back.

Cat followed them through the kitchen. In the yard, she lifted her skirt and ran to keep up with the women as they crossed the yard.

Nothing had changed at the corral except Jim had returned from the barn. Tom remained where he fell. His father knelt beside his head with Merril on the ground at Tom's side.

Amy hurried to Tom and knelt across from Merril. "Tell me what happened."

"A wasp stung both him and the wild filly just as she settled to the saddle." Merril nodded toward Tom. "He couldn't jump before she rolled."

"It's my leg," Tom said.

"Yes, it is." Amy ran a comforting hand down Tom's arm. "It doesn't look too bad from here. I'm going to take a closer look." She raised her head and her gaze touched Cat's for a moment, then locked to Nichole's.

Nichole gave Amy a single nod.

Amy blew a breath through her lips and looked back to Tom. "Here we go then, Mr. Baker. This won't hurt." She held her hands above his injured leg and closed her eyes.

Cat stood silent between Jim and Nichole. As she watched, a soft golden aura surrounded Amy's hands and extended around Tom's leg. Cat blinked, but the subtle glow, barely visible in the afternoon light, remained. "Do you—"

"Shh," Nichole whispered in Cat's ear. "Just watch."

Amy kept her eyes closed as she spoke, "Both bones are broken, but they're not through the skin." She moved one hand lower along Tom's leg to his foot, then back. Her other hand drifted to his stomach and paused. "There's no damage elsewhere—only the leg."

"I've been sayin' that," Tom said between clenched teeth.

"Hush, son." Lloyd laid his hand on Tom's forehead, his wide eyes on Amy.

Amy sat back on her heels. She exhaled sharply and rubbed her brow. When her head came up, determination shone in her eyes. Her gaze sought Merril. "I'll need two boards, the length of Tom's lower leg. They should be thin, but sturdy." Amy looked to Nichole as Merril rose and ran from the corral.

"I need my shears from the house and as much gauze padding as you can find. Ask Cookie where they are. Also, tell Jeanne to bring a bottle of the good whiskey, right away."

Next, her gaze found Lloyd and softened. "I need several soft leather strips we can soak to shrink tight around the boards and the leg. Bring a hard piece of leather for your son to bite down on."

Lloyd stared hard at Amy for a long moment, and then gave his son's shoulder a pat. "I'll be right back, Tom."

Amy turned to Jim. "I'll need you to straighten the leg. You'll have to pull his foot toward you until I say stop. We'll work together to align the bones as you ease his foot back into place."

Jim stepped forward and stopped as he stared into Amy's eyes.

"Do you trust me, Jim?" Her voice was soft.

Cat took a step closer to hear Jim's reply.

"With all my heart, Amy." Jim knelt by Tom's foot, his gaze pinned to Amy's face.

Tom's eyes had closed, and the color of his face had changed. He looked as though he might become sick with the pain.

Amy smoothed his hair back from his forehead. "Tom, if you are going to be sick, do it now. Once you start on the whiskey, it needs to stay in your stomach." Calm radiated from Amy as she stroked his hair. "Oh, and turn your head the other way if you get sick, please."

Tom chuckled despite the pain. He raised himself on his elbow, turned away from Amy and emptied his stomach.

Cat looked over as another cowboy ran into the corral and stopped beside her.

"Lloyd said I should come see if I can help." He spoke to Amy and Jim, then turned and tipped his hat to Cat. "Hello. My name's Kelly."

Cat gave the wrangler a quick nod. "Catherine Kline. Pleased to meet you."

Amy looked at Jim. "His boot and sock need to come off." She looked up at Kelly. "Can you hold Tom's leg still while Jim removes his boot?"

Kelly straddled Tom's legs, facing Jim. "Like this?"

"Yes. Hold him here." Amy indicated a point just above the top of the low boot, but beneath the fractured bone.

Kelly wrapped his hands around Tom's leg above the boot, and Tom hissed.

Jim took hold of the heel of the boot and the top of the foot and looked at Kelly. "You have him? Hold it tight. Don't let the leg move."

Kelly nodded, his gaze locked with Jim's.

In one smooth movement, Jim had the boot off, and then the sock.

Cat stepped back as Jeanne hurried into the corral with a full bottle of whiskey and a glass.

Beside her, Cookie carried linen and gauze.

Nichole followed with the shears.

Lloyd trotted back from the barn. "I've set up the camp bed in the barn. Settin' his leg might go a bit easier if we move Tom in there."

"I agree." Amy nodded and rose from her knees.

"You should bring the bed out here," Nichole commented. "Move Tom to it and then carry both back to the barn. It will be easier on his leg."

"She's right." Merril nodded and passed Lloyd on his way to retrieve the cot. When he returned, he placed it on the ground beside Tom.

The men lifted Tom while Amy raised his bare foot and moved with the men. Once Tom lay on the cot, the men carried him into the barn. They placed the cot in the center of the barn on its raised frame.

Cat followed the group and settled out of the way to watch. She couldn't take her eyes from Amy. The woman moved with an air of calm command.

Did I see the glow around her hands, or did I imagine it?

Amy directed Lloyd to place two hay bales at the foot of the bed. She asked the men to position Tom in such a way his feet rested on the bales rather than on the bed. Lloyd moved more hay bales to either side of the cot for Amy and Nichole.

Nichole sat beside Tom's head and took the glass of whiskey from Jeanne. "Now, we get you drunk."

Tom smiled weakly at Nichole and took the glass from her. "You should get a bucket, just in case I get sick again." Tom sipped from the glass.

Merril came in and set the thin boards aside. He stepped to head of the bed and looked down at Tom as he sipped the whiskey. "You're going to need to down the whole glass, and then another. That ain't sippin' whiskey."

Nichole stood, and Merril took her place beside Tom. He took the bottle from Jeanne and the glass from Nichole. "I am going to show you the medicinal application of whiskey."

Nichole said to Jeanne, "Get a bucket ready."

Jeanne nodded and disappeared into a stall, then returned with a bucket. She set it next to Merril's leg.

"Drink up." Merril encouraged.

Tom gulped the fiery liquid down, and then cringed as he handed the glass back to Merril. "I'm not much of a drinker," Tom confessed with a shiver.

Merril refilled the glass and gave it to Tom. "You'll learn. One thing though, you should never drink alone." Merril grinned. "That's what I'm here for." Merril clinked the bottle to the glass. "Here's to the ladies." He put the bottle to his lips and took a drink while he kept his gaze on Tom.

Cat looked from Merril to the other end of the cot and cringed.

Jim had split Tom's trouser leg to well above the knee, the break in the leg shown plain.

Amy's voice was softer, so she wouldn't distract Tom from Merril's antics. "Kelly, I want you to hold the leg like you did before, below the knee and above the break." Amy looked at Jim. "Hold the heel and the top of the foot and pull the foot back until the bones straighten. I'll tell you when to stop and how to turn the foot."

Jim nodded and dried his hands on his pants.

Amy looked around and spotted Lloyd. "Lloyd, would you bring the boards there, and the leather strips. Cookie, bring the gauze and linen closer. We'll need those first."

Amy raised her voice. "Merril?"

Merril looked up from entertaining Tom. His grin remained, but his eyes were sober and serious.

"It's time," Amy said to Merril. "Do you have the leather strap?"

"Yes, ma'am." Merril smiled at Tom as he took his glass away. "Enough whiskey. Let's try something else." He held up the leather strap. "Bite down on this when you need to."

Tom took the leather between his teeth and nodded to Merril. He let his head fall back and closed his eyes.

Merril gave Amy a nod to proceed.

Amy spoke to Jim, "Let's be quick. Kelly, hold his leg. Jim, get ready." Amy stood between the men and touched Tom's leg with both hands. She closed her eyes and took a deep breath and nodded. "All right, Jim. Pull."

The golden aura around her hands appeared brighter out of the sunlight. Cat heard the cook and the maid gasp, and watched Nichole hurry to them and speak softly.

"Kelly," Jim commanded. "Mind your task. Hold Tom's leg solid."

Kelly nodded and closed his eyes. He had both hands clasped below Tom's knee, his face so close to Tom's leg the perspiration on his forehead reflected the light beneath Amy's hands.

Jim had a hand under Tom's heel and the other on the top of his foot. He pulled the foot toward him slowly.

Tom cried out, and Merril braced his weight against Tom's shoulders and spoke in Tom's ear.

Amy's eyes remained closed. "You have a quarter inch to go before the bone can align. Steady. Ease it back." Her hands floated above Tom's leg inside the golden glow. "That's good, Jim. Just a bit more."

Cat had moved toward the end of the bed to watch the leg straighten under the aura of Amy's hands.

"Stop, Jim." Amy moved her hands to either side of Tom's leg. "Turn the top of the foot towards me—not too much. Slowly."

Sweat trickled down Jim's face, his gaze not on the leg, but on Amy's glowing profile.

Amy nodded. "There. The bones are aligned. Now, ease the foot back. Steady. A little more. Stop. Lloyd?" she called louder. "Would you move the hay from between Kelly and Jim? We need to get under the leg."

Cat watched Lloyd approach Amy with caution. His face as pale as his son's had been. He slid the bale straight back and out of the way. "Done," he said, and stepped back.

Eyes still closed, Amy spoke evenly. "Cookie? Wrap the gauze around the leg. Hold the linen on either side of the leg to cushion the board."

Cookie looked at Nichole, then back to Amy. "I'll have to put my hands in that light."

"It's all right, Cookie, the light won't burn you." Amy smiled, her head tipped back. "When I do this with my hands, I can see the bones in Tom's leg. I can tell how well Jim and Kelly have aligned them."

"I'll do it." Nichole said and reached for the gauze.

Cookie pulled the bandages to her chest. "No. I want to do it." She looked at Jeanne and tipped her head toward Amy. "Bring the linen."

Cookie and Jeanne stopped across from Amy. Cookie cringed when she made the first wrap, then looked at Jeanne, her eyes wide. "Well, I'll be." She finished wrapping the gauze with both hands while Jeanne waited with the linen.

Amy spoke as Cookie and Jeanne worked, "Lloyd, when she's done, put the boards on both sides of the leg, against the linen. Take a strip and wind it around the boards to hold them in place. Tie the splint together with the wet leather strips."

When Lloyd finished binding the splint, he pushed the hay bale back in place and Jim lowered the leg and released the foot.

Cat tore her gaze away from the splint and looked toward Tom and Merril. Tom looked as though he slept, but Cat suspected he lost consciousness when the screams ended.

Lloyd took the bottle from Merril, put the cork in it, and sat near the head of his son's bed.

Amy moved back and lowered her arms to her knees. The glow disappeared as she hung her head.

Jim put his arm around her shoulder and gripped her arm. "Do you need to sit down?"

Amy shook her head and looked up at Jim. Her eyes shone. "I'm good, Jim. Thank you."

Cookie gathered up the unused linens and gauze and picked up the discarded scissors. "If you're done with us, Miss Amy, we should get back to the house. You'll be wanting dinner, I expect."

"Yes. We're done. Thank you, Cookie. Thank you, Jeanne," Amy called as the two women walked out of the barn and turned toward the house.

Merril wrapped his arms around Nichole and kissed the top of her head. His gaze rose and stopped at Cat, who stood near the entrance. "Thank you for your help, Miss Kline."

"I did very little, Mr. Shilo. I've never seen a group of people work together more effectively. I found it impressive to watch." Cat fell in beside Nichole as they left the barn.

Jim and Amy followed, leaving Kelly and Lloyd to tend to Tom.

"Amy's a good leader," Merril said as he smiled back at Amy.

Amy shook her head.

"It's true. Whether you believe it or not. You gave clear, concise directions and kept a cool head under fire," Merril teased.

"Oh, go on with you." Amy laughed. "I only wish I could have done more."

"You will do more." Nichole grinned as Amy stepped beside her. She linked her arm with Amy's and leaned close. "Now that you're out of the broom closet."

Chapter 27

Alyse James

—

Alyse built up a padded seat for herself in the back of the buckboard with the blankets they had purchased on the train. She left the hard seat to her uncles. The sun had already begun to descend toward the mountains as they drove out of Denver. She knew they couldn't continue to travel after the sun set.

Two hours of dust and dirt covered Alyse's dress before the team slowed down.

Bay said over his shoulder, "Alyse, you should see this."

She came to her feet in the back of the wagon as she wiped the afternoon perspiration from her forehead. She put a hand on each of her uncles' shoulders to steady herself as the team inched forward. In the middle of the road, several yards ahead, sat two large black wolves.

"They found us." Alyse grinned and watched the wolves remain calm as the team approached. The horses ignored the animals as though they weren't there.

Bernard stopped the wagon less than ten feet from the animals.

Alyse climbed down and hurried to her familiars.

One stood and began to slowly wag her tail back and forth. The other lay down on the road and rolled onto its back. She looked up at Alyse, her tongue out of her mouth.

Alyse ignored Bernard's warning to be careful. She knew these creatures. She fell to her knees and hugged Anaïs, then reached down to scratch Sabine's chest.

Alyse heard footsteps behind her. She glanced up at Bayard.

"Why aren't they with Amy?" He knelt and scratched Sabine's neck.

"I don't know. Maybe they weren't comfortable, or maybe—"

Both animals pulled away and trotted several feet. When they stopped, they swung their heads back and looked at her and Bay.

"Maybe they thought we need their help more than Amy does," Bayard finished.

"Let's move on and find a place to camp," Bernard called from the wagon seat.

This time, Alyse sat between her uncles so she could watch her familiars. They trotted ahead, disappearing several times into the tall grass on either side of the road, only to reappear again ahead of the family's wagon.

The sun fell behind the mountains and left them in an odd twilight, the dust in the road turning purple-gray as the chill crept up her sleeves. In the sky above, the clouds still reflected the sun's light in a kaleidoscope of ever-changing colors. In the east, stars began to appear.

The decreasing visibility made it dangerous to continue. The wolves disappeared into the darkness ahead and could only be seen when they looked back, their eyes reflecting the golden glow still shining above the mountaintops.

"We need to find a place to stop," Bernard said again.

Both sets of glowing eyes turned back to them. The wolves had stopped. One stepped from the road while the other waited for the wagon. By the time Bernard halted the team, the second wolf had left the road.

Bayard jumped from the seat, crossed in front of the horses and followed the wolves into the growing darkness.

After several silent moments, movement alerted Alyse, and she pointed. "There he is."

Bayard walked toward them along the road and stopped beside Bernard. "There's a campsite nearby. I'll lead you in."

Bernard nodded and relaxed the reins.

Bayard took hold of the bridging strap between the horses. He led them several paces before he left the road. They moved down a small incline, then turned and stopped on level ground.

Alyse blinked, but all light had gone—and the air smelled suddenly of mud and wet stone. A slow stream made soft noise nearby, and when she looked up she could see stars.

Surefooted despite the darkness, Bayard gathered firewood from the back of the wagon and crossed the campsite.

Alyse heard him stack the wood a couple of yards to her right.

"How can you see?" Bernard called.

"I can't. It wasn't this dark when the familiars brought me here. There is a fire pit in the center. Be patient and I'll get a fire started," Bay replied.

"I didn't think to purchase a lantern," Alyse commented as Bay struck a match and held it to the firewood. It glimmered for a moment then went out.

"You were never any good at starting fires," Bern commented.

"Then get down here and try," Bay responded.

Alyse found herself alone on the wagon seat as she listened to her uncles argue about how best to start a fire.

"Just use your *fire-skill*." Alyse called to them in the darkness.

They were both silent for a moment.

"We need fire to manipulate fire. It isn't something we just create. You know that." Bernard sounded frustrated.

Alyse grinned. "You have matches. I don't understand the problem."

"If you think you can start this fire, then come down here and do so," Bernard retorted.

"She's trying to help," Bay told his brother.

She couldn't see them, but the tone of their voices painted such a clear picture of their familiar faces and postures—she covered her mouth to stifle a laugh. She cleared her throat. "I can do it from here." Alyse bit down on a giggle. "Strike a match and stand away from the fire pit." In the silence that followed, she heard Anaïs and Sabine pad away from the pit.

"Are you ready?" Bay's voice.

"I am." She heard the scratch and hiss of the match, and then she could see Bay's hand holding the small flame. Alyse put out her hand, and a portion of the flame jumped from the match-head to her hand. The tiny flame was warm and bright before her face—obedient, like a trained hawk perched on her palm.

Bay lowered his match to the pile of wood in the pit.

"I see it. Step back." When Bay dropped the match and moved back, she tossed the flame from her hand toward the stack of wood. As it moved, she fed it air from all sides. The flame grew when it left her hand and sailed across the camp. The fireball ignited the wood with a whoosh as it landed in the pit.

"Oh, good job!" Bay watched the fire grow as she continued to feed it air.

"Not too big," Bernard cautioned.

Immediately, the tower of fire dropped to a small steady campfire.

"Now you're just showing off." Bay grinned at her.

Bern shook his head as he unhitched the team and walked them down to the water. When Bern brought the horses back, he hobbled them, and Bayard put their feedbags on.

Alyse brought the basket of food to the fire and sat on a large stone near the pit. She handed sandwiches and apples to her uncles. The fire crackled as she ate and listened to her uncles talk about tomorrow. When she finished her sandwich, she brought her blanket near the fire and pillowed her head on her arm.

Anaïs and Sabine lay down beside her, one behind her back and one by her thighs, just like when they were cats. She scratched them deep through their thick fur.

Her uncles' conversation turned to how they would begin training Amy, and how Amy's people might react to their skills.

When Alyse opened her eyes again, the sky was the soft gray color of impending dawn. She curled her feet and arms into the warm fur of the two wolves. Positioned on either side of her, they kept the chill away.

Embers from their fire had reduced to ash. She could see her uncles huddled under their blankets in the morning chill. They had burned all the wood last night, and although she could take a flame from the matches, she knew it would be short lived without a fuel source. Using her own energy to sustain the flame would tax her strength.

Instead, she pushed Anaïs off her blanket and got up. She walked along the stream to a few denser bushes and took care of some pressing business. When she returned to the camp, both of her uncles were awake.

Bay shook out and folded his blanket, and then picked up the campsite.

Bernard walked the horses down to the stream to drink their fill before he hitched them to the wagon.

Both the wolves had disappeared.

"Where did Anaïs and Sabine go?" she asked Bayard as she shook and folded her covering.

"Dunno." Bay took her blanket on his way to the wagon. "I thought they were with you."

In short order, the three travelers were back on the road heading east. The early chill fled as soon as the sun rose in the sky, and by mid-morning they shed their greatcoats. Alyse continued to look for her familiars, but they never appeared.

They passed an abandoned ranch before noon.

"Is that the ranch?" Bernard asked.

Alyse shook her head. It didn't look as though anyone had been there for several days.

The road swung east of the ranch, turned north and began a slow incline. About an hour later, another house came into view.

"Is this it, Alyse?" Bay pointed to the ranch house ahead of them.

Anaïs and Sabine trotted into the road from either side and preceded the family toward the turnoff to the drive.

Bernard followed the wolves up the drive and slowed the team to an easy stop just before they reached the yard.

The wolves trotted forward a few more feet then stopped and sat.

There were several horses in the pen. An older man brushed one of them down. When he caught sight of their wagon, he called across the yard to someone beyond the side of the house.

A tall cowboy rounded the back of the house. He waved to the old man in the corral and headed toward the wagon. He paused for a moment when he spotted the wolves, and then his gaze lifted to the people in the wagon and settled on Alyse. He walked between the animals who turned their heads to watch his progress, but otherwise remained still. At the front of the wagon, he stopped and regarded Alyse.

"I've seen your wolves before." He lifted his hands and touched both horses. They bumped his hands in recognition. "And I recognize our horseflesh." He patted their necks and returned his gaze to Alyse. "I would, however, doubt my own eyes when it comes to you, miss."

Alyse caught her breath. His brown eyes were somehow both ancient and familiar. Her palms went damp on her skirt. She shook her head once and realized her lips had parted. She clamped her teeth together and sucked air in through her nose, but she couldn't tear her gaze from his.

"I've never seen her at a loss for words, have you, Bern?" Bay chuckled.

Bernard didn't answer. Instead, he spoke to the giant of a man before him. "We're looking for my niece, Amy Harris."

A shadow of a smile crossed the man's face as he scratched the horse's ears. "I could have guessed that. My name's Jimmy Leigh," he said to Alyse. "I'm the foreman for The Harris-Highlands. If I know Amy, she's been expecting you."

Another cowboy hurried across the yard to the wagon. He stopped short when he saw the wolves.

"They won't hurt you," Bayard called to the cowboy.

Alyse snapped her fingers, and the wolves looked at her. "Anaïs. Sabine. Let him pass."

The animals stood and padded past the wagon and continued down the drive toward the road.

The cowboy watched them trot away as he approached the wagon and reached for the bridging strap. "Those wolves are just unnatural." He tipped his hat to Alyse. "Ma'am."

Bay and Bern climbed down from the wagon.

Alyse gave her hand to Bay, and he helped her down. As soon as she set foot on the ground her head came up, and she turned toward the porch.

Amy opened the front door. She wore a bright yellow day dress with satin insets and matching shoes. Her auburn hair was pinned in a loose bun, like their mother's.

Alyse's hair hung in two dusty braids, her sturdy, dark blue farm dress, stained and worn from a week of traveling. Her shoes were low-heeled work boots, and on her head, she wore a man's bowler hat.

We are as different as night and day, and yet, we're identical.

Alyse left Bay's side and stepped onto the porch.

Amy caught her breath. Her hand trembled as it rose to her mouth. Tears filled her eyes and slid down her cheeks. "I didn't think you were real until I saw you on the train." Her voice shook, and she covered her mouth with both hands to silence a sob.

"Amy," Alyse said with a tearful smile. "Sister." Her throat closed with emotion.

"Alyse," Amy replied and opened her arms.

The sisters fell into each other's embrace.

The sound of boots approaching across the wooden porch drew them apart.

Alyse looked down, her hands still on Amy's shoulders. "I've gotten dust on your pretty dress."

"It's just a dress." Amy shook her head as their gazes met again. "It's almost like looking in the mirror in my mind, only now, instead of seeing a reflection of me, I see you."

"Is that what you see when we *twyne*—a mirror?"

Amy nodded. "You don't?"

"Not always. The first time, when you were in the box—I saw through your eyes."

Amy's brows rose, and she shook her head.

Jason came out the door and stopped behind Amy. His eyes widened as he stared at Alyse.

"I saw him, too." Alyse nodded to Jason. "When he pulled you from the box."

Amy stepped back. "Jason, this is my sister, Alyse Prescott. Alyse, my husband, Jason Harris."

Alyse held out her hand. "Alyse James, and it's nice to finally meet you." She glanced at Amy and saw her blush, and a grin crept across Alyse's face.

Bayard held out his hand to Jason. "I'm Bayard James, their uncle." He looked at Amy. "You can call me Uncle Bay." He dropped Jason's hand and swept Amy into a hug. "I never met, Amylia. I was gone with Alyse before you were born." He stepped back and pointed at his approaching brother. "Your Uncle Bernard now, you might remember him." Bayard grinned and winked at Amy. "He stayed with your Mum until you were born, and then came to the farm with your grandmother."

Bernard hopped the step and stood beside his brother. "Bernard James." He shook Jason's hand and turned to Amy. "My brother thinks he's quite funny. Hello, sweetheart." He gave Amy a gentle hug.

Jason looked between the brothers, then turned and looked at Amy and Alyse. "Two sets of identical twins." He raised an eyebrow at Bernard. "What are the chances?"

"At least once each generation, or so it seems. Best prepare yourself." Bay winked at Jason and grinned at Amy.

Jim followed Bernard onto the porch. "Kelly will see to your team. We'll work out a sleeping arrangement and move your trunks later."

"Please, come in," Amy motioned to the crowd on the porch. She took Alyse's hand and drew her into the house.

Inside, Alyse tried not to gawk at Amy's home. The polished staircase and fine furnishings in this house made her home seem rustic and worn by comparison. Although her uncles crafted this quality of furnishings, she would never have such things for herself. Voices from beyond the dining room caught her attention. A petite blonde woman gave instructions to another, before lifting her head and turning toward the entry.

"She must be your husband's sister," Alyse guessed. "Their resemblance is striking."

Amy shook her head. "Nichole is my cousin by marriage. You don't recognize her?"

Alyse watched the woman approach, crystal blue eyes above a warm smile. "No. Should I?" She glanced at Amy.

Amy whispered, "We healed her—well, you did."

"Welcome. Please, come in. I've asked Jeanne to bring refreshments." Nichole paused and looked between the sisters, delight in her eyes. "I'm Nichole." She held out her hand to Alyse.

Alyse took Nichole's hand.

She'd had no heartbeat, no breath of life. Beaten so badly, she'd been unrecognizable.

"Alyse James. I'm pleased to meet you."

Nichole tipped her head to Alyse, grinned at Amy, and then introduced herself to Bay and Bern.

"There are refreshments on the table, please, come inside and have a seat." Nichole ushered her guests into the dining room. "My husband has taken his guests on a tour of the ranches, but they will be back before supper."

Jim circled the table and stopped beside Nichole. "Have you thought about where Amy's family will sleep?" He poured a glass of water and offered it to Alyse, then poured two more and pushed them down the table toward the brothers. "The only empty beds at The Highlands are in the bunkhouse."

Nichole looked from Jim to Amy. "No. The bunkhouse won't do. June is at one end, and Bill and Kelly on the other."

"What about—The Shilo?" Amy offered tentatively.

Nichole raised her brows. "Not a bad idea. Let's discuss it with Merril at dinner. It's up to him, but I don't see why he would mind."

"Would this be the abandoned ranch we passed on the way here?" Bernard asked.

"Yes, it is," Nichole replied. "It's been empty a little over a week. In fact, everything you would need is still there—beds, bedding, linens—"

"You need to tell them why the ranch is deserted," Jason interrupted. "They may not want to sleep there."

"Why was it abandoned?" Bay asked.

Nichole exchanged a brief glance with Jason, then turned to Bayard. "The Shilo is my husband's ranch. Over the last few weeks, there have been three tragic deaths there."

"Horrific deaths, not caused by accidents." Jason looked from Nichole to Bayard. "Two were murders, and one a suicide."

"My goodness, that's awful," Alyse murmured. "Were they close to you?"

"Yes. My husband's family," Nichole explained. "His father, his brother, and his father's companion."

Alyse drew breath between her teeth and faced Nichole. "I am so sorry."

"Our condolences, also." Bernard exchanged glances with his brother and Alyse. "However, the deaths at your ranch wouldn't be an impediment to our staying there."

"Bern's right." Bayard nodded. "In fact, we would be happy to cleanse the house of any negativity that remains."

"You can do that?" Jason folded his arms and arched an eyebrow.

"Of course." Bay lifted his shoulders. "You should cleanse any house you move into, especially if you didn't build the home yourself. It's a wise precaution and allows you to begin well in your new abode."

"Huh." Jason rubbed his hand across his mouth and looked at the brothers.

"Alyse, would you like to bathe and change before dinner?" Amy asked.

"That sounds heavenly." Alyse grinned. "I'll need to get a few things from my trunk."

"You won't need a thing." Amy assured her. "I guarantee we wear the same size."

"Why don't I give your uncles a tour of the outbuildings." Jim offered. "I could show them around a bit before dinner."

"That sounds good." Bay smiled at Jim. "After dinner, we'll have plenty to discuss."

Chapter 28

Nichole Harris-Shilo

—

Nichole pulled a hairpin from her mouth and pushed it beneath the loose bun atop Alyse's head. "There. That should hold." She stood back and looked from Alyse's reflection in the mirror to Amy, who sat perched on the end of the bed. "Okay, yes." Nichole's grin grew wider, and she took a step back. "This is an excellent idea."

Jeanne moved away from Amy and shook her head. "You look so much alike." Her glance darted from one twin to the other. "Wait, you'll need gloves." She spun around and opened Nichole's dresser drawer.

Both Amy and Alyse lifted their hands, looked at their nails, and turned to Nichole with identical expressions of confusion.

Overcome with laughter, Nichole leaned against the wardrobe. "Oh my gosh. I want a twin."

"They'll know us when we talk," Alyse observed.

"True. You'll need to keep quiet." Nichole looked between the two sisters. "And remember to look at Jason like he's the brightest star in your sky." She put her hands to her heart and batted her eyelashes at the ceiling.

Amy laughed. "I don't do that."

"Yes, you do." Jeanne smiled over her shoulder. "You always have." She handed Amy and Alyse gloves that matched their dresses. "And Jason looks at you the very same way." Jeanne stepped to the door. "I'd best get downstairs and help Cookie."

"Thanks for your help." Nichole closed the door and leaned her back against it. "Jeanne's afraid to touch you," Nichole whispered and tipped her head at Amy.

"I noticed." Amy shrugged her shoulders. "But she stayed in the same room with me, and that's a start."

"Why?" Alyse rose from the chair. "What happened?"

Amy stood and straightened her dress. "I... displayed a skill the other night. Jeanne—along with a few others were—somewhat startled."

"Somewhat?" Nichole snickered as she opened the door. "Yeah, I'd say they were a bit startled." As soon as she stepped into the hallway, she heard voices from downstairs. "Merril's home." She glanced back at Amy and her twin.

Unless they give it away, no one will be able to tell them apart.

"Let's go." She rounded the banister and hurried down the stairs.

Her glance caught Merril's immediately. She bit her lip to silence a giggle as she hurried to his side.

Merril tucked her under his arm and kissed the top of her head. "Were you having fun?"

"Oh, yes." She smiled up at her husband. "I can't wait 'til you see them."

"You know what's coming, don't you?" Bayard spoke to the room, but glanced at Bern and grinned.

Bernard looked at his brother out of the corner of his eye and heaved a sigh. "Of course, I do."

"What? What are they up to?" Jason turned as the swish of material and light footsteps descended the stair behind him. He stared at the women, dressed in his wife's clothes, their hair styled into the loose bun Amy always wore.

The twins stopped at the bottom of the stairs and faced their audience. One wore a dark blue skirt and matching jacket, and the other a soft green dress.

"The challenge," Bayard told the dinner party, "is to determine which twin is which. It's a game Bern and I played as children." He set his glass on the table. "We learned to imitate each other's mannerisms in order to fool our friends." He smiled at his nieces and received two affectionate smiles back. "Oh, this will be difficult." He rested his chin on his hand as his gaze darted back and forth between the women. "Remarkable, ladies. Well done." He clapped his hands.

Nichole giggled and turned her head into Merril's shoulder.

"Can you tell them apart?" Merril asked.

"Yes, so I can't play." She caught Jason's desperate look and dissolved into laughter. "And I can't help. I promised."

"This is far better than charades." Cat nudged her brother.

Cookie stepped into the dining room and stared opened-mouthed at the two women. "Oh my stars," she declared. "Dinner's about ready." She turned and left the room, shaking her head.

Bay and Bern strolled to their nieces and looked them over. They walked around the women, and then returned to the group by the table.

"I can't tell," Bayard confessed to his nieces with a shrug. He looked at his brother.

Bern pressed his lips. "I think I know."

Bayard arched an eyebrow at Bernard. "In truth, you can tell? No guessing allowed."

Bernard crossed his arms. "Oh, all right. I cannot."

Bay looked to Jason, and his smile grew wider. "The pressure is on you, old man." He nodded to his nieces. "Can you tell which one's your wife?"

"I will in a moment," Jason boasted. He approached the women and walked around them, looking them up and down. He stopped in front of them and studied their faces.

Both women looked at Jason with such exaggerated affection, everyone in the room laughed.

Jason chuckled. "This, I could get used to." He tapped one finger against his lips and looked between the women. "You've hidden your hands, so no rings will give you away, and you're not talking."

"I suggested they not speak," Nichole told the group. "Their accents will give them away. Therefore, this is a visual game only." She began to hum a timing tune from a television game show.

"I have to say, this is remarkable." Jason held a hand toward each woman. "I can't tell you apart. You both look like Amy."

"Let me help you out, Jason." Jim pushed away from the wall and approached the twins. He crooked his arm to the woman in dark blue. "Would you join me for dinner, Miss James?"

Alyse's eyebrows rose and her face flushed as she took his arm. "Thank you, yes." She nodded to Jason and followed Jim to the table.

"And we have a winner!" Nichole clapped as Jim seated Alyse.

"How did you know?" Jason looked dumbfounded at Jim. "How could you tell them apart?"

"I can't say." Jim grinned at Jason and took his seat. "It would spoil their game the next time."

"Next time?" Jason looked concerned when Amy took his arm.

"Twins never get tired of this game." Bayard sat at the far end of the table from Nichole and Merril. "You'll tire of it long before they will."

Once everyone found a seat, Cookie, Jeanne and Lawna served roast pork loin with onions, mashed potatoes with gravy and new carrots from Henny's garden.

Conversation took second place to Cookie's delicious dinner, but as the meal wound down, Nichole broached the subject of opening The Shilo to their guests.

"I don't see why not." Merril nodded to Nichole and looked down the table to the James family. "The house has been cleaned and is only collecting dust." His gaze found Bernard. "As long as you don't mind its recent history."

"Your wife told us." Bernard bowed his head for a moment. "I'm sorry for your loss." He looked to his brother and niece. "But that won't be an issue for us. In fact, cleansing the negative energy would give us an opportunity to work together."

"Staying there would put us out from underfoot while we train Amy and Alyse." Bay gestured toward his nieces with his fork, and then speared another piece of meat.

"Train?" Jason looked around the table. "Am I the only one confused? What training?"

"I told you what I saw coming." Amy looked at Jason.

"You had a vision?" Alyse sat forward, across from her sister. "What did you see?"

Amy pressed her lips and glanced around the table. "Animals—running west as though possessed. They were a day, perhaps two, behind your train."

"That close?" Bay fell back in his chair and glanced between his nieces. "That won't give you much time."

Cat sat up straight, eyes wide, and pointed between Amy and Bernard. "You're the witches Hunter is looking for."

Sam began to cough. He sipped water as he stared at his sister. "How do you know this? What did Hunter tell you?"

Cat shrugged one shoulder. "He told me nothing. I heard the two of you talk on the train." She straightened her napkin.

"You were supposed to be asleep." Sam took another sip of water.

Cat rolled her eyes at her brother and looked to Alyse. "It's true though, you're witches?"

"Wait." Jason glared at Cat and Sam. "Who is this Hunter, and who are you calling a witch?"

Bayard cleared his throat. "I prefer the phrase 'elementally skilled', but 'witch' is the more common term."

Jason's mouth dropped open, and his eyebrows rose as he stared at Bayard. He looked across the table to Cat and Sam. "The idea of a witch doesn't bother you?"

Cat grinned. "We're from N'Orleans, Mr. Harris. Voodoo queens and magic are not as uncommon there." She rubbed her hands together and looked around the table. "I find this all very exciting." Cat turned to Sam. "Although, I do wonder when Hunter will arrive?"

Sam wiped his mouth with his napkin and set it alongside his plate. "Hunter is exceptional at locating people," Sam replied to his sister. "I would think no more than a few days."

"If what Amy's family believes is true, there's a demon on the way. You should consider returning to Denver immediately," Merril spoke to Sam and Cat. "You would be safer."

Cat shook her head.

Sam leaned back in his seat and smiled at Merril. "Unless you turn us out, we'll stay. If there's an actual demon on the loose, this may be the safest place to be." He tipped his head at Alyse and her uncles.

"There's a lot to accomplish in a very short period," Bernard told the gathering. "We need to ward both ranches—houses and barns. The ward will shield the people and animals inside."

"More importantly, Alyse is already trained in her abilities. Amy is not." Bernard took a sip of water and looked between Amy and Alyse. "You'll need to practice working together. Your abilities are split oddly between you." He glanced at Bayard. "Our instruction may not suffice for their peculiar challenge." He turned to Alyse. "Your *twyne* with Amy will be much different than between Bay and myself."

"What the hell are you talking about? Has everyone lost their minds?" Jason's face had darkened, and his brow furrowed as he stared at Bernard. "My wife has no such abilities."

"She made the water spin in our water glasses yesterday." Nichole grinned at Jason.

"She helped set Tom's leg last night." Jim looked straight at Jason.

"You healed by yourself?" Alyse looked across the table at her sister, her eyes wide.

Amy shook her head. "No. I guided Jim and Kelly to align the break. Tom will need a splint until the bone knits."

Jason threw down his napkin on the table. "This is absurd."

Alyse raised her brow at Jason. "Why absurd? I understand our skills are beyond your experience, but that doesn't make them any less real."

"I don't believe you—any of you—possess magic," Jason spoke to Alyse, then turned his gaze to the brothers, and ended at his wife. "I would know if you did."

"Jason," Alyse spoke in a sharp tone.

His scalding gaze jumped to hers.

She leaned toward him. "I don't grant wishes. I don't put spells on people or spin straw into gold." She looked up and down the table and met every eye. "If that's the magic you're thinking of, then I don't believe in it, either." Her gaze returned to Jason. "I can only tell you the truth. There is an evil being—a demon—on his way here to kill your wife." She pointed at Amy. "She has seen this demon advancing toward us in a vision."

Jason's high color had fled. He glanced to his wife by his side, and then back to her mirror image across the table.

Alyse pointed her finger at Jason. "I promise you, I have abilities that may save her life. She has abilities—skills she's never learned to use—that could save mine." She rose slightly in her seat and lowered her voice. "You don't have to take my word on faith, dear brother." She arched an eyebrow. "I'll be happy to prove my skill." Alyse lifted her hand, drawing everyone's attention as she uncurled her fingers.

As one, the gathering around the table leaned forward.

"Viens à moi, feu!" she commanded and raised her palm.

The group drew back as a tiny flare jumped from the wall lamp to dance along her palm. A collective gasp filled the room when the flame grew higher, its color evolved from a warm yellow tone to a sharp emerald hue. The fire floated just above the soft white skin of her hand. Her small display of magic held the room spellbound, as the flame danced before her face.

"That is so cool," Nichole breathed, her eyes on Alyse's flame.

Alyse smiled at Nichole, and in one swift movement, she crushed the flame with her fist. "My grandmother trained me." Alyse gestured to her uncles. "Trained us to fight using our skills. Both she, and my uncles, had to create offensive spells on their own. No coven would help us, or accept what we had to do." Her voice lowered and she stared hard at Jason. "The Prophecy of the Twins has come to pass, and we will stand or fall as a family."

Nichole's breath caught, and she swallowed. "You're like—battlemages." *Holy shit.*

Bayard leaned forward and grinned at Nichole. "Battlemages? That sounds much better than elemental manipulator."

"Tell me about this prophecy." Jason glanced at his wife's pale face, then at Alyse.

"I only learned of it myself after Amy and I *twyned.*" She cleared her throat and closed her eyes. "You will know them by their birth—crowned beneath a full moon on the witches' High Sabbat. Their *twyne* shall wake the Demon. By Fire and Earth, he shall be felled—lest the *twyne* fail—then death shall reign."

After a moment of silence, Bernard spoke, "Training will begin in the morning. While I work with the women at The Shilo, Bay can ward the buildings here. We'll ward The Shilo after the people here are sheltered."

"What can we do to help?" Merril took Nichole's hand.

"There's plenty to do." Bay looked toward Merril. "The first step will be to assemble supplies to make defensive wards. I'll make a list of what we need."

"If you give me the list tonight, I'll gather what we have," Amy told Bayard.

Jason rose from the table and retrieved pencil and paper from the office. He handed them to Bayard.

"Thank you." Bayard gave Jason a nod and began to make a list.

Merril addressed Alyse and Bernard. "For tonight, I'll take you back to The Shilo before it gets too dark."

As dinner broke up, several conversations sprang up. Bernard and Bayard worked on the list. Amy talked with Cat and Sam about Hunter.

Merril turned to Jim. "Have Kelly move their trunks to our small wagon and harness a team." Merril stood and looked down at Nichole. "I want June out of here first thing in the morning, before preparations begin in earnest. I asked Timothy to accompany June to Denver and exchange the livery horses for ours. Instead of putting June in a saddle, she can ride in their wagon. She should be pleased with that."

"You shouldn't ask Timothy to be around June," Nichole replied. "Ask Kelly or Bill."

"With Tom laid up, Lloyd will need help with the livestock and taking care of Tom." Merril shrugged. "The only hand with time to take June to Denver is Timothy."

"Poor Timothy." Nichole set her napkin on the table. "How will he stand it?"

"I asked him that same question," Merril replied. "He told me June reminds him of his mother."

"That poor kid," Nichole muttered as she came to her feet.

Alyse turned to her uncles. "Before we go, I need to get a package out of my trunk for Amy." She smiled at her sister. "It's a present for you from our grandmother."

Chapter 29

Amy Harris

—

Amy glanced over Bayard's list, and slipped it into her pocket. Most of the ingredients could be gathered tonight.

Bay turned to Merril. "Did I hear correctly? One of your cattlemen has a broken leg?"

Merril nodded. "Yes. But the bone's been set."

Bay turned to his brother. "Why don't we have the girls *twyne* tonight?"

Bern shrugged. "I don't see why not." He looked at Merril. "As long as you don't mind." He tipped his head toward Amy. "Are you willing?"

Amy cast a quick glance at Jason. He had become so silent.

What is he thinking?

Bay took Amy by the hand. "Come along, niece, we're going to try something." He glanced at Jason as they crossed the dining room. "You too, old man. Time to see what your lady can do."

Tight-lipped and obviously uneasy, Jason followed them.

Amy looked back and discovered she and Bayard led the entire group across the yard in the late afternoon sunlight.

As they stepped into the shade of the barn, Amy blinked her eyes. Both front and back double doors on the barn were open, and she could see Kelly and Bill in the back, near the wagons.

Lloyd stepped from a stall. He looked at the group, tossed down the harness in his hands and approached. He stopped just past Tom and gaped at the mirror images of Amy. Hands on his hips, he looked at Merril. "What's this?"

Merril clapped Lloyd on the back. "Let's talk for a moment." Merril steered Lloyd out and away from the group.

Amy watched Merril speak to Lloyd, but only for a moment. Lloyd wasn't her main concern. Tom didn't look better. If anything, he looked much worse. She approached his bed and touched him on the shoulder and then the forehead. "Tom? Are you awake?"

Gummy eyes blinked open and stared at her. "Amy?"

"How do you feel?" She lifted her hand from his hot, dry forehead.

What did I miss?

Lloyd stalked back inside and stopped beside his son. He shot a suspicious scowl toward Amy, then took his son's hand. "Tom, Merril says Amy and her sister want to ease the pain in your leg." He looked from Tom to Amy. "He seems to think they might be able to help the swelling and get you back on your feet." Red-rimmed eyes turned back to his son. "I won't stop them if you want them to try."

Tom struggled to his elbow and looked at the group clustered near the front of the barn. "Who are these people?" he said to Lloyd.

Lloyd looked from Amy to her twin. "Amy's family arrived from back east. She has a twin sister."

Amy smiled when Tom's gaze shifted to her. She held out her hand. "This is my sister, Alyse. We dressed alike tonight to play a joke on Jason."

"That's right. Kelly told me your family had arrived." Tom lay back down and grimaced. "Could Jason tell you apart?"

Alyse chuckled. "As a matter of fact, he couldn't."

"We want to try something to help the pain in your leg," Amy told him.

"Good." Tom closed his eyes. "I'm tired of feelin' poorly. At times, my leg hurts so much, I can't breathe. I lay here and watch my father do my work and his too."

Merril motioned to Jim. "Help me with the hay bales." They moved a bale to either side of Tom's leg and another set beside his head.

"We should remove the splint." Amy looked to Nichole "I'll need my shears."

"Hold up." Lloyd stopped Nichole. "I've got a knife. Kelly, give me a hand."

Lloyd pulled back the blanket from Tom's legs and stopped. Tom's toes extending from the splint were purple and swollen. "Damn." He glanced at Amy.

"Remove it." Amy pulled her gaze from Tom's foot and walked to the head of the bed and laid her hand across Tom's brow. "Be still, Tom. Feel my hand and listen to my voice." She nodded to Lloyd and continued to murmur to Tom.

Lloyd sliced the leather, unwound the linen and set the boards aside. He glanced once at Amy, then removed the gauze.

Amy caught her breath. Tom's leg had swollen inside the splint. His toes looked like tiny purple dumplings attached to a bruised mass of flesh. The skin on his leg stretched so tight it shone.

Lloyd covered his face with his hands and walked away.

Amy watched him go, then whispered to Tom. "I'm going to look at your leg, Tom. I want you to relax and keep your eyes closed." She pulled her skirt around the hay bale and sat beside his leg.

Alyse sat across from her.

The group of observers moved closer and formed a half-circle at the end of the camp bed.

"Should I go first?" Amy asked Alyse.

"I think so. Extend your sight and I'll try to *twyne* through you." Alyse looked from Amy to Tom's leg.

Amy held out her hands, palm down, and a warm golden glow surrounded Tom's leg.

"It feels warm." Tom pushed up on his elbow. His eyes grew wide. "What?"

"Just be still." Merril sat down on a hay bale near Tom's head.

Amy's head tipped back, and her eyes closed. "I see the break."

Alyse closed her eyes and extended her hands beside her sister's. An orange radiance formed around Alyse's hands and flowed down around Tom's leg.

Alyse shook her head and withdrew her hands. The orange glow disappeared. "I can't see inside." She opened her eyes.

Amy pulled her hands back and stared at Alyse. "Not at all?"

"You're both trying to go into the leg." Bay stepped forward and spoke to Alyse. "Once Amy has the break in sight, connect to her."

"It shouldn't matter," Bern commented, clearly disappointed. "We don't pair like that."

"No, but they have to *twyne*, not pair. Besides, they're just learning." Bay stepped back by his brother and motioned toward Tom with his hand. "Try again."

Amy took a deep breath and looked at Alyse.

This was so easy before.

Alyse nodded. "You go first."

Amy closed her eyes and extended her hands again above Tom's leg. "I see it."

Alyse leaned forward and put her hands to either side of Amy's head, and the orange glow appeared.

"I see it," they both said at the same time.

Tom's mouth dropped, and his eyes bulged.

"Easy, Tom," Merril whispered.

Amy saw the blockage and nudged Alyse with her mind. *Look there.*

An influx of warmth moved through Amy's hands and the blockage dissolved.

There's too much fluid. Can the body absorb it?

Not quickly, but I can disperse most of it. Alyse's thought replied to Amy's. *There, the bones have knit.*

Yes, I see.

That's the most I can do. The rest will heal well on its own. Alyse dropped her hands and sat back.

Amy let her hands fall to her lap. "Well done, Alyse." The swelling in Tom's leg had reduced by half, and the foot returned to its healthy color before her eyes.

"I took care of the elbows and the knot on his head as well," Alyse pointed out.

"I noticed." Amy nodded to Alyse then looked at Tom. "How do you feel?"

Tom sat up and glanced between the sisters. "My leg doesn't ache anymore." His gaze turned to his father. "The sick feeling in my gut is gone." He looked at his elbows and shook his head.

Amy's gaze met Merril's. "Help him stand."

Amy and Alyse stood and moved back as Merril and Lloyd helped Tom to his feet.

Tom stood for a moment then limped forward. "Well, I'll be!" He took another short step and raised a confused gaze to Amy and Alyse. "The pain is gone. You've healed the break." Tom shook his head. "I can't believe it."

Cat giggled and clapped as several appreciative comments echoed off the barn walls.

Lloyd turned to Bill and Kelly. "All right now, show's over. Hitch up the small wagon and get those trunks moved over."

"I'll ride over to The Shilo with Amy's family," Merril told Lloyd. "Which horse should I saddle?"

"I'll tack one up for ya." Lloyd jutted his chin toward the group at the front of the barn. "You have guests. We'll bring the wagon and your mount to the yard."

"Thanks, Lloyd." Merril tucked Nichole's hand in the crook of his arm. "Let's go back to the house, folks. They'll meet us there with the rig."

Bernard touched Lloyd on the arm. "Your son will need to go easy for a few days to finish healing."

Lloyd stepped back from Bernard. "Yep. I'll see to it." Lloyd tucked his head and hurried toward the wagons.

Bernard shook his head at Lloyd's retreating back.

Amy touched her uncle's shoulder. "He's frightened, not unappreciative." She turned and found Jason watching her. "How are you?"

"I'm dumbfounded." Jason shook his head then shrugged. "Give me a chance to acclimate."

The four of them followed Merril, Nichole, Sam and Cat toward the house. Amy looked back. Her sister and Jim trailed behind in quiet conversation.

When Amy reached the porch, Sam and Cat had already gone inside. She stopped beside Nichole and watched Kelly and Bill bring the horse and wagon to the house.

When Kelly drew rein, Jim tapped the side of the wagon. "Tie it off, Kel. We need to get into one of the trunks before they go."

Alyse pointed to her trunk and Jim pulled it to the end of the wagon.

Alyse caught Amy's gaze and signaled with her hand to her sister. "I have something for you." Alyse opened it and withdrew a soft package wrapped in brown paper and tied with twine. She handed it up to Amy.

"Is this from my grandmother?" Amy held the package to her chest.

"Her name is Chantal James. I call her *Mémé*. She asked me to give this to you and to say you were never far from her heart." Alyse wiped a tear and pressed her lips to hold the emotion back. "She said I should tell you about her, share the things she and I did while I grew up. When I share those times with you, she'll be here with us, if only in memory." Alyse brushed her shoulder against her face to catch a tear. She hugged her sister. "I'll see you tomorrow." She released Amy and looked for a long moment at Jim, then she smiled. "Thank you, Mr. Leigh."

Jim touched the brim of his hat and smiled. "My sincere pleasure, Miss James." Affection shimmered in his eyes. "I look forward to seeing you again, very soon."

Amy's heart skipped a beat and she gripped the package to her breast. Heat sparked between Alyse and Jim. Did she feel her sister's emotion in her chest, or could everyone see it?

Then Alyse turned from Jim and allowed Bay to help her to the wagon seat. He climbed up beside her as Bern took the other side and picked up the reins.

"I'll ride with you and see you settled in," Merril told Bernard and Bayard as he took the gelding's reins from Bill. Merril gave Nichole a quick kiss on her forehead. "I'll be late, sweetheart." He mounted, tugged the reins, and headed down the drive toward the road.

Amy and Nichole watched Merril and the wagon until they disappeared over the low rise in the road.

"Did you see the fireworks between Jim and your sister?" Nichole asked.

"Hmm. Felt them, too," Amy replied.

Nichole glanced around the porch, then spoke softly. "Do you think Jim is attracted to Alyse because of his feelings for you?"

"No." Amy shook her head. "It's the other way around. Alyse is the one he's waited for."

Nichole arched her eyebrow at Amy, and they turned and entered the house. Someone had lit the lamps against the coming evening.

Amy paused at the stairs and looked down at the package in her arms.

"You should open it." Nichole pulled the list from Amy's pocket and headed toward the kitchen. "I'll check with Cookie about Bay's list of ingredients."

"All right," Amy called to Nichole. "I'll be in my room."

Upstairs, Amy sat on the bed with the package in her lap. She stared at her hands on the paper for several minutes. Her grandmother had tied this knot. A woman Amy had never met, never knew existed, yet one who had charted her life from the day she was born. Tentatively, she pulled the twine bow and folded back the paper.

Inside, a crochet shawl lay folded. Blue at the top, the yarn darkened to black near the bottom. When she pulled the shawl free from the paper, two items fell to the floor. A light blue cloth pouch on a chain and a folded sheet of paper. She picked up the satchel, and the perfume of clove and pine filled her senses. The paper on the floor read—*To Amylia.*

Amy put the chain over her head and draped the shawl around her shoulders. She picked up the folded paper and stared at the unfamiliar writing. Then she unfolded the note.

My dearest Amylia,

This may be the hardest letter I've ever tried to write.

I hope you find it in your heart to forgive me for separating you and your sister. It's something no twin should have to endure, and it broke your mother's heart to realize it had to be done to save you both.

Please know I've watched you grow as I watched Alyse grow. In everything she and I did together, there was always another little girl with us, if only in my heart.

The shawl is woven with protective magic and much love. The satchel is for your protection as well. Wear it close to your heart and know it holds my love for you.

All my love,

Your Grandmother, Chantal James

Tears dotted the paper as Amy folded the letter and set it on the dresser. A lifetime of love conveyed in a brief note. Now, she understood the deep loss she sensed in Alyse on the train. Amy covered her face with her hands and cried.

Chapter 30

Nichole Harris-Shilo

—

Nichole inhaled the crisp, clear morning air as she stepped onto the porch and pulled on her leather riding gloves. Cloudless blue sky stretched west to the mountains.

She wore her rust-colored riding skirt and jacket. She had misgivings about getting back on a sidesaddle, but her legs were completely healed. She'd meant to ask Merril to find her a pair of denim trousers, but with all that had happened in the last few days, she'd forgotten about the pants until today.

Across the yard, near the barn, Timothy and June were seated on the buckboard, ready to head out. Merril stood beside the rig and spoke with Timothy. The young man nodded several times, and then Merril slapped the side of the wagon and stepped back.

Timothy shook the reins, and the wagon pulled around the yard and headed for the road. He tipped his hat to Nichole as they passed the porch.

June had her nose so far in the air, Nichole doubted she could see the road in front of the wagon.

Good riddance to the old biddy.

She met Merril at the corral. "I'm glad she's gone." She pulled the parasol from beneath her arm and opened it to shade her face. "When will Timothy be back?"

Merril leaned his arms against the top rail and rested his boot on the lower. "A couple of days. He intends to drive straight through to Denver." Merril chuckled. "I don't blame him. I wouldn't want to camp with June, either."

"All day in a wagon would be bad enough," Nichole agreed.

"I told him which boarding house would be best for June. Inexpensive, but with no bar or stable attached. Less chance for her to have a run-in with Highlands' wranglers." Merril smiled at Nichole. "He'll return the wagon and livery team, and bring back Midnight and the other horses."

"Did you tell him to stay at the house?"

"I did, but he declined. Said he wouldn't feel comfortable." Merril shook his head. "So I gave him extra money for a hotel. He'll spend one night, then head back." Merril looked into Nichole's eyes. "I suggested he stay in town until whatever happens here with Amy's family is finished, but he wants to come back and be near Lawna." He touched Nichole's face. "I must say, I understand how he feels."

The dust on the road had settled when Amy and Jason came out of the house.

Nichole and Merril turned and watched them cross the yard.

"Are all three of you going?" Merril looked from Jason to Nichole.

Nichole nodded. "I want to watch."

Jason ran a hand through his hair and reset his hat. "I thought I best go and see what they intend to teach my wife."

"Uncle Bay told me he would ride one of the horses back to set protective wards at The Highlands while we train," Amy told Merril. "If Cookie and Jeanne would be so inclined, he could use their help."

Merril nodded. "I'll mention it to them, as well as Lawna and Henny." He chuckled. "I'm sure he'll have plenty of questions and advice from everyone once he arrives."

Kelly looked out from the barn, and Merril held up three fingers. Kelly nodded and disappeared back inside.

"You're not coming?" Nichole asked.

Merril shook his head. "No. I'm going to help Lloyd house all the animals. After that, I'll ride over to the branding site. I know we can't shelter the cattle, but I want to see how many head are still close by."

Kelly walked three tacked horses over to the group.

Merril helped Nichole mount Sugar and arranged her skirt. He ran a hand along the gelding's neck as he looked up at his wife. "Be safe, sweetheart."

"I will." Nichole reset her parasol on her shoulder. "I'm not sure when we'll be back." She blew him a kiss and followed Jason and Amy down the drive to the road.

The beautiful day made the ride between ranches pass quickly for Nichole. Jason and Amy were unusually quiet during the trip.

Probably nervous about mage training.

As they rounded the house and turned into the yard, Nichole spotted Bayard seated on the bench beside the corral.

His head was down as he wound twine around white sage leaves. Bayard paused in his work and looked up at the riders when they pulled their mounts to a stop. "Good morning." He set the fragrant bundle aside. "Leave one mount saddled, if you would."

Jason nodded to Bayard and led the horses into the corral.

Nichole picked up a sage bundle and smelled the fragrance. "What is this for?"

"It's a smudge for cleansing the house." Bayard shielded his eyes and grinned up at Nichole. "Sage restores balance and releases bound negative emotions."

"Oh." Nichole glanced at Amy. "Did you know this?"

Amy lifted her shoulders. "Mother never made these and only spoke of them occasionally. I have other uses for sage."

Jason joined them. "Are you going back straight away?" Jason asked as he pulled off his riding gloves.

Bayard shook his head and pointed to the house. "Alyse said she heard a man cry in the night. She believes there's a lingering presence in the house. We're going to cleanse the house first. Make sure the fellow is sent happily on his way. I'll head to your ranch after we're done."

Alyse swept dust from the entryway out onto the porch. When she saw Amy in the yard, she waved, then disappeared back inside.

"While Alyse sweeps the house, Bernard is setting up the altar." Bay stood and picked up the sage bundle. "This is what they've been waiting for." He took a step toward the house and paused. "Oh, and Alyse wants Nichole to walk through the house before we start." Bayard grinned at Nichole. "She says you're sensitive to spirits."

Nichole blinked at Bayard. "Why would she think that?"

Bayard shrugged. "Alyse can sense things about people. She calls it *truth-reading*, but it's more than sensing a lie." Bay shrugged. "She felt something in you when the girls healed you. She mentioned it again yesterday." Bay pointed toward the house. "We can get started, if you like."

"Should I wait out here?" Jason hesitated by the bench.

"You can," Bay said over his shoulder. "This won't take long."

Nichole hadn't been inside The Shilo ranch house since her carriage accident. She walked past the library and glanced inside. Empty. The bare windows looked over the porch and side yard. She glimpsed Jason seated on the bench. She followed Bayard and Amy into the dining room.

The heavy table stood in the center of the room. The chairs were lined up against the walls. A black altar cloth covered the middle third of the table. Bernard had arranged several items on it: a water-filled chalice, a bowl of salt, a white candle, a box of matches, and a small cast-iron cauldron. In the middle of the cloth lay a well-worn book, open to a page midway through it. A red silk ribbon lay along the crease.

"Good. You're here." Bernard acknowledged Amy and Nichole with a nod. "And you have the smudge done. Excellent." He took the smudge and arranged it on the altar with the rest of the items. "Alyse, take Nichole through the house and tell her what you heard last night." He glanced at Nichole. "If she can convince the spirit to leave on his own, it will go much easier on the poor fellow." Bernard turned to the altar. "I'll set the wards and bless the cleansing."

Nichole half expected to find them in ceremonial robes, but the men wore their usual dark slacks, light shirts, and vests. Alyse wore a blue checkered day dress with light stockings and low-heeled shoes, her hair brushed and braided in one long strand down her back.

Amy and Nichole removed their hats, set them on a chair, and followed Alyse upstairs.

"Bay and Bern slept in these rooms." Alyse pointed.

Nichole knew those were Philip's and Merril's old rooms.

"I slept in the one down the hall." Alyse walked to the last room and opened the door.

Nichole stepped past Alyse and into the room. This was Kevin's room. A heavy melancholy filled her chest, and a chill touched her to the bone. "You slept in here?" She turned to Alyse in amazement. Nichole could hardly tolerate standing in the room.

Alyse nodded. "Nothing happened until the middle of the night. I woke to hear a man weeping. You feel something, don't you?"

Nichole nodded and surveyed the room. She crossed to the dresser. A wooden box held two sets of cufflinks. An empty picture frame lay on its back beside the box. Her dread of Kevin crawled up her spine, and she turned to Alyse. "What should I do?"

Alyse shook her head. "I don't know. I have no spirit magic. What I heard last night, anyone could have heard." Alyse studied Nichole for several moments. "You didn't like this man. He frightened you."

"You can sense that, or you see it in my face?" Nichole rubbed her arms.

"Both, actually." She stepped from the doorway and into the room beside Nichole. "This man was your husband's brother?" Alyse asked.

"Yes." Nichole nodded and swallowed. "Kevin Shilo. He lost his mind after their father died, and he... he did some terrible things." Nichole turned to leave, but Amy stood in the doorway.

"He wasn't always so cruel, was he? Can you remember a pleasant time with him before he lost his father? Think of positive things—good things," Alyse suggested.

Nichole shook her head. All she could see when she thought of Kevin was Toma's bloody back, and his cruel hands on her breast. She exhaled in frustration and was startled to see her breath. "He's here." She spun and searched the room. An indentation had appeared on the bed. Nichole pressed her hand to her throat as a figure began to coalesce. The color of his clothes was muted, and the outlines of his body blurred. Kevin sat on the bed, elbows on his knees, as he wept into his hands.

"You can see him?" Alyse took Nichole's hand, and she turned toward the specter.

Nichole exhaled frosted vapor through clenched teeth. "Yes," she murmured.

Kevin turned and looked at her. "Who are you?" Alarm radiated from the apparition.

"It's me, Kevin. It's Nichole." She tightened her grip on Alyse's hand.

"No." Kevin shook his head. "You're not her." He rose to his feet. Malevolent anger glared from his eyes. He took a step toward her and his voice rose to a roar. "Why does everyone lie to me?" He took another step and reached for Nichole.

Panic closed her throat. She spun free of Alyse's grip and pushed against Amy. "Let me out!" Kevin's breath was like ice down Nichole's neck. She broke past Amy, raced down the hallway and stairs, and out the front door into the sunshine.

Jason rose from the bench and caught Nichole in his arms as she fled into the yard.

The warmth of the summer sun and her cousin's arms calmed her. She wiped her face and turned as Amy and Alyse hurried to her side.

Jason looked from Nichole to Amy. "What happened?"

"Kevin's in the house." Nichole pushed away from Jason and looked at Amy and Alyse. "I'm sorry I ran like that." She pushed the hair out of her face. "He came at me, and all I could think to do was run away."

Amy looked at Nichole with sympathy. "I didn't see anything." She looked at Alyse.

Alyse nodded. "He's there, and he's angry. I understand why you ran."

Jason swore and stepped away from the women. "Kevin is dead. He's in the ground at the cemetery up that road."

Bern and Bay crossed the porch and approached the group in the yard.

"Kevin's body is buried," Alyse said to Jason, "but his spirit is lost inside this house. Nichole must help him find his way out." She looked back at Nichole. "We can't have Kevin here when the demon arrives."

"I can't go back inside." Nichole took a step back, and her legs touched the bench. "I can't face him."

"We could ward you," Bayard offered. "Then you'd be sure he can't harm you." He smiled and held out his hand to Nichole. "You'll be safe. I promise."

Nichole took Bayard's hand then hesitated and turned to Jason. "Will you come?"

Jason pressed his lips and nodded. "Of course." He took Nichole's other hand.

Together, they entered the house and continued into the dining room.

Jason gawked at the altar as Bayard drew the cousins up beside the table.

Bernard followed them across the room. "How big of a ward do you want?" Bernard asked his brother with one eyebrow raised.

"A simple call to each corner and a blessing would do, but I want all of us inside the ward." Bayard looked to Amy and Alyse, who spoke together at the side of the room. "Ladies, if you please, we need you over here."

"I've already called the corners for the cleansing. I think that should suffice," Bern said as they grouped beside the altar.

"Put a ward of salt down, bless it, and then Nichole can call the spirit." Bayard patted Nichole's hand.

Nichole looked at Bayard.

Had he lost his mind?

Anxiety slammed into her chest. "I can't call Kevin."

Bay tipped his head and gazed at her face. "Would you rather go upstairs?"

"No way." Nichole shook her head.

"Then it's best he comes to us. We will all be warded. You'll be fine." He placed a hand on her shoulder and raised his gaze to his brother.

Bernard returned from the trunk in the corner. He held a ceramic sauce boat filled with salt. "Are we ready?" Without waiting for an answer, he poured salt from the ceramic pourer onto the floor. As he walked clockwise around the group, he intoned the blessing.

"God and Goddess, be welcome in this home.
Lord and Lady, in all aspects of your creation
Hold us in your protection and offer us
The fearlessness of our father,
And the understanding of our mother.
Ensure our work this day is true and good.
Bless us with the wisdom to know your path."

Bernard completed the circle and set the sauce boat on the table. He placed his hand on Jason's shoulder.

The brothers' eyes met, and they nodded once in unison, then they both reached out a hand to their Amy and Alyse. Amy took Bay's hand, and Alyse took Bernard's, then the sisters joined hands. They formed a circle inside the circle of salt.

"Call him now," Bay and Bern spoke at the same time.

Nichole closed her eyes and took a deep breath. Bayard's warm hand on her shoulder fed her strength. She clutched Jason's hands with hers. She reached out with her mind, up the stairs and down the hall. Inside his room, Kevin sat alone and wept. "Kevin?"

A loud thump sounded in the room above their heads.

Nichole opened her eyes. Her gaze sought Jason.

His clammy hands tightened around hers. He nodded. "I heard that."

"Call him again." Bayard stared at the ceiling. "Insist he come to you."

Nichole drew a trembling breath and looked down the hall. "Kevin," Nichole called. "Come down here."

A door slammed upstairs to the sound of breaking glass. All eyes were on the ceiling as the floorboards creaked in his room to the hallway then returned to Kevin's room.

"Don't let up. Call him." Bernard nodded to Nichole. "Insist."

Nichole's legs shook as she took a deep breath and yelled, "Kevin, get your spirit ass down here and face me. Right now!"

The sound of a tornado ripped down the stairs and embodied rage entered the dining room.

"Holy Mother of God!" Jason stared at the maddened ghost of his former neighbor.

"Calm him," Bay and Bern said. "Speak to him of good times, pleasant times."

A photograph from the mantel flew across the room and detonated with a crash against the wall.

"Kevin, don't be angry." Nichole's voice shook. Her hands gripped Jason's. The temperature of the room had plummeted, and her words hung in a frozen mist before her face.

Kevin turned and pinned her with his gaze.

She gasped as tears filled her eyes and froze on her face.

"Keep talking to him," Bay whispered.

"Remember the barbecue two years ago? Remember when you danced with Nichole?" She swallowed, but the lump stayed in her throat. "Gary Bishop's daughter followed Merril all over the party and wouldn't leave him alone. What was her name?"

Kevin quieted and stared at her.

"Remember how hard you laughed at Merril?" The whirlwind of malice ebbed and the tight band around her chest untangled. "Remember when you danced to the fiddle player, and your father laughed so hard at Dale Green he fell off his chair? Remember laughing Kevin?"

Kevin calmed. The anger dissipated, but the sadness returned.

"Does he know who you are?" Jason whispered.

Nichole shook her head. "He doesn't recognize me." She could see their icy breath as they spoke.

"He sees her as the person with the spiritual ability," Amy whispered.

Jason's stare shifted from Kevin to his wife. "He sees who?"

"Urge him to move on," Alyse recommended. "Tell him where to go."

Nichole concentrated on Kevin.

He had his hands to his head and moaned with sorrow.

"Kevin," Nichole said softly, "there's a light at the end of a long hallway. Can you see it?"

Kevin raised his head and stared ahead.

"Yes," the apparition breathed.

Nichole turned her head and heard Jason gasp as she saw the hallway. It extended through the dining room wall, into infinity. Black empty doorways stood like sentinels on either side and a golden light, a beacon of warmth, glowed at its end.

"Your father is there, and your mother." Nichole rubbed a tear from the side of her face against her shoulder. Kevin had once been like an older brother to her. She remembered. "They wait for you, Kevin. Listen. Can you hear them?"

Kevin lowered his hands and took a step. He paused, and looked toward Nichole. "Why?"

"Your parents loved you, Kevin." She pointed toward the light. "They love you still."

He stared ahead into the light. "Yes," he breathed. He glanced at Nichole. "Thank you." His voice faded as his spectral body dissipated and blew into the hallway.

No one moved for several seconds. Finally, Bay patted Nichole's shoulder. "Well done."

"Could you see him?" Nichole wiped her tears and turned to Bayard.

He nodded emphatically. "Oh, yes. I think we all saw him."

Jason put his head down, hands on his knees and breathed deeply.

Amy put her arm on his back.

He stood and embraced his wife. "I have never seen anything so horrifying in my life. That was Kevin."

"I know." Amy nodded against his chest.

Alyse stepped out of the warded circle and looked back at her uncles. "Were you *twyned* the whole time?"

"Most of the time," Bernard said over his shoulder. "Something you and Amy should practice until you can *twyne* with just a thought." Bernard faced the altar. "Let's get the cleanse out of the way so we can begin some real practice. We've spent far too long on poor Kevin."

Jason and Nichole took seats along the wall and watched as the James family blessed their way around the rooms.

Bernard appointed each person an element they would represent as they removed any remaining ill-will from the home. Bayard, with the sage smudge representing air, would go first, followed by Alyse with the candle as fire. Next would be Amy, with the chalice as water, and finally Bernard, with the salt as earth.

The ritual moved swiftly as each person intoned a blessing for their element. Soon they were coming back down the stairs, saying the blessing one last time at the altar. When all four had finished, they faced Bernard for the close of the ritual.

"Blessed Lord and Lady, hear our prayers
Ensure our work this day is true and good,
Teach us with your wisdom to know your path.
And in your name, bless all who bide here.
So shall it be done."

Bayard and Alyse repeated the last phrase together.

Amy said it quickly and glanced at Jason and smiled.

Jason called from the chairs, "What now?"

Bayard picked up his hat from the seat next to Jason. "Now, I ride to your place and set up defensive wards." He rolled the bowler up his arm to his head. "I'll see you this evening." He paused and looked at Nichole. "Dinner at your place?"

Nichole raised her eyebrows at Bayard and laughed. She blew a puff of air to remove a stray hair from her eye. "Whew, yes," she breathed. "Tell Cookie we'll be home for dinner."

Bayard waved at the group and stepped out the front door, closing it soundly behind him.

"Well, that was fun." Bernard cleared his throat. "Now, then, shall we begin?"

Chapter 31

Amy Harris

—

Amy watched as Alyse and Bernard cleaned and straightened the area. Unsure of how to help, she rested her hip against the table and tried to stay out of the way.

Alyse swept the salt from the floor onto a piece of paper and poured it into the bowl.

Bernard folded the altar cloth and returned most of the cleansing tools to the trunk. Only the chalice of water remained on the table. When he finished, he leaned against the table and looked at his nieces. He appeared solemn, almost sad.

"When Bay and I were children, Mum used to tell stories about great witches who would one day be tested against an evil demon. We used to play at it, pretend we were mighty demon hunters." Bernard chuckled and shook his head. "We set a lot of things on fire."

"Years later, when Margaret became pregnant, and mother realized it would be twins born near Samhain, she told us of more of the prophecy." Bernard paused and looked at Jason and Nichole. "You should hear this. You need to know how far back this goes, and what we are facing."

Jason and Nichole rose from their seats and approached the table.

"Mum told us about The Prophecy of the Twins. Twin witches, born under a full moon on a High Sabbat, who would *twyne* for the first time and release a demon from hell. This demon would have only one goal—to kill those children and steal their witches' power. Even now, it sounds something akin to a fairy tale."

Bernard appeared lost in thought. He stared at the floor and shuffled his foot against a few salt granules. He cleared his throat and raised his gaze to Amy and Alyse. "After you were separated, your grandmother taught Bay and me her most powerful spells. Keep in mind, these spells were limited by her philosophical belief that we, as witches, would never harm another, be they witch or human."

He shifted his weight and glanced at Jason. "The three of us found ourselves not only taking care of a newborn, but crafting spells to inflict deadly harm. Without a place to begin, we were forced to experiment. Oddly enough, our childhood demon hunts began to pay off."

Bernard pushed himself away from the table, paced a few steps away, turned and looked at Amy. "What I am going to teach you is not who we are. It is not who we want to be as witches or as human beings. These skills are not something we would ever use against another living being. That being said, I'm going to teach you to be deadly."

Bernard paused and measured his nieces with his eyes. "I believe we should meet this demon in the open. Our plan is to come out of this alive, and we don't want the house to burn down around our heads."

Amy swallowed the lump in her throat.

Alyse commands fire. I grow flowers and make ointments. How deadly can I be with Earth and Water?

Bernard rested his palm on the table. "Let's make the ground itself our altar." His gaze switched to Alyse. "Go into the yard and draw a large pentacle on the ground. Gouge it deep. Put the spirit point facing the house. In front of the water and air point, I want a trough of water and a fire pit. These need to be inside the circle we will ward."

Alyse started to move, and he touched her arm. "The pentacle needs to be big. We're going to stand in the five points."

"But there are only four of us." Alyse responded.

Bernard tipped his head at Nichole. "We have our white candle right here. Nichole is our spirit element."

"Me?" Nichole touched her throat. "What good will I be?"

"When we faced the spirit today, we worked as a group in a way I never knew possible. More than a *twyne* between twins, we melded—through you.

We all saw the spirit and the passage when only you have the ability to do so."
Bern shrugged. "Your spiritual ability acts as a bridge. It may lessen Amy and
Alyse's need to *twyne*, or help them do so under pressure. With five separate
elements, we shall operate as one force."

"We were touching," Nichole argued. "We won't touch in the yard."

"True," Bernard agreed. "But even if we can't meld, you'll be able to see
and feel things that we will not." Bernard gestured with his arm. "I'll take any
advantage we have."

"I understand." Nichole nodded, then shook her head. "I know next to
nothing about magic." She exhaled through pressed lips and rubbed her forehead.

"You amaze me at every turn." Jason hugged Nichole's shoulder. "You'll
do well." He lifted his gaze and addressed Bernard, "What I need to know is
where I'll be?"

Bernard raised an eyebrow and crossed his arms. "What do you mean?"

Jason hooked his thumbs in his belt. "You're putting the two most precious
things in my life in harm's way." He shook his head. "I won't be hiding under
a bed while my wife and cousin face a demon. So, I ask you again—" Jason
stared at Bernard "—where will I be?"

Amy looked from Jason to Bernard and bit her lip. She felt intimidated by
Bernard's serious demeanor.

Yet Jason faces him without hesitation, demanding to fight by my side.

She blinked at the burning sensation in her eyes.

Alyse spoke up, "He will be in the center, along with the *grimoire*." She
tipped her head to the side with a shrug. "A gunman would be another advantage. Besides, I don't believe you'll convince Merril to stay away while his
wife is in the yard with us."

Bernard rubbed his chin. "I see your point." He crossed to the trunk, retrieved the *grimoire*, along with a quill and ink, and brought them to the table.
He paged through the book to an empty sheet. With a skilled hand, he drew a
five-pointed star and surrounded it with a circle.

"This will be our ward boundary." He continued to draw as he spoke. "This
is the corner of the porch and the corral. Here is where the bunkhouse sits."
He shrugged. "Well, approximately." He wrote their names in the angles, the
element they would represent, and sketched a small fire pit and water trough.

He raised his gaze to Jason and Alyse and pointed to the drawing. "If you two could get started on this outside, I need a moment with Amy and Nichole."

Amy and Jason exchanged quick glances, and then Jason followed Alyse out the door.

When they had gone, Bernard spoke to Amy. "*Water* and *Earth* are strong elements," he told her. "They can be a force to contend with, without *Fire* or *Air*. I'm going to teach you what I can do with just those elements." He shrugged. "If you are as strong in your elements as Alyse is with hers, you will surpass my skills very quickly." Bernard indicated the chalice of water. "Show me how you spun the water."

Nerves scraped along Amy's spine.

I don't know what to do.

She stared into the water, pushing her concentration down into the liquid. In the depth of the chalice, a battle with fire began to take shape.

Bernard covered the cup with his hand. "Spin the water, Amy. Don't read portents from it."

Amy shook her head. "I don't think I can—"

"Don't think about it." Bernard's voice grew loud. "The ability is in your blood." He pointed at the door. "Your sister's life depends on it." He slapped the table with his hand. "And now, your husband's life depends on it, and yours. *Now, try.*"

Amy blinked at her uncle and stepped back.

Nichole rounded the table and put her hand on Bernard's arm. "There's no need to shout at her."

Bernard shrugged Nichole's hand off. "No need?" Bernard glared at Nichole and turned his angry countenance toward Amy. "Bay and I grew up fighting demons in our sleep. Alyse has been trained, yelled at, and corrected her entire life until her skill surpassed even my mother's." He pointed at Amy. Disdain dripped from his voice. "This girl, with her fine Boston dresses and privileged life, will not be the weak link that gets us killed." He slapped the table again and yelled. "*NOW TRY, DAMN YOU.*"

Water from the chalice struck Bernard on the side of the head. He ducked the chalice.

Amy stepped back. With a gasp, she covered her mouth with both hands. *Oh, Goddess, what have I done?*

Bernard looked up, laughing. "Now, that's better." He picked up the chalice. "I'm lucky you haven't mastered ice daggers or throwing stones."

Amy looked from Nichole's shocked face to her uncle. "You—provoked me."

"Yes." He nodded and returned the chalice to the table. "Hold on to that fear and anger. There is power in those emotions. They'll help you learn." He turned and walked back to the chairs. "Eventually, you won't need to be goaded into using your talents." He spun and spoke sharply, pointing at the floor. "Now, clean your mess up."

Amy took a step toward the kitchen to find a mop.

Bernard's voice stopped her. "No mop. No towels. Put the water into the chalice from where you now stand." Bernard's head tipped toward the ground and to the chalice.

Amy narrowed her eyes at Bernard. Anger and frustration at his manipulation built in her chest. For several moments, nothing happened. Amy glared at Bernard and flicked her wrist. The puddle on the floor pulled together and leapt from the floor into the cup.

"Dry me off while you are at it," Bernard growled.

Amy fought a smile as she stared into Bernard's eyes. Her lips twitched. She flicked her other hand, and the moisture from her uncle's shirt and hair pulled away from him and flowed into the cup.

A look of satisfaction lit Bernard's entire face. "You used both *Water* and *Earth* skills to do what you just did." He stepped to the table and looked into the chalice. "Your fine control is as outstanding as Alyse's. I could not have done what you just accomplished." He chuckled. "I would have missed the cup with the water and set myself on fire trying to dry myself off. Well done."

"What else can I do?" Amy stepped toward Bernard with a grin. She had never imagined this skill—this power—resided inside her.

"Spin the water." Bernard nodded to the chalice.

Amy flicked her wrist, and the water spun inside the cup. She clenched her fist, and it stopped.

Bernard rewarded Amy with a nod. "Very good, niece." He turned toward Nichole. "I hope Nichole can help us speed things up a bit; at least, we're going to try." He held out his arm. "Nichole?"

Nichole rose from a chair and approached until she stood between Amy and Bernard.

"Put your hand on Nichole's shoulder and reach out with your *earth-sense*." Bernard did the same thing, and Nichole felt warmth on each shoulder, but nothing else.

"Can you sense me?" Bernard asked, and Amy nodded, her eyes closed.

"Open your eyes. Your sight will be outward, but hopefully, you will see and understand how I manipulate the water. Now, watch how I cool the water."

Bernard held his hand above the chalice and a thin film of ice appeared, and then deepened as the water froze through. Frost grew from the metal cup. He withdrew his hand and looked at Amy. "Did you see how it's done?"

Amy exchanged a glance with Nichole, then nodded to Bernard. "Yes, I did."

"Good. Now, warm it up," Bernard directed.

Amy held her hand above the vessel. The frost beaded into drops and ran down the cup to the table. In moments, steam rose from the water, and then it boiled. She pulled her hand back as steam rose from the container.

"Now," Bernard leaned forward and pressed his thumb against his finger, "pull a sliver of water from the chalice—just a sliver, mind you—and freeze it." He gestured with his hand toward the stone fireplace. "Throw the sliver of ice, like a dart, at the mantel."

One hand directed toward the chalice, Amy's other hand remained on Nichole's shoulder. A tiny trickle of water rose from the cup and hung suspended before the drop splashed back into the cup.

Amy growled with frustration.

"You'll get it." Nichole nodded at Amy and looked back to the cup. "You almost had it. Try again."

Arm extended, Amy pulled a slip of water into the air. She clenched her teeth and made a fist. The thin string of water became a shard of ice. With a flick of her wrist she sent it into the stone wall.

"Good." Bernard nodded. "Finish the rest of the water the same way, only make the ice sharp, and throw the shard hard enough to scar the stone. When the cup is empty, retrieve the water from the floor and return it to the cup."

Amy pulled another string of water from the cup, froze it and sent it toward the fireplace. One. Then two. Then six. The missiles exploded onto the stones until one frozen dart remained, hovering. With a flick from Amy's finger, the ice flashed through the air faster than the eye could follow. The dart sliced through the wick on the burning candle and the flame went out.

With a simple hand gesture, the water on the floor and chipped ice that clung to the stone came together and flew in a long stream back into the chalice.

Bernard clapped from his seat against the wall, and Amy spun to stare at him in surprise. "When did you break the meld?"

"He let go a while back," Nichole told her with a smile. "You did that all by yourself."

Amy released Nichole's shoulder and grinned as she ran a hand across her brow.

Bernard retrieved his hat. "I think it's time we go outside."

***

Bayard James

—

Bayard reined to a stop in front of the Highlands' barn and dismounted. Lloyd and Tom stepped from the shade to greet him.

"Got an early start, I see." Lloyd took the reins from Bayard.

"Up and out before breakfast is no way to live." Bayard chuckled and pulled off his gloves.

"Cookie will see you right with breakfast," Lloyd spoke over his shoulder as he led the mount into the barn. "They're waiting for you inside."

Bayard nodded to Tom. "How's the leg?"

"Better than it should be. Pa said he thought I'd lose it." Tom reset his hat and hooked his thumbs into his belt. "I want to thank you for savin' my leg, and maybe my life."

"Oh no, not I, my friend. My nieces—Alyse and Amy. Their talents far exceed mine." Bayard grinned at Tom and pointed his thumb toward the house. "Is Merril inside?"

Tom shook his head. "No. He and his guests, Sam and Catherine, rode out to check on the cattle at the branding site." Tom looked over his shoulder into the barn and took a step backward. "Merril said they'd be back around noon."

Bayard tipped his hat to Tom and crossed the yard to the house. He paused at the open front door and looked in. The entry and dining room were empty. He walked in and approached the table.

White cloth circles, about six inches in diameter, with drawstrings already woven through holes around the outside edge filled the table. The serving table held bowls filled with pine needles, cloves, bay leaves, and witch hazel. A large pan of river stones sat at the end with an artist's small brush and an inkwell.

Bayard removed his hat from his head and scratched his brow.

Everything on the list. Amazing.

Cookie entered the dining room from the kitchen with a large bowl in her hands. She gasped at the sight of Bayard. "My lands, Mr. James, you scared the life out of me." She set the bowl of marigold heads beside the pine needles and put her hand to her bosom.

"I apologize, Miss Cookie. I saw the open door, so I came inside. I should have called out." Bayard gave the cook a short bow, hooked his hat on the rack by the door and returned to the table.

"You collected marigolds." He pointed to the flower-filled bowl.

Cookie sniffed and raised her chin. "Marigolds keep pests from the garden. I thought they might keep pests from the house as well."

"I wonder why I didn't think of this. You're a marvel, Miss Cookie. This should take no time at all."

"We have something else to add as well, if you think it would be all right." Cookie waved her hand for Jeanne to approach.

Jeanne held a large flat tray at the kitchen opening. On it were small crucifixes and crosses from necklaces, rosaries and bracelet charms. Most made from inexpensive tin and pot metal, but some appeared quite valuable.

"I'm speechless, ladies." Bayard held out both hands to the room and the women. "You've exceeded all expectations."

"I told you it would be fine," Cookie said to Jeanne.

Jeanne placed the tray of crosses at the end of the serving table and stepped back.

"More than 'just fine'," Bayard declared. "It's exactly what we needed."

Henny entered the dining room through the kitchen with Katy at her side. "We would like to help," she said.

"And I have just the job for you." Bayard picked up the pan of small rocks—smooth, rounded river stones, about the size of a penny, cleansed of sand and dirt. He handed the pan to Henny. He unstopped the inkwell and then took a stone from the bowl. Dipping the tip of the brush into the ink, he quickly drew a symbol on the rock. It looked like the letter Y with a small line extended between the open branches at the top. He showed the symbol on the stone to Katy.

"Can you paint this symbol on each stone? Be sure the ink is dry before you put it back into the bowl."

"Yes, sir." Katy gave Bayard her shy smile and took the stone. "What does that letter mean?"

"It's a protection rune," Bayard told Katy. "It's been used for many years to help keep people safe."

"Is it the symbol they painted on the doors in Egypt to make the Angel of Death pass in the night?" Katy asked, eyes wide.

"I don't know," Bayard said honestly. "Perhaps so. This rune is an ancient symbol."

Henny nodded to her daughter as she crossed the room to the front porch, carrying the pan of stones. "Come along, Katy."

Katy grabbed the inkwell and brush and followed her mother outside.

"What about us?" Jeanne asked

"We can fill the satchels. How many cloth circles do we have?" He nodded to the stack of cloth cutouts sitting on a chair beside the kitchen door.

"We made over a hundred circles. Will there be enough?" Cookie asked.

"Possibly." Bayard looked from the table to the stack on the chair. "How many openings in the ranch house?"

"Forty, if we include the fireplaces. There are less for the barn and bunkhouses, but we thought you would need these for The Shilo as well, so we doubled the number."

"Miss Cookie, you are as thoughtful as you are resourceful. I will certainly be able to use most of these, if not all of them."

Cookie's plump cheeks flushed with pride at his compliment, and she patted her gray hair. "Thank you, Mr. James. Thank you."

"Let's get started." Bayard rubbed his hands together and picked up the first satchel. He tightened the draw string part way to form a cup. He stepped to the serving table and took a pinch of pine needles. "Put a pinch of everything on the table in the satchel." He glanced over his shoulder. "If you have a favorite prayer, you should say it while you add the ingredients." Bayard took a pinch of aromatic cloves.

"Even if it is a Christian prayer?" Jeanne tightened the string on her satchel and followed Bayard at the table.

"Most certainly," Bayard added a sprinkling of bay leaves and witch hazel petals.

Jeanne added a pinch of pine needles and said, "Our Father, Who art in heaven—"

Bayard picked up one of the small metal crosses and dropped it into the satchel. "The larger crosses would work better attached to the outside of the satchels. They're far too beautiful to hide away. Put the smaller ones inside."

Katy came inside with her apron full of tiny rune stones, still warm from the sun and stopped before Bayard.

He selected one, placed it in his satchel, and then drew the string tight and knotted it.

Katy emptied her apron on a chair at the end of the serving table.

"Katy, could you find a large serving tray for us?" Bernard asked.

With a nod, the girl disappeared into the kitchen. She returned with a large metal platter.

"Perfect," Bayard proclaimed. He set his knotted satchel on the tray. "If you could put the tray on the parlor table, I would certainly appreciate it."

Katy set it on the table and hurried outside.

Cookie filled her satchel, reciting Psalms, "The Lord is my shepherd, I shall not want—"

Bernard picked up another satchel, tightened it and began the circle again. "Lord and Lady, be welcome in this home—"

It took an hour to fill the satchels. Once Bayard had knotted the last white bag, he went to the barn and asked Tom for small nails and hammers, so they could hang the satchels.

Soon, Lloyd, Tom, and Kelly were in the house nailing satchels above each door and window. Cookie reminded them each hearth would require one too, and they devised a way to hang them from the wooden mantels.

While the men hung satchels, Bay took the ladies outside to collect white sage leaves to make smudges. They made three, one each for Cookie, Jeanne, and Lawna.

After a quick walk-through to be sure each satchel was in place, Bay sent the men to hang satchels in the barn and the bunkhouses. He reminded them to keep all the animals inside the barn and to give some thought as to how they would be housed, fed and watered.

Beginning at sundown tonight and through the day tomorrow, all people and animals would need to remain inside the protection of the buildings.

After the men left the house, Bayard lit a candle on the dining room table and instructed the ladies on smudging. He held his bundle of sage to the candle until it caught fire. "Extinguish the flame from your smudge, leaving the ember at the end to smoke." He blew out the flame, and a curl of fragrant smoke lifted toward the ceiling.

"We will pass through the home and pray for protection at each window or opening where we have placed a satchel." He stood before the front door and etched the rune of protection in the air. "Any symbol which provides both strength and comfort will suffice." He looked over his shoulder and smiled at the women. "If not my rune, then perhaps the sign of the cross—and recite your prayer."

Cookie and Lawna began their circuit, but Jeanne waited until the other women had left the room.

"You wanted to ask me something?" Bayard inquired softly, aware of Jeanne's hesitation.

Jeanne bit her lip, then looked up at Bayard. "This protection ritual feels like witchcraft, yet you let us participate. We aren't witches. I didn't think you would let us use the crosses, but you did. You encouraged us to pray to our God." Jeanne blushed and hung her head. "I'm confused."

Bayard leaned against the table and pressed his lips. These people had been helpful and open.

She deserves an honest answer.

He tipped his head and looked at Jeanne. "The magic in the satchels has been put there by each of us. Everyone who helped make them or hang them has put their faith into them. Your belief that God heard your prayers strengthens the protection."

He sniffed the air and smiled at Jeanne. "You can smell it. You can see it." He indicated the satchel above the door and the smoke hanging low in the room from the smudges. "If you close your eyes and open your heart, can you not feel it?"

Jeanne closed her eyes, sniffed and sighed, then looked at Bayard and said, "No. Not really."

Bayard laughed at her honesty. "That's all right, Miss Jeanne. I assure you, no evil would dare cross this threshold. I believe this is the most secure house I've ever known." He indicated her smudge. "Would you check on Tom and Lloyd? If they've finished in the barn, your prayers will help protect the animals they shelter there."

Once Cookie and Lawna finished smudging the house, Lawna left to check on Hope-Anne, who napped in the family bunk. Cookie returned to the kitchen to attend to dinner.

Bayard walked through the house. He touched each satchel and added an extra prayer to the God and Goddess to protect such good people and to allow the evil to pass their door, just as Katy had said.

He paused in the kitchen and took one of Cookie's fluffy biscuits in exchange for a smile and a wink, then headed for the barn.

As he crossed the yard, Merril, Sam, and Cat rode in and dismounted.

Lloyd stepped from the barn, greeted them, and gathered the horses' reins.

"Mr. James," Merril said, and shook Bayard's hand.

"Call me Bayard or Bay, please." Bayard grinned and released Merril's hand.

"Is everything secure then? Are you prepared to meet this demon?" Sam asked

With an easy smile, Bay nodded at Sam and his sister. "I think so. If the demon comes here, he'll find the buildings secured against him. I believe he'll pass this ranch and move to his targets, which are my nieces." Bay turned from Sam to Merril. "Your wife asked me to tell you they will return here this afternoon. After supper, they'll go back to The Shilo. We expect the demon to find us sometime tonight or tomorrow morning."

"What is the demon waiting for?" Cat asked, pulling her riding gloves from her hands.

"It apparently travels distance in much the same way we do." Bay tipped his head to acknowledge Catherine. "We came to that realization after Amy told us of the animal possessions. At the time she had the vision, she saw the demon a day and a half behind us."

"Does this thing track you by scent?" Sam asked.

"I don't know." Bay shook his head.

"What type of power does it have?" Cat asked.

"I'm not sure. Possession is all we've seen."

"For a demon hunter, you're critically short on information," Sam commented.

Bayard drew on his deep well of patience and gifted Sam with a pleasant smile. "In this instance, sir, we are most certainly not the hunter, but the hunted. None of us have faced a demon." He shrugged. "We can only prepare as best we know how, and try to keep the people here as safe as possible once the contest has begun. Please, excuse me." Bayard touched his hat and continued on his way to check the preparations in the barn. He heard their voices as he walked away.

"Sam, you're rude," Cat told her brother.

"They don't know what they're facing," Sam replied.

Merril responded, "And yet, he's here to make sure these people, who he doesn't know, are safe, rather than with his family at The Shilo, preparing to defend their lives. I don't know about you, but he gets the benefit of my doubt."

Bayard entered the barn, and the voices were lost.

Chapter 32

Morago

—

Morago paused from the long run at the crest of a small rise. Nearly spent, the body the demon inhabited raised its head above the tall grass and looked toward the valley. The animal panted and coughed, in need of water and rest. Still a day's run from its destination, the sight and scent of the human settlement hung foul in the air and burned the animal's nose. The whiskered maw curled in disgust as the coyote turned and slunk away, parallel to the town at the base of the mountains. Soon, they would arrive at the second location etched into Morago's consciousness at the moment of the *twyning*.

Wise enough to know its present form could not move unnoticed in the city, the animal perked its ears and moved south toward a rocky outcrop. Nose to the ground, the scents were alive and led Morago to a nest of rattlers. The warning rattle sent the demons tittering in Morago's mind.

Yes.

Another step forward and searing pain rocked the coyote as envenomed fangs sank deep into its snout. With a yelp, the coyote fell, and a diamondback slithered away from its den with new purpose.

In the deep summer grass, near the edge of the road, the snake tightened into a coil.

Wait.

This far from the human settlement, wagon traffic appeared sporadic.

Patience.

Morago required a particular type of vessel. A lone traveler, in good physical condition, would be the choice. Patience, a necessity.

A wheeled conveyance passed his hiding spot. A family. Then another wagon, this one populated by a group of women. The snake's tail rattled in frustration.

Any human will do.

Morago silenced his demonic horde with a hiss. He refused to ride, unnoticed, behind the eyes of these mewling creatures. Not this time. Only a specific type of body would be acceptable.

A young male with an older female approached his hiding spot. A chorus went up from the demon horde. *Take them now.* But Morago chose to wait. A better choice approached.

A lone man on a horse, head down, almost asleep in the saddle. With no more than a thought, Morago jumped from the snake to a man. The man's head came up violently, knocking the hat from his head.

One of Morago's demons took control of the animal, and their pace quickened.

Traffic increased as they drew closer to town. They had been about to pass the wagon ahead when the old woman's bitter hatred brushed against Morago's mind. Once she caught the demon's attention, the resentful loathing that radiated from her aura filled his blackened soul with glee. Morago slowed his pace and remained behind the wagon. He absorbed her rancor with each breath, her venom titillated his soul. Morago followed the woman into town. When the wagon stopped, Morago halted across the road from the woman and observed her with baleful eyes.

The young man unloaded the trunks and helped the woman from the vehicle. As soon as she stood on the boardwalk, the man climbed back into his seat and shook the reins.

The hate-filled female glared from the walkway at the man in the retreating wagon. Disgust, malignant with vindictive thoughts, and self-absorption flowed from her self-righteous rage.

Morago's soul inhaled deeply and reveled in her hatred. She was ripe with loathing, through and through—like old wood filled with worm, rank and ready to burst wide with rot.

A man at the boarding house opened the door and spoke to her. Immediately, her countenance changed. She became a poor old woman, betrayed by those she'd spent her life serving. Abandoned by the ones she trusted the most. Pitifully, she begged for a room.

Morago snickered and noted the house she entered. After she went inside, the horse and rider moved ahead with one mind, ever forward, toward the beacon.

Two wagons ahead of Morago, the young man who had helped the bitter woman caught his attention. The lad had only thoughts of a wife and young daughter who waited for his safe return. When the wagon stopped beside a livery, Morago and the horse turned right, off the diagonal and onto a residential street. The beacon lay just up ahead.

The horde gibbered in Morago's mind, filled with excitement as they moved closer to the landmark. The child would not be there, of course. Too much time had passed since the *twyning*. But the search must begin somewhere, and the beacon where the prophecy freed him might offer a clue.

Horse and man stopped in the road before a house with a large 'H' on the door. The man's bloodshot gaze rose to the second-floor window. The pair sat motionless for quite some time.

With a thought from the master, the horse moved toward the house, along the narrow side, and into the back yard. No longer did he feel a stranger's eyes upon him.

Morago turned to contemplate the empty building while his horde chattered maniacally inside his head.

***

Hunter

—

Hunter had spent every waking moment since Sam and Cat departed surveying Denver and researching the surrounding area. He'd rented a mount from the livery and rode the main arteries of the city, sketchbook in hand.

He'd asked for, and been granted, access to Denver's General Land Office records. He made a sketch of the eastern plains using homestead entries,

Commissioners' letters, and land grants. The various rail lines that served Denver provided a scale based on towns along their route—one roughly every ten miles. The piecemeal map of Eastern Colorado included the Shilo and Harris family ranches. The drawing wasn't as complete as he would have liked, but it did show train lines, small towns, and plots of lands filed with the Land Office. He'd made do with less.

He unfolded the map of the plains east of the mountains, each sketch carefully tied to the next with string. He spread the map on his bed, slid the pendulum from its silk bag into his hand, and gripped it in his fist. He checked the location of his bounty several times each day. Once they ceased to move, he could make plans to approach them.

Eyes closed, he exhaled through pressed lips.

Seeress, again I beseech you. Show me the location of those foretold in your prophecy.

The voice in the back of his mind, never completely silent, erupted with urgent warnings. *Be careful. Be cautious.*

"*Mon Dieu,* be silent," he muttered, and ran his free hand through his hair. "I've come too far to stop now."

With the rose quartz held tight, he let the arrowhead slide between his fingers and swing freely over the map. The pendulum circled wide, spiraling oblong until it swung side to side in a straight line. The easternmost point was over The Shilo Ranch, north of Kiowa Crossing; the western point, somewhere in Denver.

The same as this afternoon.

Hunter rubbed his face and rested a hand on his hip.

They may have stopped moving.

He spread the Denver map on the bed and swung the pendulum again. He hadn't bothered with the Denver map earlier. When the bob slowed, he opened his eyes. The arrowhead curled in one direction. He moved the pendulum until the arrowhead became still, and he let the tip touch the map.

"Huh." Hunter rubbed his eyes with forefinger and thumb, then pushed his hair from his face.

An incredible coincidence, perhaps?

He stowed the maps and pendulum, slid his flat-brimmed hat on his head, and left his room with a familiar destination in mind. He hurried down the stairs and waved to the clerk behind the desk. Once outside, he rounded the building to the hotel's small stable.

He flipped the stable boy a penny to tack up his horse, and then checked the cinch strap before he mounted. He smiled at the wide-eyed lad. "*Merci.*"

Hunter followed the same route as he and Sam had the other day. He turned on the diagonal and continued past the livery stable at Park and Pence. As he rode along Pence Street toward the Harris house, he realized the shadows stretched long across the street in front of him. The day had passed more quickly than he realized.

He reined the horse to a stop in front of the house. No lights shone from the windows. Along the street ahead, the soft glow from neighbors' windows made the Harris home appear empty.

Perhaps they've already departed.

The other point was close to the Harris Ranch. Tomorrow, he would check the telegraph office for a reply to his application as a field agent, and then he would ride east, toward Cat and Sam.

The voice at the back of his mind repeated an unrelenting dialogue. *Stop. Stop. Stop.*

He ran his hand behind his neck and looked back along the road. *Stop what?* He questioned the voice as a brief movement caught his eye. When he blinked, the road behind him was empty.

There's no one there. You play with my imagination and fray my nerves. Be silent.

He urged his mount forward and approached the house. Curiosity compelled him to continue into the back yard despite the frantic warning to stop. He pulled back on the reins when he saw a rider near the back door.

Is this one of the witches?

In the deepening shadow, the man appeared to be a wrangler by his clothing. He must have heard Hunter approach, yet the man stared endlessly at the back of the house.

Hunter cleared his throat. "*Bonjour.* My name is Hunter." He looked from the wrangler to the house, then back.

What is he staring at?

"I've been contracted to find several individuals that are of interest to my client."

Could the man be ill?

"I believe they may be in some danger."

The man turned his head as the voice in Hunter's head erupted with a frantic plea.

Run.

The hair on Hunter's neck rose, and his mount pranced as he involuntarily tightened the reins.

Run.

Not a cricket chirped. No bird sang nearby.

Run.

Adrenaline hit Hunter's heart like a sledgehammer, and he pulled hard on the reins a moment too late.

Ru—

He watched the wrangler and the horse collapse to the ground in boneless heaps. The voice that had been inside his head, his companion, for as long as he could remember, went silent. Instead, he heard a cackling chorus at the back of his mind and the lonely sound of a woman weeping.

Sainte Mère de Dieu, the demon had him.

He heard his own laughter and felt his recent thoughts invaded and plundered.

East of Denver, north of Kiowa Crossing. The sight of the pendulum's swing, the arrowhead stopped above The Shilo Ranch.

The horse turned to retrace its path along the side of the house without Hunter's urging. Trapped inside his mind, panic overwhelmed him. There would be no escape. Forced to watch, he couldn't even close his eyes.

Someone stood in the shadow along the side of the house. A man Hunter didn't recognize blocked their exit. Although Hunter didn't know the man, he shared enough of the demon's consciousness to realize the demon recognized the man.

"What are you doing back here?" the young man demanded. "You can see no one is home—"

With a flick of Hunter's wrist, the boy flew head-first into the brick wall.

The chorus of laughter intensified as the young man collapsed into a heap beside the building.

They rode past the body and turned onto the street. "East it is, then." Hunter heard himself murmur. "We should reach them by dawn."

Chapter 33

Nichole Harris-Shilo

—

Nichole and Bernard rode up the Highlands' drive and drew back on their reins. In the middle of the wide dirt yard between the house and the corral, two long tables covered in bright white spreads blocked their path. Nichole recognized her dining room table. Someone, probably her husband, had brought it outside. The picnic bench from the kitchen yard had been placed end to end with another just like it.

Cookie and Jeanne rushed to set place settings. Jeanne waved, then disappeared back inside the house.

"What's this?" Bernard asked.

"I don't know." Nichole shrugged. "Dinner outside, for sure. Looks like we'll need to ride around the corral to get past."

As she spoke, Kelly and Bill emerged from the barn and hurried toward the riders. Behind her, Nichole could hear Jason and the wagon turning into the drive.

Bernard dismounted, then helped Nichole from her saddle.

Kelly arrived and captured both reins. "I'll take care of these."

Bill hurried past them, waving at Jason to stop. "The yard is blocked. I'll take the wagon around the back way."

The afternoon had cooled considerably for late June, and Nichole turned her face to the cool breeze as she waited for Amy and Alyse to walk up the short drive to the house. She fell in between the sisters as they continued along the house to the kitchen yard.

Jim and Merril stood beneath the shade of the tarp with Cookie and Henny.

Nichole slipped her arm around her husband's waist, and he settled an arm around her shoulders, pulling her close for a brief hug.

"How did it go?" Merril asked.

"Surprisingly well." Nichole smiled up at him then turned and pointed at the yard. "What are we doing?"

"We, my darling wife, are having dinner with our very large family." Merril pulled her close again and kissed her forehead.

"With everyone?" Nichole looked to Cookie and Henny. "What a marvelous idea. What can I do to help?"

Cookie shook her head. "Everything's well in hand. We were just waitin' for you."

Henny nodded. "Wash up. We'll get the vittles on the table."

Nichole turned to watch the people in the yard. Cat joked with Amy and Alyse as Sam looked on. Jim approached the group, and like a moth to a flame, stopped beside Alyse. Bayard and Kelly talked beside the corral. Behind Nichole, Katy and Hope-Anne's laughter filled the air.

Merril spoke soft, for only Nichole to hear. "I need to do this."

"The dinner?" Nichole glanced up.

Merril gazed at the people in the yard. A few began to take their seats. "For everyone. These people." He nodded toward the yard. "I need them to know how important they are to me." He looked at Nichole. "They've filled a place in my heart that's been empty my whole life." He wrapped both arms around her and whispered into her hair. "I'm afraid by this time tomorrow—"

"I know you're newlyweds, but can you smooch with my cousin after dinner?" Jason chuckled as he walked from the house toward Amy.

Nichole looked up at Merril and very deliberately pulled his mouth to hers for a tender kiss, then took his hand and led him from beneath the tarp.

Cookie and Henny had placed two bowls of mashed potatoes and two platters of spiced beef at each table, along with fresh baked bread and greens.

Merril seated Nichole at one end of the dining room table, strolled to the other end and waited as everyone settled. One by one, faces turned toward Merril, who remained standing. Conversations quieted as he gained everyone's attention.

Nichole held her breath. Stepping into the role of leader could not be easy for him. She didn't know what he planned to say, but she trusted his instincts.

"Before we eat, I'd like to say a few words," Merril began. "The last few weeks have been both heartbreaking and joyous for me. The loss of my family and the gift of having all of you with me today, my new family and my wife. It first rends, and then fills my heart with gratitude. Thank you for taking those of us from The Shilo into your home and allowing us to be a part of the Highlands family." He gestured to Henny, Katy, and Bill.

They nodded in agreement to those at their table.

"Our family continues to grow, and we welcome Amy's sister, Alyse, and their uncles, Bayard and Bernard James. I've never met individuals more giving and caring of strangers, and so willing to share their miraculous talents. Without you and your abilities, I know, beyond doubt, my beautiful wife would not be with us today." He swallowed, ran a hand across his mouth, and then looked up and smiled. "For that, I am forever in your debt." He paused, but no one spoke. Then he raised his gaze and looked at Jimmy Leigh.

"Oh, no." Jim shook his head and leaned back.

Merril grinned. "If Jason and Nichole are the brains of The Highlands Ranch, then you, my friend, are its heart."

Jim wagged his finger at Merril. "I'm not," he protested over applause from both tables. "I've done nothing special. I just do my job."

Hands on his hips, Merril turned to Jim. "You went out a second-floor window, without hesitation, to save my wife. How can you say you've done nothing special?"

Jim's face flushed. "You don't think I intended to go out the window, do ya?" He shook his head at Merril and grinned. "I was just too big, and movin' too fast, to stop."

When the laughter died down, Merril bowed to Jim. "Nevertheless, thank you, my friend."

"You're welcome," Jim replied with a dip of his head.

Then Merril looked to Sam. "I've also been reunited with a man I thought of as family many years ago. It amazes me how years can part us, and yet when we find each other again, it's as if no time had passed at all." Merril walked toward Sam. "I never had the opportunity to tell you how important you were to me, and how much I cherished our friendship. Allow me to say thank you now, for putting up with a foolish lost kid, and for being a mentor and an example of the man I hoped to become."

Sam stood, and the men gripped hands.

"Welcome Samuel Kline. I also welcome your sister, Catherine. You are forever a part of my family."

"Thank you, Merril."

"You better wrap it up," Lloyd spoke up from his seat beside Nichole. "Your wife is crying, and I can hear Tom's stomach growl from here."

Nichole motioned for Lloyd to hush as she laughed and dabbed her eyes.

My husband's a natural leader, whether he sees it or not.

She sniffed and smiled at Merril.

"You're right." Merril nodded to Lloyd as he returned to his seat. "I've said more than I intended. But there's one more thing. We don't always say a blessing before our meals. Today—especially today, I think we should say two." He looked around and his gaze landed on Katy.

"Katy, would you say our first grace please?" Merril smiled at the girl and took his seat.

Katy looked from Merril to her mother.

Henny nodded.

Katy folded her hands together and closed her eyes.

"From the sky above look down on me.

Save my soul from sin and greed.

Bless our food and bless our home.

Show us that we're not alone. Amen."

The group echoed, "Amen."

"Beautiful, Katy. Thank you." Merril looked down the table. "Bernard, would you say our second grace?"

Bernard inclined his head.

"Lord and Lady, be welcome at our table.

Watch over us and bless us.

Bless this food we are about to receive

from the bounty of your earth."

Those seated around the table hesitated when Bernard finished, unsure if he was done with his prayer.

Amy quickly added, "Amen."

"Amen," echoed around the table, and then everyone helped themselves to the dishes nearest to them and passed the plate down.

Eating took precedence, and once they all filled their plates, conversation slowed. As the meal wound down, talk began to turn to the coming evening and the preparations still to be made tonight.

Nichole laid her napkin beside her plate and spoke down the long table. "I'm going back to The Shilo tonight, Merril. It seems I have a few special abilities myself. I can help them fight, and I owe them my life." She reached over and took Amy's hand. "Any help I can give, I will."

"I'm going, too." Jason leaned his elbow on the table and turned to Merril. "I thought you might decide to join us as well."

Merril nodded. "Wherever Nicki goes, I'll be beside her. I thought she told you that already."

Jason gave an amused huff and shook his head. "As a matter of fact, she did."

"Your guns will not be unappreciated." Bernard pushed back from the table. "To speak plainly, we don't know precisely what we'll face."

Jim stood. "If there's room for another, I'd like to tag along." He gave Alyse one of his rare and wonderful smiles. "Whatever you need."

"I'll stand with you." Sam rose and nodded to Merril.

"I'm coming too," Cat announced.

"You will not. You'll stay here, where you'll be safe," Sam told his sister.

Cat came to her feet beside her brother and hooked her arm with his. "I'm safer beside you than trailing behind. Besides, I already spoke with Amy and Alyse. They welcome my help."

Nichole covered her mouth with her hand and locked gazes with Merril. Almost half of those present planned to stand with the James family at The Shilo. The rest would protect The Highlands.

How can I ever repay such devotion and friendship?

Merril stood and laid his napkin beside his plate. "Everyone, whether you come with us or protect our home here, you have my gratitude." His gaze met those who would shelter at the Highlands. "I recommend everyone stay in the main house overnight—even if your rooms have been warded." He looked from Kelly and Bill to Henny and Lawna. "You'll find strength by being together."

"I'm not leavin' the animals," Lloyd stated. "They'll need my care."

Merril nodded. "I agree, but you'll need to stay put. Take what you need into the barn for both you and the animals tonight." He looked around the group. "No one should leave their shelter until at least sunset tomorrow night."

"I'll make food baskets for Lloyd and Tom, as well as your group." Cookie pushed herself to her feet. "I don't want anyone to worry about food or water. Enough for one day, you say?"

Merril nodded. "Our adversary should arrive sometime between sunset tonight and tomorrow night."

"I'm surprised Hunter hasn't arrived," Sam said to Merril. "He uses a map and a pendulum to find people. I've worked with him before, and his ability is, well—unnerving."

Bay and Bern exchanged startled glances.

Nichole caught their exchange and sat forward. "Speak up, gentlemen. We hold no secrets at this table, not today."

Bayard cleared his throat and looked from Nichole to Sam. "The power to track people, or souls, using objects held by or owned by those individuals is usually associated with spiritual magic. Similar to what we saw this morning in Nichole."

Nichole's gaze shot from Bayard, touched on Cat and ended at Merril.

Merril's brow furrowed. "Spiritual magic?"

Lloyd stood and stepped away from the table. "Yup. That's all very interesting. We'll keep an eye out for this Hunter fella." He brushed at his shirt. "I'd best get movin'. By sunset, you say?" He patted Tom's shoulder as he passed. "Time to get busy."

Lloyd's words set the people in the yard in motion.

Cookie picked up several empty plates and headed toward the kitchen. "I'll get those baskets ready."

Lawna handed Hope-Anne to Katy, then cleared the table with Jeanne and Henny.

Merril spoke above the commotion in the yard. "Bill, Kelly, would you saddle four horses and hitch up the buckboard? We'll leave for The Shilo as soon as Cookie packs our supplies."

Nichole took hold of Merril's arm. "I'm going to pack a bag. Do you need anything?"

"I'll come with you." He followed her across the porch, his hand resting on her lower back.

In their room, Nichole pulled the carpetbag from the base of the wardrobe and opened it on the bed. "I'm not sure what I'll need."

"Not much of anything. We'll be back tomorrow night."

Nichole paused when Merril closed the door and turned to her. "Tell me about this spiritual ability Bernard says you have. What happened?"

"Oh, that." Nichole put her brush and several hairpins in the bag. "I can see and interact with spirits." She opened the dresser drawer and tossed a camisole and underdrawers into the bag. "I should have suspected, of course."

Merril stepped forward and touched her arm. "Stop. Tell me what happened." He wrapped his arms around her waist.

Nichole looked into his eyes and pushed a strand of hair behind his ear. "We found Kevin's spirit lost in the house. I helped him find his way out." She laid her hand along his face. "I could see him, the same way I saw you in my other life."

Merril kissed her hand, never taking his gaze from hers. "How is that possible?"

Nichole's sighed and tried to relax in Merril's arms.

Trust he will understand.

She bowed her head to the soft voice in the back of her mind. "My future self, the one who came back to be with you—her name was Courtney Veau. My father—Courtney's father—had a strong spiritual ability. He tried to trace our family history, but the furthest ancestor he could find was Alexander and Catherine Veau."

Merril's brows lifted, and his eyes widened.

"I suspect the bounty hunter Cat is so taken with may be Alexander Veau."

"You think Sam's sister and this Hunter fellow are your ancestors?"

"Courtney's ancestors, but yes. The ability to hear and see spirits must be inherited. Courtney's father had it, and she could hear you—see you. It's how I knew I could find my way back."

Merril studied his wife's face but remained silent.

"I thought I recognized Cat. I even asked her if we'd met before. She must be my great, great—something, grandmother. Courtney looked very similar to Catherine Kline."

Merril shook his head and smiled, love shone in his eyes. "You astound me. Continuously."

She tipped her face up and rose on her toes to kiss him. "And you are the very beat of my heart."

"Enough, in there." Jason rapped two times on the door. "We're ready to go." His boots beat a staccato down the stairs.

Merril closed the bag and opened the door. "Come, my dear, let's go meet the Devil."

Nichole preceded him out the door and down the stairs, song lyrics from another time playing inside her head.

Outside, the tables were gone, and the wagon and horses stood ready. Jason and Amy took the buckboard seat with the James family. Cat sat in the back of the wagon with the food and weapons. The rest mounted and trailed behind the wagon down the drive.

Nichole rode beside Merril, but they didn't speak. Instead, they listened to Sam and Jim discuss the finer merits of the various firearms they carried.

The setting sun tickled the distant hills as they arrived in The Shilo yard. Merril directed Bayard and Sam to move the wagon and horses to the large, empty barn. The rest carried supplies into the house.

Bayard secured the barn with protection satchels, weaving magic and prayers together, and laying down the salt barrier at each opening. When he finished, he and Bernard shut and secured the barn doors, and then followed Sam back to the house.

Alyse and her uncles worked quickly to ward the house. Everyone else stayed out of their way and remained on the front porch as the color faded from the sky, east to west.

After he secured the house, Bernard called everyone to the dining room to discuss his strategy for the coming battle. He brushed his hand over the drawing of the pentacle to press it flat. "You all saw the circle in the yard. When the demon arrives, we'll move out there. Although the circle will be warded against evil, people and animals will be able to cross the boundary." He met the gaze of the gunmen. "Your main job will be to keep anything from crossing that line. Guard our ward, and our backs."

"What do you expect to attack us?" Sam asked.

Bernard gave a partial shrug. "He'll use animals. He uses them already. We'll aid the gunmen with our magic, but I believe our main task will be to counter the demon's powers."

"What powers does he have?" Merril checked the chamber of his Colt, then holstered his weapon.

"We don't know." Bernard shook his head. "My hope is, with the warded house behind us, he can only approach from the direction of the corral and bunkhouse. Remember, you can move freely within the circle, but do not cross the warded line." He looked around the room and stopped his search at Cat. "Your role will be to reload the weapons from your place in the center of the star. I also ask that you maintain the warded boundary line."

Cat nodded, wide-eyed. "I can do that."

"Will we post guards tonight?" Jim asked.

"You're welcome to do so. I'll leave the lookouts to you." Bernard tipped his head to Jim. "While you assign duties, I'll cast the ward boundaries for the circle. Please, once I finish, be careful of the salt circle, especially as you rush across the boundary once the demon arrives."

The empty library became their ready room with the basket of food, a cask of fresh water, as well as their extra weapons and ammunition. Bernard picked up his warding supplies, then went outside.

Jim set the watch schedule and assigned which items each person would bring to the circle at the first sign of trouble. When he finished, everyone returned to the porch to watch Bernard cast the ward.

He moved from compass point to compass point, calling the elements for each direction and invoking their protection. He ended with a blessing, and asked the God and Goddess to be present during their battle. When he finished the ward, he turned to his audience on the porch. "Would those of you wielding magic join me in the circle?" He spread his arm wide and stepped into one of the far angles of the star.

"Bay, I'd have you up front with me. Amy and Alyse, please take the air and water points. Nichole, you will have the Goddess or spirit point in back."

Once the casters stood in place, Bernard tossed Alyse a box of matches. "We'll keep the fire burning throughout the night."

Alyse smiled at her uncle and struck the match. Fire ignited in her hand and jumped into the pit.

"Gunmen and Miss Kline, there are no assigned places. We stand now in the elements each of us will represent, but we are not limited to those elements. As we are free to move about the circle, so will you be. These are but our starting positions."

Nichole hid her trembling hands in the folds of her skirt. Bernard had taunted Amy with being the weak link, but deep inside her heart, she knew herself to be the untrained weak link.

Be brave, a voice whispered. *When the time comes, you will know what to do.*

"Those of you on the porch will bring the items from the library and place them in the center, here." Bernard indicated the large open area in the middle of the star. "Catherine, keep the bag of salt and pouring bowl with you. Keeping the circle secure will be our best defense."

Cat nodded. Her stare caught Nichole's, and they gazed at one another for several moments.

"This could be a long fight—I don't know. I believe we're as prepared as we can be." Bernard crossed the pentagram and stepped over the salt circle. "We should try to get some rest." He turned back to the circle. "Oh, Alyse, if you would lower the flames and bank the coals before you come inside?" He smiled at his niece.

The rest of the casters in the yard stepped carefully over Bernard's ward and followed him inside. As they passed the library, Sam stepped inside. He had been assigned first watch.

Chapter 34

Alyse James

—

Unable to sleep, Alyse slipped from the room she shared with Cat. She tiptoed down the hall, past the closed doors where Amy and Nichole slept with their husbands. Fully dressed in her dark blue skirt and jacket, shoes in hand, she padded down the stairs and paused outside the library door.

Although a lamp burned in the main room, the library remained dark. No reflection in the windows would impede the watchers' view. The water keg and food basket were stacked inside the door. Beside those were the weapons and ammunition they would take into the circle. In the center of the room were two chairs and the man she'd come to find—Jimmy Leigh.

Jim ran his hand over his face and stared out into the night.

She'd never met anyone like Jim before. Although, she'd be the first to admit the customers her uncles brought to the farm were far too old, and their sons too young, to spark her interest. This man though—his first glance had made her soul sing. He acted as though he knew her, made no secret of the fact he had recognized her, even though they had never met. Given—she looked just like Amy—and perhaps that's what he meant. Yet, her familiars allowed his touch. That, alone, she found shocking.

How do I know this man?

Her gaze caressed his profile. He wore his hair trimmed at the collar, but longer on top. His nose was long and straight, with a strong chin she longed to touch. Although handsome, in her mind, what set him apart from the rest was his height. Nichole's husband was a tall man, but Jim stood several inches taller still. A giant of a man with sad, ancient eyes.

"I know you're there," Jim said softly. "Come sit with me."

Thankful the darkness covered the heat that bloomed in her face, Alyse crossed to the chair beside him and took a seat. She bent and slipped on her low-heeled work boots and laced them. Sitting beside this intriguing man, she wished she were dressed like her sister, stylish and elegant, instead of practical and boring.

When she sat up, she could see the reflection in his eyes as he watched her.

"Did you sleep?" His voice touched each part of her—his words a gentle hand along every nerve in her body.

It took all the control she could muster to nod and respond. "Some, yes. Cat still sleeps. I didn't want to wake her."

Jim turned back to the window.

In the darkened room, she could see the outline of his hand. His elbow rested on the arm of the chair, his palm open and facing up.

An invitation.

Her breath caught. By slow degrees, she lifted her hand from her skirt and slid it onto his palm. His fingers closed softly over hers, and she exhaled. Neither spoke as they stared at the embers in the yard. The quiet and the dark would have been peaceful, had she not known what stalked the night.

"It feels calm." His voice came, soft and low.

"It does. Still, the storm approaches," she whispered.

"It's as though you read my mind." He chuckled.

They fell silent and watched the banked embers in the fire pit flare and die back.

"Could I ask about your name?" She glanced at him and then back to the embers.

"Of course," Jim replied. "You can ask me anything."

"Should I call you Jim or Jimmy? I've heard you addressed both ways." Could he hear the tremor in her voice? Would he think her frightened by the coming battle, or would he know the touch of his hand made her tremble? She looked up at him and found his gaze on her.

He didn't answer. Instead, they studied each other's silhouettes in the dark. He raised his other hand and ran his knuckles down the angle of her jaw to her chin, then tilted her head back and lowered his mouth to hers. His lips were warm. A soft pressure. A question.

Alyse responded with a question of her own. Her hand explored the side of his face as she tasted his lips this time. The threat was too imminent for passion to ignite. Instead, they exchanged a promise. One more taste, and the kiss ended.

Jim raised his head and looked down at her face. "Call me anything you like," he whispered. "I will always answer."

The sudden howl of wolves inside the house startled them both.

"It's here." Alyse rose to her feet.

"How did your wolves get inside the house?" Jim grabbed his rifle and two boxes of ammunition.

"They're not always wolves, and they go where they please." Alyse rushed out of the library and opened the front door. Both wolves ran past her. Their howls echoed long after they disappeared into the murkiness of the night.

Alyse yelled toward the main room, "Bay? Bern?"

"Right here." Bay stepped into the library and picked up the *grimoire* and the keg of drinking water, then followed Jim out the door.

***

Nichole Harris-Shilo

—

The baying shocked Nichole awake. She and Merril rolled from the bed at the same time. Fully dressed. She slid her feet into her shoes, pulled the strings tight, and knotted them.

Merril opened their door and buckled on his gun belt in the dark. "Let's go."

Nichole rose and took his hand. There was enough light from the room below to navigate the stairs. As she followed Merril down and out into the night, flames blossomed in the fire pit. She paused at the edge of the porch.

Outlined by the blaze, Alyse stood before the fire, hands raised to the night sky.

From near the door, Jason called to Amy, "Go ahead and take your place. I'll be there in a moment."

Then Amy was beside Nichole. Together, they stepped over the salt circle and took their place in the pentagram.

Jason carried weapons outside, handed Merril several rifles, then went back for more.

Merril stacked them near the center, then helped Cat step over the ward.

Cat moved to the center of the circle and arranged the guns, ammunition, and precious salt containers to be within easy reach.

Jason brought several boxes of ammunition and set them where Cat pointed, then backed toward Amy, checking his rifle.

Bernard came last with the basket of food. He closed the door of the house, then strode into the circle. He placed the food between Nichole and Amy and took his place beside his brother.

"Check the ward." Bayard pointed to the circle they had all just crossed. He spoke over his shoulder to Alyse. "Lower the flame—conserve your fuel."

Cat walked the circle and returned to her place. She crouched beside the food and extra rifles, her head turned in nervous twitches from side to side.

The couples grouped together. Sam stood beside Cat in the middle. He leaned down to whisper to her, and she nodded. The brothers took their stand alone in front and stared into the night.

"Where are the wolves?" Jim searched the shadows to his left.

"They're here." Alyse looked up and scanned the night sky. "Somewhere."

A sound alerted Nichole, and she cocked her head. "Do you hear that?" To the west, beyond the bunkhouse, a buzzing approached. "What is it?" A black cloud flowed over the building and took aim at the circle in the yard. The bunkhouse disappeared behind the cloud.

"Get down," Merril said to Nichole as he moved in front of her.

"Insects," the brothers spoke in unison. "Alyse."

"Yes." Alyse thrust her hands forward and pushed a wall of air at the swarm. The insects divided around the air burst. Most diverted away from the group, but their sheer number overwhelmed the wall of air and dozens of bugs flooded into the circle.

Alyse sent a burst of flame overhead, but the flame did little good. Cinders and bits of wings fell all around.

Cat jumped to her feet and screamed as she pulled locusts from her hair and threw them into the fire.

The brothers ignored the pests to stare into the darkness. "A distraction."

Except for a few lingering flies, the insects disappeared as quickly as they came.

"They're out there." Nichole pointed across the corral. At the edge of the fire's light, countless silvery eyes reflected. More joined as she watched, then crept forward.

Merril turned and searched in all directions. "Jim—the road."

Nichole looked where Merril pointed. Dozens of shining eyes circled in the dark.

Jim cocked the lever action on his rifle and moved forward. "Step back," he said to Alyse. He touched her arm and put himself between her and the growing threat. He dropped to his knee, steadied his arm against his leg and looked down the barrel of his rifle.

"Trade me places," Merril said close to Nichole's ear.

She looked from Jim to Merril, nodded and moved toward the center.

What now?

Merril knelt in a stance similar to Jim, the barrel of his rifle pointed down the other side of the house.

Jason and Amy traded places, and Sam stepped between the brothers and knelt in front of Cat.

"They'll rush us," Bay and Bern said. "Drop them before they reach the circle." As though their words released them, the animals rushed in from all sides.

Horror engulfed Nichole's senses as she turned in every direction. Everyone around her fought against the onslaught except her. She observed.

Terrified animals of all types—deer, skunks, and coyotes—raced away from a threat, rather than attacking the group with rage. At the edge of her vision, shadows moved. A dozen of them wormed among the frightened beasts.

More than one demon?

Gunfire erupted, and the scent of gunpowder filled the ring. Alyse threw missiles of fire at the largest animals while Amy released dozens of ice darts. Bay and Bern used fire as well, and their attack filled the corral with flaming light.

Coyotes, badgers, and whitetail deer were among the animals that raced at the group. Some changed course at the last moment, and some fell as they charged toward the circle.

Catherine passed forward loaded rifles to Merril and Jim, then reloaded their empty weapons.

A red fox ran past Jason as he exchanged rifles with Cat. The small animal hunched down near the ammunition supply, panting with fear—confused and frightened.

"Salt!" Bay and Bern yelled.

Cat picked up the salt boat and stepped over the fox. She knelt beside Jason and repaired the circle. The animal had barely smudged it, but she filled the impression of its footprint, mounding the salt to match the line on either side. When she returned to her place in the center, the fox had fled.

"Cat." Jim motioned to her. "It went this way."

Cat inspected the circle and shook her head. "It must have jumped over the line." She returned to the center and reloaded weapons.

"Southwest, between the bunk and the corral." Nichole pointed. Shadows moved from mound to mound. "Do you see them?" Then, the ground began to shake.

"Damn," Jim swore. He stood and looked in the direction of the rumble.

Dawn approached. The fire pit's brightness dimmed as the gray half-light filled the yard.

Funneled between the bunkhouse and the corral came the horned animals.

"I can see them. The demons," Nichole screamed. Spaced throughout the cattle, hunched shadows urged the animals forward.

"Stampede," Merril shouted and shoved Nichole behind him as he came to his feet and took aim between the brothers.

The animals were panicked, their eyes wide and rolling with terror. They brayed in fright and ran toward Bay and Bernard.

Fire rolled from Bay, Bern and Alyse toward the front of the stampede, but it only served to terrorize the animals more. They were packed too tightly between the bunkhouse and the corral to swerve and were driven forward by the scared animals behind.

"Get down!" Sam shouted as he continued to fire into the herd, dropping several beasts that disappeared beneath the hooves of the oncoming horde.

The front of the stampede passed the corner of the bunkhouse as a sheet of water blocked the view of the animals in front of Bay and Bern. The water formed into an angle outside the circle, the liquid pointed forward with water extending to either side of the circle. In an instant the fluid hardened to ice.

Amy fell to her knees, eyes closed, her arms extended. Her hoarse cry filled the pentacle as power flowed from her to strengthen the ice. The hand pump exploded from the top of the well, pushed upward by water pressure, and the ice wall thickened.

Bay and Bern paired their ability with hers to harden the barrier and repair the cracks as cattle, unable to turn, were driven into the ice structure.

Divided, the stampede channeled along the side of the group.

Alyse stretched out her palms to the air and created a shield of flame where the ice wall ended. The large beasts pounded their hooves into the ground as they turned away in fright.

Amy fell forward onto her hands. Her hair, escaped from her braid, fell in waves around her face and hung in the dust.

Jason wrapped his arms around her as Nichole reached down and touched Amy's shoulder.

"She's exhausted," Nichole said to Alyse. "She pushed too hard."

Alyse held out her hand.

As Nichole grasped Alyse's hand, Amy raised her head. "That's better," Amy said softly as Alyse echoed the same words.

Jason pulled the hair from her face, brushing at the tears and dust on her cheeks. "Are you injured?" He looked from his wife to Alyse, helped Amy to her feet, and exchanged a look with Nichole. Assured by all his wife was well, he stepped away from the women to check his ammunition.

Nichole released Amy's shoulder and took her hand.

The ice and fire were gone. The rumble of cattle faded in the distance.

Cat finished reloading another round of rifles and pushed her hair out of her eyes. She glanced up at the three women linked behind her and smiled.

Movement in the swirling, gray dust caught Nichole's attention. A dark figure approached between the bunkhouse and corral. She pointed. "Someone's there. Straight ahead of us."

A woman's voice called across the yard. "No need to fret, dear hearts. My beloved twins. My dear, sweet granddaughters. We'll be together soon. Very soon." Chantal's voice echoed in the silence.

"Bay, it's not her!" Bernard yelled at his brother.

Bayard nodded. "I know." Tears streamed from his eyes. "But it means she's gone."

"That we stand with Amy means her plan succeeded," Alyse shouted at her uncles, tears scored lines in the dust on her face as she gripped Nichole's hand. "It's not her we hear. It's the demon."

"It mimics her voice," Nichole said. She stared at the figure as it walked toward them through the cloud of dust. In a whisper she added, "But she's there. I can feel her."

The man continued forward. He walked around dead animals and stopped near the end of the bunkhouse. Broad shouldered, he wore a dark suit coated gray with dust. As he took another step, light touched his face.

"Son-of-a-bitch," Sam swore as the man moved from the dust cloud into the light.

"Hunter?" Cat whispered, then jumped to her feet and tried to rush past her brother. "Hunter!"

Sam caught her around the waist and lifted her from her feet before she came close to the edge of the circle.

"It's not Hunter," he said with regret into her hair. "Not anymore."

Catherine didn't fight her brother. Instead, she crumpled to the ground at his feet. Her hands covered her face. A scream tore from her chest and echoed from the buildings across the yard.

Sam wrapped his arms around her and nodded at Hunter. "How the hell did this happen?"

Hunter's legs trudged forward with a slow, faltering step. His eyes reflected the fire's red glow as they peered up through his long, tangled hair. Parched lips cracked and bled when he smiled. His knees dripped blood through holes torn in his trouser legs. He staggered to a stop and laughed. "My darling Cat. So sweet. So innocent, and oh, so curious." Morago unbuckled Hunter's belt and gave a hoarse, rasping laugh. "Would you have me now, sweet Catherine?" He lurched forward another step and grabbed his crotch as he thrust his hips toward her.

Jimmy Leigh cocked the lever action on his rifle and stepped forward, taking aim at the man in the yard.

"Jim, wait," Merril said

Jim looked at Merril in confusion.

"We can't kill him," Nichole murmured.

Save him. Don't let him pass into the light. A voice whispered into Nichole's mind.

Nichole shook her head. *Who are you?*

No answer.

"He's not alive anymore. He's the demon," Jason replied sharply "Shoot the bastard."

A fireball flew at the circle and extinguished several feet from the ring.

Amy stood, one hand clutched her sister's, and the other stretched toward the demon.

"We have to kill him." Amy looked at Nichole. "We can't let him live."

"What happens if he dies?" Merril gripped Nichole's shoulders and spun her to face him. "What happens to you?"

"I don't know," Nichole replied. "I don't know what the future looks like without him. For me, there won't be one." Her gaze locked with Amy's. "He's my ancestor—Courtney's ancestor. My line of descent will disappear when he dies. He's not dead now because I'm still here." She looked across the yard. "He's being controlled by the monster."

Another fireball flew at them, but Alyse countered easily. She pushed it toward the hillside beside the bunkhouse. The field exploded in flames.

Bay and Bern hurled fire at the demon.

Morago caught the flares, one in each hand and laughed. "You boys were never as good at playing with fire as your mother was." He combined the two balls above his head and launched it back at them.

Amy met it with a jet of water just feet in front of Bernard. The explosion knocked him backward into Sam and Catherine.

"Merril?" Jim said. His rifle still sighted between the demon's eyes. "I need to know."

"When he goes down, I'll go down." Nichole looked from Merril to Jim. "But you have no choice."

Snarling growls turned Merril's head. "Wolves. Behind us." He released Nichole, dropped to his knee and lifted his rifle in one movement. Then he took aim.

A golden flash of light swooped down from above and sped past Merril. From the flicker of light leapt a large black wolf. It landed near the side of the house, between the warded circle and the wolves, and charged into the threatening pack of grays. With its hackles raised, the black wolf was twice the size of the other wolves. It seized the first gray by the head and tossed it aside, and then snarled and jumped at another.

"Your wolves are here," Jim said to Alyse.

Nichole turned at Jim's words. A second black wolf chased a pack of grays along the other side of the house toward the road. The grays' shadowed riders sprang from their backs and arched toward Hunter's body. Nichole followed the shadows flight, then faced the man in the yard.

Laughter erupted from the demon, and a low rumbling began beneath their feet.

"Our pets are playing. How nice." Hunter laughed and raised his bloody palms toward the circle. Fist-sized rocks burst from the ground and flew toward them.

Amy raised one hand and half the rocks burst into dust.

The other rocks were blown to the side by Bayard and Alyse.

Bernard launched flaming arcs in the direction of the demon from his kneeling position.

The beast laughed and stepped closer, juggling flames back faster than Bernard could counter.

Amy blocked the fireball coursing toward her uncle and sank to her knees.

Nichole backed up until she bumped against Merril's chest. "Take him out," Nichole ordered Jim.

"Not in the head," Amy yelled and glanced up at Jim. "In the chest."

Jim nodded, dropped his line of sight, and fired.

A small hole appeared in Hunter's vest. The demon laughter ended in a cough of blood. He fell to his knees and collapsed onto his face in the dirt.

Chapter 35

Morago

—

How?

Morago reeled in confusion inside the dead man.

How did this happen?

Demons howled, and a woman's brash laughter added to his disorientation. Deprived of choice, Morago slithered from the body and raised his head to look back at the witches.

A fireball soared across the yard toward him, and he retreated in terror. Fire scorched along his delicate scaled skin, blistering his hide. He slithered blindly across the prairie, afraid the witches and the gunman would pursue him. His vulnerability enraged him, blinded him to his surroundings.

I must escape.

Pain raked his body anew as a hawk's talons tore into his skin.

The demon changed to vapor just as the bird tried to rend him with her beak. Morago released the empty snakeskin and lifted into the sky, turning away from the powerful elemental magic he continued to covet.

Full of hubris after the easy victory over the witches' grandmother, he hadn't anticipated his prizes' allies or their weapons. But they had not defeated him, only driven him away. For that single mistake, he swore to make them pay. He vowed to learn more about the era he now inhabited. He would study this age and discover allies of his own. A plan took shape in his mind.

He shrieked loudly in triumph and tipped his wings to head west.

Next time, there would be no defeat.

Next time, he would obtain all he desired.

Chapter 36

Amy Harris

—

Merril caught Nichole as she collapsed and eased her to the ground. He pushed the golden curls from her face and searched for a pulse. "I can't keep doing this." He shook his head and looked at Amy. "I can't."

Amy crawled to Merril and put her hand on Nichole's forehead and quickly scanned her for wounds.

No injury to her body.

Bayard helped his brother to his feet and they both stared at Nichole.

"What happened?" Jason demanded and dropped to his knees beside his wife. "Why did Nichole fall?" He looked from Merril to Amy. "Can you heal her?"

Amy's gaze turned to Alyse. "No, but we can heal Hunter."

Bernard's face twisted as he looked at Amy. "Have you lost your mind?"

"We shouldn't step out of the ward yet," Bayard replied. "We don't know if the demon's gone."

Amy watched the yard for a moment. "Set the prairie on fire if you must, but we need that man inside this circle immediately. Every second counts."

Bernard gave her a hard stare then stepped across the ward and hurried to the fallen man.

Bay followed, and together they lifted the larger man's dead weight and carried him into the circle, careful to step over the salt boundary.

Cat remained motionless where she had fallen. Both hands over her mouth, her eyes bled tears. Her gaze never wavered from Hunter.

Sam stood beside her. He reset his hat and shook his head. "Damn."

As soon as they placed the body on the ground, Amy and Alyse were beside him. Amy put her hands on his back and looked up at her uncles.

"Turn him to his side." She raised her hand over the body and a golden glow radiated from her palms.

Bay and Bern shifted the body, and Amy put her hands to either side of Hunter's chest.

Alyse mirrored Amy, placing her palms on the back of Amy's hands. The gold and orange glow wove together, as the group looked on in silence.

***

Courtney Veau

—

Courtney stood with one foot in the Passage. Half of her ethereal form lay trapped beyond the blackened doorway. Unable to move, she raised her gaze and searched along the hall.

Several doorways ahead stood the incorporeal form of Alexander Veau. He turned his head slowly toward the light.

"Hunter, stop," Courtney called.

Hunter's spirit turned and looked at her. "Cat?" He glanced over his shoulder at the light again, then back toward Courtney.

"Don't go down the hallway, Hunter. Stay with me."

He shook his head, stared hard at her for a moment, and then turned back toward the light.

"Alexander Veau, look at me," Courtney demanded.

The spirit turned toward her. "How do you know that name?"

"Catherine needs you. I need you. Stay with me, please, for just a few moments."

Courtney could feel herself begin to fade. With each passing moment, the reality of her existence became less and less certain. If Alexander left and walked into the light, she would disappear.

She would never have existed.

Hunter hesitated, one hand rose toward Courtney. "You're so like Catherine," he murmured.

"I'm like you too, Alexander. It's how I'm here." She felt her existence evaporate. "Cat needs you, Hunter. Wait here, beside the doorway." The hallway dissolved before her eyes. "You need to wait," she whispered. "Give them time."

***

Amy Harris

—

"*Do you see it?*" Amy thought to Alyse, her eyes closed, her head tipped back.

"*I see it.*" Alyse wove her fire magic through Amy's *earth-sight* and cauterized the tear in Hunter's lung. The bullet had passed through his chest, missing his heart by a fraction of an inch. The metal tore the large vessel that led to his lungs. "*You need to align the tear. Push the torn edge closer to the vessel.*"

"*How?*" Amy floundered for a moment, then understood. *Earth-magic* allowed her to move the vessel. When the edges aligned, she felt Alyse press through her and close the tear.

"*He needs fluids.*" Alyse mended the skin, front and back. "*His blood's too thick.*"

"*Can I do that?*" Amy sensed the water in the trough and the keg. *Either will do*. She absorbed the water into herself, then directed it through her magic into his bloodstream.

"*That's good.*" Alyse thought to her. "*I'm going to clear his lungs and spark his heart.*"

A spray of blood shot from Hunter's mouth and nose.

Cat's gasp of shock was cut short.

"*What's wrong?*" Amy wondered to Alyse.

"*I don't know. I'll try again.*" Alyse pushed air into Hunter's lungs and sent a spark into his heart.

Hunter curled his knees to his chest and coughed more blood from his lungs.

Amy released her bond with Hunter and opened her eyes. She watched Alyse open hers, and the twins stared at each other. Her mirror image smiled, and Amy smiled back.

"Amy?" Merril called. He looked at the sisters, then back at Nichole. "Nicki, wake up."

Amy moved beside Nichole and ran her hand over her forehead. "Nichole?"

Nichole's eyes opened, and her brow furrowed. She looked from Merril to Amy, then back at Merril. "What—" Her body convulsed, her head fell back, and her eyelids fluttered closed.

"Nicki?" Merril lifted her into his lap. "Damn it, Nic." He looked at Amy. "What happened? Why isn't she awake?" Merril's glare cut to Hunter. "He's awake."

Amy took Nichole's face between her palms. "Nicki." Amy patted Nichole's cheek then looked back at Hunter.

Hunter struggled to his hands and knees. His head down, his dark hair hung in the dust.

Around the circle, everyone stepped back, except for Cat. Sam held her when she tried to reach for Hunter.

"Cat," Amy called. "Hunter needs water, badly. We couldn't heal him completely." Amy looked from Cat to Sam. "Please, he needs our help. They both do."

Cat shrugged off Sam's hand, pushed to her feet and lurched toward the keg of water. She filled a tin cup and hurried to Hunter's side. She sank to her knees and pushed the hair back from his face. "Hunter? Alexander? Can you drink?"

Hunter turned over and sat, dark hair clung to his face, his lips cracked and bloody. *"Petit chat?"* he rasped and raised a hand toward her. "I saw you."

"You need to drink." Cat shuffled forward on her knees, placed the cup in Hunter's hand and guided it to his lips.

Hunter took a sip, coughed, then took another sip. "I died." He tore his gaze away from Cat and looked around the circle of faces. He stopped at Jim. "I saw you fire your rifle at me. I knew you would. You had to." He rocked forward and groaned in pain. After a moment, he turned his head and looked Cat. "How am I alive?"

Cat pointed to Amy and Alyse. "They're witches. They healed you."

Hunter looked from Amy and Alyse and his brows rose. "Yes, that's right. The witches." He switched his gaze to Bayard and Bernard. "And you're witches as well."

The brothers nodded.

Hunter coughed and shook his head. "The demon didn't know the gun would kill me." He drained the cup and returned it to Cat. *"Merci."* He looked up at the witches. "But he knows now." He raised a hand to Sam. "Help me stand, *mon ami.*"

Sam took his hand, pulled him up, and steadied him. "Are you all right?"

Hunter nodded and pushed the rest of the hair out of his face. "I think so." Then he shook his head and bent, hands to his knees. "I don't know."

***

Nichole Harris-Shilo

—

Nichole struggled to regain her mind and body from the dark nothingness surrounding her. She'd watched the passage of light disappear as she'd faded from existence. What had brought her back? *Alexander.*

"Amy—do something!"

She latched onto Merril's frantic voice and fought her way forward. The rumble of his chest against her head filled Nichole with joyful motivation.

My love.

She drew a shuddering breath and blinked. "Holy shit," she muttered as Amy's worried expression came into focus, inches from her face.

Amy sat back and scrubbed her hands across her eyes, then smiled at Jason. "She's back."

Merril tightened his grip on Nichole. "I'm damned tired of you dying." He kissed the top of her head and pressed her curls close to his chest with a sigh of relief.

When his hold eased, Nichole turned and found both Jason and Amy remained on the ground beside her. She smiled at her cousin's dust-covered face and put her hand out toward Amy. "You did it." Nichole included Alyse in her gaze. "Thank you."

Nichole turned and laid her palm against Merril's cheek. "I'm sorry that happened."

"It wasn't your fault." He kissed her hand. "Are you well?"

She searched his eyes and caressed the stubble on his chin. "Yes, my love, I am." She touched her lips to his, then pushed upright. "Help me stand."

Merril rose and lifted Nichole to her feet.

She dusted her skirt and looked at Bay and Bern. "The demon's not gone." Nichole's words caught everyone's attention. "He's still out there."

"What do you mean?" Bernard questioned. "We defeated him."

"No," Nichole pointed southeast. "He went that way."

"She's right," Hunter touched his lip and looked at the blood on his finger. "The demon won't give up. He calls himself Morago... and he's learning." Hunter stared at Amy and Alyse. "He'll be back for you. He craves your abilities."

Hunter turned to Cat and opened his arms, catching her as she rushed into them. *"Mon Dieu. Ma belle Cat. Mon amour."* He held her head to his shoulder as she sobbed. "Shh. *Tout va bien.* Shh." His gaze lifted, and he stared at Nichole.

Nichole met and held his regard. *Do you know me, Alexander?*

Hunter tipped his head to Nichole. The intensity of his dark eyes burned into hers before they closed, and he buried his face in Cat's hair.

"Well, then, what are we going to do?" Bayard asked. "He could have our mother."

"He does," Hunter confirmed, and everyone looked to him. "I could sense her—hear her. He controls a horde of demons that do his bidding. Your mother's soul is a prisoner among them."

"Ah, no." Bayard turned away. He lifted his hat and held his wrist to his head. "No."

Nichole wrapped her arms around Merril, her head against his muscular chest.

It's not over.

"Your bunkhouse is on fire," Jason stated calmly.

Alyse squawked in alarm and clenched her fist, smothering the flames.

Hunter kissed Cat's head and whispered in her hair.

Cat nodded and helped Hunter walk out of the circle and ease himself to the wooden planks of the porch. Cat refilled the cup with water and returned to Hunter. He took the tin from her hands, set it beside him, then reached for Cat. He wrapped his arm around her as she settled beside him on the porch.

"Is it safe to leave the ring?" Jason asked Hunter.

"Yes." Hunter grasped the cup beside him and took a sip of water. "Morago will need time to plan before he returns. He was—unprepared for defeat."

"We can't leave Mum with him." Bayard pressed his lips together and stared at Hunter. "What are we going to do?"

Jim stepped forward. "First thing will be to head back to the Highlands. They need to know it's over, for now." He looked down at Alyse and took her hand. "I don't know about demons, but I know about getting beat in a fight. You don't come back for more until you think you have a chance at winning." He tipped his head in the direction Nichole had pointed. "He's running scared for now." He gave Alyse a reassuring smile. "We have time to make plans of our own."

Nichole took Merril's hand and led him over to the porch. She settled beside Hunter on the wooden planks. "Do you know—" She cleared her throat, looked into his dark blue eyes and held out her hand. "Hi. My name is Nichole." She glanced at Merril as he sat beside her. "This is my husband, Merril Shilo."

Hunter nodded and took her hand. "*Bonjour,* Nichole. Merril." Hunter nodded to Merril. "My name is Hunter."

"Yeah." Nichole felt a foolish grin spread across her face, and her heart rate doubled as he squeezed her fingers. She looked from their joined hands to his battered face. "I've heard a lot about you." She glanced at Cat, and the memory of an aged postcard addressed to Alexander Veau crossed her mind. "I'm very pleased to make your acquaintance."

Hunter's eyes narrowed as he gazed at Nichole. "Perhaps... we've met?"

"Yes." Nichole took a breath and nodded. "Perhaps we have."

Sneak Peek at Paradox

The Soul of the Witch Saga continues in Book 5:
Paradox

Chapter 1

Morago

—

The broad-winged hawk soared across the empty blue Colorado sky. Anger and frustration beat in the bird's chest with every downward stroke of its wings.

Morago, the demon entity in possession of the feathered raptor, fumed with impotence and abject failure.

The demon-servants Morago held in thrall were unusually quiet in the aftermath of their master's defeat. Only the old woman's soft laughter remained to mock his fury.

Quiet!

Morago struck his prisoner's soul with his thoughts, lashing her battered spirit.

In the silence that followed, the master inside the gold-breasted bird could sense the hawk's gnawing hunger.

Desperate for nourishment, the young raptor had attacked Morago's primordial snake form as he fled the witches across the prairie.

Pinned beneath the bird's talons, Morago had transformed into a mist and passed into his new host's mind, possessing the predator's healthy young body.

Deprived of its meal, the hunger inside this body remained.

Never before concerned with his host's needs, Morago paused to reconsider.

I will need living slaves. Corporeal fighters to defeat the witches' allies.

He loosened his grip on the hawk, riding behind the bird's instinctual mind instead of exerting complete control.

The broad-winged hawk dropped from its lofty height and slowed, surveying the ground.

A peep from a prairie dog below warned the entire animal village to scurry for shelter.

The hawk banked and skimmed the prairie sage, uttering a sudden piercing shriek. Its keen eye focused on a dove his cry had flushed from the brush. Talons extended, it plucked the smaller bird from the air and forced it to the ground. The raptor's ravenous appetite took control and it ripped the flesh from the tiny creature. The hawk's curved beak slashed at tissue until feathers scattered and blood soaked into the hard soil.

Morago delighted in the rending of flesh and the bird's satiation as the raw meat slid down the hawk's gullet to fill the emptiness inside.

Giving this raptor the strength to serve me further.

The bird ate its fill from the downed dove, then lifted into the sky. Gorged, it searched for a place to roost for the night.

Not yet, Morago conveyed with his mind, imposing his will. *Fly West.*

A slight adjustment to its feathered wings and the hawk turned toward the distant hills.

An inkling of a plan took shape in the demon's mind. With renewed enthusiasm, Morago fed the bird a new destination—a house in the human settlement along the mountains. The place where he had possessed his last human host, the dead man who thought of himself as Hunter.

***

Nichole Harris-Shilo

—

After the group of witches and gunmen had beaten back the demon and revived Hunter, Nichole and Cat escorted the weakened man into the ranch house, out of the sun.

Amy and Alyse followed them inside.

They gathered at one end of the large family table, exhausted from their ordeal.

Nichole leaned forward in her chair and placed her elbow on the edge of the long table. Her chin rested on her palm while her gaze stayed glued with fascination on Hunter.

The fatigued man acted on her like a magnet, focusing her attention as though he were the only other person in the room. She'd read about Alexander Veau, the man known as Hunter, in her father's genealogy research. In fact, she'd slipped Catherine Veau's postcard to her husband from a pile of her dad's old documents and hid the frayed card inside her personal treasure box as a young girl. She'd read the short missive, again and again, always wondering who Alexander Veau was, and why the Veau family history dead-ended at Alexander and Catherine Veau.

And now he sits across from me. They both do.

Nichole couldn't look away. She pressed fingers to her lips to hide a fangirl grin as she took stock of Courtney's ancestor.

At first, Hunter's eyes appeared as black as their pupils, but when the light fell across his face, they were the darkest blue she'd ever seen. His eyes were only slightly less fascinating than the jagged scar that ran from the outside of his left eye down his cheek to his chin. He probably wore his long hair tied back the same way Nichole's husband wore his, but right now Hunter's dark strands hung in dusty tangles across his shoulders and down his back.

Dehydrated and exhausted from his horrific ordeal, Hunter downed a third glass of water and nodded his thanks to Cat.

"Thank you," Hunter spoke to Cat as the tall brunette placed yet another glass of water on the table near his hand, but his gaze darted to Nichole, catching her stare. "You implied we had met, Mrs. Shilo. I apologize, but I'm at a loss to recall where that might have been."

Amy and Alyse sat to Nichole's left. The identical twin witches were dust-covered and drained by their recent efforts against the monster.

Catherine Kline, equally bedraggled, hovered beside Hunter. She tracked each shift and gesture of the bounty hunter. A slight blush colored her cheeks.

Nichole couldn't remember a striking resemblance to Hunter in any of Courtney's family photographs. Hunter's dark skin and hair must have lightened with each passing generation. But Nichole had seen Catherine Kline, or her near image, in Courtney's makeup mirror every day.

Before the car accident. Before she returned to her past life as Nichole Harris.

"Where we met?" Nichole raised her eyebrows and shrugged. "I'm not sure how to describe it." She paused and studied his profile.

I'm going to sound like a complete psycho to him.

Beside her, Amy lowered her head into her arms on the table and closed her eyes.

Alyse relaxed back and grinned at Nichole giving her a nod of encouragement.

"All righty then." Nichole cleared her throat and lowered her chin to address Hunter. "When Jimmy Leigh shot you, well—shot the demon inside you—your death put my future existence in jeopardy. As I expected, that act knocked a portion of me into what I call *The Passage*. I knew it would."

Cat sank into the chair next to Hunter, hand over her mouth, her gaze now fixed on Nichole.

Hunter narrowed his eyes. "Go on."

"Anyway, in this passage, I don't look like I do now because—" Nichole searched for a clear and concise explanation. Not finding one, she held out her hand as though in supplication for Hunter's trust. "Because Nichole, the person seated before you, would have remained alive even if you died. But the reality of Courtney's life would have ended with yours." She glanced at the sisters. "I had to give Amy and Alyse a chance to heal you by stopping your spirit from moving out of reach."

Hunter's brow furrowed as he rested his arm on his knee and leaned forward, searching Nichole's face and eyes. "Then—that was you."

"Yes," Nichole whispered.

"How did you change your appearance?" His voice lowered. "How did you know the resemblance to Cat would make me hesitate?"

"I didn't. I appeared as myself." Nichole shrugged and exhaled through tense lips. "I'm also Courtney Veau. Your descendant. I-uh, returned to my past life, my life as Nichole Harris, to be with Merril. In my future life, I bear a strong resemblance to one of my ancestors." Her gaze flicked to Cat and back to Hunter. "Apparently."

Hunter raised a brow as he looked from Nichole to Cat, then he leaned back in the chair and ran a tanned hand over his face. Although he'd washed the blood and grime from his skin, his clothes remained tattered and stained from his ordeal. "You claim to be my descendant. And you're here because you spirit-walked into this life and chose to stay. You gave up your future existence to return here."

Nichole closed her mouth. *He understood.* "To be with the man I love. Yes."

"Who taught you?"

Nichole's mind went blank. "Who taught me what?"

"To spirit-walk. That is a difficult and dangerous skill. Someone must have guided you, showed you how." He wasn't angry, only exhausted and curious. He pushed back his thick black hair and reached for Cat.

She grasped his hand with both of hers and tucked her fingers under his palm, resting his hand and her elbows on the table.

Nichole shook her head. "I didn't have a teacher. My father would have, I'm sure, but my parents died when I was young. My grandmother raised me. My mother's mother. Grandma Curtis knew nothing of my father's skills." Nichole's spine straightened as a thought occurred. "But my father spoke with spirits. And I saw Kevin Shilo." Her attention darted to the sisters and found both sets of identical eyes on her. "Kevin was Merril's brother. He died in this house."

Hunter closed his eyes for a moment. "He's not here now."

"Exactly. I showed Kevin *The Passage,* so he could move on."

The conversation ended when the front door opened. Merril and Jason removed their hats as they entered the dining room.

Merril rounded the table and dropped an easy kiss on Nichole's forehead. "We're going to head back to the Highlands." He addressed Amy and Alyse, "Most of the small animals and insects are burning in a fire your uncles started in the corral. The large animals are too heavy to move." He shook his head. "I'm not sure what we'll do. Butcher them where they fell, I suppose."

Jason squeezed his wife's shoulder. "Amy, would you and Alyse care to ride back to the ranch with us? Whatever Jim decides, he'll need help. Merril and I plan to return with men from The Highlands once everyone at home knows the threat is over, at least for now."

"Wait a minute." Nichole held up her hand. "Go back to what you said about the large animals." She raised an eyebrow at Amy. "Why don't you sink them into the ground?" She grinned at their various expressions. "I'm serious. You and your uncles manipulate earth. Why not change the density of the ground underneath the bodies and quicksand them underground? Suck 'em right down."

Amy rose from her chair. "I'm not sure it would work." Her gaze circled the table. "But it's worth a try." Chairs scraped back as Amy turned and led the group to the front porch.

In the yard, Jimmy Leigh, the Highlands' foreman, and Marshal Sam Kline worked together to drag a deer carcass toward the fire pit in the corral. They paused when the group filed onto the porch.

Jim pushed up the brim of his hat with his thumb, setting it back on his head. "What's happened?"

"Nichole has an idea," Merril explained.

"A good one," Amy added. "We're going to sink the large animals into the ground where they lie or at least make an attempt."

"I'm not." Alyse passed Jim and Sam on her way into the corral. Her smile lingered on Jim. "This *Fire* and *Air* witch will tend the flame."

"What's this?" Bayard wiped an arm across his head and reset his bowler hat. "Sink the animals?" He leaned his arms on the split rail fence and stared at the group on the porch.

"I never considered that." Bernard joined his twin at the rail.

"It should be possible," Bayard agreed. He gestured toward the deer at the foreman's feet. "Let's try with that one."

Jim and Sam stepped back as the brothers approached the carcass.

After a few moments, the twins held their hands out, palms down, and closed their eyes. Each movement, including the rise of their chests, mirrored the other.

By infinitesimal degrees, the carcass sank into the ground. The area where the animal had lain shimmered for a moment, appearing liquid, then hardened, leaving no trace the hard-packed yard had been disturbed.

Bay and Bern continued to concentrate for several minutes after the animal disappeared, then lowered their arms.

Bay leaned over, hands on his knees. "Not as easy as it looks, folks."

"That doesn't look easy at all," Jason replied, shaking his head in wonder.

"If Amy wasn't tired, she could do this by herself." Bernard pointed at a two-year-old heifer across the yard. "That one next."

"I want to help." Amy gripped Nichole's arm and pulled her along as she followed the brothers across the yard. "You don't mind, do you?" she asked Nichole. "I want to watch what they're doing."

"No problem, just glad I can help."

"How do you assist them?" Hunter called.

Both Amy and Nichole looked back, but it was Bernard who answered. "She acts as a bridge between us. Although Bayard and I can twyne our magic together, Amy would not be able to observe how we use our gifts. Our white candle makes that possible."

"They could see Kevin's ghost when they touched me," Nichole called to Hunter.

Nichole placed her hand on Bernard's shoulder and held Amy's hand.

"Wait." Hunter hurried to the group. "I want to observe their work."

"Unless you have their type of magic, you won't witness anything," Nichole explained.

"That's all right." Hunter's hands rested lightly on Nichole's shoulders. "I want to watch what you do."

"Okay." Nichole shrugged. "But there's nothing to see."

A throaty French scoff, deep in Hunter's throat, sounded behind her.

"Now." Bayard and Bernard said in unison, and the heifer lowered into the ground.

Several moments after the animal sank beneath the yard, the brothers broke their twyne and dropped their hands.

"Do you understand what we did?" Bayard asked Amy.

"Yes, I do." She pointed to a large steer on the far side of the corral. "I'm going to try that one."

"You go girl." Nichole waved her on. "Did you learn anything?" she asked Hunter.

Hunter shook his head. "Not a thing."

"Yeah, I don't understand how I help, or what I do." She shrugged. "But if I can lend a hand, even a little bit, it's cool."

Hunter's brow furrowed at her words.

"Oh, sorry." Her face warmed under his stare. "The Courtney side of me is super jazzed to meet you. I know better than to use her words. Amy says I freak her out when I talk like this." She rolled her eyes. "And now I chatter like an idiot, saying things you won't understand."

"You are no idiot, *ma chère*."

Nichole's gaze met Hunter's.

His grin stretched the scar on his cheek, and his eyes danced. "And I do understand your meaning, if not your words." He tipped his head. "I am flattered." He walked beside Nichole as they returned to the porch. "Unfortunately, I continue to suffer symptoms from my ordeal. The afternoon heat has made my head swim." His face paled beneath his tan and perspiration dotted his forehead.

"Go inside and rest," Nichole advised. She caught Cat's watchful eye and tipped her head at Hunter.

Cat stepped up and took Hunter's arm, escorting him into the cool interior of the ranch house.

In the yard, Alyse spoke with Merril near the corral fire, then left the pen and headed toward her sister.

Nichole put her concern for Hunter aside and hurried to join the twins. New to *twyning*, the twins would appreciate the help a spiritual bridge would provide.

It's the least I can do. The only thing I can do.

By mid-afternoon, the teams had cleared the animals from the yard, either by sinking or burning them.

Jim and Merril saddled the horses and hitched the wagon for their return home.

Few had slept before the battle with the demon, and the work of clearing The Shilo showed on everyone's face.

"We look like a horde of zombies," Nichole commented to Amy as she mounted her gelding.

Amy blinked at Nichole. "I'm too tired to ask."

Chapter 2

Morago

—

The hawk perched on the balcony rail of a familiar house. It overlooked a small yard facing west into the sunset. Although the bird slept, the entity inside remained awake.

Morago considered the talents of his adversaries and everything he'd learned in defeat. The witches were formidable. Together, they displayed more elemental power than the old woman had possessed, which was considerable. Two male witches had fought beside his targets, but that alone had not defeated him.

It had been the human servants and their weapons that brought me down.

The encounter had been uneven from the beginning. Morago knew that now.

But that would change.

The bird's head swiveled, and its keen vision focused on a thin older man rounding the side of the house.

"Well, I'll be damned if she wasn't right." The stranger paused and lifted his hat with one hand and scratched his balding head with his fingers. "Wilma said she saw something big fly back here." He settled the hat and threw out his arms. "Scat, ya filthy vulture. You'll eat Wilma's little finches." He jumped forward. "Scat, I say."

The broad-winged hawk cocked its head.

The man picked up a stone. "Now, off with you." His arm froze, and the rock fell from his fingers.

Take Albert Fielding back to his wife.

Morago instructed the lesser demon that now dwelt inside the neighbor.

Tell her you chased the raptor from the yard.

The old man tottered around the side of the house, but Morago's demonic magic allowed him to look through the eyes of his slave with only a thought.

You may watch through your vessel's eyes, Morago instructed his servant, but allow him the freedom to go about his daily tasks. Report to me all you learn.

With a cry, the hawk rose into the evening sky. This body was too unusual within the human settlement. He required a less remarkable host. Beneath the hawk's watchful eye, Albert Fielding returned to his house.

Behind Albert's house, several small, colorful birds chirped at a feeding area.

The broad-winged dipped toward the tiny birds, frightening them into the air. With a single thought, Morago released the hawk and rose inside a little yellow finch above the rooftops.

***

Hunter

—

Hunter stifled a groan as the wagon bounced over another rut. The magical care provided by the dark-haired twin sisters had returned him to life, but in their exhaustion, the healing had remained incomplete.

Or perhaps my soul is scarred, forever marked to show my failures, like my face.

The brother witches, another set of twins, introduced themselves as Bayard and Bernard and shared the wagon bed with Hunter and Cat. They spoke in hushed tones about rescuing their mother from the demon. They were worried for the old woman's soul.

With good reason.

At Hunter's back, a light-haired man, who resembled the blue-eyed, golden-haired Nichole, drove the wagon. On the buckboard seat beside him sat Amy, and her twin, Alyse.

The witches I was hired to kill are the ones who saved my life.

The towering man who fired the rifle, freeing him from the demon, rode beside Alyse, never straying far from her side.

There were so many people. Far too many for a solitary man like himself to recall their names, especially with his physical and spiritual injuries.

Riding behind the wagon were the Shilos, Merril and his wife, Nichole, who had magic in her soul from another life. His descendant, if she were to be believed.

And do you believe her? Noticeably absent since the demon possession, the voice in his head had returned.

I can't doubt her. I've seen the evidence of her power with my own eyes. Hunter's gaze flicked to Cat.

On the other side of Nichole rode Marshal Sam Kline, Cat's older brother, and Hunter's friend. Sam narrowed his eyes as his little sister grasped Hunter's hand.

He worries about the demon.

Cat held firm to Hunter's hand and glared defiance at her brother.

Hunter closed his eyes and leaned close to her. "*Mon amour,*" he whispered in her hair. "It does no good to make your brother angry. Give him time, *mon beau petit chat.*"

"I don't care what Sam thinks."

"Yes, you do. And so do I." He set aside her hand and listened to the murmured words between the brothers, what he could hear. His eyes closed, and the wagon rocked him to sleep.

A sharp jolt woke him as the wagon pulled up a low incline and into a wide yard. They rolled past a white clapboard house. A long, covered porch wrapped the front entry and continued along the side of the building.

Faces peeked from behind the curtains, and then the back door opened. A portly gray-haired woman in an apron hurried down into the yard waving her hands and following the wagon. "Is everyone safe? Is it over?"

Merril and Nichole reined their mounts to speak with the woman as more people spilled from the house into the yard.

"How many people live here?" Hunter asked Cat.

The wagon stopped, and Cat pulled herself to her feet. She slapped at her skirt with a sharp left to right motion and lifted her chin to push several strands of dark hair from her face. "I'm sure you'll get the full tour and introductions. Although, I don't know where they'll put you. All the rooms in the house are taken." Her words were polite and distant.

I've hurt her feelings.

"Cat—"

Two workers from the large stable unlatched the back of the wagon and helped Cat to the ground. She walked to Nichole and Merril without turning around.

"She's right about the house."

Hunter tore his attention from Cat and looked at the tall, muscular cowboy who had put a bullet through his chest.

"We weren't introduced before. I'm Jimmy Leigh, Foreman here at The Highlands. Most folks call me Jim."

"Jim." Hunter stood in the wagon bed and held out his hand to the tall, mounted man. "I'm Hunter."

"So I understand." Jim shook his hand. "Sam and Cat spoke of you before we battened down the ranch and rode to The Shilo."

Hunter hopped over the side of the wagon as Jim dismounted. Normally the tallest man in the room, except for Sam, Hunter had to tip his head back to meet Jim's eye. "Six foot four?"

"Just shy of six five." Jim pointed at the house. "Like Miss Kline said, the guest rooms are filled. If you don't mind, I'll settle you in the bunkhouse. There's only Kelly and Bill in there now, though I've no doubt we'll need more if Merril decides to drive to market."

The workers, father and son, by the look of them, led the animals and wagon to the large stable as soon as Hunter stepped away from the wheels.

"That's Lloyd and Tom Baker. They take care of the livestock and equipment." Jim waved back at the men then held the door to the dormitory for Hunter.

Inside, the long building housed a dozen or more bunks with a small storage box beside each bed. Jim opened an inside door beside the entrance. "My bunk's in here. Bill and Kelly have the first two beds, but you have your choice of the remainder."

"I don't know how long I'll be staying. My things—" His heart rate accelerated. "I've left important items at my hotel in Denver. I'll need to retrieve them."

"Denver's a fair distance. We can make arrangements if you want to head back, but you won't be leaving today." Jim walked down the aisle between rows of beds beside Hunter. "It would be quicker to send a telegram from Kiowa Crossing. The hotel could hold your things until you return."

Hunter nodded and pointed to the last bed. "I'll take that one."

Jim gave Hunter a nod and retraced his path through the bunkhouse. "Cookie will have dinner early, I expect, and the James family will return to The Shilo before sunset." He paused at the door. "Between dinner and their departure, they'll want to make plans."

Hunter lifted his chin. "Am I to have a part in these plans?"

"That would be up to you." Jim shrugged. "You have a unique perspective." Jim's lips thinned. "I know they could use your help, and if it were me, I'd want a bit of revenge."

You'll stay, came the voice in his head.

Hunter nodded to Jim. "You're right."

"There's a large metal tub out back with a hand pump for washing up." Jim pointed to the door across from Hunter's bunk. "I'll talk with Sam and Merril about a change of clothes for you. They're about your size."

Hunter examined the long room after Jim had left and scrubbed a hand down his face.

I'll be no help to them without my pendulum.

Your pendulum won't help with this. You'll have to delve deeper. Dark times call for dark magic.

Do you use my grandmother's words against me?

They were my words before they were hers.

"And what does that mean?" Hunter's voice echoed back to him from the empty room. "*Mon Dieu,* now I talk to myself." He half expected the voice to respond, but this time, the whisper inside his head chose to remain silent.

Later that evening, after the dishes were cleared from the dining room table, the family and guests grew quiet, and their gazes turned to the head of the table—to Merril and Nichole.

Hunter sat nearer the other end, beside the James family.

Bayard, the more outspoken of the brothers, leaned forward. "Has anyone given any thought to what we're going to do next? That monster holds my mother's soul." He looked at Hunter for confirmation.

"He holds the soul of a woman," Hunter replied to Bayard. "That much is true." He lifted his voice and spoke to the rest of the table. "Her soul is captive but not broken. I could hear her taunts but did not communicate with her." He shrugged and stared at his hand. His knuckles whitened as he pressed hard on the table beside his water glass. "While he possessed my body, I remained a prisoner inside my mind. The woman, your mother, for lack of a better description, appeared to be a prisoner inside the demon's—"

"We need to go after him!" Bayard pounded his fist on the table. "We must avenge our mother's murder and free her spirit."

"How will you find him?" Jim asked from beside Merril. "He could be any-where. The only thing you know for certain is he will return for your nieces." A look, heavy with significance, passed between Alyse and Jim. "He wants them more than anything, am I right?" Jim asked Bernard. "According to this Prophecy, he'll have to come after them. I say we lay a trap."

"We laid a trap last night," Amy countered. "And he nearly had us."

"Where does he get his magic?" Merril asked. "Why would he desire your elemental magic if he already has those abilities?"

"He has our mother's magic," Bernard said.

"And her knowledge," Hunter added. "I've no doubt this demon can pillage her thoughts as he did mine. He learned where to find you because I knew where you were."

Beside him, Sam nodded as if it all finally made sense, and his eyes widened. "Then he has your skills as well?"

"He wasn't interested in my gifts," Hunter admitted. "Only where he could find the twin witches. But now that you mention it, his actions make no sense. If he covets magic, why not take mine?"

"Maybe he already has yours," Jason said.

"No." Hunter shook his head. "If that were true, he wouldn't have needed my insight to their location, information I gained by the use of my skills."

"It could be because of the Prophecy." Alyse ran her finger around the rim of her glass. "If he had killed you like he did grandmother, the demon would have inherited your power, but the only thing he wants is the magic of the twins." The sisters stared at each other.

"How long do we have until the demon comes back?" Jason asked.

All eyes turned again to Hunter.

They wait for you, the whisper prompted.

I don't have their answers.

No. But you know more than you say. They need you.

I swore never to use the dark arts.

Even to save those you love?

Hunter's gaze lifted to Cat, and then grudgingly slid to Nichole. "I would say you have time. He must make plans, gather his strength, and prepare for his next assault. Your advantage is familiar ground. You should wait for him to come to you."

"Like Amy said, a trap didn't work last night. What's changed?" Bernard asked.

Hunter swallowed and acquiesced to the voice gone silent inside his head. "Now you have me."

Also by

Soul of the Witch Saga

Prodigy – Book 1

Pyromancer – Book 2

Passage – Book 3

Prophecy – Book 4

Paradox – Book 5

Patriarch – Book 6

—

J.L.'s Timeless Quest

Aubrielle's Call

The Corsair's Tempest

Hawthorn and Mistletoe

—

The Hunter Chronicles

Hunter's Gamble

Hunter and Lily Graham

The Kid in Black

Penelope's Heart

All of these stories take place within the same shared universe.

About the Author

C. (Connie) Marie Bowen writes paranormal romance and historical fantasy set within a richly layered, persistent universe. Her award-winning novel *Passage* launched the *Soul of the Witch* series, introducing a world where magic, loyalty, and sacrifice intertwine.

Bowen's stories span multiple series, with characters crossing paths and timelines within the shared universe of the Soul of the Witch Saga. Figures such as Hunter from *The Hunter Chronicles* and J.L. from *The Timeless Quest* play meaningful roles within this interconnected world.

Born in Denver, Colorado, Bowen grew up with a love of ghost stories and storytelling. She now lives in the greater Chicagoland area with her husband and two rescue pets, Abigail and Rousseaux.

Visit https://www.cmariebowen.com to explore her connected series and learn more.

www.ingramcontent.com/pod-product-compliance
Lightning Source LLC
Chambersburg PA
CBHW060855250626
47159CB00008B/2744